Billy'O

Lost in the
Promised Land
Book I

John E. Sheehan

This Amazon paperback edition of Billy'O
Lost in the Promised Land Book I
was written, edited, designed and published
by John E. Sheehan

ISBN: 9781673609226

The cover illustration is a reproduction from an original
acrylic painting titled: Sanctuary
by the author, John E. Sheehan

From the Author
About the Cover

The cover jacket of this book includes two separate works of original art that I created for Billy'O, Book I. The cover illustration is an original painting titled: "Sanctuary" The illustration on the back of the jacket is a detail cropping from a larger painting titled: "August island" The view on the cover offers you the vantage point of the sanctuary house and August island from the top of the hill looking west. The cove with the Inn and the pier are seen in the distance below. The picture on the back of the jacket shows you the vantage point from the west looking east from the cove offering a view of the pier, the Inn and the sanctuary house on top of the hill from a distance.

August island is located about 15 miles east off the coast of Portland, Maine in Casco Bay. The island serves as an important setting for pivotal events that take place in all four Billy'O books. It has the most significance in Book I as you will discover beginning in chapter 10.

You will not find this island on any map because it is too small to be significant enough to be included. The island is only noted on navigational maps of an earlier era and my imagination.

Introduction:

The Billy'O Epic is a story of the Irish American experience beginning with the Great Famine and following onward to the perilous Atlantic crossing to America. I considered writing the book in the third person but when Billy O'Shea made himself known to me, I knew he was the only one who could tell the story and bring the realism of those events forward. I knew he was a good story teller and a good observer and I chose him to relay this epic story to you as he saw it through his eyes and experiences. In the last two volumes, Billy's son James offers his account of events as a counterpoint to his father's story.

The Billy'O Epic took more than twelve years to complete. The original story was to be encompassed in a single novel, but as the research progressed and the story line grew in scope and breadth, I realized that the Billy'O Epic could not be compressed into a single novel. Even with strict editing standards, the story and its vast scope of historical events and locations took up nearly twelve hundred pages upon the final editing so I decided to break it down into four separate novels. I have created a bibliography of the research material used to write this epic. Because the list was so extensive, I created a partial bibliography of the most important books and historical information used to write this epic that will be included in the final installment of the story in Book IV.

There is some graphic language, violence and sexual situations throughout the story. I would recommend this set of books for young people in their early teens with some parental guidance and discussion.

To enter the world of Billy O'Shea and follow his story you must open up your imagination and transport yourself back in time to the mid nineteenth century to the year 1846. The story begins in south central Ireland in the County of Kilkenny. The small farm villages south of Kilkenny dot the banks of the Nore River. The farm plots are further divided into tiny squares of land surrounded by stone fences and groupings of little thatch roofed huts that are huddled together along the road. Although the western counties of Ireland suffered the worst of the potato blight, other counties in Ireland suffered just as many hardships.

It was the second winter of the famine in Ireland and the O'Shea family had struggled through a year to manage to pay their rent on Gale day each November and May. The potato crop had failed again and by November 1846, there were not enough resources to pay the rent on the plot and the O'Shea family was visited by the county magistrate and, not long after the reading of the writ, they found themselves turned out of their little plot and out of their home.

Billy O'Shea was middle son out of eight children. There were five boys and three girls ranging in age from three to nineteen. Billy was 13 years old at the time of the eviction. He was left angry and bewildered by the progress of events that led to his homelessness. He begins his story on the day of the eviction.

Chapter 1

First you must understand it was a miracle that my family survived through the winter of eighteen forty six and forty seven, living out on the road as we did after the eviction from our home. Next I should explain that we were not a close knit family. I was the middle child out of eight and the fourth boy. At the time of our eviction, I was thirteen years old. I was not old enough to be kept privy to the family secrets or troubles so that when the eviction came about, I was taken completely by surprise. No one bothered to tell me that Gale Day had come and gone and the rent was due and there was no crop to pay the landlord because all the potatoes had turned to a rotted stinking pile of black mush.

   I remember that it was so early of a cold morning in late November of eighteen and forty six. I was sleeping in the loft above the kitchen. I shared a bed of straw with my three older brothers, Eamon, Paul and Sean. There was a pounding at the door that roused us from our sleep. My father was not about, so it was left to my eldest brother Eamon to gather us up out of our beds and lead us out into the chilly dew of the morning with only our nightshirts to offer us cover from the cold.

We watched from the road as the county officials handed mother a piece of paper and spoke some words about the order of the magistrate. My mother then placed her hands over her face and began to weep.

I wondered why Eamon and my other brothers had not tried to put up a fight. But then I saw that battering ram placed against the front wall of the house. I had seen it used before to break down the wall of the McCreary's house the week before and I knew it was hopeless to resist.

My father found us out on the road after we were forced to abandon the house. When he heard about the eviction, he went into one of his tirades right out there in the middle of the road for all to hear.

There are things you should know about my father, Gerald O'Shea. First I should tell you that he was never much of a father or a provider to the family. Mother could not keep that family secret from me. I knew he was the black sheep of the O'Shea family with his drinking and thieving ways. What made it worse, he was possessed by a dark moody spirit and his fits of violent temper put the fear into us all. It's a terrible thing to admit and I knew it was a sin to hate, but I hated my father and there were times when I wished that something terrible would happen to him so that we would not have to suffer his presence in our house.

I dared tell mother how I felt one day and she got very angry with me and tried to explain why my father was like he was. "No man can keep his sanity or his sense of manhood once his dignity has been stripped from him," she told me. But at the time, I was too angry to listen or to try and understand her words.

The eviction meant the breakup of the family. I said that we were not a close knit family, and that was true. But it was still hard to watch my older brothers take leave of us.

Eamon had gone into Kilkenny and found places at the workhouse for Paul, Sean and himself. Father had gone away again and that left me as the remaining eldest son to become the man of the family. I so wanted to go away with my brothers. I knew that life at the workhouse was very hard but at least I would have a roof over my head and food to eat.

I still cannot forget the sight of watching my three older brothers waving to us and walking as threesome away from us toward town. I wanted so much to join them, but mother told me that I had to stay and take care of my little brother Terrance and my sisters, Ann, Lisa and Geraldine.

I suppose I should tell you a little bit about each of them; the ones that were left to care for. I'll start with Ann. She was sixteen and oh how she loved to lord it over the rest of us. That was fine with me. I was more than willing to defer to her the duties of wiping the bottoms and the runny noses of the littlest ones. At times, Ann could be as loud and moody as my father and other times she would not say a word for days on end.

We were all terribly thin. We never had enough to fill our stomachs and our faces were always drawn and pale. My little sisters, Lisa and Geraldine were undersized for their ages and had tiny spindly legs. Geraldine was just three and was so frail that I carried her up on my shoulders because her little legs could not support her with so little food to eat. Lisa was just six and it was left to Ann to keep a hold of her hand to prevent her from wandering away.

The youngest of us resembled my mother with our dark red hair and fair, freckled faces and the oldest boys possessed dark features like my father. And then there was Terrance. He didn't look much like my father or my mother. He had almost white hair that was soft as corn silk. He was eleven at the time of the eviction but he appeared so much younger. He was as frail of the body as the little ones.

My little brother lived in holy terror of my father. I once heard a story about the day when Terry was born. I'm not sure it was true, but it was said that my father took one look at the pitiful newborn baby in my mother's arms and was ready to take the baby down to the river and drown it to put the poor thing out of its misery. My father called Terrance the runt of the litter.

My mother favored the little Terrance above all of us. We all called him mother's little angel because that is what he looked like. He had a pretty little oval face that was girlish and he was always taunted for his fair looks especially by my older brothers and my father. Because he was mother's favorite, Terrance drew the worst kind of attentions from my father. He loved to rap Terrance across the head or against the ear for crying too loud or for his whining but, the result was, Terrance wined all the more.

When I think back to the day of our eviction, I have to confess that my memory of the events of life that took place before that day is vague to me now. It was as if the eviction had wiped away all that had come before. I could not understand why I never had a chance to meet other members of our family that lived up the road. And, at the time of our eviction, I could not understand why we were not offered help by them or by any of our neighbors. My mother had always told me that we had a close knit family but I never saw any evidence of it. I never knew my uncles or aunts and I wondered why we were shunned. Of course, I know what the truth is now. It was my father's doing. He made the rest of the family angry at him and we suffered for it.

After my brothers left us out on the road on that cold November day, we walked and searched for food and some kind of shelter. It would be a very long walk indeed before we came upon a soup kitchen and more often than not, they wanted us to pay for the food. Mother would send me in to get the food. We had no money. I had to beg them for something. They took one look at me and knew that I did not lie. I explained to them that my whole family had been evicted from our house and that we were five children. All they had to offer was this soup made from water and ground up corn. It was hardly enough to satisfy our hunger, but it was better than nothing at all.

We passed some frightening sights out there on the road. Mother told me to keep the little ones away from the strangers who slept by the side of the road. I knew better. From the stench that rose from them; by the look of their thin skeleton like bodies, their gaping mouths and their sightless eyes gazing up to the sky, I knew that their slumber was eternal. At least, I thought, their sufferings had come to an end.

We passed upon people piling up furniture and clothes beside a house and it was all being set on fire. I knew that it was because of the fever. Out here on the road there was more a fear of catching the fever than of going hungry. But I thought it might be better to die quickly of the fever than to suffer long with the hunger.

The sight of the dead people along the road and the burning flames of that fire gave me terrible dreams at night. I found myself lying in a bed of straw beside my mother, sisters and brothers. People were covering us all up with sticks and bits of turf. Women were keening over us. I heard their wails and cries so clearly. I couldn't move or utter a sound because I was so weak from hunger and fever. I was still alive and they were about to set me on fire.

The most terrifying part of that dream was that my father was standing on the outside looking down at all of us. He held a lit ember and threw it upon us and the flames grew around us. I could feel the searing heat and the lick of the flames curled about my arms and legs. My sisters had begun to scream in my ears as the flames swept over us.

I would wake suddenly and feel hot all over as if I was claimed by the fire. I would stare up at the open sky and reach up with my arms to fend off the flames but then, I realized that I was not on fire and that it had been just bad dream.

That was not the only dream I had. Sometimes I would dream of being found on the side of the road and thought to be dead. I would then find myself being buried alive.

I don't know where these dreams came from. I thought it must be because of the hunger. I could think of nothing else but to get something to satisfy my gnawing hunger. It was getting to the point that I was ready to abandon my family and run off to find something on my own. On some days, I could barely muster the strength to lift little Geraldine upon my shoulders.

There were times when I thought about stealing some food. I couldn't understand why others seemed to get their stomachs filled with food and so many more went hungry. It just wasn't fair. It wasn't our fault that the potatoes went black and turned to mush.

I thought it might almost be worth going to jail to get my family the proper food. But I was thinking of myself most of all. It is difficult now to explain the feelings of desperation when you had an empty stomach and had no future prospect of finding something to eat. All sense of human decency and dignity was stripped away. I would act as an animal might. I had to hunt down what I needed to survive. That it would be a sin no longer mattered. I had more of a fear of dying of hunger than dying of old age and going to hell for my sinning as a thief. I wondered then, could hell have been any worse than this?

I tried to pass the time by looking out beyond the road to the plots owned by others. It seemed as if we had ventured many miles on those roads during those days and weeks after our eviction. But you know, it turned out we were actually walking in a great wide circle, and in time, I came to recognize the familiar sights of our own village, the same ditches and plots of land marked off with piles of stone and the tiny whitewashed houses with straw roofs.

It must have been many weeks that had passed; Eamon came out to find us to tell mother that he, Paul and Sean had settled in at the workhouse. He had good news for us. There were places for all of us at the workhouse. But mother was against it. She told Eamon that they would take the little ones away from her and send them to orphanages. She was worried about Ann working among the roguish men. No one could persuade mother that going to the workhouse was the best for us all.

It was about that time, the temperatures outside were feeling a little warmer. The chill damp air was changing to a balmy coolness. That and the smell of manure of the new planting were signs that we had survived the winter.

Mother saw it as a sign from God that we were going to survive. I was angry with mother. I couldn't understand her refusal to take us all to the workhouse. I was ready to go with Eamon but then my father made his appearance out there on the road. He announced to us all that we were going to leave the country. Mother didn't believe him. No one did. He was always making promises that he never kept. In fact, he told us the same thing the day we were evicted but no one believed him back then either.

He gathered us up together after Eamon left us. He told us we were going to go aboard a ship that would take us to a place called America. Mother asked him where he got the money to pay our passage. He would not tell her. I suppose that he stole the money.

"And what about the older boys?" mother asked him.

"They'll have to stay behind," my father replied. "They have work. They will survive well enough on their own."

This made mother very upset. She told father she wasn't about to travel across an entire ocean and leave her boys behind. But my father would not take no for an answer and I knew that sooner or later, my mother would give in to him.

America, I had heard a little bit of talk about that place that was so far away and on the other side of an angry sea. Some I heard call it the promised land or the land of milk and honey. It was said that if you managed to survive the crossing, you would reach the gates of paradise on the other side.

My father was trying to persuade my mother to go by telling her about the plenty in America. "None of our family would ever face hunger and want again once we reached her shores," he told us. He was even trying to put on the charm, something I had not a chance to see before. His act was very good. He almost had me believing that he cared about what happened to us.

Father finally persuaded mother to obey his command by agreeing to go to Kilkenny to tell the older boys that we were going to America and that, if they could come up with their own passage money, they could follow us later on. That seemed to satisfy my mother. Father then told us to proceed south on the road following the Nore River until we reached New Ross. We were supposed to wait there for my father. He told us he had already made the arrangements for our passage on a cargo ship called the Saint Gerard. The ship would be docked along the quay and we should seek her out and find the captain; a man named Zachariah Wilkins.

I had never before traveled beyond the borders of my own village and I wondered how far we would have to travel to reach New Ross. Father told us it would take at least three days to make the journey on foot. Mother told my father that we had to have food to sustain us or we could never make such a journey. Father promised to bring us some food soon but that we had to leave right away. The Saint Gerard would be leaving for America in a week's time.

I didn't want to go to America. I told mother that I wanted to go back to Kilkenny to live at the workhouse with my older brothers. I did not trust my father. I wondered if there really was a ship waiting for us as he had told us there would be. I was convinced that it must be another one of his lies or a cruel joke.

Even though I was feeling desperate, I could not be so heartless as my father. I would never abandon my little sisters or brother to go my own way, so I took father's instructions and led the way south.

Mother tried to put the best face on things: "What was back in Kilkenny that was worth staying for?" she asked us. "We had lost out house and our plot. The other O'Shea's shunned us. What was the use of looking back?" But then, I could see the sad look on mother's face as we moved farther and farther away from the place where we had lived out our lives. Mother knew that part of her was being left behind. No matter how hard she tried to hide her sorrow from us, I knew from the look in her eyes, that she was already missing her first born babies.

Walking to New Ross was not as easy as my father told us it would be. It was not just a matter of following one road along the Nore River. We soon encountered many towns and crossroads. I had no map. Even if I had a map I could not have read it, nor could I read what the signs were telling me that had been posted along the road.

Mother had tried to teach me something of the language of Erin and even a bit of English while I was growing up. Only my elder brothers had seen any schooling and it was a very short session held outside among the hedgerows. Mother had a book called the holy bible and she read to us from it and tried to give us lessons. Honestly, I never felt myself stupid because I couldn't read or write. It just wasn't necessary to work the plot.

It turned out that my little brother Terrance had the keenest sense of direction among us. It was he who figured out which road to take that would lead us in the right direction to New Ross. I noticed that as a long as father was not about, Terrance would stop his whining. Even though he was as tired and hungry as the rest of us, he could laugh and carry on as if he were out on a holiday instead of struggling to survive. There was something about his happy manner that caught the fancy of strangers.

A singing merchantman came along toward us in his horse drawn wagon. He stopped and asked us where we were going. My brother had the courage to ask the man if he had any food to share with us. The merchantman laughed and took an immediate fancy to my brother. He told us to climb aboard his wagon. He pulled a sack out from the back of his wagon and handed out pieces of bread and offered us drinks from a jug of fresh water he had. He wanted to know where we had come from and Terrance told him we had been evicted from our home and were going to a place called America.

The merchantman took pity on us after hearing my brother explain that we had spent an entire winter out wandering the roads. He offered to take us to New Ross in the back of his wagon. It was crowded in the back of that wagon, to say the least, but it was better for the little ones.

It turned out that we were not so far from New Ross. It was not long before we caught our first view of the harbor. I had never been to a seaport before and I had never seen a sailing ship. They appeared to mc like big houses floating on the water. I tried to imagine what it would be like to climb onto the deck of one of those houses and go out to sea. I had a fear that once that house went out to sea there would be no way to get back to land. We would be at the mercy of the ship's captain. What if he looked upon my family with disfavor and decided to throw us over the side. If I could not trust my own father, how could I trust some stranger to take us such a long distance?

We said goodbye to the merchantman as he left us beside the quay. He never even told us his name. He wished us God Speed on our journey to America and then disappeared among the many other wagons that gathered on the street beside the quay.

My sister Ann took one good look at one of those floating houses and began to complain loudly that she was not going to go out to sea on one of those big floating houses. She had been so quiet as of late and had not complained much during our journey to New Ross. But, after seeing the way we would travel, Ann put up such a fuss, it was all mother could do to shut her up, for she was getting the little ones upset and they had started to cry. Ann had them convinced that we would all be drowned at sea.

Terrance was usually the most timid among us, but the prospect of going aboard one of those floating houses and riding it out to sea appeared to excite him. He begged mother to let him run up a plank that led up toward one of the houses. Before mother could order him to stay off, Terrance headed for the end of the wharf and up a long wooden plank that led to the deck of the big house

Just as Terrance had started to run up the plank, a man appeared at the other end. He was a scary looking fellow with a black beard and he had this long yellow pipe clenched between his teeth. He stood there for a long time and said not a word until my brother dared to run up the plank until he was just a few feet away from the stranger.

"Sir, might you be the captain of the ship?" asked Terrance.

The man pulled the pipe from his mouth. "Be off with you beggar boy," he said.

My brother gazed up at the man with his mouth open.

"What are you filthy beggars doing here?" the man shouted down to us. "I have nothing to give you."

My sister Ann was feeling her courage. She stepped forward and brushed away strands of red hair from her face. She raised her chin in a defiant way and told him. "We are not beggar's sir."

The man smiled down at Ann and I did not like the look of his smile. I thought I caught him winking at her. Even though my sister and I were always at odds, I felt duty bound to protect her from a man like this.

"Well, the pretty young lass has a tart mouth, don't she?" said the man after giving her another wink and flashing an even broader smile, revealing a mouthful of different colored teeth; some yellow, some black and some that shined like gold and silver.

I rushed up to Ann and pulled her back. And then, I walked up to the man and asked if he was Captain Wilkins and might this be the Saint Gerard?

"Who would you be?" asked the man.

"I am Billy O'Shea," I told him. "This is my family. My father told us we should come here and find a captain named Zachariah Wilkins."

"Oh he did, did he? Where is your father?" asked the man. He pulled the pipe from his lips again. He offered us a devilish smile and tapped the shiniest tooth in his mouth with the pipe.

"He is on his way," I said.

"Well, he had better hurry up. This ship is leaving tomorrow morning after the tide rises and if the wind agrees," said the man.

"Then this is the Saint Gerard?"

The man nodded. "And I am her first mate. My name is Morley Stoddard."

"Where is Captain Wilkins?" I asked.

"You'll meet him in due time. If you all be passengers you had better come aboard," said Stoddard.

My mother told me it was divine providence that we made our way here so quickly and that we found the ship so easily. I was no so sure. I didn't like the manner or the looks of that man Stoddard or the way he gazed down at Ann and my mother.

I didn't much like the look of this house that would be a ship. It creaked and groaned like some live animal and smelled of rot. I began to share Ann's fears that we might all be drowned out at sea.

Just as we began to make our way onto the ship, other men appeared behind the first mate. There were also some boys among them that were not much older than I. Every one of them had their roguish eyes cast down on my sister Ann and my mother in a way that made me feel uneasy.

The group of men parted to either side of the first mate and then Stoddard turned and moved aside to allow another man to come forward. He looked to me to be more of a threatening presence than the first mate. Much of his face was covered with a long, gray beard and there was a fierceness about the look in his dark eyes that gave me a bad feeling in the pit of my stomach.

The first mate turned and said something to the captain before he came toward us. I was leading the way up the plank and I was the first to meet face to face with him.

"I am Captain Wilkins," said the man.

Mother came up beside me to speak.

"My husband had bought passage for us to go to America on your ship," she said.

"Oh did he now, and where is the bloke?" asked the captain.

"He is on his way," mother replied.

"Well he had better come soon," said the captain and then, he turned his attention to me. He eyed me strangely and reached down to grab my shoulder but I stood away from him before he could reach me.

He was gazing and studying me from head to foot. I wondered why.

"Yes, I suppose you'll do," said the captain to me.

"Do what?" I dared to ask him.

"Your father agreed to let you two older boys work your way across as members of my crew."

"My father didn't tell me about that," I said.

"Well now you know," the captain replied.

"And what if I refuse?" I said.

"Then we'll be leaving you behind," he replied.

"I'll gladly stay behind," I said.

"And you would leave your family?" asked the captain.

"They don't want to leave either," I said.

"Billy you have to obey your father's wishes," said mother.

"I don't know anything about working on a ship," I said. "What good would I be as part of the crew except to get underfoot?"

"You and your brother can work as fetch boys," said the captain. "You don't need to know much to do that. All you have to do is follow orders."

I was bent on refusing him. I walked back down to the quay and mother told me to come back.

"I'm going back to Kilkenny to live with my brothers at the work house," I said. "I don't want to go to America. I don't trust father or this stranger."

Mother gave me that look she gave when she wanted to put on the guilt. "It is your duty to stay with the family and watch over the little ones in your father's absence."

It was hopeless to defy my mother's will. I knew I couldn't go off and leave the family behind, never to see my mother, sisters or brother again. How could I allow them to travel alone across that wide sea in the company of men who might do them harm?

My father did not make his appearance until the very morning that we were to depart. He ignored us as if we were strangers in his midst. Terrance and I had been shown the way about the big floating house and I was told to keep a memory of every part of it. Terrance was actually excited at the prospect of becoming a member of the crew.

Every time I thought I knew who my little brother was, he did something to surprise me and make me see something different about him that I had never known before. He did not seem to be frightened by the other members of the crew or even the captain. And yet, he was still so afraid of his own father.

After going about this ship, I was soon to discover that this big house was actually a very small world. It was cramped with so many men and cargo that there was hardly a place to lay one's body to rest. There were no beds for the family in the dark smelly bottom rooms of the ship.

I followed mother down into what the captain called the hold of the ship. I could not imagine that they would expect humans to live down there for even a single day let alone a number of weeks. With no privy, no fresh water and no real bed except the platforms of the cargo crates, how could anyone have been foolish enough to pay money to make a voyage aboard this ship? And yet, my father had chosen this ship to take his family to America. I couldn't imagine how we would survive the journey.

We were not yet out to sea, but the constant roll of the ship caused my stomach to turn about. Ann was the first to get sick and then mother and the little girls followed. They all had to come up on deck to get air and to hang their heads over the side to puke into the water below.

The orders from the captain were; that once we got out to sea, all passengers would be restricted to the hold and that food and fresh water would be carried down to us.

Mine was not the only family to share the hold. Four other families had paid to make the voyage along with ours. I overheard one of the other fathers complain to the captain that conditions in the hold were uninhabitable and that he should provide a proper berth fit for humans. The captain laughed in his face and told him to take what was offered or leave the ship and that there would be no refunding of their passage fare.

I stood on the ship's deck while listening to the captain argue with the other passengers and I watched as some members of the crew pulled away the gangplank that broke our last connection with the land that had once been our home. I didn't want to show my fear to any of the men aboard the Saint Gerard, but as the ship moved slowly away from the quay and headed her way down through the wide channel to the sea, I felt a shiver rise up my back and I had to swallow hard to loosen a very tight lump in my throat.

As I looked about the deck, there was not a familiar face. I was alone to deal with my fears. My mother and sisters had already gone down below deck into the hold and Terrance was off somewhere below, on the part of the ship they called the quarterdeck. The land moved away from me as the wooden planking under my bare feet swayed and rolled. It was a most uncertain feeling. I had to dig my toes inward and spread my knees outward to keep from falling sideways.

The thing that frightened me the most was leaving the land behind. It was such a new experience to feel the world move beneath my feet. The deck was so narrow that there was no place to run far. It took only a few strides to reach from one side of the deck to the other. I rushed over to deck rail and looked down to see the blackness of the waves and the white froth of foam at their tops as they washed against the hull of the ship far below. I gazed back toward the land as it disappeared from my sight. I realized then that I was on my way to that place called America and there was no turning back.

Chapter 2

A shout came from behind me as I stood and watched the land of my birth fade from view.

"Hey you boy!"

I turned quickly, lost my balance and almost fell over the deck rail and into the waves below.

"Go fetch me a drink of water and be quick boy!"

I struggled to rise and to regain my balance. I looked up behind me to see the first mate, Mister Stoddard, standing over me. He was once again tapping his broad shiny tooth with the end of his pipe and grinning at me. His smile made me feel uneasy. He winked at me with his right eye and then moved closer to me.

"And why are you just sitting there?" he shouted.

I got up on my feet.

His smile faded. I saw a glint of anger in his eyes and before I could move away, he raised his right arm and swept it outward to strike me on the cheek with the back of his hand. I lost my balance again and fell backward onto the deck. I felt a burning in my cheek and my ear. My head was reeling from the force of the blow. I lay sprawled out on the deck and was afraid to move. I looked up, saw the man's angry face and for an instant, I thought it must be my father. I had seen that angry look before and waited for the next blow to fall.

"Get on your feet!" Stoddard shouted.

Other members of the crew had come over to see what was happening. They all stood there and smiled down at me. They were not smiles of good cheer.

They smiled at me as the devil might. One of them quipped that I should be made to climb the mainmast and forced to sit up there for a day and a night and another sailor suggested that I be tied fast to a yard arm and whipped.

Captain Wilkins came strutting across the deck and saw me sitting down and surrounded by half the crew. Wilkins shouted to the crew to get to their labors. Stoddard came forward and told the captain that I had disobeyed his orders and refused to fetch him water. I made no effort to defend myself. In fact, I could not utter a sound. Fear had frozen my tongue.

The captain stared down at me and shook his head. "You'll be useless to me as a fetch boy," he said. "Get below with the women. I haven't the time to train you. Go on now boy. Get below. You'll not be seeing the deck or the sunshine again until we arrive in Boston."

At the time, I was relieved to depart from the presence of the first mate. To go below was better than facing another blow from that man or to be at the mercy of the rest of the crew. I felt much regret though, once I had climbed down the ladder into the darkness of the lower regions of the ship and got a nose full of the terrible odors down there. I looked up one last time and cherished the last sight of daylight before the hatch was closed and then I was surrounded in darkness so that I had to feel my way down the rest of the way to the bottom. Once I felt my way down the ladder to the hold, I looked up and could see that there was just a tiny crack of light that filtered down from high above my head. It was just enough light so that I could make out the darker shapes that were people sitting about on stacks of barrels and crates that filled the spaces.

Once my feet touched off the bottom of the ladder, they sank into a slippery, watery ooze that reached to the top of my ankles. One good sniff of the air made me sick to my stomach. I waded forward through the darkness and called out for mother.

"Billy," I heard mother call.

I made my way between the crates and saw some black shapes in the dim light coming from above. I strained my eyes to find them in the darkness. I thought I could see my mother's form with her long dress and she was holding Geraldine in her arms. As I moved closer, mother called out to me again and I was sure the shape I saw was mother. Geraldine was sleeping in her arms that had a hold of her. Lisa was lying curled up beside her. Ann was standing on the other side and leaning against a barrel.

"I want to go back to Kilkenny," I said as I felt about to find a place to sit.

"Where is Terrance?" asked mother. She had not even paid attention to what I had said to her. I told her that I had not seen him since we left port and that I thought he was somewhere in the quarterdeck. "I want to go home," I said again.

"There is no home," mother replied. "Not until we reach America."

And how long would it be before we reached America? I wondered about this but said nothing to mother. I could see that her mind was preoccupied with worries about her little angel.

As for how long it would take to reach America. I had made the mistake of asking some men of the crew that question. They told me it would be six weeks at sea or longer depending on the wind and the current. They also warned me about the storms. One of the sailors described what he called a big blow that lasted four days and how it almost led them to their deaths. Another sailor spoke with great seriousness about the sighting of ice mountains that put ships in harms way. He vowed that he witnessed such a collision and saw the ship break into splinters. He was shaking his head slowly back and forth and hung his head down as he told us about the many men that had drowned in the icy waters. They had gone to pick up survivors and found only three who had lived.

I guessed that some of the stories were told just to frighten me. They called me a landlubber and said I'd be lucky if I lived to see the shores of America. After surviving such a hard winter after our eviction I wondered, could things could get any worse than they had been?

We were just starting out on this long voyage and yet it seemed as if I had been down in the hold already for such a long time. My sister Lisa had started to cry and so had Geraldine for want of food and some warmth. Mother could do nothing to sooth their needs or their fears. Mother started to rock Geraldine in her arms and sang a little ditty that she used to sing to me when I was a baby. I found it soothing again to hear her soft voice and it had calming influence on all of us.

After the littlest ones finally fell asleep, mother asked Ann and me to pray with her. She had in her possession a long set of rosary beads that she kept in a tiny bag that was tied with a ribbon to her right wrist at all times. It was too dark to see, but I heard the sound of them as mother rubbed them together in her hands.

I would never dare tell mother what I thought about a God who would allow such a suffering of his own people. How could he be a kind forgiving God, so mother had always taught me? Look where we ended up? Did prayers do us any good? Did God prevent our eviction or get us food to eat when we needed it? Were I to ask mother these questions, I would get a slap across the face and a stern order to pray to God to forgive my sinning for saying such a thing. So despite my true feelings and lack of faith, I bowed my head along with my mother and sister Ann that first night aboard the Saint Gerard and prayed for deliverance as we spent our first night aboard the Saint Gerard.

And a frightening first night it was for all of us living down in the hold of the ship. None of the other families that shared that dark space had ever been aboard a sailing ship. The floor of the hold would not be still. It rose up and down and heaved from side to side. I could hear such loud groans. It sounded as if the ship might split apart at any moment. Where there had been cracks in the deck above us to let in a bit of light had now let in a shower of water and there was no escaping it.

Everyone had been terrified into utter silence. The most frightful thing was the total blackness at night. That combined with the terrible noises, made me feel as if I was in the belly of a great beast. I feared that this beast might devour us before we arrived in America.

My mother told us to huddle together and for me to take the hands of the little ones and not let go of them no matter what. I could hear them breathing close to me.

I had an urgency but I couldn't leave to find a place to relieve myself. What an indignity it was. I just let it go in my pants. I couldn't squat behind a bush like we had along the roadside. How could any of us ever feel like human beings again after living like animals? What would become of us after living six weeks in our own filth and not having the sun to shine down on our faces?

We knew morning had come when one of the crew brought down a bucket of water and some shreds of bread in tin bowls. Mother complained to him. "And this is what you expect us to survive on?" But her complaints fell on deaf ears. The man left without saying a word.

By that morning, my eyes had adjusted to the darkness so that I could see more about my mother and my sisters. I watched as mother took her finger, poked it into the water, and then brought it up to taste it. She then took the bucket and dumped its contents out.

"Go up and find the captain," said mother in an angry voice. "Take the bucket with you. You tell him that we need good water. You do that now and then go and find your brother and bring him here to me."

"Yes mother," I replied.

"What will become of him?" she said. "He's at the mercy of those roguish members of the crew."

I didn't tell mother this, but I thought that Terrance was much better off than we were down in the hold. It was my guess that mother's little angel was being afforded special protection from God. Maybe it was because he was the weakest child and needed to be looked after more than the rest of us.

I climbed the ladder to the closed hatch with bucket in hand. I banged on the hatch but no one came to lift it up. I supposed that no one heard me. I could not budge the hatch open by myself. I began to feel weak in the legs. Very slowly, I lowered myself back down the ladder. I went back to mother with the empty bucket and told her there was no way out.

"Lord help us all," mother replied.

During the second night at sea, I feared sleep. I worried that if I closed my eyes, I might not live to open them again. In the blackness of night, I was tossed about and drenched in cold sea water. I could feel the cold grasp of the little hands of my sisters wrapped tightly around my fingers. We all clung to the tops of crates from which we were perched to keep from being thrown into the stinking water of the bottom of the hold.

My head felt weary and my eyelids were so heavy with sleep that I didn't think I could stay awake a minute longer. I wished that this was a nightmare and that I might wake up and find myself lying under a tree by the roadside. I was hoping that the sun would blind my sight when they first opened to see the new day.

When I finally did drop off to sleep, the real nightmares came. It was the same bad dream I had back out on the road. My mother, brothers, sisters and I were laid upon a funeral pyre and my father was standing there with the lit ember and he threw it in on us. I could only see his eyes. The red glow of the fire was reflected back in my father's eyes. The next thing I knew, I was in a dark tunnel and I was running hard to reach the white light that appeared at the other end. I looked back and could see only a pair of red glowing eyes peering from a wild black dog like creature that advanced upon me. I knew it was my father as the devil and he was chasing me. My legs grew so weary I could run no more and my father was catching up with me. I looked back again and could see those eyes glare at me like those of some wild dog ready to attack. Suddenly, the tunnel was filled with a raging fire and the face of my father was surrounded in flames. His arms were extended like the licks of flame and curled outward to grab me. The flames touched my arm and I felt a searing pain as my flesh started to burn. And then, my father's hands reached out and took hold of me and I felt as if I was being consumed by the fire.

Someone was shaking me. I opened my eyes and saw nothing but blackness and yet, I felt as if the fire was still consuming me. A soft hand touched my forehead.

"Is that you, mother?" I whispered.

"You burn with the fever," she whispered back to me. "We have to move you away from the girls."

Mother could not carry me herself so she and Ann had to help me to my feet and lead me away to another place. I did not want to leave them. What were they going to do, leave me aside to die alone?

I heard mother tell Ann to return to watch over the little girls. Mother said she was going to stay with me. I heard the sound of ripping cloth and then I felt something cool and soft being placed against my forehead. In the darkness I could not see my mother's face but I could sense her presence. She had a hold of my hand. "You keep very still, Billy," she whispered. "Lie here and try to sleep. I don't know what else I can do for you except pray and hope that the fever breaks soon."

Having the fever might have been God's way of saving me. I don't know. I had lost account of the passing days and nights. At times though, I still awoke from tortured dreams of fire only to find myself still in the blackness with the fire raging inside my head and body. I found myself praying. Please God let me live. If I agree to do what you ask of me, will you put out this fire and bring me back to see the light of day once more?

"Billy...Billy!"

I heard a familiar voice through a haze of sleep. I opened my eyes slowly and I thought I saw a flame before my face. It startled me at first and then I opened my eyes wider to see that it was the singular flame of a lighted candle. In the glow of the light, I saw the thin pale face of my brother Terrance. He held the candle in one hand and something wrapped in a cloth in the other.

"I stole food from the galley," said Terrance. "I heard from the captain that you had the fever."

Maybe my prayer had been answered. Perhaps Terrance was my living guardian angel to see to my wants and needs. In the candlelight, his small innocent face appeared like what an angel might look like.

I didn't know if the worst had passed for me. I still felt consumed by fire and my lips were swollen and split. I felt as if someone had twisted my body and wrung out all the water like a wash rag.

Terrance opened the cloth and revealed to me a piece of bread and a slice of an apple. Mother came near and I could see her in the candlelight. Strands of red and silver hair hung down over her careworn face.

"Take only a little bit now," she said.

Terrance put a piece of apple into my mouth but I could not swallow it. I started to cough and choke. I spit out the piece of apple but I did savor the sweet taste of it.

What was to become of me I wondered? Was I going to just waste away and die? If I could not swallow to eat or to drink then I could not survive.

"Am I going to die?" I asked mother.

My question made Terrance very upset and he looked away from both of us.

Mother gently wiped my face with a cloth. In the light of the candle flame, I could see that it was a shred torn from the skirt of her dress.

"Don't you be saying those things now," she said. "You just lie still and get your rest. Once the fever breaks, we'll know you'll be fine."

While I was going through the worst of it, I could not know that my little sister Lisa had also caught the fever and that other passengers had been stricken as well. I found myself begging God to put an end to this fire that was torturing me even if it meant the end of my life.

One night, I awoke from another one of my bad dreams. The fire had left my body but it was replaced with a cold chill. I found myself floating on the water and more water was rushing down upon me. The water had drenched me to the bone and my teeth were chattering with the cold that had replaced the fire. The cold was so sharp that it hurt every muscle of my body as I tried to move about. I felt a heavy weight of water pushing down on me. I then heard a thrashing and splashing about me and someone screamed that they were drowning.

I had little strength in my body to resist the downward pull of the water's current. I fought as hard as I could to keep my head above the water. I reached out with my arms to grab a hold of something. I felt a piece of wood before me. It was part of a crate and I reached out and grabbed it and held on to it tightly. It helped me stay above the water. The raging waters made a deafening roar in my ears. I strained to listen for the sound of a human voice. Suddenly a cold hand reached out and grabbed my arm.

"Billy is that you?" It was the voice of my sister Ann.

"Hold on to me!" I shouted. "Where is mother?"

"I don't know!" Ann screamed back in my ear.

"Billy?" It was my mother's voice and sounding so far away.

"I can't see you. Where are you?" I shouted back.

"Over here on a crate. I've got Geraldine with me. Have you seen Ann?" mother cried out.

"I'm here with Billy," Ann shouted.

"Where's Lisa?" I shouted.

There was no answer.

"Mother, are you still there?" I shouted. "Do you have Lisa with you?"

"Lisa was lost," Ann shouted over the rage of water. "The fever took her a day ago."

Poor little Lisa, I was so deep into my own sickness, I could not even be present to see her before she left us. I was thinking that it would not be long before we all joined her.

It was a miracle that any of us survived through that storm at sea. Ann and I held onto that bit of crate for what seemed like an eternity. I have no true accounting of the amount of time that had passed. That is the way it was during the entire voyage to America. There was not enough light of day to measure the passing of time. An eternity could have been a minute, a day or a week in length, I only know that I lived to see the end of it.

I was in a state of numbness and disbelief when the cargo hatch was finally opened one day and the sunlight came streaming down upon us. Captain Wilkins came down and barked an order to us that we should all come up to the deck. I was sure that the vision of the sunlight shining down on the shape of that figure standing before us might have been God himself come down from the heavens to take us to his house.

The light revealed a terrible scene. Until now, I did not have but the dimmest view of the other passengers. With the sunlight shining down from above, some among us wore not a shred of clothing. Men rushed to offer their wives cover from their nakedness, but the children just stood bare skinned and filthy black all over. We all had to reach up and hold our arms over our eyes because the fierceness of the sunlight hurt them.

Captain Wilkins announced that we would be arriving in Boston in two days time and that he wanted us all to come up to the deck to be washed down and given clothing. There would also be proper food and drink.

My mother came forward and demanded to know why we had been neglected for so long and why were only now being offered the proper food and water. The captain ignored my mother's complaints and explained that the port officials would want to inspect us all to make sure that we were healthy and would not bring fever to the city. And then, Captain Wilkins posed the question to all of us. "Which of you has been sick?"

Mother pointed to a little mound on the floor of the hold that was covered with scraps of wood from a splintered crate. "My daughter lies there," mother said. "And the fate of her poor soul should be on your conscience for the rest of your days for, as God is our witness, you are the man responsible for her death." Her angry voice echoed throughout the hold of the ship. The captain said nothing in response. He stared down at the mound and shook his head.

Another man came forward and pointed to a dark figure lying on the floor of the hold not far from him. This time, there was no covering. The sunlight revealed the figure of a naked woman curled up as if asleep. Her long hair was swept over her face to hide her mask of death.

"That was my wife," the man said with a slight whimper in his voice and then he pointed to two naked little boys that huddled near his legs and clung to him with their hands. "And now," said the man. "These little boys have no mother to take care of them."

The captain refused to look at the dead woman or the poor boys that had lost their mother. "They will have to be buried at sea," said the captain. "Come up ye all now and prepare yourselves for the landing in Boston."

My eyes had a hard time adjusting to the daylight. Slowly I pulled my hands away from my eyes so that I could get them used to the brightness of it. I saw the faces of my sister Ann, my mother, and little Geraldine. It was not long ago that I was sure I would not see them again.

We were all so filthy. Our bodies were slathered with black stinking grime from head to foot. Mother had just enough left of her dress to cover herself and I could see the ripped hole on the bottom of the skirt. I knew she had ripped away that part of her dress to use to wipe my face when I had the fever. I was almost wishing that the fever would return because I had only a shred of cloth to cover my privates and it was freezing cold down there in the hold.

Ann had enough left of her dress to cover her but she had to hold onto the front to keep it from falling to reveal her bosom. Poor little Geraldine had nothing to cover her at all. Mother held her close and pulled up her dress skirt to keep the baby warm. Geraldine clung to mother tightly and began to whimper and moan.

"Can you carry Geraldine up to the deck on your shoulders?" mother asked me. I nodded and took hold of Geraldine in my arms. She reached out and hugged my neck. I had carried her for untold miles of walking during our days out on the road. It was almost as if Geraldine had been part of me so that she felt familiar and comfortable perched up on my shoulders and her frail little body provided me warmth. I looked up at the stream of sunlight coming in from above.

I saw it as a blessing. With the return of the light, there was renewed hope and, with the return of hope, there was a newly found strength in my arms.

We were the last passengers to climb the ladder to the deck. I told mother and Ann that they should go first but mother insisted that I take the lead. I stood at the bottom of the ladder and stared straight up into the light. I felt a great warmth and comfort from it. As my eyes became accustomed to the daylight, the bright blue sky appeared and little puffs of clouds floated by and then there were faces turned down to gaze at me as I climbed up the ladder.

Once I had reached the top of the ladder, I found myself surrounded by the dark green ocean that stretched out beyond the edges of the deck rails. The sky was so large and blue and the sun was so bright, gleaming like a star high above my head. It was such a dumbfounding experience to see the world appear so bright before my eyes after living in enclosed darkness for so long. I searched the faces of those who surrounded me on deck, looking for Terrance.

"Billy!" my brother shouted as he ran toward me. He was dressed in an oversized pair of seaman's pants and a plaid shirt that was many sizes too big that billowed from his back in the breezes. His face was red from long exposure to the sun and it made his white hair stand out. He appeared fitter that I had ever seen him in his life. I had never seen him look so happy.

Terrance's joy faded quickly upon the arrival of my father. He bullied his way through the crowd that surrounded me and wanted to know where mother was. He then surprised me by offering to take Geraldine from my shoulders and carry her. My father reached out for her and Geraldine clung tighter to my neck and I felt her body tremble with fear. My father took hold of her and lifted her away from me and Geraldine began to scream and cry as if her father was some stranger. My father lifted her up and then held her away from him and wrinkled his nose at the smell of her.

"Hush little one," he told Geraldine to stop her crying. But it did no good.

"Might I hold her?" asked Terrance.

My father glared back at him. "You? Why you would drop her for sure."

I saw a look in Terrance's eyes that I had never seen before. It was an angry look of defiance.

Geraldine was putting up such a fuss that my father gave in finally and Terrance came to take Geraldine. He lifted her up to carry her in his arms. Geraldine stopped her crying as soon as Terrance had a hold of her.

I turned and looked down into the hatch. I wondered why mother had not come up but then, I realized that she must be down there with my poor sister Lisa, preparing her for a burial at sea. A crewmember went down and helped mother carry up the lifeless body of my sister. They had been thoughtful enough to bring down a part of a sail to use as a shroud.

I reached down to grab mother's hand as she emerged from the hatch. Ann was right behind her and then appeared the sailor who carried the little bundle that contained the body of my sister Lisa.

My father saw the shroud covered bundle and I supposed that he had already been told that his daughter had died of the fever. I could see that he had no tears to shed for his poor little daughter. When mother reached the deck, she saw father and burst into tears when the sailor brought up the bundle. But father did not make a move to comfort my mother. What was wrong with him? I just couldn't understand his coldness toward his own family.

I was staring at my father and he turned his gaze toward me.

"You," he said. "What are you looking at?"

I hated him more now than ever before. I hated him for bringing us to this place of hell. I hated him because my little sister had died of the fever and he had no tears to spare for her…hated him because I too had almost died…hated him for all his selfish arrogance and I let him see how I felt in the look I gave him.

I knew I was at his mercy. My older brothers were no longer around to protect me from my father and I was the only one left to offer protection to Terrance. I didn't want to be anyone's protector. I didn't even want to be part of this family anymore.

My God, why wouldn't mother just stand up to him? She should be so angry with him. He didn't lift a finger to help the family. And what was to become of us? We had no money and no place to live in this new land of America. Father certainly wasn't going to work to support us. We had no other family or friends to turn to in this strange land so far away from our home. But even that was a joke. Home indeed, should I still regard Eire as my homeland when our home consisted of a roadside ditch?

I began to think that it might have been better that I had not survived the fever because I could see no hope for the future. Not even the sight of the open blue sky, the feel of the sun's warmth or the ability to take a strong breath of fresh clean air, could give me hope that life would be better in America.

Despite my deep feelings of dread and melancholy, I could not deny that I felt a little bit of excitement when the Saint Gerard sailed into Boston Harbor a day after we were allowed to come up to the deck. We were given food and allowed to wash the filth off our bodies. The captain offered us some spare sailor's garb to cover our nakedness.

I stood alone on the deck away from my family as the ship made its way through the morning fog that surrounded us. There was the loud report of a horn that came from the distant shore. Through the swirling mists, I could see the faded images of other ships in our midst. Behind me, there was the soft light of the sun trying to burn its way through the mists that cast everything about me in a golden glow. As we moved farther into the harbor, the veil of mist began to disappear and there stood before us in the distance, the faintest outline of a city rising up on a hill.

Chapter 3

Poor little Lisa, I was thinking about my departed sister as the Saint Gerard made its way into Boston Harbor. I could still remember her pretty young face framed in crimson colored curls. But then I thought about her when I saw her last, her tiny body was sewed into a section of canvas sail and tossed overboard into the sea like some bit of ships refuse. I looked down upon the blue sea waters and watched as my sister's body floated away back in the direction toward the land where she had been born.

All of the surviving passengers were allowed to come up from the dark hold and stand on the open deck. Mother and father stood together and Ann was just behind them holding Geraldine in her arms. I stood as far away from them as I could and Terrance chose to stay at my side. He stood so very close to me that I could feel his breath on my neck. I noticed that he was constantly looking over at our father and frowning. I couldn't tell if my brother was feeling fear, resentment or perhaps a bit of both. I understood his feelings only too well. I didn't want to draw near to my father either.

We were all given clothes to wear to be presentable to the port officials. Mother and Ann looked rather odd wearing seaman's pants and shirts. Were it not for their long hair, they might have been mistaken for members of the crew. The captain told me that I would have to return my clothes once the port officials had passed us through. And what was I supposed to do after that? Was I going to be forced to walk the streets of this new land naked as the day I was born?

I was already beginning to think about my new life here in America as the Saint Gerard neared the wharf where we would make our landing. I was determined that I would not live in the same house as my father. I would strike out on my own here in Boston. I would find work on a farm. I hoped they had plenty of farms in Boston but as the Saint Gerard came up near to the wharf, I got a closer look at the city through the clearing mists. There were so many buildings and no sight of open land anywhere to make one think that a farm could exist.

I looked over at mother. She appeared to be pleased at the sight of so many church spires and she pointed to them. In her hands were clutched that string of rosary beads. She had a very tight grip on them. Her eyes then closed and her lips moved just a little as she murmured a prayer to herself.

The sun was high in the sky and all the fog had burned away by the time the Saint Gerard had found her berth beside the wharf. We were told to stay put and wait until the port officials arrived to inspect us before we could leave the ship. I had the greatest fear that these officials might refuse to let us come ashore. I knew that I would not survive a return journey. It was a terrible thing to imagine that we would come this far and be at the mercy of these strange men. I would be ready to beg to stay or steal away onto the land beyond their sight.

Three men in dark blue uniforms climbed up the gangway. One of them came directly toward me. He had a kind enough face but his questions were harsh. "You look frail and sickly young man," he began. "Have you fever in your body?"

"I had," I replied. "It broke."

"Open your mouth wide," he ordered.

I obeyed him.

"Mouth sores," he said.

"Bad water," I replied.

He grunted. "Hmm," He then looked about the deck as if he was searching for someone. He asked where the rest of my family was. I pointed to them across the deck.

"Why aren't you with them?"

I shrugged my shoulders.

He pointed to my father. "What work skills does your father have to support your family?"

"Why don't you ask him?" I said.

"Don't be insolent with me young man, I'm asking you."

"He's a farmer," I said. And a drunken thief to boot, I wanted to add.

"There's no farming here," said the official. "But if he can make use of a pick and shovel, he can dig ditches."

I couldn't imagine my father ever bothering to pick up a shovel to turn one solitary spade of dirt in his life unless he was offered a drink of whiskey in return.

"I'll work," I said. "I'll dig ditches if that is what is needed, but please don't send me back to Eire. I'll die for certain."

"I don't know about you. You look pretty sick to me," said the official. He then walked away without asking Terrance any questions.

One of the other men positioned himself in front of all of us and announced that we were going to have to wait aboard the ship until a final decision was made as to whether we would be allowed to leave or be denied entry at the port.

Captain Wilkins angrily stormed across the deck, stood before the official and demanded to know why we were being detained. He argued that he had a schedule to keep and had to make his way to New Haven in a few days and then he was going on to New York City. The Port official told the captain not to try his patience and that a decision would be forthcoming in a few hours time.

After the port officials left the ship, one of the passengers asked captain Wilkins what would happen if we were denied entry into Boston. Captain Wilkins replied that he would take us all to New Haven if we were refused entry into Boston. He explained that New Haven was a much smaller port and we could slip ashore quite easily without being discovered.

My father came forward and asked the captain if it would not be better for us just to wait and go to New Haven? Captain Wilkins grunted and stared at my father through squinted eyes. By that look, I guessed that captain Wilkins would rather that my father jump ship and swim to New Haven under his own power.

One of the port officials returned to the ship just after sunset. It had been a hot day on board waiting there. We were not allowed to leave the open deck, so we found places to sit under the hot sun. None of us were used to this kind of heat and water to drink was not offered to us.

As for the date, the captain told us when we arrived in port that it was the seventeenth of June in the year of our Lord eighteen and forty seven. Dates and years meant nothing to me then. I only knew that it was the summer season.

The official who returned after sunset was the same one who questioned me. From the grave look on the man's face, I was certain that we were going to be refused entry into Boston. The official paced the deck before us with his hands clasped behind his back. He stopped in the middle of the deck and turned to face us.

"Who among you has money?" he asked.

My father raised his arm. "I have a few quid in gold," he said.

It was I'll gotten money I was sure, but if it got the family ashore, what did it matter?

"Are you prepared to find work for yourself and your sons?" asked the official.

"They'll do what I tell them," my father replied.

"Being that you have a supply of money to support your family and you're willing to work, I'm going to allow you and your family to go ashore," said the official. "But let me warn you. I don't want to hear that you've caused any trouble. If you land in jail for any reason, I'll have you and your family placed on another ship and sent away from these shores. Do you understand?"

My father nodded to him.

I don't know what fate awaited the rest of the passengers. I only knew that we were allowed to leave the Saint Gerard just minutes after the port inspector told us we could go ashore. My father wasn't going to wait any longer, worrying that the man might suddenly change his mind.

Captain Wilkins stopped us before we left the ship and demanded that the clothes we borrowed be returned. Father turned toward Terrance and me and ordered us to strip off the sailor's pants and shirts. Captain Wilkins pointed to Terrance before he began to remove his shirt. "Young lad, you can keep your clothes. You've earned them," he said.

But I had to leave my clothes on the deck. I stood there naked as a baby. I reached down to cover myself with my hands in front of the ladies. Terrance reached down and pulled the long shirt over his head and handed it to me.

"That's for you boy," said the captain.

"If it's mine than I can give it to who I like," Terrance replied.

"You have a very fine son there," The captain told my father.

My father grunted a reply.

The captain softened his standing when it came to the women. He was not about to order them to remove their clothes. So as we left the ship, Terrance was naked from the waist up and I wore a shirt that covered me to just above the knees.

As I expected, once we left the ship, father disappeared into the night and left us standing on the pier with no money and no place to go. Mother told me that he had gone off to find us a place to sleep. I knew it was a lie. I was sure he had gone off to find himself a drink of whiskey with the money that would have afforded us food and shelter

We spent the first night in America sleeping behind a shed that stood beside the pier. There were stacks of folded sails that made a fairly comfortable bed. No one came to bother us or to help us. Captain Wilkins had been generous enough to give us a few pieces of what was called pilot bread; thin hard chips of tasteless food that had to be soaked in water before it could be chewed without breaking the teeth.

We had no fresh water to drink. We did not have a place to wash ourselves, nor did we have the use of a privy closet. I stood on the side of the pier and peed right into the harbor. It was much harder on the women of course.

I tried to sleep, but the hunger was gnawing at me again. I had spent too many times with that empty feeling in my stomach and I was growing impatient. We were in America, where was the milk and honey that was supposed to flow from her? Where were the maidens with pitchers of milk and baskets of bread? I told mother and Ann that I was going to search for food. I could not be satisfied with this hard bread that broke the teeth to chew.

Terrance wanted to come with me but I told him he must stay and protect the family while I was gone. Terrance began to whimper and whine and I was about to rap him on the ear like father would have but I stopped myself. Just the thought of doing anything like my father frightened me.

Mother had persuaded me to wait until morning to go out on a search for food. I spent the entire night awake wondering what the future would hold for me. I wanted to know what the world was like beyond this pier.

I thought about my older brothers Eamon, Paul and Sean. They were so very far away and I was sure that I would never see them again. But I also realized that I was not going to be lorded over by them. Nor would I allow my sister Ann to rule over me. As for my father, I wanted nothing to do with him at all. I had decided on that first night in America that I would succeed on my own and by my own labors and when the dawn came; I would leave the family and begin my new life. I did feel a certain responsibility for the rest of my family. I loved my mother in spite of the way she let my father treat us. Still, it was a man's duty to go out and start his own life sometime. I promised myself I would return to make sure my mother brother and sisters had found a home for themselves.

A chilling fog surrounded us by early morning. My thin shirt offered scant protection from the cold. I wanted to go out and find something extra to wear while it was still dark enough not to be seen. I didn't want to tell mother that I sought something to steal. But I was not going to remain exposed and have a chance to catch the fever again.

I left the family as they all slept, huddled together against the chill of the fog. I could see nothing about me but the swirling grey mists. I felt my way along the pier toward the city. I walked past some small shacks. There was white smoke rising through a pipe in the roof and I was sure I could smell something good cooking and it made my hunger worse. By now, I was more than familiar with the sounds of my own growling stomach.

I saw a rope line that stretched from one shed to a pole. Hanging on the line was a shirt, pants and a blanket. I crept around to be as quiet as I could. I was thinking that I would just borrow the pants until I could get some of my own and I would come back and leave them. That was borrowing, not stealing. I reached up and grabbed the pants. They were heavy canvas sailor's pants like the one's I had to give back. I stole around the corner into an alley, pulled them up and secured them. No one had seen me and yet, my heart pounded in my chest with the fear that I might be caught, sent to jail and then put back on that ship and sent away.

I fought the urge to run. I walked farther down the dark alley and came upon another street. On the corner I saw what I was sure was a tavern with a sign hanging from above a pair of doors. There was a picture painted of a tankard and some lettering I couldn't read. I drew close to the doors and could hear the laughter of men inside. I could detect the strong odor of whiskey. I thought about my father and rushed from the doors. I worried that I might find him inside.

I walked down the dark alley beside the tavern and saw a pile of bones lying in a gutter just outside the back door. Meat, I thought. I leaned down and picked up one of the bones and smelled it. The bones must have been lately cooked, but the bit of meat that still clung to the edges looked dirty. I could not stop myself. I couldn't stand the hunger yearnings. I had to taste it. I took the bone between my teeth and began to chew the shreds of meat that were left.

The back door to the tavern swung open with a loud crash and this boy appeared clad only in pants. I could see from the burly look of his bared chest, broad shoulders, and muscular arms, that he was a strong boy and not much older than I. In the dim light, I could only see parts of his dark, brutish looking face. He had a long mane of shiny black hair that fell down below the back of his neck.

The boy came directly toward me. He reached forward, grabbed the front of my shirt and pulled me toward him. I could smell whiskey on his breath.

"Those bones are for my dog," said the boy.

I threw the bone on the ground. I was too weak to fight for them.

"Aye...you that hungry?" asked the boy.

"For my dog," I replied.

The boy let out a chuckle. He pulled me closer and then wrinkled his nose. "You stink," he said.

"Not as bad as your whiskey breath," I told him.

I raised my hands and then I reached out to push him away. The boy had faster reflexes than I. He moved around me quickly, wrapped his arms about me and wrestled me to the ground. I had no strength to resist him. He had me in a tight hold with his right arm holding me about the neck and shoulders while he used his left hand to hold my arm against my back.

"What's your name?" asked the boy.

"Let me go and I'll tell you," I said.

The boy pulled my arm hard so that it hurt, but I made no sound.

"I could break your arm," he said. "Now tell me your name."

"Billy O'Shea," I replied.

"You wanted those bones for yourself, didn't you?" he asked while tightening his grip.

I refused to let him think that he was hurting me, even though I could hear the bones strain in my arm with a crackling sound.

"For my dog," I said.

"You're a liar," he replied. He then tightened his hold around my neck to make it harder to catch a breath. "Tell me the truth or I'll choke the life out of you."

"Alright," I gasped. "The bones were for me."

The boy released his grip and let me get back on my feet. But he stood close in a threatening way. He put his fist to my face. The daylight was brightening around us and I could see his face more clearly and the deep red scars on his knuckles that were just a few inches from my face. I stared back at him and I thought I could detect a smile emerging on his lips and his eyes sparkled with mirth.

"My father owns this tavern," said the boy as he shook his fist in front of my face. "And everything about it including the bones in this alley."

"Good for him," I replied.

"Aye, I can hear a bit of the Irish in you. Did you just come off the boat?" he asked.

"Who are you?" I asked him.

"I'm Jason Brody. I lead a gang of boys that rule these alleys," he said. "Now what about you, boyo? Did you just come off a boat?"

"Maybe" I said.

"No maybe about it...I can see you're a dirty stinking Irish thief," he replied with a growing smile on his lips. His mouth opened to laugh and he showed a lot of yellow teeth. He then looked past me toward something he was seeing in the alley behind me.

"Who is that?" he asked.

I heard footsteps behind me. I turned and saw my sister Ann standing in the alley. I could see that this Brody fellow was giving her the eye. He reached up and slicked back his long hair with his fingers.

"My sister Ann," I said.

Jason nodded with approval.

Ann offered Jason an up and down look and then averted her eyes as if to dismiss him. "Mother wants you to come back to the pier," she said.

Jason reached out and pushed my shoulder. "You come back here sometime. Oh, and make sure to bring your dog," he said and then he laughed out loud.

His laughter caught my fancy and I started to laugh with him. My sister looked at the both of us as if we were daft. I hadn't had a good laugh in such a long time. Jason was shaking with it and his eyes were watering with tears. There was something about him that made me take a liking to him even though he had tried to beat me up.

"Come along now," said Ann.

"Aye, you let your sister lead you by the chin, boyo?" asked Jason.

"You go," I told Ann. "I'll come along later."

"You find your own way," Ann replied. "I don't care."

I turned to Jason. "I'll come back sometime," I said.

He reached out to shake my hand. He clasped my fingers in a tight grip that was meant to bring pain. And yet, he was still smiling at me and flashing those big yellow teeth. "Next time you come back," he said after releasing his grip on my hand. "Forget about the dog, bring her," he said as he gestured to Ann. He winked at her and then laughed again.

Ann offered him a cold stare and walked away.

I followed Ann down the alley. I turned and waved back at Jason but he had his eyes directed at Ann. She refused to turn and acknowledge his attentions.

I don't know what Jason saw in my sister. I never looked upon my sister Ann as an object of beauty. We both had red hair and hers was frizzy and tied up in braids. She was dressed up in a man's set of pants and a sailorman's shirt so that what ever womanly qualities she had were hidden beneath the billowing cloth of that plaid shirt and oversized pants that were held up with twine tied about her skinny waist.

She glanced back at me and saw the pants I was wearing.

"Where did you get those pants?" she asked me.

"I borrowed them," I replied.

"From that boy?"

"Yes," I replied. And why not, I thought? One lie was as good as another.

"You stole them, didn't you?"

I waved my hand to dismiss her. "Get along sister," I said.

"I'm going to tell mother," she replied.

Why was I going with her? I didn't want to go back with the family. I wanted to be on my own. I might even have made my first friend in America. At least this boy Jason could laugh. That was more than I could say for our own melancholy souls, having just arrived from Eire. But then again, I realized that it was hard to laugh on an empty stomach.

I could still taste the musty grease of that bone in my mouth and I would have given anything to have a bowl of that thin watery corn meal gruel offered up by the soup kitchens back in Eire. It was better than that hard bit of moldy bread that captain Wilkins had given to us. I had survived on only that and bad tasting water during the entire voyage to America. I had my mouth set to taste some of that milk and honey that was promised.

So where were the gates of paradise? All I could see were tall brick buildings with their tiny windows and some shops that displayed ship's wares and lengths of sailcloth. Between the shops were the taverns and I knew what kind of refreshments that were offered within those doors. I'm sure that my father was sitting in one of those taverns and getting his fill of the whiskey. He was spending the money that would have afforded us some decent food and shelter. I'm sure that those swinging doors to the tavern were the gates of paradise to my father. From what I had seen so far of America, I knew already that there were no gates to be found and that this was not a paradise.

I followed my sister back to the pier where we had arrived the previous day. By now, the sun had risen and the fog had cleared. I could see mother standing beside this man who wore the collar and the cross of a Catholic priest. Despite the warm weather, he wore a heavy black wool cloak that reached the ground about his feet and it had a hood that was draped over his head that covered all but his face.

I had a sense already that this priest was strict in the matter of redemption of lost souls. From the first look that the priest offered me when Ann and I approached them, I knew I was already being scolded. Mother and the priest regarded me with those accusing eyes. Mother looked down and saw the pants I was wearing. She knew that I had stolen them but she was not going to let on to the priest that she knew.

Terrance ran toward me and asked where I had been. "Did you see the city?" he asked with an excited voice.

I was in a dour mood and hungry to boot, but meeting Jason had an effect on me. I pointed back toward the warehouses. "I saw the gates of paradise," I said with the biggest smile I could muster. "And brother, you should see them. They are all covered in gold and silver!"

Terrance's eyes grew wide with excitement as he looked off in that direction.

"And" I added quickly. "You should see the pretty maidens all dressed up in white that are offering bowls of milk and big slices of bread heaped with butter."

"Mother is it true?" asked Terrance.

Mother glared at me. Her eyes were sending me a message, stop your lying, she was telling me.

"Gates of Paradise indeed," said Ann as she rolled her eyes at me and nudged me in the stomach with her elbow.

Mother turned our attention to the priest and introduced me to father Thomas Donahue. The priest's long bony hands protruded from the sleeves of the cloak. And as I approached him, he reached out to shake my hand. The expression on his face did not change. It was as if he was trying to see through me to my very soul with those dark brown eyes. He was not a young man, there were wrinkles about his forehead and the bit of hair I could see was gray even though his eyebrows were still bushy and black.

"You shouldn't be telling such tall tales to your young brother," said father Donahue. "And you should appreciate the fact that you are here in America now. You shouldn't be poking fun at your new home."

New home, what home? I wanted to ask. We had no money for a roof over our heads or to buy food with. Was it again charity that would save us? Not for me, I wanted to work to pay my own way.

"Father Donahue is going to find us a place to live," said mother.

What about food? I wanted to know where there was food but I said nothing because I didn't want to upset mother.

Father Donahue led us away from the waterfront through the busy streets of Boston. The noise from the wagon traffic was so loud that it made it hard to hear what Father Donahue had to say. I did catch enough of it to know that he was taking us to his church that was located in a place called the north end.

I did not want to show my ignorance by asking Father Donahue what were all those colorful signs saying, the ones that were tacked above the windows of the many shops that we passed. I was not a bit happy about the way these strange Americans looked at me and my family as we ventured across town. I suppose we were objects of curiosity as much as they were to me. It didn't help that my mother and sister were dressed up in sailor's pants and shirts.

Terrance seemed to be the most excited among us. He would crane his neck to gaze up at the church spires that reached up so high above our heads as we passed them. He would catch sight of every curiosity and want to explore like some cat on the prowl, so mother kept a tight rein on him.

I didn't see anything more remarkable than what I had seen during visits to Kilkenny back in Eire. They had shops and fine churches as well. There wasn't even a castle about.

I asked Father Donahue where the farms were. We walked through so many streets that were crowded with tall buildings on either side. "Was there no open land in this place called Boston, for a farm?"

I watched father Donahue's grim face break out into a smile all at once. "I'm sorry Billy," he said. "But there are no farms in downtown Boston."

"No farms?" I asked. "Then how do men make their living?"

"The trades," Father Donahue replied. "You shall learn a trade. But first you will have to work at hard labor to prove your worth and..." He stopped speaking suddenly. His smile faded. He was about to say something and thought the better of it. I don't know what caused him to frown.

He turned from me and went to mother's side and pointed to a large house that stood on a street corner just a block from a much taller red brick church. Mother asked if the tall brick church was the father's church. Father Donahue shook his head and told mother that it was a protestant church. He directed our attention to a smaller house on the opposite corner and told us that it was his church. He told us that it had once been an old meeting hall and that his parish had started there just a few years ago and that one day in the future, they would have the means to build a fine brick church in it's place.

"There is another house down the street," said Father Donahue. "There is one tiny room vacant but there is no stove. There is a privy in the rear and running water from a back yard spigot."

"We have no money," said mother.

"The church rents that room and four others in that house for those who need shelter and cannot afford to pay," said Father Donahue. "I'll take you there now. After you have a bit of a rest, you can come to the church. We have a kitchen set up in the basement where we have soup and bread to offer the hungry and we have a selection of donated clothes. I'm sure we can find dresses for you and your daughter and a swaddling blanket for the little one."

I did not like this part of Boston called the north end. The streets were crowded with small children and the place smelled of garbage. I would have preferred the aroma of farm manure to this human kind. The streets smelled as foul as the dark ship's hold we had recently left.

Father Donahue led us to this narrow house that was three stories high. It appeared as if it was leaning to the left and it looked as though one part of the roof might collapse down upon us. There were just a few small openings for windows and two of them had boards nailed across them. The entrance door was missing and there was nothing to greet us but a dark hole to walk through that led us into an even darker hall.

There were piles of garbage lying about the floor just inside the hall. Flies buzzed about in a swarm and a terrible stench rose from them. I was almost tripped backward by a squealing pig that came running down the hall toward me. It was being chased by a couple of naked children. They were so covered from head to toe with muck, that I could not tell whether they be girls or boys.

The house made sounds like the ship we had left. The floors groaned and creaked. I could hear all the mixed sounds of those who lived upstairs; crying babies, angry oaths, coughs and other human noises. It was so hot inside the hall even though it was so dark. It was a smothering kind of heat that made it hard to catch one's breath. I would rather have stayed out in the street and found a place to rest in the gutter. At least I would be out under the open sky to see the bright sun.

Father Donahue led the way up a narrow staircase that swayed back and forth each time he took a step. I had no shoes and my bare feet slid across this black ooze that covered the floor and made the steps slippery. I followed directly behind Father Donahue and Terrance was right behind me. Mother had told us to go on ahead of her. I climbed the steps and felt them sway under my feet almost as if I was on the deck of the Saint Gerard again. I had to dig my toes inward and spread my knees to keep from falling backward.

Chapter 4

I reached out to the wall with my right hand to regain my balance and I felt the wall move away from me. Once I got up to the top of the stairs, I noticed that there was only one tiny window at the end of the upstairs hall that let a bit of sunlight in. There was just enough light so that I could see many doors and that the floors were bare and dirty as the downstairs hall.

Father Donahue led us to the end of the hall, away from the light. He pushed open a door into a room that was as small as one of the sailor's berths that I had seen aboard the Saint Gerard. At least in the sailor's quarters, there had been a bunk and a sea chest. There was nothing in this room but the bare four walls, covered with strips of stained brown paper.

Mother took a look at the tiny room and sighed. "At least it's a roof over our heads," she said. "...and we should give thanks for that."

I didn't want to stay with the family in this tiny room. It was so crowded with the five of us, that there was not enough room for all of us to sit on the floor at the same time. Before he left us, Father Donahue promised to get us some straw filled mattresses and a candle for light.

I knew that food was waiting for us back at the church and I didn't want to spend another minute in this dark, smelly, noisy house. Ann agreed to stay behind with Geraldine and we would bring food back to them.

Father Donahue met us in the church basement. I will admit I did like the new smell that greeted our noses there, that of cooked cabbage soup and freshly baked bread. A few other pour souls sat upon long wooden benches at a table and dipped their bread into hot steaming bowls of soup. I could hardly wait to have the young lady there dip the bowl into the big pot and hand it to me. I nodded my thanks and rushed over to the table to eat.

Mother told us to wait. "We shall say grace first," she said. She told me to lead the prayer. I wasn't sure what to say. I sat there and stared at her.

"Forget how to pray have you?" she asked me. "Well, Father Donahue will have a cure for that soon I'm sure. You'll be going to church and confession every Sunday now that we are in America."

I sat there with the bowl of soup under my nose. The steam rose up to my face and the smell of cabbage filled my senses. I picked up the bowl and started to swallow the thin watery soup.

Mother shook her head at me. "There is a lot you have to learn about table manners," she said in a tone of disgust.

I swallowed until my mouth was full and I could swallow no more. There were just bits and shreds of cabbage and little more that was solid, and yet, it was better than anything I had eaten since I left Eire.

"There's a school here," mother said to me. "You, Terrance and Ann will have to learn how to read and write."

"I'm going to work, mother," I replied as I took a bite of bread into my mouth.

"And what will you do?" mother asked. "You don't have a trade."

"The port officer said that there was work digging ditches," I said. "I can use a shovel well."

Mother shook her head. "And you'll get in with the working crowd. You'll start to drink and carry on like your father."

"No," I replied. "I'll never be like him." I resented the very suggestion that I might start to drink and carry on like my father.

"Father Donahue told me he has work for me as a laundress," mother announced.

"Father would have a fit if he found out you were working," I said.

"We have to have money," said mother. "Ann will stay home and take care of Geraldine and Terrance."

"I want to work too," said Terrance.

I patted Terrance on the shoulder. "You'll stay home and be the man of the family," I said.

"But you'll be there too, won't you?" he asked.

"I'm going my own way soon," I said after swallowing the last mouthful of soup.

Mother was silent at first, after hearing me say this. She then leaned forward suddenly and raised her hand to point a finger at me. "While your father is away, it is your duty to stay with your family," she said. "Terrance is too young to take your place."

"And what happens when father returns and he comes to stay? Where will we all sleep?" I asked.

Terrance looked terrified at the mere mention of my father's coming home. He pushed his half eaten bowl of soup away from him and pouted.

"You finish your soup," mother told him.

"I don't want father to come home ever," Terrance whined.

Mother looked away from him in disgust.

After finishing our soup and bread, mother led us over to a table piled high with clothes. Someone had given mother a tin bucket to carry soup home to Ann and Geraldine. She gave it to Terrance to carry. Mother reached into the pile of clothes and found some dresses, all very large and somber in color. She also found some coats without their buttons. Leave it to my mother to be already planning for winter as the summer had just begun.

Father Donahue met us at the door before we left the church basement. He asked to speak with me alone. I stayed to talk to father while mother and Terrance went back to the house.

"I can find you work if you still want it," he said.

"Yes, I would like that very much."

"But with your father away and your mother working, perhaps you ought to stay at home and take care of your brother and sisters."

"Ann can take care of them," I said. "I've decided to go my own way. I'll get work and find my own place to live soon."

"And leave the family?"

"There's not enough room for me, especially if father returns," I said.

"Where is your father, Billy?"

"I don't know," I replied. I wanted to add; and I don't care.

"I wanted to speak with you alone because I felt I should warn you," said Father Donahue. "There are many ways for a young man like you to get into trouble. If I were you, I would keep away from the waterfront and Fort Hill. There is a bad element there. Gangs of boys roam the streets and piers and get into all kinds of trouble."

Boys like Jason Brody, I was thinking. Jason told me he was leader of a gang. I wasn't afraid of them.

"Where is Fort Hill?" I asked.

"It's where I found you and your family by the waterfront," he replied.

I nodded.

"You can't read or write can you?" he asked.

I shook my head slowly and looked down at my feet in shame. Father Donahue reached out with his hand, tapped my shoulder gently and told me to raise my chin. "You should not feel shame," he told me. "At least you have the will and the desire to work. You can go to school here to learn those things soon. Get along now, but remember what I told you. Stay away from Fort Hill and the gangs. You'll find nothing but trouble down there."

I went back to the house. I stood out in front of that rickety old place and had to swallow hard to get the courage to go back inside. I felt as if I was returning to the dark hold of that ship back at the pier. I looked down at the pile of garbage and kicked away at it. Why must people live like pigs? Was there no better way? I thought America should be a better place. At least it should be cleaner than the hold of the Saint Gerard.

I found my way back up the unwieldy staircase to the dark little room. Mother had managed somehow to get two straw filled burlap mats into the room, one for us boys and the other for mother, Ann and Geraldine. There was a narrow path between them where mother set the candle on its side. Mother would not let us light it. She told us that we should save it for an occasion when we will really have need of it.

There was one tiny window in our room about one foot square and the outside was covered with dust and grime so that the sun's light could not penetrate fully. I stood up and looked out through the glass. I could only see the shapes of the privy shed below in the back yard. I tried to lift the sash to bring some fresh air into the room but I discovered that the window was nailed shut and could not be opened.

Mother sat on the straw mat beside Ann and Geraldine. The poor baby had a terrible cough and mother was cradling her in her arms and singing that soft ditty she sang before to calm her while in the hold of the ship. It didn't do much this time to quiet Geraldine's wails and cries; nothing seemed to sooth her suffering.

Ann had the dresses in her grasp. She told me to look away as she stripped off the sailor's pants and shirt and then she pulled one of those dresses over her head. I turned and saw her disappear into the big folds of that dress. She spread the skirt with her hands but nothing was going to make the dress fit her.

"I'll get some pins," said mother. "It looks better on you than the sailor's clothes. At least you look like a lady again."

"She looks like an old maid," I said.

"Billy," mother scolded.

Ann was quick with her foot and brought it out to kick me in the shin of my leg. I moved quickly backward but her toe nails dug into my skin.

"Enough!" said mother. She gazed over at the fading light from the window. "It's getting near suppertime," she said. "Billy, you go back to the church and tell Father Donahue that you will be bringing the food home. Tell him that Geraldine has taken a turn for the worse and I don't want to leave her. He'll understand."

But I had questions for mother. I wanted to speak with her alone.

"Why can't Ann and Terrance go to the church and get food?" I asked her.

"I haven't been out yet," said Ann. "May I go? Billy can stay here this time."

"Very well," mother replied. "Terrance, you go with Ann to help carry the food."

I felt a sense of relief after they left. At last, I would have a chance to speak with mother alone without Ann or Terrance to get in the middle of it. I waited until Ann and Terrance were well down the stairs before I asked mother the first important question. "What is our future going to be here in America?" I asked her.

"I don't know, Billy," she replied. "You should be thankful that we made it here alive and that we have a roof over our heads. Thanks be to God and the church."

"I don't like America very much," I said. "It's crowded and it smells bad."

"You've been living with the smell of manure all your life and you shared a bed with four brothers. What is so different here?" said mother in reply.

"Can't there be something better?" I asked. "Must I always be satisfied with what I have? Can't I hope for more?"

"Oh Billy, why do you bother me with those kinds of questions?" mother replied. "I don't have the answers for you."

"What if father returns?" I asked her. "Will you let him in as if nothing has happened?"

"Let him in?" Mother replied. "Of course I'll let him in. He's my husband and your father. Never forget that."

"He hates me," I said.

Mother shook her head at me. "Hate you? How could you say such a thing about your father? He has his own weaknesses, but hate, that is a very strong word. Hating is a sin."

"Father is a terrible sinner," I said.

"Billy, stop this. It'll get you nowhere but trouble," said mother.

"I hate him," I said it without thinking.

"Hate who?"

"I hate Father," I said.

Mother was on her feet. "You get down on your knees right now and pray to God for forgiveness. Hate your father? Where have these thoughts come from? How could you say such a thing?"

I realized I had gone too far. I had to say something to soften that fierce look in my mother's eyes and to lighten her anger.

"I'm sorry," I said. But I didn't mean it.

Terrance and Ann returned shortly with our dinner. I was glad that my time alone with mother was at an end. I had no desire to spend another time like that with her. Mother could not stop looking at me. I wondered what was in her mind. Did she think less of me because I told her the truth about how I felt about my father?

I had decided right then that I was going to leave my family soon. But I wasn't yet sure about what I was going to do or where I was going to go. I only knew that I could not bear to spend more than a few nights in this tiny cramped room and on that narrow straw mat with my brother Terrance who most certainly would pee all over me with fright, knowing that his father was coming back to get him.

We finally settled in for our second night in America. I suppose I was grateful that at last, it was under some kind of roof. The truth is, I would have preferred sleeping outside in the fresh air. I was finding it hard to breathe in this hot, airless little room.

I lay myself down beside Terrance. He was already asleep but thrashing about in the dark. He must be having another one of his bad dreams and I knew what was to follow. I felt that warm liquid seep under me and spread through the mat. I could smell it among the odors of left over cabbage soup, the stale straw and the stench of our unwashed bodies. As I lay there in the dark unable to sleep. I looked across the room toward the window. There was just the slightest bit of light coming in through the window from the moon in the sky that allowed me to see the sill and the darker figures of my mother and sister Ann lying on the mattress side by side. Little Geraldine had fallen asleep after all her coughing and crying and was tucked in the crook of mother's arm.

Terrance had finally become still. Other sounds came from beyond the walls; the grumbles and snores from inhabitants of the next room. Outside, wagons rolled over the cobbled streets and you could hear distant honking of a fog horn.

I was the first one to hear the heavy footsteps in the hall just outside our room. I got a clot in my throat upon hearing those footsteps as they approached our room. A man's voice grumbled something. It was just outside the door. Someone knocked. Mother stirred and Geraldine began to cough again. "Who is there?" mother called out in a whisper. "Billy, get up and see who is at the door."

I dared not move an inch.

Mother got to her feet and Geraldine was crying louder. "Shh," mother said to the baby and tried to calm her. I watched as mother's dark figure passed me as she went to the door. I was saying a prayer. "Please don't open that door." I knew who was on the other side. Mother opened the door and I held my breath.

"Gerald," she said. "Where have you been? How did you find us?"

Where had he been? Only mother would ask such a stupid question with the stench of my father's whisky breath filling the room.

My father staggered into the room. His feet slid across the floor and I held my breath even tighter as he came closer, until his dark form hovered over me. The smell of the whiskey on him overpowered the other odors of the room.

Mother moved back to her bed.

A bright light flashed before my eyes. Mother had lit the candle and she placed it in the sill of the window. Of all the special occasions to light it, I wished she would not have chosen this particular time. I looked up and saw my father's face in the flickering glow of the candlelight. Although much of his face was still concealed in dark shadows, what I could see sent shivers down my spine.

He had a growth of beard on his chin. His darkened face was blotched red in the cheeks and nose and there were flecks of white spittle at the corners of his mouth. His eyes appeared as dark holes tucked under his hooded brow. He towered over me and leaned forward as if he was about to fall onto me.

"Get out of that bed," he growled at me.

Terrance squealed with fright.

My father reached out and tried to rap Terrance's ear but he was so drunk that instead, he slapped the air above our heads.

I grabbed Terrance's arm and pulled him out of bed. I knew the bed was wet with Terrance's pee. I hoped father didn't notice.

Terrance and I slid away from the bed toward mother and Ann. We were all crowded into the corner of the room. Ann awoke and looked up to see father. Her eyes widened at the sight of him and I saw her shudder with fear.

My father then lowered himself down on the bed. He put one hand down onto the mat. "Damn little son of a bitch," my father growled. He turned and glared at Terrance. Terrance rushed toward the corner of the room and cowered. His whining filled the room and drowned out Geraldine's wails.

"What's wrong?" mother asked father.

"The boy peed in the bed," my father replied.

Terrance's' whines became louder.

Father headed for him.

Mother was holding Geraldine. She and Ann slid away in the opposite corner, leaving Terrance alone and unprotected. The candlelight did not reach the corners of the room so that I could only see part of Terrance's dark form but his sounds gave his position away. If only he would shut up, father might not find him. I couldn't let this happen. I rushed to stand in front of Terrance.

"Stand aside," said my father.

"Leave my brother alone," I replied. "Go away."

"What's that you say? You are telling me, your father, what to do in my own house?" my father raised his hand, swung it out and caught me on the left cheek before I could move away. There was no place to go. My head snapped to the side and my cheek burned, but I stood my ground.

My father reached out and grabbed my arm. He pulled me aside with such force, that I fell to the floor and hit my head against the wall. I felt dizzy and my head began to ache. I was stunned long enough for my father to reach Terrance.

My brother screamed at the top of his lungs and his wails pierced the night. My father swung out with the back of his hand and hit Terrance hard across the face. Terrance squealed and whimpered and then, he started choking. It sounded as if he was unable to get his breath.

I couldn't see my brother's face clearly to see what damage my father had done until Terrance lurched forward into the light and I saw the blood streaming from his nose and the side of his mouth.

Just as my father was about to make a fist to strike a harder blow, I got to my feet, grabbed at my father's arm and pulled at it with all my might to prevent another blow to fall.

"Get up and run!" I shouted to Terrance.

Terrance was shaking all over. He looked toward mother who was cowering in the other corner. I couldn't understand it. Mother's little angel was being tortured and she didn't lift a finger or say a word to help him.

"Go down to the church," I told Terrance. "Leave now! I can't hold him back much longer."

Terrance ran to the door. Just as he left the room, I lost my hold on my father's arm. He took hold of my arm then. His rough fingers dug into my skin. His hold was so strong, I could not pull myself away. "I'll show you. You'll not defy your father again," he growled.

I closed my eyes for a second and winced for the blow that was to come. I then felt an explosion in my nose as his fist smashed into my face. I was dazed by its force. I opened my eyes to see bright flashing lights and then I felt sharp pains shooting through my skull. I tasted the hot blood that soon filled my mouth and I could not get air through my nose. I dared not cry out. I ripped my arm from his grip. I could feel my own hot blood of anger rise to my face. I could have killed him right then, if only I had the strength. The will was there for certain.

My father staggered away from me and then his eyelids drooped. He had expended all his energy on me. He was so drunk, his legs began to fold under him and he faltered on his feet. He managed to guide himself over to the pee soaked straw mat and fell down upon it with a loud thud. One of his arms swung outward to hit the wall with a thump and he was out cold.

Mother came to me and reached up to touch my face. I pulled back before her hand could reach me. I turned away from her.

"Billy, I'm so sorry," she murmured softly.

I couldn't speak, but if I could, I would ask. Why didn't you try and stop him? Thank God he was drunk to the point of senselessness, otherwise, he might have killed me and would she have stopped him then?

I knew I couldn't stay in this room one more minute, even though it was the middle of the night and I had no place to go. I grabbed my pants and shirt from the floor and ran out of the room into the hall. I was so dizzy I had to lean against the wall for support. I looked back into the room and saw Ann's face in the dim candlelight. There was no pity for me in her eyes and I turned away.

I tried to regain my senses. It was so much darker in the hall. I had to feel my way along the wall to the stairs. I could feel my own warm blood dripping from my chin onto my bare chest. Pain struck me hard every time I tried to take a breath through my nose. I looked out into the blackness of the night. Where was I going to go, to the church? I wanted nothing to do with the church or God. I didn't feel any sense of protection from him. Terrance was one of his angels. I was sure he would be watched over. I was not that kind. I suppose I hadn't measured up. I didn't deserve to be protected.

I made my way slowly down the swaying staircase to the back yard. There was a lantern that offered a feeble light near the privy. I kneeled down to the water spigot so I could wash the blood off my face. I ripped away part of my shirt sleeve to wash my face. I touched the end of my nose with the cloth and the pain made me cry out. I knew it was broken. I gazed up to the second floor to that tiny window where mother had placed the candle. The light was out. They had gone back to sleep. I turned and staggered away from the house.

Chapter 5

I was awakened by a loud scream. I opened my eyes and saw something dark swoop down toward me. I raised my arms over my face to ward off the attacker but the dark object flew past me and I saw the shape of wings glide across the sky above me. A large bird, a seagull, had come to roost on the roof of a large wooden shed that cast a long shadow over me. I lay in a pile of old canvas sails. I recognized it as the place where my family had spent our first night after leaving the Saint Gerard.

For a moment, I thought I was back in that little room and that my father had come at me to strike me once more. I could still see his face; the dark eyes, the flecks of spittle at the corners of his mouth and I could still smell his whisky breath. I remembered that blinding pain of the impact when his fist reached my face and I could still taste the blood in my mouth.

I wished it had been another bad dream. I reached up to touch the end of my nose and I let out a cry that frightened the gulls. I could feel the tenderness and the swelling and my head ached something terrible. The gull swooped down and screamed out to me and three or four more gulls came to join the other and they started screaming. I wanted them all to shut up. I put my hands over my ears to block out the sounds.

I got up on my feet and looked down toward the end of the pier. The Saint Gerard was still moored there. I thought of running down to the ship and begging Captain Wilkins to take me back home. I would work for him. I would do anything. If I could not go home, then I thought perhaps that I should take a leap into the dark waters of the harbor and end my life.

I walked over to the edge of the pier and gazed down into the black water. A stranger stared back up at me. Who was that red haired boy with the bloodied and swollen face?

It was all so hopeless, I thought. America didn't want me. They didn't want any of us to come. The gates of paradise might just as well be the door to a jail cell and the plenty was hoarded by those who possessed the power and the money.

I leaned farther over to the water's edge. I felt an overwhelming urge to jump into the water below my feet. I was never a good swimmer. I wondered what it would be like to drown. How long would it take and how hard would it be to die and relieve this terrible pain...not just the pain in my body but the deep pain in my heart.

"Aye you there!"

I heard the voice calling from the other end of the pier. I turned about but could not see anyone. I looked back toward the water. "Mother, I hope you will forgive me for what I am about to do," I said as I stepped to the very edge and leaned out toward the water. I was about to leap, when I heard footsteps. I turned to look and I saw five boys approach me from the street. The boy leading the other four was Jason Brody, the same boy who had wrestled me the day before.

All five boys were stripped to the waist and had their shirts tied about their stomachs. They all had brawny chests and arms with tough looking faces. Jason strutted a few steps ahead of the rest and had his chin raised in a look of grim determination.

I turned toward the beginning of the pier and started to run. I thought perhaps that Jason was not my friend after all. Maybe he was going to have these boys hold me down while he could beat me again.

"Aye there, stop!" Jason called out. He then strode directly toward me. His face broke out into a smile and he pointed to my nose. "Got caught, didn't you?" he asked. "Stealing food for your dog?" He looked around. "Where is the pooch?"

I shook my head.

He came forward and dared to touch the end of my nose with his finger.

"Ouch!" I cried out. I pulled my head back and he quickly recoiled his hand.

"Sorry," he said. "It's broken you know."

I didn't reply.

"Can't you talk?" he asked.

"Yed," I said. My voice sounded strange as if it was coming from faraway. As I moved my jaw to speak, a sharp pain shot through my head.

"Who broke your nose?" asked Jason.

"My father," I managed to say. The effort to speak brought more pain and I reached up to rub my jaw.

The smile faded from Jason's face and it was replaced with a look of anger. He surprised me by reaching out to wrap his right arm around my shoulder. "I'm sorry," he said. He sounded like he meant it.

The other boys were standing some yards away from us and called out to Jason to come along. Jason waved at them and told them to go on ahead without him. "We're going for a swim," said Jason. "Why don't you come with us? You can wash that blood off your face. A dip in the cold water might make you feel better."

I could have told him that I was just about to take a dip into the water but the purpose was not to feel better. I was dizzy and hungry and I just wanted to be left alone. No, that wasn't true; I didn't really want to be left alone. Jason's bit of brotherly affection had brought me to the brink of tears. But, I gathered that he was not someone who would allow me to put my arms around him and cry on his shoulder as if he was my mother.

"Hang the swimming," said Jason. "Why don't you come home with me? Mother will know what to do about your face. Dinner will be ready in a few hours. I can hear by the growls of your stomach that you could stand to eat something."

Jason shouted over to the boys who were still waiting at the street end to the pier that they should go ahead and that he was going home to wait for dinner. They went running off and disappeared among the storage sheds.

Jason led me to the alley where we had first met. I noticed that the bones still lay there in the gutter.

"Where is your dog?" I managed to mumble through my sore jaw.

"My dog?" Jason replied with a wily grin.

I pointed to the bones.

Jason let out a chuckle and slapped me on the back. "I don't have a dog either, boyo." He then invited me to enter the back door of the tavern. We walked into a small room that was crowded with stacked barrels that reeked of whiskey fumes. The odor made my stomach queasy. We then climbed a stairway to a small landing and then Jason led me into what appeared to be a kitchen.

"Can you smell the ham and cabbage cooking boyo? A feast awaits us," he said and he then remembered my nose and shook his head. "Sorry boyo, I forgot. Does it still hurt?"

"Jason is that you?" A woman's voice called from a distant room and then there was the shuffling of feet. Through the kitchen door from the hall appeared a short stout woman wearing a brightly colored flowery dress with a yellow apron tied about her waist. Her features appeared to me to be too compassionate looking to be the mother of this tall brute of a son. She saw me first and frowned at the sight of my face. "Now Jason, haven't you done enough fighting?" she asked. "What have you done to this poor boy?"

"Oh ma, I didn't lay a hand on him. He was robbed and got beat up," said Jason. "I found him on the pier."

The woman came over quickly. I saw a mother's concern in her moist black eyes. "Poor thing," she said as she reached up and tapped my cheek. "Come over to the sink," she said as she gently touched my arm.

I followed her to the other side of the room. There was a deep wooden trough set upon some legs. Beside the trough was set a water pump with a long handle. She grabbed a cloth that hung from a hook above the sink. She then pulled the handle of the pump to release a narrow stream of water into the trough. She wet the cloth and was about to touch my face when I pulled back from her.

"Oh I know it hurts," she said. "I promise I'll be gentle with you." She then turned to Jason. "If he was robbed, shouldn't this boy see a constable?"

Jason shrugged his shoulders. "They wouldn't care about some poor Irish boy, mama, you know that. They might just end up accusing him of being a thief."

"Just off the boat are you?" she asked me and I nodded.

"And your family?"

"They all died," Jason said it so quickly. I had no chance to reply.

"Well now, why don't you let the boy speak for himself?" she said.

I thought it was as good a lie as any I could think of. "Jason is right," I said. "They didn't survive the voyage. The fever took them all." I then stared down at the floor.

"You raise that chin," said Jason's mother. "You have nothing to be ashamed of. Dear me, no family? What's to become of all these children who come from the ships with no mothers or fathers to take care of them?"

She tried to approach me once again with the cloth to clean the blood from my face and I stood there and bore the pain without allowing myself to flinch. I wanted this woman to be my mother. But then, I thought about my real mother and how she tore off a part of her dress to wipe my face and she watched over me when I had the fever. But then again, she had also stood by and had done nothing to stop my father from beating me or my brother.

"You have such a handsome face," she said. "I think your nose will heal well."

I looked about the kitchen as she wiped the blood from my face. There was such a comforting air about the room. Is this what it was like to have a real home? To be able to look about and see familiar walls, to see the fine lace curtains and the pretty clay pots of flowers that stood on the windowsill. A mother in her kitchen having her gentle ways with her children, even a tall brute of a boy like Jason and a stranger like me?

After Mrs. Brody had finished cleaning my face, Jason took me through the rest of the house atop the tavern. I thought Jason and his family must be very rich people. The other rooms were filled with store bought furniture and fine colorful carpets spread upon the floors.

I chanced to pass a tall looking glass in the hall and I stared back at myself. I saw the damage that my father had done to my face. My tangled and dirty red hair hung down to my shoulders. My nose was a wide flat nub that disappeared into my fat swollen cheeks. Dark shadows surrounded each eye. I didn't think I was handsome at all. I thought I looked like a freak.

Jason tugged at my arm and directed me up a narrow stairway to an attic room that was furnished with a big soft looking bed, which was covered with a red and blue checked quilt. Atop the quilt lay some big pillows. Beside the bed there stood a chest of drawers. A desk and chair stood opposite from the bed. There were two windows at one end of the room that faced east and the bright rays of the late morning sun came shining through.

"This is my room," said Jason. He ran over and jumped on the bed, landing square in the middle. He stretched himself out and let his feet hang out beyond the end of the bed.

"Fit for a king," I muttered. And then I remembered the straw filled mat I shared with four brothers in that loft above the kitchen in our old home. I would have still settled for that rather than the hard surface of a ditch beside the road.

Jason pointed to what looked to be a pillowy stuffed armchair covered with green cloth. "Sit down," he said. "Make yourself at home. It'll be a few more hours till dinner time." He sat up in his bed and then he reached over to grab a deck of playing cards from atop the chest of drawers. I knew them by sight because my father had a set that he kept in a little box and he would not let anyone else touch them.

Jason shuffled them deftly and then he performed magic movements with his fingers allowing the cards to slide from one hand to the other with great ease.

"You ever play cards?" he asked me.

I shook my head.

"Never?" he asked, sounding surprised.

I shrugged my shoulders.

Jason leaned over and lay the cards out on his bed. "I'll teach you," he said.

"Nothing beats four aces, boyo," said Jason. He held them up in his hand and flashed them at me. "I'm going to teach you a lot of things," he added. "Maybe you would like to join my gang? We have a little club room in the cellar below a warehouse. My father uses it to store whiskey and I use it set up card games. I'll take you to see it after dinner."

Jason went on to talk about his gang. He talked about the good times they had drinking, playing cards and carrying on with the girls. He mentioned a place called Audrey's house. He talked about the fine young women who offered pleasure for just a few bits. He then began to tell me how he made his money. He talked about the rich schoolboys from the other side of Boston who like to come down to the waterfront and mix it up with the Irish boys.

"They love to gamble away their allowances," said Jason. "They are not good card players and the house always wins the pot. I don't even have to cheat them. I just bluff them." Jason made a fist with his right hand. "Sometimes they don't want to pay and I have to use this," he raised his fist. "To get the money out of them."

The mean look in Jason's eyes made me shiver.

"I hate to have to beat them up," Jason went on to say. "After all, I can only spend their money. I can't profit from the blood they leave on my floor."

Jason's mother called us from below to come down for dinner. Jason threw the cards on the bed and was up on his feet and headed to the door before I could rise from the chair.

Jason's mother had prepared a feast fit for a king. I had never sat down to such a fine table. China dishes were laid out on a large table beside sparkling silver and crystal. Platters of steaming food were placed upon a side table against the wall. I wished I could smell the food. I bet the whole house was filled with the aroma of the ham and cabbage. I noticed that there were plates set out for six. I felt some dread at meeting Jason's father. I hoped that all fathers would not be like my own.

The sound of footsteps, rambling voices and laughter came up from the stairs leading from the tavern below. Two men entered the dining room. Their faces were flush with laughter. They both nodded toward me. Jason quickly made the introductions.

"Pa, this is my friend Billy," said Jason. "Billy, this is my father, Sam Brody."

I gazed up at the man who would be Jason's father. He was a taller man than his son but with the similar dark features. He had a head of short coarse gray hair that stood up on his head like a scrub brush. His eyes were deep brown and still shiny with moisture from the tears of laughter. I saw no threat in his expression of glee. So unlike my own father, Mister Brody was the picture of a happy man.

He took my hand and shook it. I could already see that he wondered about my face. "What happened to you son?" he asked.

"Someone robbed and beat him," said Jason. "I found him out on the waterfront."

The man standing beside Jason's father was shaking his head back and forth. "What are we coming to in this city? Young boys being beaten and robbed?" he asked. He offered his hand to shake. "I am Tory Odwyer. You know, son, you should go see a constable. We can't have this go on."

I studied Tory's face. He appeared to be younger than Jason's father. He had reddish blonde hair was just turning white at the temples and he had a lighter skin color and blue eyes like mine.

"The city watch doesn't give a damn about poor Irish boys coming in off the boats," said Jason's father. "That's where you had come from isn't it?"

I nodded.

"Do you have a family?" he asked.

"They all died," said Jason.

"Let the boy speak for himself," said Mister Brody.

"Jason speaks the truth," I replied. "They all got the fever and died aboard ship." The lie sounded convincing and Sam Brody accepted it as readily as Jason's mother.

Jason's mother entered the room carrying a plate full of sliced bread. "You take your seats now," she said. She then looked about the room. "Where's Maddy?" she asked.

"She says to keep something warm for her," said Tory. "She's not hungry now."

Jason's mother lay the plate down on the side table with a loud clatter. "Jason, go down and get Maddy. Tell her to come up and eat now or she'll get it cold later on."

"Let her be," said Jason's father. "She's been working hard. She's napping in the downstairs pantry. Let her have her rest will you please?"

"Oh well then have a seat and let's get started before everything gets cold," said Jason's mother. She then turned her gaze toward me and offered me a smile of reassurance.

Samuel Brody sat at the head of the table. I sat beside Jason on the left side by the windows and Tory sat opposite me. Jason's mother sat at the other end of the table opposite her husband. Jason's father led us in a few words of quiet grace and he put in a few words about the sad loss of my family and wishes for my own safe future as a newcomer in America.

My mouth was watering at the sight of the plates heaped with slices of ham and boiled cabbage as well as the bowl of potatoes swimming in melted butter.

"Eat plenty," said Jason's mother.

I couldn't taste anything that went into my mouth and yet, I managed to devour two platefuls of everything and drank several glasses of milk. I never had such a full feeling in my stomach. I was sure I had found heaven. Jason's mother seemed to enjoy watching me stuff myself with food.

There was such a clatter and sounds of chewing. Not a word was spoken. Jason's father finally lowered his fork, uttered a sigh, leaned back in his chair and dug his thumbs into his belt. "A fine dinner," he told his wife. He then took a finger and used it to pry a bit of something from between his teeth. He leaned forward and turned his attention toward me. "So, young man, Billy is it?"

I nodded.

"Who's going to take care of you now that your parents are gone?"

"Pa, he's just been robbed," said Jason.

"Now Sam," said Jason's mother. "Let's leave the boy alone for now and let him digest his dinner. Let's not spoil dessert for him." Jason's mother rose from her chair and excused herself. She walked out of the room and returned shortly afterward carrying a big steaming pie that was colored a rich golden brown. I watched the juice of apples bubble through the slits made in the top of the crust. I dearly would have loved to smell that.

The pie was cut up, served and devoured in quick order. I didn't think I could find the room in my stomach. And yet, I managed to gobble down two whole slices of pie and another glass of milk. I thought my stomach might burst at the seams.

Jason rose from his chair at the table first and excused himself. He told his parents that he was taking me out to show me more of the waterfront. This before his father had a chance to ask me any more probing questions.

Before I left the room, I thanked Jason's parents for the fine dinner.

"You're welcome anytime," Jason's mother replied.

"Where are you going to spend the night, young man?" asked Jason's father. "You can't sleep out there on the waterfront. You'll be at the mercy of the same men who robbed you."

"He can stay with us can't he, pa?" asked Jason. "We got so much room. We can pull out that trundle bed that rests under mine."

Before Sam could utter a reply, Jason's mother chimed in. "Well of course he must come and stay with us."

Sam nodded approval. "You both go off now. We'll talk more about Billy's future later on."

"Jason," said his mother. "Please, while you are on your way out, wake up Maddy and tell her that I am keeping her dinner warm on the stove."

"Who is Maddy?" I asked as we headed down the stairs to the tavern. We had gotten halfway down the stairs when this tawny haired teenage girl came up toward us. She had a face full of freckles like my sister Ann. This girl had a prettier face and a look in her eyes that showed me that she was more knowing of the things that most young woman her age might not yet be privy to. The kind of girl my mother would scorn.

"Ma wants you upstairs, Maddy," said Jason.

"Who is this?" said the girl.

"Billy, this is Maddy Odwyer," said Jason. "She's Tory Odwyer's daughter."

Maddy had a devilish smile and roving eyes. She wore a tight yellow dress that showed much of her womanly shape. She was staring at Jason as if he was naked. Her eyes roamed over his body and stopped at his crotch. Jason was giving her the same look. He reached out to touch her bosom. She responded by slapping his hand playfully. Still, she did not appear to mind his attentions. She then turned her eyes on me. She stared down at my crotch and I felt my cheeks grow hot.

"So what happened to red here," asked Maddy, pointing to my face."

"He got robbed and beat up," Jason told her.

Maddy reached out to touch my cheek. "Poor boy," she said as she gazed into my eyes and then winked at me.

Something was happening down below and I couldn't stop it or hide it. Maddy glanced down quickly and her smile became broader.

"Ma's got dinner waiting for you," said Jason.

Maddy continued up the stairs and waved at us. "I'll see you both later."

"Ma asked Billy to come stay with us," said Jason.

Maddy raised her eyebrows at me and then winked again. And then, she turned away and ran the rest up the way up the stairs.

Jason and I reached the door leading out into the alley and then he grabbed my shoulder from behind, moved in beside me and looked downward. "Maddy got to you, I see. She has that effect on all the boys she meets," said Jason.

"She's a beauty," I said.

"Your voice sounds better," said Jason. "It must have been those two helpings of apple pie."

"Is she your girl?" I asked Jason.

"Maddy is no one's girl," Jason replied. "She loves to tease and play with you but she'll never let you go farther than she wants to."

Jason led me away from the tavern into an area of warehouses a few blocks away. It was a hot afternoon and the streets were dusty. Jason picked up a stone from the street and threw it up high toward a rooftop. It bounced off a brick chimney and danced across the air, disappearing from our sight.

"Is Maddy her real name?" I asked.

"Madeleine is her real name," Jason replied. "But don't ever call her that. She hates her name."

I reached down and picked up a rock and tried to throw it up high. My arm was so weak, I couldn't manage to throw it as far as Jason.

"A few more dinners of cabbage and ham and you'll get some strength back in those arms, boyo," Jason said and then he began to run ahead of me. "Come on boyo, let me show you where I have my fun."

Chapter 6

We continued to walk through the deserted streets between the long rows of warehouses. By now, I was feeling lost. I looked down the alley in both directions and could not tell where we had come from. I wondered where all the people had gone in the middle of the day.

"Here it is," said Jason. He ran down a set of stairs to a small basement door located below the street under the warehouse. Beside the short little wooden door, there was a window that was protected by a wire cage. Jason pulled a small key from his pocket and showed it to me. "It took a lot of doing to get this extra key, boyo, " said Jason "My father doesn't know that this is the best little gambling club on the waterfront." Jason unlocked the door and pushed it open. "You first," he said.

I passed him to enter the dark room. I first ran into a tangled veil of spider webs that hung down from the ceiling rafters. The dirt floor was covered with straw and something else. The bare soles of my feet came into contact with something sticky but I could not see what it was in the darkness.

"Watch where you step boyo," Jason warned. "Our club does not yet own a spittoon. The boys love to spit their chewings on the floor. I've been meaning to steal one from my father's tavern."

I stepped carefully over the straw on tiptoe until I reached a part of the floor that was hard dirt.

"This place stinks of rye whiskey," said Jason. "Course you can't smell anything with that busted up nose of yours can you?

It was just as well, I thought. The odor of whiskey made my stomach queasy.

Jason felt his way through the semidarkness to the opposite corner of the room to a stack of barrels set against the wall. He pulled one of the barrels away from the wall, reached in behind it and pulled out a bottle of what I guessed was whiskey. Jason shook the bottle back and forth and grinned. "This is from my father's best stock. I drink only the good stuff boyo," He then pulled the cork, brought the mouth of the bottle to his lips and took a long swallow. He squinted his eyes as he drank and then pulled the bottle away. He wiped his mouth with the sleeve of his shirt. "God that's so good," he said and then gestured to me to take the bottle from him. "Have some," he said.

"No," I said. "I don't like whiskey. It makes my stomach churn."

"Aw come on, this is good stuff," said Jason. "It's real smooth going down. You must still be hurting. It will make the pain go away, boyo."

"No, I can't," I said.

"Have some beer then," said Jason. He reached down behind the barrel again and pulled out a slender brown glass bottle with a wax seal. "Beer won't hurt you and it's easy on the stomach. Try it boyo," said Jason as he handed me the bottle.

I grabbed the bottle from him and pulled the cork out of the wax seal and it popped. A gush of foam ran out over my fingers. I brought the mouth of the bottle to my lips and caught some of the foam on my tongue and it tasted bitter. I took a swallow. The liquid was cool and smooth going down. Tiny bubbles tickled my lips and tongue.

"You never had beer?" asked Jason.

I shook my head.

Jason reached behind the barrel again and brought out a small wooden box. He lifted the lid to reveal a deck of cards whose corners were folded or curled back. He handed the box over to me. "Count them for me, boyo. There are supposed to be fifty two of them. Make sure they are all there," Jason flashed a broad smile. I wouldn't want to be accused of playing with a short deck, now would I?"

I took another taste of the beer. I was getting used to the bitter flavor and liking the tingly feeling I got from it.

"Help me get this place ready for the boys. They'll be coming soon. Let's get these barrels set up to make a table. I'll take that board over there to use as a top. We'll use some of the smaller barrels for seats."

I helped Jason arrange things so that in a short time, the table was set up. Jason brought out a candle that was already burned down to a flat mass of wax on the plate with the black wick sticking out.

"I'm going to have to steal another candle from mama," said Jason as he drew a long match and struck it against the table to light the candle. Jason brought out another package from the hiding place in the wall behind the barrels. I wondered what else he had back there. Jason pulled a plug of what looked like dried up shit from a black wrapper. He tore off a chunk and placed it in his cheek. He offered a piece of the brown stuff to me.

"It's tobacco, boyo. Here, have a chunk," said Jason. "Put it in your cheek. Oh that's right, your jaw is sore. Not a good time to try it...maybe later."

I watched Jason as he worked his jaw back and forth and produced a stream of dark yellow juice on the edge of his lower lip. He then pursed his lips and spat out a stream of vile looking yellow juice from his mouth onto the floor. I thought about the fact that it was what I had stepped in and I immediately started to rub the soles of my bare feet on the dirt floor to remove the slime.

"Finish that beer boyo. I've got more."

I swallowed the last drop of beer and lay the bottle down. I was getting more of a tingly feeling in the tips of my fingers, through my feet and down to my toes. It was a new sensation of restfulness that I had never experienced before and my face was feeling hot. I wondered if this is what my father felt when he drank his whiskey? Was this what it was like to be drunk?

There was a flurry of sounds coming from outside, laughter and footsteps. Through the window, I spotted the face of one of the boys that had been with Jason earlier this morning. He was accompanied by three other boys. There was little light left from the setting sun so that I did not see the boys clearly until they had bounded forth into the cellar, slamming the door backward in their wake.

"Boys, we got a new member here," said Jason. "This is Billy."

"What happened to his face, looks like he ran into a wall?" asked one of the boys. It was still rather dark in spite of the candle. The boy's faces were cast in dark shadows so that I could not get a good look at any of them.

"His father beat him up," said Jason.

"Aye that's a badge of honor," said one of the boys. He stepped forward and offered his hand. "I'm Olny," he said. "My father kicked the shit out of me just this mornin. You ought to see my back."

"Come on," said another boy who did not bother to introduce himself. "Let's get the game going. I want to win back what I lost yesterday."

"Aye let's forget the fucking game and go see Audrey," said another boy who sat back in the shadows."

"That's Ray," said Jason. "He's the lady killer."

"It's the Sabbath," said Jason. "Audrey don't let any boys in on the Sabbath, remember?"

"Who's Audrey?" I asked.

"I thought I told you about Audrey," said Jason. "You pay your way and you get to spend time with a girl."

I had never been with a girl. But I wasn't about to admit that to these boys.

"I'll have to take you to see Lucy," said Jason. He put an arm on my shoulder. "Lucy is great with beginners."

The beer was doing strange things to me. Jason brought me a second bottle and I drank it down quickly while the boys played cards. There was no more talk about Audrey's. They argued amongst each other about their card hands this while I stood aside and watched.

"Hey, why ain't Billy playing?" asked Olny. I finally got a better look at him in the candlelight. His hair was yellow and his face was long and slim with a short stubby nose and wide brown eyes. There was a dark round splotch on his right cheek like a large freckle and he had a habit of scratching it every time he spoke up.

"He's just learning," said Jason. "Plus he's got no money for the pot."

"Why don't you stake him then?" asked Olney.

"Next time," said Jason. "That alright with you Billy…you just watch this time, ok?" asked Jason.

I nodded sleepily. The beer was getting to me and I had a funny feeling in my stomach. It was still full of food and I was burping it up. I went over to the wall by the door to get some air. It was so hot in that room. I slid down against the wall and let my head rest against the stone. I looked at the gang of card players and my view of them was getting fuzzy so that there was more than one image of them before my eyes.

"Wake up!" I felt someone tug on my arm. I opened my eyes and a dark figure hovered over me. For a moment I thought it was my father.

"Get away from me!" I shouted. I tried to pull myself up. But my head hurt and my arms and legs wouldn't work.

"Billy, it's me, Jason. Wake up. It's time to go home."

"Home?"

"Game is over. The boys left," said Jason.

My stomach was churning and I had to swallow hard to keep what was in there from coming up. I looked about, but could not see much. The candle had been snuffed out so I could only see the barest outlines of the cellar window and door.

"Get up. Let's go home," said Jason.

"Oh God," I said. I rose up and felt for the door opening. I ran up the stairs to the street and could not hold what was in my stomach any longer. I bent over and puked out all the fine dinner and dessert onto the cobblestone street.

Jason came up the cellar stairs and stood beside me. "Sorry boyo," he said. "I thought you could hold it."

"Just let me be," I said after spitting out the last of what was left in my stomach.

Jason reached out and rubbed my back with his hand. "Are we still friends?" he asked.

"Still friends," I replied and then I wiped my mouth with my shirt sleeve. I forgot about my sore jaw and brought more pain by accidentally hitting my nose with my hand.

"I am really sorry. You don't usually get drunk on beer, but if you never had any before, well after having some more you'll get used to it," said Jason.

"Don't worry," I said. "I feel better."

I looked up at Jason. I couldn't see his face clearly, but I noticed that he was leaning to the side and wavering on his feet. I stood up straight and reached out to catch him just as he was about to fall sideways.

"Oh I'll be fine," said Jason. "Just lead me home to bed." He then put his arm around my shoulder and leaned heavily on me.

"Which way back to the tavern?" I asked him. And then I heard Jason snore in my ear.

I found my way back to the tavern and had to lead Jason most of the way in spite of my own dizziness. I helped him through the back door to the tavern and Tory Odwyer was standing just inside the back room by the door. Tory offered Jason a once over glance and nodded with a smile. "Up the stairs both of you. Go sleep it off."

Jason grumbled and moved about under his own power again. He opened his eyes and offered Tory a sheepish grin and a little wave. I then directed Jason toward the stairs. I followed him up each step to make sure he didn't fall backward. Jason aimed his body forward up the stairs to the landing. I had to turn him in the direction of the next set of stairs to his room. He headed up the stairs directly and I followed him until he reached the end of the bed. He then fell forward, his head hitting the pillows and his arms stretched out and there was not another move or sound from him. I went over to the big stuffed chair, curled up in it, closed my eyes and the next thing I knew, day light was shining in my face.

That's how it had all begun. I brought Jason home that first night and his mother and father were grateful that Jason had made a friend who would take care of him.

Jason slept until the middle of the afternoon and then his mother called us down to have dinner. They made no mention of Jason's drunken condition. They did not offer to scold him or punish him in any way.

I learned that first day that all the members of Jason's family except Jason, contributed their labors to the running of the tavern. Jason's mother Mary cooked food for the patrons in another kitchen that was located in the basement. And

Maddy Odwyer was the server. Jason's father, Sam, took care of bookkeeping and managing while Tory worked as the bartender.

No one spoke to Jason about what his plans were for the day. In fact, no one even bothered to inquire further into my own background. They accepted the fact that I was orphaned at sea and were quite willing to accept me as a new member of the family without any official invitation. I just fell into their routine of life. After we ate dinner, the other members of the family returned to work. Jason was left to his own devices.

After that first day, I realized that Jason did not really lord over that gang of boys. In fact, he was pretty much of a loner. I soon learned that those boys came only to drink Jason's whiskey and chew his tobacco and that none of them were his real friends. I couldn't understand it. He was not a bad person. He was generous with what he had. He liked to push people around, that's true, but it was always in a fun loving way.

After dinner, Jason and I would go back to that cellar room. He would get out the deck of cards and play tricks for hours. Of course he had his bottle of whiskey at his side always and by the end of the evening he had finished it off and had opened another. I could not imagine drinking so much whiskey in such a short time. What amazed me was how long it took him to get drunk. It was that way all the first week of my stay and then that first weekend, the boys came back to play poker and drink more of Jason's whiskey.

On a hot Saturday afternoon, I went swimming at the docks with Jason and the other boys. Jason told me he wanted to teach me how to fight and defend myself. He announced to me that from now on, I was in training and that I should eat extra helpings of food each day. He promised he would run it off me and that he did. He ordered me to run back and forth up and down each pier from one end of the waterfront to the other and he was right behind me urging me all the way.

I don't know where his energy came from. He drank so much whiskey and yet it did not slow him down. He had such a powerful body. I would watch him dive and swim in the harbor. He could lift boys bigger than himself up on his shoulders and throw them over.

I got a chance to speak with Olny Madsen while Jason was busy counting his winnings on a Saturday night in the cellar. By then, I had been living with Jason's family for a few weeks. He told me that Jason had another friend who used to take care of him like I did, but that the boy's father told him to stay away from Jason after he found out that Jason was a bad influence. Olny told me that Jason was a thief.

I knew that Jason was stealing his father's whiskey, but after what Olny told me, I realized that Jason was stealing much more than that. Olney told me to watch my step. Jason was not so good a friend if you crossed him in any way. And then he told me the story about a boy that Jason had killed with a knife. He took his body and threw it into the harbor. Jason told the boy's parents that their son had drowned. His body was never found. Jason even had the nerve to tell the boys parents that he had jumped in and tried to save their son.

I listened to Olney and then gazed over at Jason who was busily counting gold coins and flashing that big smile. I remembered that first time I met him. The look he had in his eyes. I didn't think about the possibility that he really meant me harm, but after hearing what Olney had to say, it sent chills up my spine. I tried not to let the things Olney told me affect the way I thought of Jason. He was still a good friend and his family took good care of me while I took care of Jason.

The days and weeks were passing so quickly. My face had healed and there was a dent in my nose as a permanent reminder of what my father had done. Jason asked me more than once if I thought about going back to see my family. He knew that I was still afraid to confront my father.

There were times when I sat among Jason's family at that big table arranged with so much good food and I thought about my family and wondered how they were getting along. Did they have enough to eat? Winter would be coming soon and I knew that the room where they lived had no stove.

I saw myself again in that looking glass. So much had changed since that day Jason had brought me to his house. I had let Maddy cut my hair short. My scrawny body had turned to muscle. When no one was about to see me, I flexed my arms and turned to and fro. My mother would not recognize her own son.

Jason was excited that the summer was ending. He told me that the rich boys from Beacon Hill would be returning from their summer vacations. "We'll earn our money now, boyo," said Jason. "We'll have the gold to buy the attentions of all the women we want. We will have plenty of whiskey to drink and tobacco to chew."

I might have asked Jason, if I had the courage, what did he need with gold when he found ways to steal everything he wanted?

"You can take some of that money to help your family," said Jason. What he said surprised me. "You should go home to see your mother," Jason added. "I know my mother would miss me if I stayed away."

I made every kind of excuse why I shouldn't go back. The best excuse was that my father would be there.

"You have to face him some day," said Jason. "I taught you how to defend yourself. Why are you still scared?"

I couldn't think of a good answer. I just was.

"I know what the cure is," Jason told me. "The only way to lose your fear is to put the fear into someone else."

I wasn't sure what he meant until that Saturday night in the last week of September. We went through our usual ritual of having dinner with the family and then we went down to the cellar. Jason was unusually excited that night. He told me that the rich boys were coming to play poker. He had me sweeping the floor and getting the room ready for our guests. He managed to steal three more candles and a couple of silver candleholders that we placed upon some barrels. The room was brighter than it had ever been.

"You're going to stand guard at the door," Jason told me. "No one leaves without paying his debts."

"What if they don't want to pay up?" I asked.

Jason made a fist with his right hand and raised it up before him. "Remember, no hitting the face," he said. "Aim for the stomach and below. Use your fist or your knee. We can't mess up the pretty faces of these rich boys. Their mothers wouldn't like that."

The rich boys behaved no differently from the boys of the waterfront. They drank, they cussed, and they chewed and spit tobacco. The main difference was what they wore; sporting their fine frock coats, fancy pants and leather shoes. They all had clean faces and hands as well.

It was a pleasure to watch Jason lure these boys into a false sense of security. He let them win a few hands to get their confidence up. He made them think it was their lucky night. Each of the boys thought he had a good chance to win the stacks of gold coins that were piled high on the table. All of their monthly allowances were riding on this game.

Jason plied them with the best whiskey his father had to offer. They were allowed to drink all they could hold and then some. After a while, the boys began to get sloppy with their cards and Jason started to play his tricks.

It was well into the night. Many of the boys had fallen asleep and were lying about the floor of the cellar. There was one boy left standing who played on after all the other boys had passed out. Timothy Gardner was tall, blond and about sixteen years old. He had a smug snobbish way about him and I didn't like him from the start. I didn't like the way he looked at me and turned up his nose. I would be ready to have a go at him with my fists if the chance came.

Tim Gardner was the only boy who refused to drink whiskey. He had bragged openly that he could beat Jason at his own game, but by now, he had already lost all his allowance and he was trying to win it back.

Jason let him play on; knowing that there would be a debt to be paid on top of what Tim Gardner had already lost tonight in the pot. Jason had persuaded Timothy to cut the deck for a double or nothing bet. High card would win.

Jason drew the high card. Timothy swore at Jason and called him a cheat. Jason turned and looked in my direction. He gave me a wink. It was my signal to guard the door.

Tim Gardner reached into the pile of gold coins that were spread out on the table. Jason grabbed Tim Gardner's arm and wrenched it away.

"I'll go and get a watchman," said Timothy. "You can't have all my money. It's my whole allowance for the month." Timothy headed for the door and I stood in his way. We exchanged glances. He was angry and not yet afraid. "Get out of my way," said Timothy.

I stared back at Jason. He gave me a nod. I reached out, grabbed Timothy by the shoulders and pushed him backward into the room. He fell back and tripped over the legs of one of his friends who was stretched out on the floor asleep. Jason grabbed Timothy as he was lurching backward and prevented him from falling. He had a hold of Timothy's right arm. He jerked it sideways and up and then twisted it until I could hear the bone cracking. Timothy let out a cry and struggled to break Jason's grip with his other arm. But Jason pulled even harder.

"You're breaking my arm," Timothy cried.

"You owe me," said Jason. "You bet double or nothing. You lost. You owe me another two hundred in quid."

"You're crazy," said Timothy. "I can't get that kind of money."

"You will or it will go bad for you," said Jason.

"Bob, Steve!" Timothy cried out. Those were the names of his friends passed out on the floor.

"Your friends can't help you now. No one can," said Jason.

"I'm going to tell my father about you," said Timothy as tears started to roll down his cheeks.

"You're not going to tell your father anything," said Jason. He twisted Timothy's arm in the opposite direction and spun him around. And then, he let go of Timothy's arm and threw a hard punch into Timothy's stomach. He groaned and was doubled over by the blow. Jason nodded back to me and I threw a punch into Timothy's side. I felt his ribs bend under my knuckles. He let out another groan and his face turned bright red.

"You're going to get me that money aren't you?" asked Jason. He was hovering over Timothy with both fists clenched. Timothy gazed up at the fists. The look of anger in his eyes had been replaced with fear.

"Yes," he said.

"Just so you know we mean business," said Jason. "I am the kind of son of a bitch who will kick a man when he is down." And, with that said, Jason brought his foot up and kicked Timothy in the groin with such force that he was lifted up in the air. Timothy squealed loudly and grabbed himself as he fell and rolled around on the floor.

I didn't like Timothy, but I thought Jason had gone too far. I kept thinking about poor Terrance and how my father came at him and struck him in the face. And then I took the hit in the nose. But I was too afraid myself to let Jason think that I was not on his side. What would he do to me if I crossed him? I didn't want to find out.

Timothy slowly got back up on his feet. "No more please," said Timothy. "I'll get you the money somehow."

"Have it here by tomorrow night or you'll get more of the same. If you don't come here, I'll come and get you," said Jason.

Timothy was headed to the door. Jason caught my eye and gestured for me to kick him, by lifting his own foot up. I thought Timothy had had enough so I raised my foot and playfully kicked Timothy in his bottom as he was headed out of the door. Timothy reached back to rub himself and ran up the stairs.

Jason went over to the table and sat down. He grabbed the bottle of whiskey and took a long swallow. He then drove his hand into the pile of gold coins and shuffled through them. His face broke out into a broad smile and then he began to laugh out loud. He picked up one of the gold coins and threw it at me. I reached out and caught it. I stared at the shining yellow disk and hefted its weight in my fingers.

"That's a whole twenty dollar gold piece you've got there in your hand, boyo. Don't spend it all in one place."

"Twenty dollars," I said as I studied the coin.

"I bet you don't even know how much that is," said Jason. "I'll tell you," he added. "It will buy you dozens of visits to Audrey's. A whole lot of whiskey to boot and some left over for a plug of tobacco."

"I was thinking more about a winter coat," I said.

"No...no...no...that money is for fun, boyo. I'll buy you all the coats and fancy clothes you want later on," Jason replied. He got up from the table and looked down at the floor. "Timothy left without his friends."

"Will they tell?" I asked. "Will we get into trouble?"

"Oh hell no, boyo," said Jason. "They won't remember what hit them. They will wake up tomorrow and wish they were dead. They wouldn't dare tell their mothers or fathers that they'd been out drinking and keeping company with the low down Irish boys from Fort Hill." Jason then reached down and grabbed one of the boys by his coat collar and dragged him up on his feet. "Out you go," he said as he pulled him along toward the door.

The other boys woke up and rubbed their faces. They got up one by one and left the cellar with their heads hanging down. I heard one of them puking his guts out on the street. After they had all left, Jason came to my side and grabbed my shoulder. "You did good tonight," he said. "It's time for a reward. Time to take you to Audrey's house to see Lucy. She'll take real good care of you."

Chapter 7

Lucy was the most beautiful woman I had ever met, even prettier than Maddy Odwyer. I'll admit that I was terrified of her at first. I knew what I was there for, sitting in that stuffy little parlor on the first floor of that small house in Fort Hill, tucked away behind one of those big warehouses on the waterfront.

There were other girls who came into the parlor and wooed the boys with their attentions. Jason told me to hold out for Lucy. He had told me before that she was good with beginners. I never told Jason that I had never been with a girl but somehow he knew the truth.

Miss Audrey was a kind, quiet spoken, older woman who looked more like someone's mother than the manager of a whorehouse. She knew Jason well and I wondered if they had done it together.

After having met Miss Audrey, I thought about how angry my mother would be if she knew where I was and what I was about to do. I knew that my mother and my father had to have done it in order for the children to be born. I was never really sure exactly how it was done.

My eldest brother, Eamon, used to brag about the good times he was having with a girl named Eleanor McCreary. I was just there to listen in. It was a troubling thing for me. I had seen pigs carry on but I was still not sure that men and woman did the same thing. I supposed I was to find out soon enough.

Lucy came into the parlor and Jason introduced me to her. She had such a sweet smile. Her face was framed in long blonde locks of hair that ended in ringlets about her shoulders. She reached out her hand to take mine and she led me out of the parlor. I still had not said a word to her. My throat was caught with a lump in it and I couldn't think of what to say.

She led me up the stairs to a small room located off the end of the hall that was furnished with a narrow bed and a chair. She closed the door and began to remove her dress. I was not sure what to do next.

"No need to be afraid," she said in a soft voice. She took my hand and pulled me toward her. She brought her face close to mine and our lips touched. She ran her hands down over my shoulders and down my chest to the front of my pants. She opened my pants buttons one by one and I reached down to pull them off. It was not long before we were both naked and standing close together. She felt me down there and rubbed it to get a reaction, which came quickly. She then took my hand and put it between her legs and she moved me toward the bed.

She lay down first and I climbed on top of her. It all seemed so natural and I felt very secure. When the time came for it to happen, she showed me what to do. She was very kind and gentle. I was not ready for the result. It all happened so fast. It came as a shock at first and then, after it was over, I felt a bit melancholy. I wanted to stay and spend more time with her. But, her manner changed after I rose from the bed. "Hurry up now," she told me. "I have other boys waiting. See Audrey on the way out."

"Well? Was I right about Lucy?" asked Jason as we left the house after I have given Audrey the two bits to pay for my time with Lucy.

"How many boys does she see in one night?" I asked.

"What does that matter?" said Jason.

"How can she do that?"

"Do what?"

"Let herself be used," I replied. I had to admit to myself, I was thinking about my sister Ann. I could never imagine her doing this kind of thing and for money?

"Don't worry about Lucy, boyo," said Jason. "She makes out well. Now, you still haven't told me how it was."

I felt my cheeks go hot. I didn't know how to describe it to Jason.

Jason laughed as he patted me on the back. "You don't have to tell me. I can see it on your face. Give it a few more times, boyo, it'll soon come as natural to you as breathing."

As we left Audrey's house, a cold wind blew toward us from the harbor and it reminded me that winter would be coming soon. Time was passing so quickly. September passed into October. The routine never changed though, it was always what Jason wanted to do. We had more gambling parties with the rich boys on Saturday nights. Timothy Gardner came through with the money to pay his debts but somehow he always managed to owe Jason more and he seemed to like to get himself in trouble so that Jason would be forced to punish him. I thought Timothy was a strange bird. It was almost as if he enjoyed coming back for another beating. Jason was more than happy to provide him with that pleasure and I thought there was something sick about the whole thing but I never dared say a word to Jason about it.

Jason continued to prod me to go back and pay a visit to my family in the north end. I had been thinking about going back to bring some of my newly earned money to provide for the family. But as always, I would start to think about my father and I could not rid myself of the fear of another confrontation. Jason assured me that I could take him in a fight; that I was trained and ready but, he had never met my father and he didn't feel the power in my father's punch like I did.

On a cold, rainy Saturday in late November, I got a message from Maddy Odwyer at the tavern that my sister Ann had come to find me. She left a message with Maddy that my mother wanted to see me.

Maddy Odwyer and I had become good friends. We both shared a common purpose, taking care of Jason Brody. I knew that Maddy felt sorry for Jason and she even mentioned the possibility of marrying him one day. I knew that she was strong enough to carry Jason up the stairs each night after he got falling down drunk. I told her that marrying Jason wasn't any way for her to spend her life.

There was something about Jason that you couldn't let go of. He had such a happy way about him most times and he could be so generous. You found yourself wanting to do everything he asked of you.

I told Jason about my sister's message and he told me he wanted to accompany me to the north end to see Ann. He told me not to bring it up with Maddy. I told him that I had to go alone. My mother would already be suspicious. What with my new clothes; my new wool winter box coat and beaver hat and I looking so fit and well fed. I know the first thing she would think, that I had stolen everything and she would accuse me of being just like my father.

Despite my concern about introducing Jason to my mother, I was thinking that maybe it was a good idea to invite him to come along. The both of us together could defend ourselves against my father. But there was something else that bothered me. I didn't want Jason to see how my family lived. Not after knowing what his life was like with rich parents. I didn't want him to feel sorry for me or my family.

Sleet was falling onto the street as I headed away from Fort Hill and made my way to the north end on that cold wet Saturday in November. As I was leaving the tavern, Jason patted me on the back and told me not to worry. "Go and face your fears," he said.

I reached the street near that tall brick red church that my mother admired even though it was Protestant. The alleys were just as dirty and dark in the near winter as they were last summer when I first saw them.

The wind picked up around me and I could feel the sting of the ice hitting my face as I searched the street for that house without a door. I walked another block and thought I might be lost and then I saw the meeting house where father Donahue had his church. And, not much farther down the block stood that narrow broken down three story house with the roof that looked like it might fall over at any minute. I reached the house and walked into the dark hole that was the entrance. The wind moaned up through the stairwell.

It was so dark I had to feel my way along. I had forgotten about the terrible smell of the place. I wished that my nose was still broken and clogged with blood so that I did not have to breathe the odors of this place. The stairs still swayed under my feet. But at least I had boots to wear this time so that my bare feet would not slide over the black, filthy slime that coated the steps.

I made my way up to the second floor and noticed how the cold wind blew up through the stairwell. There was another cold draft blowing through a broken window at the end of the hall. Why was it so quiet? Not a human sound. Was I in the wrong house or had everyone left?

I found that little room at the end of the hall. The door was wide open and the room was bare. The mattresses were gone. I stepped into the room. All evidence that my family had once occupied this room was removed. I turned and was about to leave, when I heard footsteps from above.

"Billy!"

I turned quickly and saw my brother Terrance standing at the other end of the hall. "Father is in jail," Terrance said in a rush of words as he ran toward me.

I had never seen Terrance look so happy.

"Is he now?" I replied.

"We have a much nicer room upstairs with a stove," Terrance said with great excitement. "Come upstairs and I'll show you."

I followed Terrance up another flight of steps. The air was so cold that I could see the vapors from my mouth and from Terrance. I looked down and noticed that Terrance's feet were bare and all that he had on to protect him from the cold was a thin dingy night shirt that came down to just below his knees.

I was still feeling cold even though I was bundled up in my new wool coat and had a scarf wrapped around my neck and ears. I had left my beaver hat back at Fort Hill. I worried that it would arouse mother's suspicions.

"Don't you have any winter clothes?" I asked Terrance as he led me to a door just across from the stairwell.

"Mother is still mending our coats," Terrance replied. "It's not so cold in where the stove is," he said as he opened the door.

I felt the wind of heat coming from the stove that stood near the center of the room. A bright orange flame glowed through the grate. I could smell cabbage cooking from a dented pot sitting atop the stove. Steam was rushing out from the lid and making it dance.

A single candle was burning in a shallow plate atop a rickety looking old wooden table set not far from the stove. There was a chair at each end of the table whose seats were torn through in the center. In the soft amber glow of the candlelight, I spotted three burlap covered mattresses spread out on the floor against each of the walls away from the door. On the nearest mat lay little Geraldine bundled up in a blanket and sleeping peacefully.

Over by a small window there stood my sister Ann. She was still wearing that old woman's dress that was so big that she was lost in the folds of it. She turned and glared at me as I entered. Her face emerged in the glow of the candlelight. She was looking very old and tired for a young woman of sixteen years.

"Where is mother?" I asked Ann.

Ann walked over to the stove. She lifted the lid of the pot and stirred the contents with a bent spoon. She's late," Ann replied with a tired voice.

Terrance was right at my side and feeling the arm of my wool coat. "Where did you get the new coat?" he asked.

"I got a job," I said. It was a half lie. I suppose you could consider taking money for gambling debts as a kind of job.

"What kind of job?" asked Terrance.

"Carrying barrels of whiskey to a tavern from a warehouse," I replied. It was partly true. Jason's father did have me helping him restock his bar on occasion.

Ann offered me one of her looks. She wore the kind of expression that told me that she wasn't fooled. I could never get a lie past her or mother.

"That coat would cost a pretty penny for the likes of a laborer," said Ann. "From which poor soul did you steal it from?"

"If you want to know the truth, it was a gift," I said.

"And you expect me to believe that?" Ann replied.

"Leave him alone," said Terrance. "He just came home."

Ann reached out and rapped Terrance on the ear. He moved quickly away from her to avoid another slap.

"So father is in jail," I said. "Is that why you came to get me? How did you know where I was?"

"I knew you would go back to that place to find that friend," said Ann. "I can see that he's taking good care of you. It was mother who told me to find you. I told her she should let you stay where you are. You're going to end up in jail just like father. It's only a matter of time."

I wished that I hadn't decided to come after all. I could sense great hostility from Ann. I felt sorry for Terrance for having to put up with her.

"Leave Billy alone. You'll make him go away again," said Terrance as he wiped his face with the back of his hand and whined out loud.

"Oh stop your whining," Ann scolded him. She was about to rap him on the ear again but then, she looked at me and thought the better of it.

Someone came lumbering up the stairs out in the hall and approached the door. Terrance ran to open it. Framed in the doorway stood a hunched over figure bundled up in two threadbare coats that were covered in a crust of wet ice. A scarf and bonnet were tied about the face and ears. The scarf fell away to reveal my mother's face, chafed red by the cold. She looked up at me and she gave me that accusing stare as she saw my new coat and boots. "So Ann found you," she said, still gazing at my coat. "You're working?" she asked.

I nodded to her.

"Come and get out of those wet things, mother," said Ann. "Have a seat. I've kept the soup hot for you."

Terrance helped mother off with her coat to reveal a dress that was just as somber and ill fitting as the one worn by Ann. My mother had become so thin; she looked as if she was wasting away. As she rubbed her hands together to warm them, I could see how red and chafed they were from scrubbing other people's clothes.

"So father is in jail?" I asked mother.

She looked away from me. "He is," she replied in a tired, faraway voice.

"Come have the soup mother. It will warm you up," said Ann.

Mother asked if everyone had eaten. Ann told her that they were waiting for her to come home so they could all eat together. Mother took a seat at the table and began to tell us about her long day working at the Gardner house. My ears perked up upon hearing the name. "Mrs. Gardner wants her house ready for a birthday celebration. I had to stay and see that the carpets were properly beaten and that the floors were scrubbed clean," said mother wearily.

Mother then turned her attention to me and asked how I was doing. She insisted that I sit at the table across from her. She wanted to know; where did I work? What kind of work was I doing? And, most important of all, how did I manage to afford to pay for a new wool coat with the wages of a laborer? To all the questions, I came up with the best lies that I could think up on short notice. I was sure she didn't believe a word of it. But, I think she was too tired to challenge me.

I had a tin cup of the soup. It tasted terrible. Mother insisted that I share some with her and the rest of the family. She couldn't know about the rich food that I had been eating as of late. It didn't seem possible that there was a time that

I would have been so grateful to have this miserable soup and be thankful. How could I manage to forget the worst of times? After the long struggle to survive through the want and hunger after our eviction, the long torturous voyage to America and our first days ashore?

"You look very fit and healthy," said mother. "You have been eating more than cabbage soup to put that kind of brawn on your arms."

I wondered if that was said to make me feel guilty. I reached into my pocket and pulled out a five dollar gold piece. I laid it out on the table in front of her. She stared at it with a look of disbelief. "Now are you going to tell me, Billy O'Shea, that you make that kind of money working as a common laborer?"

I realized too late that I had made a mistake. I should have pulled out a smaller coin. "I saved it for you, mother," I said. Hoping she would accept it without question, fat chance of that happening.

"What do you make a week?" asked mother.

"Two dollars," I replied. But I added quickly. "The tavern owner gives me a place to sleep and I eat with their family. They gave me the coat, mother, as a gift."

"Very generous of them," said mother. Her voice was full of suspicion.

Mother turned her attention to Ann. "I need you to go down to the church. Father Donahue has some potatoes for us. Take Terrance with you."

"Out there in that cold and ice?" said Ann. "Can't it wait till tomorrow?"

"Not if you want to go without breakfast," said mother.

I knew that mother had other motives for sending them out. She wanted to talk to me alone. Maybe she thought I was old enough now that I might share some of the secrets of the elders. I took off my wool coat and let Terrance borrow it to go to the church and Ann put on mother's coats, which were still wet and coated with ice.

Mother waited until she could hear Ann and Terrance descend the stairs and then she leaned forward toward me. "This family is in a great deal of trouble, Billy," She started with that and then she paused and grabbed a sack from beneath the table. She pulled out a worn out winter coat, laid some buttons on the table before her and then a tiny roll of thread, a thimble, and needle. She first threaded the needle, took one of the buttons and began to sew it onto the coat.

"What kind of trouble?" I asked.

"The Port Authorities know about your father. You remember what they told him when we came here. If anyone ends up in jail, they will come and take us and put us back on a ship. It's only a matter of time before they come, Billy."

"What did father do to get himself put in jail?" I asked.

Mother would not look directly at me. She was concentrating on the needle and the thread and held the coat in her lap while she attached another button. She talked while she worked. "They say he robbed a storekeeper and hit the poor man over the head. The storekeeper survived and fingered your father. They picked him up off the street I suppose. I heard about it from the lady downstairs before she moved out. That's another part of our troubles, Billy. We have to leave this house. It has been condemned by the city. We have only a short time to find another place. We are the last to leave. The rest of the house is already deserted."

"You think we will be sent away from America?" I asked.

Mother's hand shook. She almost dropped the coat. She looked up at me. I could see the fear in her eyes. "That is what I fear," mother replied.

"You have a job. You support the family. We don't take much charity. I am working too. They can't make us leave because of something father did, can they?"

"They seem to be able to do anything they wish to anyone," mother replied.

That was something I did not want to hear.

"I won't go," I said.

"If they want you to go, there is nothing you can do about it," mother replied.

I got up from my chair and started to pace the floor in front of the stove. "Why did you marry him?" I asked her.

The question startled her. She put the coat down and gazed up at me. "Sit down, Billy," my mother said. Her voice was edged with anger.

"Father is a bad man. He belongs in jail," I said.

I was still standing, holding the back of the chair and looking down at mother. I realized that I had grown taller over the summer months because she appeared so much smaller to me.

"That's a fine thing to say about your father," she replied as she pushed the coat away. "You're father is not a bad man."

"Look at my nose, mother," I said. "I'll have this scar forever on the top of my nose. Tell me now that he is a good man. You tell me that."

My mother stared up at me without offering a word in response, just a look of disgust.

"Father might have killed Terrance if I had not tried to stop him," I said.

"No...no, how could you say such a thing?" said mother. "For Gerald to kill one of his own sons?" Mother shook her head at me. And then, she looked off into space and her eyes focused on some faraway point towards the ceiling. "I can remember what your father was like when we were first married. He was such a handsome young man and he had a kind way about him. He could be such a fine gentleman. I had come down from County Mayo with my father after my mother died. My father went to work with your father in the fields. Your father set about trying to woo me into marrying him just a short time after we met."

"When did he start to drink?"

Mother was still gazing up into space. She had managed to transport herself back to those earlier days in Kilkenny and she was smiling with her fond memories.

"Mother," I said, trying to get her to return to me. "When did father begin to change?"

Mother turned toward me. Her smile faded. "I knew that your father had a hard streak in him from the beginning and the drink brought it out," she replied. "When times were good, he was not so hard and cruel a man as he has become."

"Then you admit he can be cruel," I said.

Mother eyes closed to a squint and her lips formed an ugly sneer. But her anger was not directed at me this time. "You have no idea what has been done to us by the English," said mother in a bitter voice. "They took our land. They kept us from our church. They robbed us of our very dignity as human beings. What can you expect to happen to a man who has had his dignity stripped from him?"

"You told me about that before, mother," I said. "I still don't understand. Why would it cause him to turn against his own family?" I asked her. "Why couldn't he take his anger out on the English? They deserved it, we didn't," I said.

"You just don't understand how things were. Your father had lost all hope for the future," said mother. "It didn't happen all at once. Oh Billy, you're too young to understand. Thank god you won't have to live the life that your father had. We have a better chance at life here in America."

"Oh do we really? Father is in jail and we might all be deported. What has changed, mother? I don't see any difference between the Americans and the English. We don't have any more control over our own future here than we did back in Eire."

Mother turned away from me. She knew I spoke the truth. But I had one more important question that I wanted answered. "Was there ever a time when my father loved me?"

Mother was disturbed by the question. She continued to look away. She picked up the coat and began to sew on another button.

"You can't answer me, can you?"

"What do you want me to say Billy? We both know that your father is a very sick man. But in his own way, I'm sure he loves all his children," mother replied.

I stood there watching her. I knew that she loved my father despite his faults. There was no way I was going to be able to get her to see things my way.

Mother looked up from her work sewing the button. "Ann and Terrance should be coming back by now," she said.

There was a sound of rapid footsteps coming from the stairs.

"That is them now, I think," I said.

"This friend you made down in Fort Hill," said mother. "I want to meet him. What is his name?"'

"Jason Brody," I replied.

"That is a nice family you are staying with to be so generous. This boy, does he work with you?"

"Yes," I replied. At least that wasn't a lie.

Mother squinted her eyes at me again. "Tell me the truth, Billy. You aren't thieving are you?"

"No mother," I said.

"Why don't you invite that young man here for dinner sometime?" said mother. "I want to meet him. We can use some of that money you gave me to buy a ham."

"I'll buy dinner and bring it here," I said. "You use that money for new dresses for you and Ann and clothes for Terrance and Geraldine," I said. "I'll be bringing you more money as soon as I can save more."

Terrance came bursting into the room carrying a brown sack that was torn and ready to split open. He had just made it to the table when the sack ripped open and potatoes came falling out and rolled across the floor.

Ann came in afterward. She glared at me as if to ask, why are you still here?

Terrance had gotten dirt from the potatoes smeared all over the front of my new coat, but I said nothing.

"I have to get back to Fort Hill," I said.

"Can I come with you?" asked Terrance. "I want to see where you live."

"Some other time. It's too late tonight," I replied.

"Please," said Terrance.

"It's late and there is a storm outside. I need my coat now," I said.

Terrance unbuttoned the coat, took it off and handed it to me.

"Don't forget to ask your friend about dinner. Next Sunday would be fine," said mother.

Ann turned to me with one of her cross looks. "You're bringing that other boy here?"

"I told him to," mother replied.

"Please Billy, take me with you now?" said Terrance.

"Next Saturday, I will come and take you somewhere. I'll take you about the city of Boston. You'd like that wouldn't you?"

Terrance pouted. "I want to go see where you live."

"I don't want you taking him down there to the waterfront," said mother.

"Billy lives there now," Terrance whined louder.

"Next Saturday, I promise, we'll do something together," I said. "I have to go now." I headed to the door and nearly tripped over one of the potatoes lying in my path. Terrance followed me to the door. He was hiccupping with each sob.

I turned toward him. I wanted to take him with me. He was almost twelve years old and he still carried on like a baby. How was he going to become a man without the guidance of an older brother? He had no father. As I started to walk down the stairs, I looked back and saw Terrance's tear streaked face framed in the crack of the open door. His cries filled the hall. I waved back at him. It was so hard to turn away. But then I made myself a promise that I was going to come back and take him away.

I left the north end that night thinking about my father and the fact that he was in jail and that I had the threat of deportation hanging over me. I knew that none of us would survive another sea voyage back to Eire. I would fight with all the strength in my body to prevent that from happening. American was not such great place, but at least I was alive.

Chapter 8

I returned to the tavern at Fort Hill. Maddy met me at the back door. She told me that Jason had already left for the cellar. I went to the cellar and found Jason sitting alone and already partly drunk, even though it was still early in the evening. My visit to the north end had only taken a few hours time, but it seemed so much longer. I took a seat on a barrel across from Jason. I watched him shiver. He wore no coat despite the fact that there was no heat in the room save for the candle flame and the whiskey inside of him.

"Have any beer?" I asked him.

Jason got up, reached behind him pulled out a bottle and handed it to me. "Not like you, asking for a beer," he said. "What happened back at home? Did you see your father?"

I opened the beer and took a long swallow. I had become accustomed to the bitter flavor and the bubbles, but I loved beer most because it helped me sooth my fears.

"My father is in jail," I replied.

"You don't look happy about it, boyo," said Jason.

"I'm afraid that the port officials are going to send my family back to Eire. They told us before we left the ship that if any of our family landed in jail, we would be sent away."

"My father won't let that happen, boyo, so don't you worry," said Jason.

"We lied to your father, remember? He thinks my family died at sea," I replied.

"Trust me, boyo. No one is going to send you away. I'll find a place to hide you," said Jason.

"And what about my mother, my brother Terrance and my sisters Ann and Geraldine? I can't stand by and let it happen to them while I hide away."

"I thought your mother had a job," said Jason.

"She does. She works as a laundress for the Gardner family," I said.

Jason raised his eyebrows. "She doesn't know, does she?"

I knew what Jason meant. "No, and she must never find out," I replied.

Jason then smiled. "Does your sister Ann have a beau yet?"

"Don't get any ideas," I said. "Ann wouldn't associate with the likes of you."

Jason's smile faded.

"You wouldn't want her anyway," I was quick to add. "She's as cold as the winter ice falling outside on the street."

"You're her brother, that's not a nice thing to say about your sister," said Jason.

"I'm just telling you the truth," I replied.

"I'd like to see her again anyway," said Jason. "I have charms you haven't yet seen, boyo. I know how to melt that ice."

"Oh do you now? And what do you think Maddy would have to say about that?" I replied.

Jason looked about him as if Maddy might be present. "Shh," He put his finger to his lips. "She doesn't need to know about it."

"You might just get your chance," I said. "My mother wants to meet you. She wants me to invite you to come to dinner with my family next Sunday."

Jason took another swig from the whiskey bottle and grinned from ear to ear. "I accept your mother's gracious invitation."

"You had better be on your best behavior," I said. "My mother can't know about what I have been doing. There must not be any talk about gambling or how I've been earning my money. My mother is already suspicious."

Jason did not say a word to Maddy about his invitation to have dinner with my family. I told her about it. And I asked her to accompany us. I was sure that my mother would be more than willing to welcome her as well. But Maddy told me she had to work that day at the tavern. It was probably just as well. The minute my mother met her, she would wonder what I was doing associating with the likes of a barmaid with roving eyes and a devilish wit. I spent the remainder of the week worrying about that Sunday dinner. I worried that one slip of the tongue from Jason or myself would ruin everything.

I headed back to the north end of Boston on Saturday morning to take my brother out and spend some time with him like I had promised. The snow had begun to fall earlier that morning so that by the time I had left the tavern, the ground was coated with white. It did present a pretty picture to watch the horse carriages and wagons glide along through the snow covered streets. The air smelled so clean and the chill was invigorating.

Despite the prettiness of the view, I was happier about the fact that I was bundled warmly against the cold, and that I had a full stomach. I still had a great fear of the winter. I could not forget the hunger and the terror that I lived through last winter. What made it worse was the fear that some men would come and tell me and my family that we would have to return to that hell. It would be a fate worse than death for us all.

I had not yet found much to admire about this place called America. I learned quickly after my arrival, that the people here were just as willing and able to act cruelly and hard hearted as the English who lorded it over us back in the old country. I had to admit though, at least in America, we had a roof over our heads and some protection and charity from the church. Mother and I had work to support the family and, I could not ignore the generosity of the Brody family.

I was ready to tell mother that I was taking Terrance to live with me at Fort Hill. I would insist on it. Father was in jail and it was up to me to do what was best for my brother. Someone had to teach him how to be a man and how to take care of himself. I planned to teach him how to use his fists to defend himself against our father if the need ever arose again. I hoped that need would never come. As far as I was concerned, Terrance need not ever have to come face to face with our father again.

Terrance was beside himself with excitement when I arrived. Mother had finished sewing the buttons back on an old coat that was many sizes too big for my brother's slight frame. His arms and hands disappeared somewhere inside the long sleeves and mother had to roll them up. I looked down at what Terrance wore on his feet. Mother had found an old pair of worn out shoes. They had to stuff old newspapers in them so that Terrance could walk normally without his feet slipping out of the shoes. They had big gaping holes near the toes so that Terrance's feet were still exposed to the cold and wet.

I said nothing to my mother about my plans to take Terrance back to Fort Hill. I promised mother that I would bring Terrance home before dark. This was the first time in my memory that I had the chance to spend time alone with my brother. During our days out there on the road, we were always together of course, but it was not the same. It is strange to think that I never really shared any private moments or talks with Terrance since he had been born.

Terrance ran ahead of me on the street. He skipped along and tilted his head back to try to catch snowflakes on his tongue. It was the first time I had seen him act this happy since we had arrived in America.

I took Terrance to the nearest cobbler I could find to buy him a new pair of shoes. The cobbler told me it would take a few days to fashion a new pair of shoes for my brother and suggested that we choose a pair already made. I told the cobbler that I wanted my brother to have shoes that fit him perfectly. The cobbler measured Terrance's feet and he went out back and returned with a pair of fine looking leather brogans. Terrance tried them on. They fit him well. I insisted that Terrance wear them but he was afraid that they would get wet in the snow. The cobbler suggested that I buy him some India rubber overshoes. He had a pair that would fit me too. So I bought both pairs.

It was a good feeling to have the money I needed to buy what I wanted. Terrance was wide eyed with curiosity when I handed the cobbler the gold coins from my little purse.

Even though he had new shoes and rubber boots, Terrance still looked like a street urchin with his tattered coat and ripped pants. I was actually embarrassed to be seen with him like that, so I took him to a clothing emporium and bought him a new suit of clothes and a new winter coat. I could not forget that day when we first arrived in America. Terrance had given me the shirt off his back.

I was about to ask the clerk to throw away the old clothes Terrance had worn, but my brother wanted to have what was in the pockets. The clerk pulled out a wad of paper scraps that were decorated with drawings. I recognized the faces of my mother and sisters drawn so carefully on each little scrap. There were also some sketches of the room in which they lived. They were incredible little works of art and the clerk was astonished at their beauty.

Terrance admitted that he had pulled the paper from the walls. He told me he had used bits of charcoal taken from the wood stove with which to make his drawings. I decided that Terrance should have some real paper. I took him to a stationer and bought him a little bound book of paper and some real pencils. I had never seen him look so excited. He held the package close to him like some great treasure as we walked the streets.

During this time, Terrance had spoken few words except thank you. He was so filled with awe at the outside world that he had seen so little of before this outing.

We ventured farther into the city as the snow fell harder. I asked Terrance if he was feeling cold. His face was flush red and his teeth were chattering but he shook his head back and forth and trudged forward with his left arm swinging and his right arm holding his treasures close to him.

A kind old lady told us how to find the Boston Common. Maddy had suggested that I take Terrance to see the great pond where there were ice skaters and that the park made a pretty scene in the snow. She was so right. The ground was covered with white and long icicles hung from the bare tree branches. Terrance was dancing about and trying to catch more snow on his tongue. I leaped upward to a tree branch, broke off an icicle and handed it to Terrance. He bit off the pointed end and chewed it to pieces with a great smile of joy. I grabbed another one for myself. The ice tasted so cool in my mouth and the water was so refreshing to swallow.

"Wait till mother sees my new shoes," said Terrance. It was the most words he had spoken since we left the north end.

"I'm glad you like them," I said.

"Billy, when are you going to take me to your home? I want to see where you live," asked Terrance.

"On a finer day than this. When the streets are not so snowy," I replied.

"I want to come and live with you, Billy," said Terrance.

I turned and looked at him. His smile had faded and he was pouting again.

"Ann hates me," he said. "She treats me like a baby and hits me when I cry, like father does. When I try to draw, she grabs my paper and throws it into the stove. I go down and hide in the woodshed behind the house. It's my own little place where I can draw in peace. But I really want to live with you, Billy. I know you wouldn't stop me from drawing."

"I'll put a stop to that as soon as we return," I said. "Ann won't bother you anymore. I'll promise you that."

"But I want to come with you," he said.

"You have to understand something, Terry," I said. "I don't own my own house. I live with a family that invited me to stay. I am planning on getting my own little room. As soon as I move there, I'll come and get you and we can share that room together. But until then, you'll have to stay with mother."

"Please," said Terrance. "Why can't I come with you now?"

"I just can't take you right away. I would have to ask Mrs. Brody first. I can't ask them to take care of my family. I'm going to do that. You'll just have to trust me, Terry. I mean what I say. We will have our own place in a month or two. It won't be so long and I'll make sure that Ann leaves you alone."

"But what about father? He's going to come back and kill me some day," said Terrance.

Terrance's words frightened me. He spoke them without blinking an eye.

"Father is in jail," I said. "He can't hurt anyone there."

"He'll get out someday," said Terrance. "He'll come after me then."

I didn't want to talk about it anymore. I tried to change the subject by asking him where he learned how to draw such fine pictures. He told me he first started to draw pictures in the ground with a stick while we were out there on the road.

I looked at my brother as we sat there on the park bench. I couldn't resist the urge to run my hand through his silken white hair that was now topped off with a thin layer of snow. I had never touched my brother in any affectionate way before. It was something that only my mother did with the children. We never thought about hugging each other, brother and sister, to show each other affection. I saw Terrance sitting there and felt the urge to show him that I cared about him.

The time had passed so quickly that afternoon and before I knew it, the daylight was fading. I told Terrance it was time for me to take him home. He offered me a look of sadness. I tried to brighten his spirits by telling him that I would take him out again next Saturday and each following Saturday until the time would come when I could take him to Fort Hill to live with me.

On our way back to the north end, I found a butcher and ordered a ham to be cooked with all the fixings. He agreed to allow me to come and pick up the dinner basket the next Sabbath day.

"Billy bought us a feast!" Terrance shouted once we returned. He then displayed the new shoes and boasted about his new suit of clothes and winter coat. Mother was not about. Ann stood there with a jealous expression on her face upon seeing the new things I bought for Terrance.

I pulled a small package out of my pocket and handed it to her with a grin on my face. "There's peppermint candy for all," I said.

Ann dropped the candy on the table and turned away.

I left Terrance in his glory. He promised that he would make a drawing of the sights we had seen in the little book of paper that I had bought him. There was such a bright look in his eyes. I felt the better for my visit.

I returned to Fort Hill still dreading the next day's dinner. I made Jason promise to be on his best behavior. He had slicked his hair down with some kind of scented oil and had shaved his face very close. In fact, I had never seen him look so clean and gentlemanly looking. He wore a finely tailored frock coat and a dark brown beaver hat that his parents had bought him. He even had a watch fob and chain hanging from his dark green vest and had a red cravat tied about his collar. Maddy asked him why he was so well dressed and he just smiled at her and tipped his hat as we left the tavern together.

Jason insisted on bringing a bottle of wine to dinner. I was sure it was stolen from his father's best stock. He tucked it under his coat as we headed to the north end of Boston early that Sunday afternoon. He accompanied me to the butcher's to pick up the dinner basket. Jason bought a fresh loaf of bread and tucked it in the flap on the other side of his coat tail.

I warned Jason in advance not to expect much. I described to him as best I could, how bad the circumstances were in which my family lived and that the house we were going to enter was already condemned and was going to be torn down by the city soon.

"So where is your family going to go?" he asked me as we approached the house.

"I don't know," I replied. "The church got them that room. I think Father Donahue will try to find them another place soon if we are allowed to stay."

"Boyo, I told you not to worry. They're not going to deport you, or your family," said Jason.

"Please don't say anything about that to my mother," I said as we entered that black hole of an entrance. Jason looked up at the flimsy staircase and then back at me. "Is it safe to climb those stairs?" he asked.

"If you take it slowly," I replied.

We went up to the third floor. Jason went first. He took each step carefully as if he was expecting the entire structure to collapse under his feet at any minute. I heard him breathe an audible sigh of relief when he reached the landing.

The door to my family's room opened and little Geraldine stood there sucking her thumb. She saw Jason and ran into the room. I went in and Jason followed. He reached back into his coattail and lifted out the bread and placed it on the table and then he pulled out the bottle of wine that was hidden under his coat and placed it beside the bread.

Little Geraldine had gone over to one of the mattresses and instead of sucking her thumb; she was sucking on a piece of peppermint candy that I had brought yesterday. Ann was standing over by the window again and looking out. She did not bother to offer either of us a greeting. But she did turn to look at the bottle of wine sitting atop the table. "You had better hide that from mother," said Ann.

"Where is she?" I asked.

"At the church. Terrance is with her," Ann said as she moved away from the window and walked over to the stove. She pulled open the grate, stoked the fire with a stick of wood, and then closed it again. She gazed over toward the basket of food I had in my hand.

"It's the dinner," I said. "Should I put it on the stove to keep it warm until mother and Terrance return?"

"I don't care what you do with it," Ann replied. She still had her eyes focused on the bottle of wine.

"Don't you remember me?" Jason asked Ann.

Ann turned toward Jason and scowled at him. "Where is your dog?"

Jason let out a chuckle. "Very good," he said. "You do remember me."

Ann averted her eyes from him. I wanted to go over to her and slap her face for her rudeness. Jason didn't appear to mind. He was still smiling at her behind her back.

"I'm telling you," said Ann. "You had better hide that wine. Mother..."

The door flew open wider and Terrance came running in. He was carrying his new shoes tucked under his arm. "I'm going to be an altar boy!" he announced.

Mother came in after him. There was such pride in the expression on her face. I suppose she had always dreamed that one of her sons might achieve such an honor.

I introduced her to Jason. He offered her a polite greeting with a slight bow from the waist. It was a bit overdone. He was putting on his best Sunday show of gentlemanly charm. I just hoped he wouldn't take it too far.

Ann stood by the table and picked up the bottle of wine so mother could see it.

"I'm sorry," said Jason. "I should have asked first."

"Nonsense," said mother. "There is nothing wrong with having a bit of wine with our dinner."

Mother's reply made Ann furious. I could see the anger blazing in her eyes. She turned her head away from mother to avoid allowing her to see her look of rage.

I pointed to the basket that I had placed atop the stove. "It's warming there," I said. "Baked ham and all the fixings."

"It'll be a fitting feast to celebrate my son's good fortune," said mother.

I was sure she meant Terrance's good fortune and not my own. I was going to tell my mother on this occasion that I was going to take Terrance down to Fort Hill to live with me. I had given the matter a lot of thought the night before, and had told Jason of my idea. He told me that his parents would not mind if I brought Terrance to the house.

I was determined to find my own lodgings. I had lied to Jason's parents about not having a family. How would I explain my brother to them? Jason realized that I was right. Maddy told me about a rooming house down the next block, that it was inhabited mostly by sailors, but she thought we could get a room there very cheaply.

I could see now that mother had other plans for Terrance's future, perhaps the priesthood. Maybe, I thought, that was the best thing for him. He was such a kind and meek young boy. The church might offer him the best refuge from my father and the greater dangers of the outside world.

Mother told Ann to open up the basket and bring out the food. She insisted that Jason and I sit at the table while the rest of the family sat down on the mattresses to eat their dinner.

I had not thought about bringing dishes, forks to eat with, or goblets to drink the wine. Mother had one fork and she shared it between Ann, Terrance and herself. Mother sat Geraldine in her lap and fed her with her fingers. It was an embarrassing thing to watch, but Jason said nothing about it. He had brought with him some tin cups from the tavern to serve the wine. He poured a cup for each member of the family. Mother even allowed little Geraldine to have a sip of the wine from her own cup.

Ann emptied her cup in one long swallow. I did not like the expression on her face. I saw the growing anger in her eyes and waited for her to say something. She got up from the mattress and went over to the table. She picked up the bottle of wine and refilled her cup to the brim. She drank from the cup so quickly and then poured more wine into her cup.

Mother wasn't watching her as Ann looked down at Jason.

"It was very generous of your family to take Billy in and give him that coat and a job so he could earn the money to buy us this fine dinner and Terrance his clothes," said mother.

Jason gazed across the table at me and raised his left eyebrow.

Ann had drunk another cup full of wine and was about to pour herself another. I grabbed the bottle from her hand and placed it on the table. "Don't you think you have had enough?" I said.

"Well now," said Ann. She held her cup high in the air with her right hand and had placed her other hand on her hip. "Billy is worried that I might drink too much wine." she then reached for the bottle and lifted it up high. "It can serve to loosen the tongue."

"Mind your manners, Ann," said Mother.

Ann began to walk about the table with the bottle in her hand. She poured herself another cupful.

"Mister Brody, Did you know that mother works for the Gardner family?" said Ann. "She washes their clothes and sometimes does their sewing. I must say, she must be doing a lot of mending. Young Tim Gardner does come home these days with a lot of rips in his clothes."

"What are you babbling about?" said mother to Ann. "Sit down and put that wine back on the table. Billy is right. You've had too much to drink."

"Have you see Tim Gardner lately, mother?" asked Ann. She was still standing by the stove. The wine bottle was still clutched tightly in her hand.

"Daughter, I don't know what you are up to," said Mother. "We have a guest. Now you put that wine bottle back on the table and come here and sit down."

"I will not," Ann replied. She had raised her voice to a shout. "This is the Sabbath. I think the time has come for the confession of our sins."

"You had better come here and sit down," said mother. "There will be no confessions, but I can see a young woman who is asking for trouble."

"Why mother, don't you want to know where Billy is getting all this money?" asked Ann. She tipped the bottle and poured more wine into her cup. She glared back at me as she poured.

I gazed across the table at Jason. His smile had faded and he was sending me signals with his eyes trying to tell me that it was time to leave.

I rubbed my stomach. "That was such a big meal," I said. "I'm in need of a walk. Mother, Terrance, why don't we all go out for a walk. The fresh air might do us all some good."

Terrance jumped up and ran over to get his coat. As Terrance passed Ann, she grabbed hold of his coat and pulled it away from him. She rushed over to confront mother. Geraldine was frightened and began to cry. Ann waved the coat in mother's face.

"Imagine what this wool coat must have cost?" Ann shouted. "Could anyone afford to buy this coat with the wages that come from sweeping the floors of a tavern?" she said. "Feel the cloth. It's real wool."

"Lie down and calm yourself," mother told Ann.

Ann dropped the coat on the floor and stepped on it. "This coat was bought with the wages of sin. Gambling and stealing," she shouted.

Jason rose quickly from his chair.

Mother lay Geraldine on the mattress and then stood up to grab Ann by the arm. "Get a hold of yourself, young lady."

Ann wrenched her arm free from mother's grasp. "Must I make it clearer for you mother?" Ann shouted.

Jason put his coat on and was headed for the door. I got up and followed him.

"Billy, what is all this about?" asked mother. She turned to me with accusing eyes.

"I'll tell you," said Ann.

"You've said enough!" I shouted back to Ann.

Ann raised her chin in a bold look of defiance. "Billy and his friend here run a gambling cellar down at Fort Hill," Ann began. "They coax those rich boys like Timothy Gardner to gamble away their allowances on card games. When the boys can't pay their debts, Billy and Jason beat it out of them."

Mother was already shaking her head at me. "Billy, Billy, I hoped you would know better. I didn't think you would take after your father."

"My father?" I replied. "Why mother, just last week, you were telling me that father was once a kind and honorable man. That he was a victim of circumstances beyond his control."

"That he was," mother replied.

"So it is alright to steal to provide for the family, is it not?" I asked.

"I never told you that," mother replied.

"I didn't steal this money," I said. "No one twists the arms of those boys to play cards and gamble away their money."

"Gambling is a sin," mother replied.

"So is drinking and thieving," I said. "Do you know what is the worst of sins, Mother? For a man like our father to consider killing one of his own children or to sell us all out for a drink of whiskey."

"It's time for you to leave, Billy," said mother. She would not look me in the eye. She knew I was telling the truth.

I glared back at Ann. She smiled back at me. I wanted to strike her across the face with the back of my hand to wipe that smug grin from her mouth. Father would have done that. I wasn't going to be like him. I turned away from her and walked toward the door.

Terrance ran up to Ann and tried to beat on her with his fists. "I hate you!" he screamed. "I hate you. I hate you!"

Ann grabbed his flailing arms and pushed him back.

Terrance ran to me and grabbed the sleeve of my coat. Jason had already gone out and was waiting for me in the hall.

"Take me with you, please!" Terrance cried.

I gazed down into his tear streaked face. I wanted so much to pick him up in my arms and take him with me.

"You're not going away with Billy," said mother. "I'll not have you cavorting with the likes of him and his friends, with their sinning and gambling ways. You are going to be an altar boy."

Terrance turned to face mother. "I don't want to be an altar boy," he replied. "I want to go away with Billy."

"Get out of here, Billy," said mother. I was shaken by the harsh tone she used.

Terrance was looking up at me with eyes that were pleading. I reached out and ran my fingers through his hair. "I'm sorry Terry. Mother knows what's best for you," I said it, but I didn't believe it.

"No...Please take me with youuuuu!" Terrance uttered with a loud pitiful whine.

I went out into the hall. Terrance had his tear streaked face framed in the partly open door, as he had done the Saturday before. I followed Jason down the stairs. I turned back to take another look. My mother was standing there peering out through the door behind Terrance. She grabbed him by the shoulder and pulled him in and then she closed the door with a loud slam that felt like a hard slap on the face.

Chapter 9

I could still hear my brother's muffled cries from behind the closed door as I made my way down the stairs.

"Go back and get him," Jason told me. He was speaking to me from the bottom of the stairs. It was so dark in the stair well, that I could only hear his voice.

"The church will take care of him now," I said. "They will protect him from my father."

"But who will teach him how to be a man?" asked Jason as I reached him at the bottom of the stairs.

"And what do I have to teach him…how to drink and gamble? Do I train him in the manly art of how to beat up boys who don't pay their debts? Do I take him to Lucy to make sure he knows how to pleasure a woman?"

"Just be a brother to him," Jason replied.

The stench in the downstairs hall was so bad I had to rush out into the street to get some fresh air to breathe. Jason followed close behind me.

I looked up at the third floor window. I thought I could see Ann's face staring down at me. It had all gone wrong just as I had feared and it was all my fault. But there was nothing I could do to fix things. Mother didn't want me anymore. I had shamed the family just like my father had. And yet, were he to be released from jail, mother would welcome him back with open arms.

"Terry will be better off without me," I told Jason as I began to walk away from the house.

I heard my brother's cries in my sleep for many days after that Sunday. I heard that door slam over and over again. There were times when I had mustered enough courage to go back to get my brother only to walk a few blocks in that direction and then turn about. I could not forget the look on my mother's face peering at me through that door. I knew it was hopeless.

It was getting near Christmas time and a deep winter chill had settled in over the city of Boston. The waterfront down around Fort Hill was especially cold with the wind whipping in from the harbor.

Our little clubhouse in the cellar had turned into an ice cave and we had to abandon it. The rich schoolboys were gone on their holiday vacations. The gambling money dried up and Jason and I found ourselves without a farthing between us. Jason went back to stealing his father's whiskey to drink instead of buying his own. I had doubts whether he really had paid for it anyway.

Jason took to spending his days either up in his room or down in the back room of the tavern cavorting with Maddy. I took to helping Tory Odwyer sweep the floors and carry kegs of beer and whiskey from the cellar warehouse to the tavern.

Much as I tried to forget about the row with my mother, I could not stop worrying about how my brother was getting along and if my father was still in jail. No one had come to tell me that I was going to be put back on a ship and sent back to Eire. I had come to the conclusion that I had done the right thing by not taking Terrance with me to Fort Hill. I had no more money or a job to support him or myself. I lived off the generosity of the Brody family and I wondered how long that would last.

On Christmas Eve, I fell into a melancholy mood when everyone else about me was smiling and full of frolic. I had never known a true Christmas, not like the ones Jason's mother described to me. Mary Brody was very excited about the holiday and she worked hard to put out a great feast for the family that afternoon.

I tried my best to put on a happy front. I had no understanding of why this should be such a joyous time. I could remember last December and the struggle that my family had endured. It was enough for me to find some food to satisfy my hunger and some covering from the cold to keep from catching the fever. We had lost everything that winter. And what did I have a year later that would give me cause for celebration? At least I was still alive; I supposed that was something to be thankful for.

It was a custom in the Brody family to gather downstairs in the tavern after dinner with their friends from the surrounding neighborhood. Once gathered, they would have a glass of the nog, share stories and dance to music of the old country.

Jason handed me a glass of nog mixed with a healthy dose of his father's best Irish whiskey. After a few cups of the spirits, my sorrows melted away and I got caught up in the mood of frolic. A fiddle player stood by the bar and beside him was a man who played the squeeze box. The floor shook with the stomping of feet as the men played a lively jig.

I let myself be persuaded into joining Jason and Maddy in an uproarious dance that had everyone clapping their hands. Jason's father and mother came out into the middle of the floor. Mary lifted her skirt and twirled upon one foot while her husband clapped his hands and pranced about her like a gleeful child.

Maddy grabbed me about the waist with her hands and pulled me back out to the floor to do another jig. We twirled round and round while the lively music echoed in my ears. Maddy and I were laughing. The world became a blur of bright colors of the ruddy faces of the guests and the flickering amber light of the lantern hanging above our heads from the ceiling.

The music stop suddenly and I noticed that everyone's attention was focused toward the back of the tavern. I turned my head and there stood my sister Ann. She was bundled up in my mother's coats and bonnet and frosted with a covering of snow from head to foot. Crystals of snow frosted the ends of her eyelashes and nose.

"Who is she?" someone in the crowd inquired.

Jason was the only one left smiling.

"She looks half frozen, the poor dear," said Jason's mother. She moved toward Ann and invited her to come in and get warm.

Ann glared at me. She did not say a word or move an inch. "Billy," she said as she finally broke her silence. "Father has been released from jail," she said it loud enough for everyone to hear.

My face grew hot.

Sam Brody came to my side. "Who is that?" he asked me.

"My sister," I replied.

"So you do have family?" he said.

I had to confess the lie. I nodded yes.

"Terrance is missing," said Ann.

The other guests stood in silence. I wished that the fiddle player would start another tune. Maddy came to my side, grabbed my arm and pulled me toward the back of the tavern. Ann had not moved. The snow had begun to melt on her face and was dripping from her nose and chin. Jason's father frowned at me. I wanted to run somewhere and hide. But there was no place to escape. Ann turned and headed toward the back door.

"Where are you going?" Maddy asked after her.

"Home," Ann replied. "I've delivered the message. I can see Billy is occupied with more important matters. Why don't you have another drink, Billy, do another jig will you?"

"When was father released?" I asked Ann.

"This afternoon," Ann replied. "He got thirty days in jail. He came home and told mother that we don't have much time left. We are all going to be deported," Ann said and then headed to the door.

"Wait," said Jason. He turned to me. "You've got to go with her and try to find Terrance. I'll get my coat and come with you."

"Did you check the church?" I asked Ann.

"Father Donahue hasn't seen him all day," Ann replied. "He's been gone ever since he heard from mother that father was released from jail."

Poor Terrance, I was thinking, He must be terrified. I wondered where he could have gone to hide in the middle of this storm. "I'll go myself," I told Jason. "No need for you to miss your family celebration."

Ann started toward the door. A blast of wind driven snow flew inside as she opened it to leave.

"Wait for me," I said and grabbed my coat from the hook on the wall by the door. She would not wait. She was already out in the storm and had disappeared into a wall of white before I could step outside.

I stepped out into the raging wind that tore at my face. Jason called after me. "If you do not come back in a few hours time, I'm going to go to the north end and get you."

I managed to catch up with Ann. I saw her hunched over against the wind and walking slowly beside the shelter of the warehouses along the waterfront.

"Stay away from me," she shouted back to me. I could barely hear her above the howl of the wind.

Each time I got close to her, she would run away from me. I stayed a short distance behind her, just close enough to keep her within my sight and followed her all the way back to the north end of Boston. Ann went directly to the house and ran inside through the dark entrance. I stopped and looked up at the third floor window. I wondered if my father was up there. I knew I was capable of taking care of myself this time. But I did not feel up to the task of having another violent confrontation with him.

A figure emerged from the house entrance bundled up in mother's coats and bonnet. I reached out to grab Ann's shoulder to stop her from running. The figure turned. It was still very dark and yet I knew it was not Ann, but my mother.

"So you've decided to come to look for your brother have you?" said mother.

"So he hasn't returned yet?" I asked.

"Go back to Fort Hill," said mother. She walked away from me and headed down the block toward the church.

"Wait," I said and followed her.

Mother would not stop walking and I had to run to keep up with her.

"Has he been found?" I asked. "Why won't you answer me?"

Mother stopped walking and turned toward me. "Go back to Fort Hill, Billy. We don't need you here."

"Where is father?" I asked.

"I don't know," she replied.

"He's out of jail. Ann told me," I said.

Mother started walking again.

This time, I moved quickly enough to get ahead of her and then I blocked her path. "Tell me mother, has Terrance been found?"

"I'm sure he's at the church," mother replied. "If you will stand out of my way, I shall go and find him there. You may come along. A visit to a church might do your sinning soul some good."

I walked backwards ahead of her. "Ann says that we are going to be deported," I said.

"I want to see my boys again," said mother.

"You want to go back?" I asked

"There's no good life for any of us here," mother replied.

"We barely survived the voyage. We lost Lisa at sea. We might not be so fortunate to survive the return voyage," I said.

"I'll put my faith in the Holy Spirit," said mother. "If it is ordained that we return to Eire or if it is God's will that we die at sea, let it be so."

"Is it that easy for you mother, to just give up like that?" I said.

"It is easy for one who has faith, Billy," mother replied as we reached the church steps.

A light flickered from inside the doorway and Father Donahue appeared holding a lantern. "Kathleen, where is Terrance?" he said and then he saw me.

"So the sinner has come to repent," said Father Donahue.

"I've only come to find my brother," I replied.

"Terrance hasn't been here?" asked mother.

Father Donahue shook his head. "I haven't seen him since this morning. I've decided to cancel midnight mass because of the storm. I don't want anyone venturing out on a night like this. Let us hope the storm passes quickly, so I can hold Christmas mass tomorrow morning."

"Why are you two just standing there talking about a religious service when my brother is lost out there in the storm? Why isn't anyone doing something to find my brother?" I asked them both.

"You would do better to keep a civil tongue young man," said father Donahue. "I'm sure the good Lord will keep a watch out for his little lamb. I bet the boy has found a place to sleep."

"You both can rely on your faith if you want to. I'm going to go look for him myself," I said and then I walked away from the church and didn't turn back. Neither of them said a word to me as I departed.

I had the worst feeling in the pit of my stomach. I tried to imagine where Terrance might hide himself and then I remembered he told me that he took to hiding himself in the wood shed behind the house. At least that was a place to start looking. I walked through the blinding snow and then began to run. I stumbled into the side of a deep drift leading into the alley beside the house where my family lived. I had to feel my way up and over the snow bank and down through the dark alley to the back of the house.

There was a lantern hanging above the privy door. Someone had lit it but the wick was low and the light was feeble, but it did show me the way to the woodshed, located just a few feet away. The terrible stench from the privy made my stomach churn even more. I had to swallow hard to keep all that Christmas feast and glasses of thick nog down in my stomach. It was no time to get sick.

I grabbed the lantern from the hook above the privy door and carried it to the woodshed. I noticed that the door was slightly ajar. I peered down into the snow to look for footsteps. I held the lantern downward and noticed dark spots in the snow. At first, I thought it might be bits of dripped mud. There were footsteps near the spots. I lowered the lantern further and noticed that the spots were colored dark red. My heart started to thump in my chest and there was a clot formed in my throat that no amount of swallowing could clear. Please let it not be, I told myself.

I moved closer to the shed door. The drops formed a trail into the shed. They also formed a trail that led back to the house. I wanted to see what was in the shed first. I took a deep breath to steady my nerves, grabbed the door and pulled it open wider. I entered the shed and waved the lantern about. There was a pile of wood standing against the wall and near that was a pile of straw. The trail of spots led to the straw but there was nothing there.

I was about to leave the shed, when I noticed something grey lying under the straw. I went back over and dug through the straw with my free hand and felt the wool cloth of the coat that I had bought my brother. I pulled it out of the straw. There were dark splotches on the coat front. I knew it must be blood.

"If my father did anything to Terrance, I'll kill him with my bare hands," I said aloud. I held the coat close to my face. I pressed my nose into the wool. It smelled like Terrance. I don't know how you describe something like that. You just know the scent of your own kin.

I was thinking the worst, but trying at the same time to hope that he was only hurt. I hoped that he had the sense to get away and that he was wounded and hiding someplace where our father couldn't find him.

I remembered the blood trail to the house. I tucked the coat under my arm and used the lantern to guide my way to the back door of the house. The door was wide open and I could see the glow of a fire down the hall. I entered the hall and crept down toward the first open door. Someone was moving about inside that room and I could hear the crackle and snap of a fire.

A man grunted and the sound of the voice was familiar. I placed the lantern on the floor and peeked around inside the door. There, my father was crouched before a stove. A raging fire had been lit and the flames curled outside the grate. The light made the whole room glow red and my father's figure cast a giant ominous shadow upon the wall and ceiling.

I watched him as he ripped off his shirt. There were blood stains on the sleeves and the shirt front. He bundled it up and stuffed it into the fire. A shower of sparks flew out of the grate and my father jumped back. His face and chest were all aglow in the light of the fire, glistening with sweat from the fire's heat.

He turned his head to look my way. I pulled back so that he couldn't see me. Out of the corner of my eye I got a look at his face. His eyes were hidden in the dark shadows like the sockets of a skull. My father was breathing heavily and I could smell his whiskey breath above the odors of burning wood and smoke.

I felt my blood rise and grow as hot as the fire with the anger. What had he done to my poor brother? I couldn't let him get away with this. I had visions of when I last saw my brother. His tear stained face framed in that doorway and I had left him thinking that God would protect him.

"Who is there?"

The voice startled me. At first I thought about running away. But I couldn't do that this time. I knew I had to face him. I moved into the doorway and let my father see me. He stared at me and then blinked.

"It's you," he said.

"Where is Terrance?" I asked him. "What have you done with my brother?"

"Done? I've done nothing. I haven't seen Terrance," my father replied.

"What was that you were burning? I saw that shirt. It had blood on it didn't it?"

"I cut myself," he replied.

"You're lying. I have Terrance's coat. Here," I raised my arm and waved the coat before him. "It has blood on it too."

My father looked surprised. "Where did you get that?"

"You finally did it, didn't you? You killed my brother," I said.

"You're daft," my father replied.

"You won't get away with it," I said.

"Shut up," my father replied. "Come in here."

"I'm going to get a watchman," I said.

"And what will he do? Do you think they care one bit what happens to a little Irish boy who's just come off the boat?" my father replied.

"Then you admit it, you killed him?"

"I didn't kill him," my father replied.

"Where is he then?"

My father didn't reply. He looked away from me and toward the stove.

"You won't get away with this," I said as I took a step inside the room. I dropped the coat on the floor. "I'll kill you myself," I said.

"Oh will you now?" my father replied, turning back toward me. He pulled a knife from the waistband of his pants and pointed the tip of the blade toward me.

"Is that what you used on my brother?" I said.

"Go away. Leave me be if you know what's good for you," he replied. "You won't fight me. You don't have the guts, boy."

"I can and I will," I said. "Drop the knife. It's the weapon of a coward. Fight me with your fists. Let's see if you can hit me in the nose again. Just try."

My father dropped the knife on the floor and then raised his fists in front of him. "You come forward boy. I'll show you a thing or two about fighting that those boys down in Fort Hill never thought to teach you."

There was venom in the look from my father's eyes and his voice. He would kill me too if he could. I raised my fists and moved toward him. He swung out toward my face with his right arm and fist. I saw it coming and I moved right, just in time to avoid the blow. I countered with my left arm and used all the power I had in my body to propel my fist forward. My knuckles slid across his sweat stained face as his head snapped to the side to avoid the blow. I had not even stunned him.

I expected him to throw another punch but instead, he surprised me by grabbing my arm. He pulled me forward to shift my feet off balance and then pushed me toward the stove. I reached out with my hand to keep myself from falling into the stove and my hand made contact with the hot iron. The searing heat burned my palm and I let out a scream. I regained my balance and moved farther into the room. I realized that I was backed into a corner and had no way of escape except through my father.

My father reached down, picked up the knife and held it firmly in his right hand. He came toward me holding the knife blade downward and slashed the air before me. I moved backward against the far wall. I had no place to go. I had to figure a way to get around him. I knew he was drunk. I was going to have to make a run for it and hope that his reactions were slower than mine. Talking to him was of no use. I didn't think that there was any part left of him that was human. I was convinced that the devil had taken over his body and soul.

I took a deep breath and then ran forward. My action surprised him so that I had an advantage. Just as I thought I had freed myself, I felt something tug at my coat. My father had a grasp of it and he pulled me backward toward him. I turned, and out of the corner of my eye, I saw his other hand holding the knife. He had it poised to drive it into my back.

I thought I heard someone moving out in the hall. I called out for help. I tried to break the hold my father had on my coat by trying to let the coat fall from my shoulder. But I had my arm caught in the sleeve.

He finally let go and then lunged toward me with the knife. I reached out with both arms to push him away with all my might, just as the knife slid across my coat sleeve and left a slash in the cloth. He stumbled backward and hit the stove. He yelled out as his back hit the hot iron and then his backward fall propelled the stove off it's feet and the stovepipe came crashing down from the ceiling. The stove erupted in flames that curled up the walls and arched over the ceiling.

My father let out a scream as the flames engulfed his body. I watched as his flesh crawled with the flames. They curled about his arms, his neck and then his face. His figure turned red and then black, melting before my very eyes. His head shriveled down to a grotesque skull, fire filled the spaces where his eyes and nose had once been.

The heat was searing my throat and I could not catch my breath. I was surrounded by flames and smoke and I could see no way out. Something tugged at me from behind. A pair of arms wrapped themselves around my waist and pulled me out of the flames. I could not turn my head to look back. I closed my eyes tightly because the heat burned them so. I was dragged out into the hall. I could feel my flesh burning. I looked down and saw flames curl about my left arm. I had no voice left to make a sound. I was dragged down the hall by some unseen force and out into the snow. Someone pushed me down and rolled me about in the snow to put out the fire that was consuming me.

I heard other screams. I looked up and saw that the entire house was engulfed in flames. I remembered that my sister Ann and Geraldine were still in the house. I had to get them out. I got to my feet and moved toward the flames. But someone grabbed my arm and pulled me back.

"Let me go," I tried to say but no sound came out of my mouth. I turned around and saw Jason Brody standing behind me. He grabbed my shoulder and held me fast.

"It's too late, boyo," he said. "You can't save anyone in there."

I gazed up at the advancing flames. The house was crumbling before my eyes. Sparks and bits of flaming wood rained down on our heads. Jason grabbed me by my coat and pulled me back farther and farther away from the fire.

A great crackling sound filled the air and was followed by the sudden collapse of the roof into the house and then the entire frame crumbled inward. A part of the house came falling downward in our direction. Jason grabbed me and threw me to the ground and he crouched over me as a flaming timber crashed down into the snow just inches away from us.

More screams could be heard and then the night was filled with the sounds of shouting and ringing bells from a distance. I looked up again and saw that the fire had reached over to the adjoining house. It looked as if the entire world was on fire. The brightness of the flames turned night into day.

I had a searing pain running through my left arm. I felt as if I was still on fire. I was fast losing all my strength. I couldn't even muster the will to stand on my own feet. I fell into the snow. Someone grabbed me by the arms and then I was lifted upward. Someone had picked me up and threw me over his shoulders. I knew it was Jason Brody. I closed my eyes tightly because the smoke burned them. The ringing of bells grew fainter as we moved away from the fire. The pain was so terrible. It was making me sick to my stomach and I felt like I had to puke, but I couldn't muster the strength. Everything suddenly went black.

"Here drink this," I heard someone say.

I opened my eyes, looked up and saw Jason hovering over me. He had the mouth of a bottle pushed up against my lips.

"Take some of this," he said. "I'll help make the pain go away."

"Where am I?" I mouthed the words.

"Drink," he said.

I opened my mouth and swallowed. The liquid filled my mouth and then pain filled my skull. I could not swallow. The liquid ran out of my mouth. My throat felt as if it was on fire along with the rest of my body. I opened my mouth to scream but nothing came out.

"You're going to be alright, boyo. Don't worry. I'll take care of you. Here's my coat. It'll keep you warm."

"Warm? Jason, I'm burning up," I wanted to tell him.

I looked up and noticed that Jason's hands were covered with pink and red blotches. He took the bottle from me and drank from it. He winced each time he moved his fingers about.

I glanced farther upward and saw that I was back in that cellar room under the warehouse. Parts of my body felt as if they were still on fire and other parts were numb with the cold. I wished that the numbness would spread all over to make the pain go away. I remembered the fire. My sisters, I couldn't save them. I couldn't grasp the fact that they were gone. My father was gone too, and my little brother Terrance. Only mother and I were left alive. What would she think of me when she found out that I had started the fire that killed her husband and children? She would hate me for the rest of her life. No amount of repentance could save my soul after this.

It took all the strength I could muster to rise from the floor and get my balance.

"Where do you think you are going?" asked Jason.

I mouthed the words, "I have to go find mother and tell her what happened."

"You can't go back to the north end, boyo. They'll arrest you for sure," said Jason.

Of course he was right. But what did it matter now if they sent me to jail or deported me? It was all lost tonight. And it was my fault. If I had taken Terrance to live with me last November, none of this would have happened. I saw those flames eating away at the other houses. How many innocent children and their parents had died tonight because of what I had done? I didn't deserve to survive.

Chapter 10

I waited until Jason fell asleep so that he wouldn't stop me from doing what I knew I had to do. I left the cellar and dragged myself up the steps through the ice and snow to the street. The snow had stopped falling and the wind had died down. I didn't know what hour of night it was or how long it had been since Jason had carried me to the cellar. I gazed toward the northern sky and saw a red glow. The fire still burned.

I found my way to one of the piers. I leaned over into the darkness and could hear the gentle lapping of the waves below my feet. I suddenly became stricken with an overwhelming sadness. "Mother, if you could only be here now so that I could tell you how sorry I am. I didn't mean to hurt you or anyone else. I was just trying to protect my own brother from harm. Please forgive me for what I am about to do. I can't endure this pain any longer."

I leaped forward into the blackness and felt a crushing blow as my body plunged deep into the icy waters of the harbor. As my body descended deep into the water, so many images rushed through my mind all at once. The faces of my older brothers, Eamon, Paul and Sean, appeared before me and then I found myself standing outside the little rented house by the bank of the Nore River where I had been born. And then, the faces of my sisters appeared. They were all still alive and calling out for me. And then, as suddenly as they appeared, their faces and voices faded into the blackness, as if I was falling away from them. And then, my mother appeared. She was calling out for me too. In that instant, I realized what a terrible mistake I had made. I didn't really want to die.

I struggled to raise my head above the water and tried to move my arms and legs. They were numb and I could not manage to swim about. It should have been so easy. I should have died by now. I felt a sharp pain in my chest and I couldn't get my breath. I had to find a way to get my head up above the water. Even if I could manage that, I had no voice to call out for help and the waterfront was deserted. It was no use. And yet, I couldn't stop fighting. I knew my death would not be easy or peaceful as I had hoped. It was not so easy to die as I thought. I used ever bit of energy I had left to propel my body upward through the water. Finally, my head broke above the surface. I strained my throat to get out a sound.

I saw a flicker of light above my head. A man was running down the pier carrying a lantern. Two other men appeared at his side. I struggled to keep my head above water and made a screeching sound with my throat. I hoped they heard it. There was a splash and someone was churning the waters near me and then a pair of arms wrapped themselves around my waist and pulled at me, dragging me through the water.

"Let's get a hold of him and pull him out!" someone shouted from above.

I looked up to see hands reaching down to grab me. I felt myself lifted up and carried upon the pier and laid out there. I looked up to see the faces of two teenage boys illuminated by the lantern that the younger one of them carried in his hand.

At first, I thought the boys might be some of Jason's friends. But these boys were dressed differently. They both wore the long slicker coats and dark wool caps of the fisherman I had chance to watch earlier in the year when Jason and I swam out beside the piers on Saturday afternoons.

An older man appeared. His face was covered with a growth of thick curly beard that was dripping wet. I think he was the man who had jumped in to save me. One of the boys handed the man his coat. He came forward and laid it over me.

"Pa, will he live?" asked the younger boy.

"We have to get him warm," the man replied. He then knelt down beside me. "Boy, can you hear me? My name is Jack Wolcott. There's no need to be afraid. These are my son's Roddy and Jarrod. We're going to carry you aboard our boat and get you warmed up. Can you speak boy?"

I shook my head.

"I think he understands us," the man said. I closed my eyes. I couldn't muster the strength to stay awake and his voice drifted away.

I awoke to the sensation of floating on water. For a moment, I thought I was back aboard the Saint Gerard. I opened my eyes and gazed up to see a lantern swaying gently from the low ceiling above my head. The lantern gave off a dim yellow glow to reveal the cramped interior of a ship's cabin. I lay in a narrow bunk and was bundled up in blankets. A rope was tied across my chest and fastened to each side of the wooden berth to prevent me from falling out.

I tried to move my feet and wiggle my toes but there was no feeling down there. My left arm was draped across my stomach. I saw the blackened hole in my shirt sleeve that revealed a dark mass of burned skin. I tried to raise my hand up just a little and flexed my fingers. A shooting pain ran up through my arm. It was as if the fire was burning again. I opened my mouth and tried to scream but I could not muster more than a weak grunt. Oh God, couldn't anything or anyone come and stop this pain? Why hadn't I died? Death would have been better than this agony. I closed my eyes again and prayed for sleep and for an end to the pain.

I awoke again to hear the sound of a woman's voice singing in my ear. For a moment, I thought it was my mother singing that little ditty that brought me such comfort when I was feeling frightened. I opened my eyes and turned my head to see that it was not my mother, but a pretty young woman I had never seen before. She was rocking back and forth in a chair and singing to herself.

I looked about me and saw that I was lying in a bed and covered to the neck with layers of colorful quilts. My head rested in a big, soft white pillow that smelled of the fresh air. I gazed down at the foot of the bed to see daylight filtered through the frost covered panes of a long narrow window. The wind howled outside causing the whole room to shudder with each gust. I heard the crackling sound of a fire and looked across the room from the left side of the bed and saw flames rising inside the hearth of a fireplace. I tried to lift my left arm to fend off the flames and the effort brought an incredible wave of pain. I let out a hoarse grunt that startled the young woman. She rose to her feet from the chair and rushed to the door.

"Mister Wolcott, he's awake," she said.

The door opened and there stood the man with the beard. I remembered him as the one who had saved me. He ambled forward into the room. He had that gait of a sailor like one of the crew of the Saint Gerard and his skin was weathered by long exposure to the wind and the sun. He came by the bed, reached down and touched my shoulder. "Do you remember me?" he asked. "I am Jack Wolcott. I saved you from drowning in the harbor."

I tried to raise my head a little and the room appeared to me as if it was turning in circles. Mister Wolcott pressed his hand on my shoulder. "Just lie back," he said with a calm soothing voice. "You're safe now. Get some rest. Your arm has been badly burned. I'm sure it still hurts a great deal."

I nodded.

"I've taken you to my home," said Jack. "You are on August Island. It is located some hundred miles north of Boston in the outer reaches of Casco Bay. You probably have no idea of where that is."

I shook my head.

"No need to worry," he said. "You just lie there and get your rest so that arm will heal up."

I mouthed the words. "How long?"

"What is that?" he asked.

"How long?" I tried to whisper but no sound came out.

"Oh, I understand. You're asking how long you've been here."

I nodded.

"Well, it's been a few days since we returned from Boston. You're very lucky, you know. No one was about the harbor when you fell in. My boys and I were held up by the storm. In fact, we don't make many trips to Boston. But we don't need to go into that now. You probably don't even remember my carrying you up here from the boat, do you?"

I shook my head.

"No need to worry. You may stay as long as you need to recover," said Jack and then he gestured toward the young woman with his other hand.

"This is Erin O'Neill. She'll be keeping a watch over you. You are resting in the attic room of the Inn run by her aunt Constance."

I shifted my gaze to the young woman named Erin. What a pretty sight to behold she was. I tried to raise my head again to get a better look at her.

Jason Brody would have complained to me that her features were plain and her figure was of modest shape. But to me, Erin O'Neill was a vision of beauty; far prettier than those young ladies who sold their attentions for a few bits at Audrey's house and even prettier than Lucy. I was hoping that Jack would leave soon so that I could be alone with this young lady.

"I'll leave you to rest," he said. "Let me know if there is anything you need. I hope you get well soon," he said and then headed toward the door and went out into the hall.

After Jack Wolcott left the room, Erin lifted a cup and saucer from a small table located near the head of the bed beside the chair. She moved to the side of the bed and leaned down. "Aunty Constance made this special tea to heal your throat," she said as she sat down in the chair and brought the cup to my lips. "Sip it slowly now."

I studied her hands. They were so slender and her fingers were so delicate. I gazed up into her eyes. Now that I could see them more closely, I noticed that her eyes were green mixed with bits of gray and she had a nice little nose that turned slightly upward. I turned my eyes away quickly once I thought she saw that I was taking stock of her.

"Roddy!" someone screamed from the hall. It was the high pitched voice of another girl. Erin turned her head toward the door. Laughter echoed through the outside hall and then there was a quick patter of footsteps. The door burst open and a plumpish young girl came running into the middle of the room. She had a round face with fat rosy cheeks. Her lips were formed into a cheerful smile. The skirt of her bright green dress flew upward as she slipped on the floor. She grabbed the corner post of the bed with one hand to steady herself. She pointed to the door with her other hand and then uttered a little giggle.

"Oh, I'm sorry," she said. "I'm trying to find a place to hide. Roddy is chasing after me."

"I know where you are," a deeper boy's voice could be heard from the hall.

"Cassie," said Erin. "This is no way to behave in front of strangers."

Cassie turned, smiled at me and giggled again. "He has pretty red hair, don't you think?"

"Sister," Erin scolded her. "Mind your manners."

Cassie offered a little curtsey. "Pleased to meet you," she said. And then, she placed her fingers to her mouth and let out another giggle.

The door was pushed open wider. First I saw a head of curly black hair appear and then the smiling, ruddy cheeked face of a teenage boy. "I found you!" he shouted as he entered the room. I knew from the look of his hair and face that he was the son of the man who had saved me. And then I remembered that this was the young boy who held the lantern over me at the pier.

Cassie let out a squeal and ran to the window. The boy came running in toward her. "I've got you trapped now," he said. Cassie let out another shriek.

"I want you both to leave at once," said Erin. "Can't you see that our guest needs his rest?"

The boy advanced on Cassie, reached out to grab her and drew her close to him. He leaned toward her and pecked a kiss on her cheek.

"That's quite enough," said Erin. She pointed to the door. "Out with the both of you or I'll call Aunty Constance."

Cassie giggled again and then stuck her tongue out at her sister. I could not help but smile.

"Look," said Cassie. "We made the stranger smile."

The boy put his arm around Cassie's waist and pulled her along. "Let's take our leave," he said. As they passed the bed, the boy turned to me and smiled. "You had better behave with Erin. For a girl, she packs a fine wallop. Ask my brother Jarrod."

Erin pointed to the door. "Out you go."

"I'll come back later," said the boy. "My name is Roddy Wolcott. It was my father who saved you. As soon as you are on your feet again, I'll come and take you for a tour about the island."

"A tour around the island?" said Erin. "Why, you could easily stand in one place atop the hill behind the Inn and take in all there is to see of this windswept pile of rocks."

Roddy frowned at Erin and then shifted his gaze to Cassie. A mischievous smile appeared on his face. He reached out and pinched Cassie's arm and she let out another squeal. Cassie then ran out of the room and Roddy left to follow her. I heard another distant squeal from Cassie followed by Roddy's hearty laughter.

"Will they ever grow up?" asked Erin as she rolled her eyes upward and shook her head at me. She walked over to the window and rubbed the frost off one of the glass panes with her fingers. She blew onto one spot of the glass, rubbed it again to clear some of the ice. And then, she peered through the tiny opening she had made in the frost. "I cannot wait to take leave of this island," said Erin. "If I am forced to spend one more winter here, I think I shall go completely mad." She then turned and gazed back at me. "Oh the tea, it's getting cold," she said and then walked back toward the bed. She picked up the cup from the table and sat down beside me. "If it's too cold, give me a nod," she said. "I'll go and get some more." And then she brought the cup to my lips again.

The liquid was cool but I didn't care. It still felt soothing to swallow something wet. I think it had more to do with who was serving it to me. I took the time to study her face some more. Even though I had only seen her since I had waken such a short time ago, I was beginning to take a fancy to this young woman named Erin O'Neill.

I couldn't remember how I had drifted off to sleep. I opened my eyes again after a new wave of pain ran through my arm. It would start at my left hand and go up through my shoulder to my back and then up to my neck. And then it came back again and again. Calling out was no use because my throat was still so sore. I could only muster a grunt. I gazed down toward the end of the bed. The window was dark. The only light in the room was from the soft glow of a single candle that burned on a plate set atop the mantle of the fireplace. The fire had been allowed to run low in the hearth.

I noticed that a painting hung on the wall just above the hearth. In the dim light of the candle flame, I could see the shape of a hill and an evergreen forest rising from the sea above a rock sheltered cove. I turned my head and saw that Erin was still sitting in the chair beside my bed. Her face was hidden in the shadows and I could not see if she was awake.

The door opened and an older woman entered the room carrying a small bundle of clothing under her arm. She was a very tall woman, almost as tall as Jack Wolcott. She wore a green bonnet that was pushed back onto her graying brown hair. She wore a black overcoat over her dress and gloves over her hands. Vapor came out of her mouth when she breathed. She turned to stare at the cold hearth. "Erin. The fire is low. We must get more wood. It's cold up here," she said.

"Oh Aunty," said Erin. "You startled me."

"You should be in bed," said the woman. "You go ahead; I'll get the fire started again."

"I fell asleep," said Erin. "I'm sorry."

"How is the stranger? Has he told anyone his name?" asked the woman.

"He still cannot speak," said Erin. "I gave him the tea. But he can only grunt a reply or nod and shake his head. I think he still feels a lot of pain in his arm."

"It was a very serious burn," said the woman. "If it had been much deeper, he might have lost his arm entirely."

"How do you think it happened?" asked Erin.

"I don't know. Jack found him drowning in Boston Harbor. It was a very strange place to find a young man at that time of night on Christmas Eve," the woman replied.

"I think I know what he was doing there," said Erin.

"Oh, do you now?"

"He was trying to take his own life," said Erin.

"Now you must never say such a thing, not in front of the young man. How could you think such a terrible thing?"

"I don't know," Erin replied. "I just have a very sad feeling about him. I can't explain it."

"You go on to bed now," said the woman. "And please don't say anything to this boy about what you have told me. I'm sure there is a better explanation."

"Good night, Aunty," said Erin as she leaned over to kiss the woman's cheek.

After Erin left, the older woman went to the hearth and began to lift some small logs from the wood scuttle and shoved them into the grate. I couldn't keep silent for long. The pain returned and I let out a loud grunt that made her turn and look at me.

"So you're awake," she said. "I bet you are chilled to the bone. I'll get another fire started quickly. As long as you're awake, I'd like to take a look at the poultice that I wrapped around your arm."

The woman turned and went back to work preparing to start the fire. Soon after, I saw a glow rise from the hearth and heard a crackling of flames. She got up and turned toward me.

"There now, it should warm up in here shortly," she said. "Now, let me take a look at that arm." She came over toward the bed and first pulled off her gloves and then she grabbed a corner of the cover to pull it down.

I glared back at her.

"Now, now," she said. "You're among friends. My name is Constance O'Neill. I run the Inn with the help of my two nieces Erin and Cassie. You can trust me. I've been doctoring the men and boys on this island for many years. So there is no need to be modest."

My burned arm had been tucked under the covers. I was afraid to look at it again. I allowed the woman to lift the quilt to expose my arm. I looked down and saw that it was wrapped in a thick white cloth. The stench coming from it made my stomach churn.

"This is going to hurt at first when I unwrap the cloth," she said. And then, she gently unwrapped the cloth from my arm. Each turn of the cloth was an agony. I looked away from her as tears came to my eyes. "There," she said in a soothing voice.

I looked down at my left arm and saw the long red gash that stretched from my elbow to the wrist.

"It's coming along well," she said and then began to rewrap it. I grunted again as the cloth touched the burned skin.

"Does your throat feel any better?" she asked.

I nodded.

"That tea should help. I'll have Erin serve you more tea tomorrow. Right now I'd like you to try and say something to me. Not in your normal voice though. I want you to just whisper. You might begin by telling me your name."

"My name is Billy," I replied in a faint whisper.

"Very good," she said.

"How long have I been here?" I whispered.

"A few days," she replied. "Tomorrow is New Year's eve."

"And I am on an island?"

"Now, you mustn't strain your voice to speak," she said. "After a few more cups of tea, I think your voice will come back soon. Don't force it now, Billy. I'll answer all your questions tomorrow. I've brought you some things to wear that were borrowed from the Wolcott boys. The best thing for you to do now is to get plenty of rest so that you can get back on your feet as soon as possible. I'm sure you are anxious to return home to your family. They must be terribly worried about you."

I lowered my eyes from her gaze.

"What's wrong, Billy?" she asked.

"They are all dead," I whispered.

"Oh dear Lord, I am so sorry," Constance said as she reached down, took hold of my right hand and gently rubbed my fingers with hers.

I shouldn't have lied about my mother. It was a terrible thing to say that she was dead. But, I was feeling so melancholy. I wanted to say something so that this woman would feel sorry for me. I'm sure, if she ever found out the truth, that I had started the fire that had killed so many innocent people, she would not be so compassionate towards me.

Constance pulled the quilts over me and tucked in the corners snugly about my shoulders. She left the side of the bed and went over to snuff out the candle with her finger. The room still glowed with the fire in the hearth. I couldn't muster the words to tell her that I didn't want her to leave me alone with the fire. By the time I was going to say something, she was at the door. "Goodnight Billy," she said. "Pleasant dreams."

I lay awake and could not keep my eyes off the fire in the hearth. I wondered where my mother was. She must know the truth by now, that my father had murdered her little angel. How terrible it must be for her to be alone. All her children are gone. She must be searching for me. But then, I thought, maybe she isn't looking for me after all. She thinks I am a sinner, a black sheep, to be shunned as my father had been back in the old country by the rest of our family.

A heavy drowsiness overcame me all at once and I could not keep my eyes open. But there was always the pain to wake me up once again to remind me of the terrible thing I had done. I was sure I was bound for hell. After sleep finally came, I found myself in the midst of a nightmare. I opened my eyes and found myself once again surrounded by walls of flame. The voices of my sisters and my little brother, Terrance, were calling out to me from above. I looked up and could see hands outstretched, ready to rescue me from the flames but, as I tried to reach up to them, someone from below grabbed me from around the waist and pulled me down.

I looked down to see who it was, and there stood my father. His arms, hands and fingers were formed of the flames that curled about my legs and began to consume my body. I could smell my flesh burning. The pain was so great and yet I could not summon any sounds from my throat to scream for help. My father called out to me from below. "I've got you right where I want you. You'll live here with me in hell for all eternity."

I tried to pull free from my father's grasp. I screamed out for help but no sound came from my throat. I opened my eyes and the flames had disappeared. In their place, there were rays of sunshine streaming through the window at the end of the bed where I lay. I didn't want to spend another minute lying in this bed. I had a fear that the bad dream would return if I fell asleep again. I wanted to see what the world looked like outside that window. I threw back the quilts with my right hand. I grit my teeth and raised my burned arm so that I could pull myself up and let my feet drop over the side to the floor. I looked over at the hearth. The fire had gone low again and it was freezing cold in the room. My bare feet touched the cold floor and I shivered all over. I grabbed a quilt with my right hand and gingerly pulled it up over my shoulders. I pressed my feet against the floor and raised myself up. I was glad no one was about to see me attempt to take my first awkward steps away from the bed. I held my burned arm stiffly to my side worried that I might bump it against something. I slid my way beside the bed until I reached the end post. I decided to rest. I grabbed hold of the post and sat on the edge of the bed.

I gazed up above the hearth and noticed that painting again. This time, I could see every detail that had been hidden by the darkness. It was the scene of an island partly covered with an evergreen forest, whose rocky shore was surrounded by clouds of mist. The green land and the mists reminded me of my old home. But I could see that this was a foreign place, a tiny little world surrounded by the sea.

In the center of the painting, a steep hill rose up from the middle of the island that over looked a cove. At the water's edge, there stretched a long pier that jutted out into the cove and berthed there, was a small ship. On the waterfront street beyond the pier, there stood a shed, and a white, two story building with black shutters. There was a broad clearing in the forest that stretched up along the side of the hill facing the cove, and it was blanketed with tall green grasses and bright colored wildflowers. A narrow foot path was worn through the grass leading up to the top of the hill where there stood a red, two story house with a steep sloping gray roof.

I got up from the edge of the bed. I steadied myself by holding on to the bed post and then I stood alone with no support and took a few steps to the window. The sunshine had melted away some of the frost on the windowpanes. I peered through the oval clearing in the glass to get a look at the world outside the window. I gazed outward through the window and there before me lay the same cove that I had seen in the painting. To the right, there stretched a long narrow neck of land that rose to a snowcapped hillock that sloped down to a long curved rocky beach that formed one end of the cove. A shroud of gray mist obscured the sights beyond the cove.

Looking out just below the window, a wide street ran parallel to the shore of the cove along the waterfront. A stone wall ran along the water's edge to the entrance of a pier. It was the same pier as in the painting hanging above the hearth. I turned my gaze back inward toward the painting above the hearth. I realized that I was inside that white house with the black shutters and looking out from the attic window. I turned and then gazed back out through the window. I followed the length of the pier with my eye and there lay that small ship with two tall masts. Her rigging was all coated with ice that glistened in the sun. That must have been the very boat that brought me to this island.

I was fogging the window with my breath. I wiped the cloud from the glass with my fingers when the door opened and Erin appeared.

"You are up," she said. "I see that your curiosity got the better of you. I hope you're not too disappointed. There isn't much to see out there."

"What time of day is it?" I whispered.

"Oh, so you can speak," said Erin. "I've brought you more tea. In a few days your voice will get stronger."

"It is the afternoon is it not?"

"You shouldn't strain your voice," Erin replied "Yes it's past noon."

I couldn't stop staring at her. I hoped she didn't notice.

"You should get back into bed. It's cold in here. Oh the fire is out. I'll get it started again," said Erin.

"No," I said. "Please, it's not that cold. I'll use the quilt to keep me warm."

"Your afraid of the fire aren't you?"

I looked away from her.

"No need to be afraid," said Erin. "I'll make a small fire."

I took a few steps toward the bed and I suddenly felt very dizzy and wavered on my feet. Erin saw that I was about to fall and rushed toward me. She put her arm around my shoulder and leaned toward me to offer support.

"Let's walk slowly to the bed," she said. "Take your time."

Once she escorted me to the bed, she looked away so that I could get back under the quilts. I moved my burned arm and let out a howl as the worst of the pain returned.

"I'm sorry," she said. "The pain must be very bad."

I nodded to her. I wanted to get away from the subject of pain and fire. I pointed to the painting of the island.

"You like the painting?" she said.

"When was it painted? Everything is so green," I whispered.

"Last summer," she replied. "Captain Wolcott took me out on the Dorothy and I painted it from out at sea."

"You painted it?"

"Yes," Erin replied. "But it's not one of my best. It's difficult to keep hold of a brush when you are sitting on the moving deck of a schooner."

"Where did you learn to paint?" I asked her.

"My father taught me. He is a great painter. He lives in Amsterdam. You must have heard of James O'Neill. He is one of the greatest painters of our time."

"I don't know much about painters," I said.

"One day, I hope to be as famous as my father," said Erin.

Erin walked over to the window. She looked out and breathed a long sigh. "I hate this island," she said. "Aunty Constance has promised me that this is the last winter we will spend here." She then turned toward me again. "Aunty told me what you told her last night about losing your family in that fire. Do you have any surviving relatives back in Eire?"

"I have three older brothers," I replied.

"Might you go back to live with them?"

"No, I'll never go back there. It's a place of death. I don't even know if my brothers are still alive," I replied.

"I do miss my father and mother," said Erin. "My sister and I were brought here two years ago when the famine began," she added. "My father was afraid that we would catch the fever. I wanted him to take me to live with him at his studio in Amsterdam. I wanted him to teach me so much more about painting. But instead, he insisted that we come to live here in America with our Aunt Constance, my father's older sister. We come from the county of Donegal. Do you know where that is?"

I shook my head.

"You don't know very much about the world do you?" she asked.

I didn't know how to answer her.

"You should stop talking. The tea I brought is getting cold," said Erin as she moved away from the window. "I have been rather rude, haven't I?" Erin added. "You're a guest, and you've been through a terrible time, losing your family. I can't imagine losing my sister or my aunt in such a terrible way. Oh, but I'm sure you don't want to talk about that either. Enough of this talking, please allow me to serve you more of that tea."

She had placed the cup on the table. She again sat beside the bed and brought it over to me. I got another chance to look into her eyes.

"It is hot enough?" she asked after I took my first sip.

The tea was cold, but I nodded anyway.

"There are some things you should know about the Wolcott family," said Erin. "I think you will be better off if you take leave of this island as soon as you are well enough."

"Jack Wolcott saved my life," I said.

"Captain Wolcott has a brother named Daniel," said Erin. "He's a very rich man. He manages a bank back in Boston and he owns a lot of property. He hates the Irish and the Catholic Church. He charges the poor Irish immigrants a fortune to live in those terrible hovels. It is no wonder that there are so many terrible fires."

I moved my head abruptly when she said that and the tea spilled on my chin.

"Oh I am sorry. I am so stupid. I promised not to say anything more about fire, didn't I?" said Erin.

I looked away from her then.

"But you should be told the truth about Daniel Wolcott," said Erin. "He's a very dangerous man. If you intend to remain for any length of time on this island, you must keep your distance from him and his wife and children."

"I don't know what I will do next," I replied.

Erin seemed to forget about me. She was looking directly at me, but her mind was elsewhere. "Daniel Wolcott comes to August Island every summer about the week of the fourth of July and brings his wife and children," Erin went on to say. "He does it to make his brother and the rest of us suffer. No one wants him to come. But no one has the courage to tell him to stay away. You see, he owns half the island. Every year he comes and threatens to build a hotel in the place where Jack wants to build a catholic chapel in memory of his departed wife, Dorothy. In fact, that is how the captain and his sons came to be in Boston to find you. He wasn't about to tell you that he rushed to Boston in the middle of a storm and so near Christmas because his brother threatened to sell part of the island to strangers. Lord I wonder what Daniel Wolcott was thinking. I don't know why anyone would want to come out here for a vacation. I suppose he was going to build the hotel just to spite his brother whether it would ever be used or not."

"I don't think I will be here that long," I replied.

"You'll be much better off back in Boston," said Erin. "I do love Boston. Aunty promised me that she would take me to Boston to live some day."

"I hate Boston," I said. "The people there don't like the Irish."

"Oh not everyone," said Erin. "Daniel Wolcott's kind of people don't occupy the whole of Boston."

I didn't want to argue with her, but I did want to know why she hated this island so much.

"If you hate August Island, why did you paint it?" I asked her.

"Because there was nothing else to paint," Erin replied.

"I like the painting very much. I wish it was summer so I could see it like that, with all the green," I whispered.

"I already told you," said Erin. "You don't want to be here during the summer when Daniel Walcott makes his visit with his family. Oh, and I didn't finish telling you about his family. You see, Daniel Wolcott has a very religious wife who wears a black veil so no one can see her face. She carries a bible with her at all times. She sits in the parlor and reads it aloud all day long. None of us are allowed to say a word to her. We are supposed to be invisible. Well I'll tell you something," said Erin as she pointed a finger at me. "This summer I'm not going to stay and become lady in waiting to those people."

I still had not said a word and she went on talking.

"You should meet their little daughter Victoria," said Erin. "She is the most spoiled little child. She screams and rants and pulls my hair. Last summer, I nearly took her out to the cove to throw her off the end of the pier. And then there is their baby boy, Brent. He's not really a baby. He's almost a man in size; seventeen years old and he still blubbers. He does everything his father tells him.

He's going to grow up to be a just like his daddy, a petty, arrogant..." Erin suddenly stared down at me and noticed that I was smiling at her.

"What do you think is so funny?" she asked me.

I couldn't help it. With the way Erin went on, she didn't realize how funny she sounded talking about the family of Wolcotts. I wanted to tell her that she looked even prettier when she was angry.

Chapter 11

I scrambled up the steep hill through the snow, past the old red house, toward a tall stand of evergreen trees. I was gasping for breath by the time I reached the top of the hill. Once I stood at the summit, bright rays of the morning sun streamed through the gaps in the trees that towered over me. I found my way through a sunlit passage under the tree canopy to a jumble of rocks that lay on the other side. I walked among the rocks and the twisted, wind stunted trees toward an opening to the sky. Once I reached the end of the path, I was stunned by the view of the great sea that stretched out before my eyes. It was like standing on the edge of the world.

I could hear and feel the pounding fury of the sea as it rolled against the cliffs that lay below my feet. I walked to the very edge and looked straight down to see bright splashes of foam rush upward as each wave hit the dark stone walls below. A brisk gust of wind carried the salty spray of the sea upward to wash over me from below. I found a place to sit on one of the rocks a few feet back from the edge of the cliff. I pulled up the collar of my coat to protect my face from the biting wind and the salty mists.

This was my first journey outside the confines of my bed at the Inn. I had quietly slipped out through the back door in the kitchen, took a coat that was hanging there and wrapped it around myself. Once outside the inn, the cold wind stole my breath away. I looked up behind the Inn and there arose that hill that I had seen in the painting. It was not covered with green grasses and wildflowers but instead, blanketed with a thick covering of snow. I was so anxious to see more of the world that Erin O'Neill had painted. I was determined to get a view that world from the top of the hill. I could not have imagined such a sight as the one I had found, to reach what appeared like the very end of the earth.

Somewhere out there, across that wide open sea where the sun rises, there lay the land where I was born. I was determined that I would not return there. I had no happy memory of that place. My future in America was most uncertain. If Jack Wolcott decided to take me back to Boston, I would be left at the mercy of the port authorities and they would surely send me back across the sea in another ship. I knew I would not survive another crossing if it was to be like the voyage on the Saint Gerard.

I had been on this island for a little more than a week's time and just a few days had passed since I awoke from my long sleep. I had spent the time in the confines of that small attic room at the Inn. Erin explained to me, when I mentioned my desire to go out for a walk that the harsh winter weather was unyielding and I was warned not to venture out of doors in my weakened condition.

Erin O'Neill was the prettiest young woman I had met since coming to America. I know I said that already but it bears repeating. I could sense that she was lonely, frustrated and desperately wanting of someone to talk to. Even though I was a stranger, she dared to speak openly about everything that was on her mind.

After many cups of Constance O'Neill's special tea, my voice returned after a few days. I was surprised to hear myself speak. I had always heard myself sound like a boy. The fire had changed all that. My voice was lower and deeper when it returned and henceforth, I heard myself speak as a man.

I didn't have much of a chance to talk when Erin was about, for she loved to dominate the discussion. She was so anxious to tell me about the history of the Wolcott family. She was doing her best to talk me out of staying on August Island. I do not know what I had said to make her think that I planned to live with the Wolcott's. No one had yet invited me to stay.

I allowed Erin to continue to feed me even though my right hand was strong and I could have fed myself. I liked having her take care of me. It was the second or third day after I had awakened that she began to talk openly about the Wolcott family, and the rivalry between Jack and his brother Daniel. Before she began, she made me promise never to repeat the things she told me.

So far, I had taken a liking to Roddy Wolcott and I really didn't want to hear Erin speak badly about the family and the man who saved my life. But I knew there was nothing I could say to stop her. I didn't want to hurt her feelings either.

Erin was serving me broth for supper and she started in like she always did. There was no warning. I did not ask her to talk about the Wolcotts. She did not need to be encouraged. "You see, the brotherly rivalry between Jack and Daniel began with their father, Barnabas Wolcott. He prefers to be addressed as the commodore," Erin began to say as I sipped my broth. She was sitting in the chair beside my bed. She leaned over toward me as she spoke to make sure I heard every word.

"Barnabas had just returned to his family home in Marblehead Massachusetts after serving in the Navy during the second war with the British," Erin went on to say. "I believe it was the winter of eighteen and fifteen. His family was wealthy and owned many ships in the China trade. Barnabas had no interest in taking his place as a part of the Wolcott shipping empire. He came out of the navy wanting to start his own business in the fishing trade. He met and courted Mildred Schuster, the daughter of a wealthy shipping magnate.

Barnabas was a coarse type of man; lacking in the social graces. Mildred was a delicate, graceful lady and accustomed to the trappings of wealth. I don't know how Barnabas persuaded Mildred to leave the comforts of her Marblehead mansion and the benefits of society to start a new life out on what was then a deserted island, located far off the coast of Maine, abandoned by some English colonists a century before.

    The only structure that stood on August Island at that time was the roofless shell of an old English manor house. It was unfit for human habitation. Barnabas promised Mildred that he would have the house restored. Until the house was made livable, they had to reside in a tiny shack on the beach. Barnabas's first order of business was not to restore the house, but to build a fishing boat. And once the boat was completed, Barnabas went out for weeks at a time to the fishing banks and left Mildred alone to fend for herself.

    There was no fresh water on that island other than the rain that was captured in barrels. The only food was the fish that Barnabas brought back, along with the lobsters that were trapped along the shore. Barnabas refused to spend precious dollars bringing the comforts of civilization to the island and yet, he always made promises to make things better.

    A year after their arrival on August Island, Mildred gave birth to their first son. Mildred named him Daniel, after her father as an act of defiance. Barnabas made no protest and accepted the name. He took little interest in the boy as an infant. I don't know how she managed. Barnabas was a cruel man to leave her alone in childbirth. It was unforgivable. I can understand why Daniel hates his father," said Erin.

    I didn't know why she needed to tell me this about the Wolcotts. What did it have to do with me? But I could not stop her. She was determined to tell me the rest of the story, whether I wanted to hear it or not.

    "You must never repeat to anyone what I am about to tell you, Billy," said Erin. She got up from the chair and went to the door to make sure no one was in the outer hall or on the stairs and then, she came back and sat down. "No one knows about this," she whispered. "I overhead the truth told last summer, during an argument between Jack and his brother Daniel. I know I wasn't supposed to hear it. I've never told anyone else," said Erin. "You see, Barnabas told everyone that Mildred had been lost in a storm that carried away their little shack on the beach and that her body was swept away by the sea and never found. But that's not the way it really happened," Erin went on to say.

    Erin got up from the chair again, walked over to the hearth and stoked the fire. She reached down and grabbed a piece of wood and threw it into the fireplace. She then walked over to the window to gaze out at the darkness beyond and then she turned back to gaze at me. "Billy, please listen carefully to what I have to say now," she said. "This the saddest part of the tragedy. Barnabas was away at the fishing banks," Erin went on to say as she turned about again and had her attention focused outside the window. "Seven years had passed since he had brought Mildred to August Island. He had still done nothing to improve the living conditions on the island. Mildred was going mad. Barnabas knew it, but he left her alone with their son. Daniel was only six years old at the time."

"Mildred Wolcott didn't drown in a storm, Billy," said Erin as she turned to face me. "She threw herself off the cliff behind the manor house, and her son Daniel was a witness to it. Barnabas returned and his son blurted out the whole story of what he had seen. Barnabas was comforted by the fact that no one would believe the rantings of a child. He made up his own story and threatened to beat his son if the boy ever told the truth to anyone. Daniel never forgave his father for causing the death of his mother and forcing him to hide the truth about how she met her end. After Daniel grew to be a young man, he returned to the mainland on his own and convinced the Schuster family that what he had witnessed was not the figment of a child's imagination. But there was no way Daniel could prove his story." Erin shook her head while still looking out of the window and then she turned again to face me. "That was not the end of it, Billy," said Erin. "Barnabas was a stubborn man. He had no concerns with regard to what the family back in Marblehead thought of him. To add more troubles to an already strained relationship, Barnabas took an Irish Catholic wife in Portland, Maine, a year after Mildred killed herself," said Erin. "Ida McKennon was the exact opposite of Mildred Schuster. She was a hearty soul who thrived in the primitive ways of the island. She worked side by side with Barnabas and a crew of carpenters brought over from the mainland to complete the restoration of the manor house. Barnabas had the sea wall constructed and the pier that stands today."

I hoped Erin would stop to take a breath but she went on and on and I think she forgot I was in the room she was so determined to tell the whole story. She continued to go on without interruption. I was not going to interrupt her for fear of making her angry with me.

"The trouble began when Ida insisted that Daniel be sent to the mainland to attend school after Jack was born. The truth was Ida wanted to get rid of Daniel," Erin went on to say. "Daniel hated his stepmother and was doing everything he could to make her life miserable. He reserved his worst tantrums for the times when Barnabas was away at the fishing banks. Daniel hated the way Ida forced him to study the Catholic catechism. Ida insisted that Daniel should be prepared to be confirmed as a Catholic. Daniel managed to sneak out a letter to the Schuster's in Marblehead and asked to be taken in by them. That was when Daniel told them the truth about his mother's death. Barnabas returned from the fishing banks to discover that the family feud had grown worse and his son had been the cause of it."

"Daniel was fourteen years old at the time of the feud," said Erin. "It was the beginning of his hatred for all things Irish and Catholic. Daniel chose to accept the offer of the Marblehead Wolcott's and the Schuster family to leave his father and August Island to be brought up in the protestant surroundings on the mainland."

"Is Barnabas still alive?" I asked.

"Oh yes," Erin replied. "And he is just as impossible to deal with now as he ever was. The only man I have met that is more arrogant than Daniel Wolcott is his father, Barnabas. You would do well to stay out of his way too."

Erin walked away from the window and returned to sit in the chair beside the bed. "They are all mad, you see," said Erin as she placed a finger next to her ear and twirled it about. "It is carried along in the family. Daniel's daughter Victoria is also touched by the madness."

"You told me a day ago that Daniel was a wealthy man and owned the houses rented by the Irish in Boston?" I said. "How can such a mad man become so rich and powerful?"

"Daniel went to all the best schools and was given a position early in life of great power. Wealth and power in the hands of a mad man such as he is very dangerous to those with whom he would focus his wrath, by that, I mean the Irish Catholics," said Erin.

"I'm not afraid of him," I said.

"You should be," Erin replied. "I am."

"How is it that Jack is such a kind man, if his father is so mean?"

"His wife Dorothy tamed him before she was killed in a steamboat accident eight years ago," Erin replied with a curious grin.

"Tamed him?" I said.

"She was a very strong woman. Jack loved her and was devoted to her. He would obey her every wish or command."

I was thinking and wishing that my mother had had that kind of power over my father. Life might have been quite different for all of us.

Erin shook her head and went on to say: "Jack has not been the same since his wife died. Still, he has a terrible temper. When he gets his Irish up, he can be just as mean as his father."

I thought about my own father and the things that my mother had told me about him. Gerald O'Shea had once been a kind man but that he had turned mean because of the way he was treated by the English. I hoped nothing could change me into a monster like that. But I did wonder if the devil had a way of taking over a man's soul.

"There is so much more I should tell you about Jack. He is not the kind man you think he is," said Erin.

"I don't want to hear anymore," I said. Why don't you tell me something about your own family?"

Erin stifled a yawn. "Oh very well," she said. "I've already told you about my father, the painter. There's not much to say about my mother other than she follows my father where ever he goes and acts as his obedient servant."

"She is his wife. Isn't that is how it should be?" I said.

Erin glared back at me. "We women do have minds of our own, don't you know?"

I dared not reply to that question.

Erin went on to tell me about her Aunty Constance. She spoke with pride about her aunt's worldly accomplishments. "My aunt Constance holds a very high position among the reformers here in America," Erin began. "She leads a temperance group that sends messengers to the immigrant poor and leads them away from the evils of drink and gambling."

I gulped. If Erin's aunt Constance knew what I had been doing down at the waterfront of Boston, I wondered if I would still be welcome at her Inn.

"Aunty Constance is also part of a woman's suffrage group and she is an avowed abolitionist. She has met with some of the great leaders of the Abolitionist movement here in America. She is acquainted with people such as Abby Kelly, William Lloyd Garrison and Wendell Phillips."

I guessed that these were names offered to impress me. I did not want to disappoint her by telling her that I had never heard of any of these people and did not even know what an abolitionist was.

"My Aunt has promised to take me to Seneca, New York, for a very important woman's conference this summer," said Erin. "I am hoping that we will win the right to vote some day. It will be a hard fought battle. My aunt is a very powerful woman. If anyone can lead and win the battle, it will be my aunty Constance."

I wondered how powerful her aunt could be or if it was just boastful talk. Why would a powerful woman live so far out on a lonely island to run a deserted Inn?

Erin quickly provided an answer as if she was reading my thoughts.

"That's why we need to leave this island soon," said Erin. "Aunty Constance came here to fulfill a promise made to her best friend, Dorothy, Jack's late wife. You see Aunty Constance and Dorothy came across the sea from Donegal together almost twenty years ago. Dorothy asked my aunt to watch over Jack and his sons before she died."

I was about to ask how Dorothy Wolcott died and again Erin seemed to know what my next question was going to be.

"Oh and I haven't yet told you the story about the steamboat sinking in Casco Bay," said Erin. "Dorothy was taken ashore by rescuers. She had almost drowned during the steamship accident. She was carrying a child inside of her. The baby boy was born prematurely and died in birth and Dorothy was not strong enough to survive. My aunt promised to spend her winters out on August island. She has done so ever since the accident. I should tell you that Aunty Constance owns a house on the mainland in Portland," Erin went on to say. "She lets out the rooms during the winter to women who have no other home. They take care of the house for her and she returns there during the warmer months. Last summer, she stayed here on August island. It was such a mistake. Daniel Wolcott was here with his family. I don't think Aunty will ever make that mistake again. We'll be leaving before the spring thaw this year."

I waited to hear if she had more to say. I was getting tired just listening to her talk. "I'll miss you when it comes time for you to leave," I told her not long after she had stopped talking.

"Miss me? Why, you hardly know me," Erin replied. "Besides, you'll be going back to Boston soon. You'll find work and a place to live. I know you'll make out well. I can tell that you are not stupid. You'll forget about me very soon."

Oh how wrong she was. I was not going to forget her anytime soon.

It was getting late and Erin left me alone after that long talk. I felt more strongly for Erin than ever after spending this time with her. I began to think of ways of how I might be allowed to stay here on August Island just so I could spend more time with her.

My attention quickly returned to the present by the scream of a seagull flying overhead in the sky beyond the edge of the cliff. I had become so lost in my memory of the first days I spent in that attic room with Erin as my nurse that I had forgotten where I was. I got up and nearly stumbled over the cliff and into the sea below.

I thought about what Erin told be about Mildred and then I recalled my own effort to end my life. I would never tell Erin about that. I could understand Mildred's desperation to escape her pain by any means necessary. I looked back down at the sea below the cliff's edge. I was happy to admit that my own feelings about dying so soon had changed after meeting Erin O'Neill.

After hearing all her boasts, I dared not ask Erin about when she would take a husband. I had begun to have dreams about Erin that replaced the nightmares of the fire my father and the devil. I began to fancy her as my wife and my thoughts became filled with visions of what it would be like to share the rest of my life with her. She was so unlike my mother. I loved her for her feistiness and her strong will.

The seagull called out to me again. It swooped high over my head and joined a group of other birds that flew up into the trees and nested there. I moved farther back from the edge of the cliff. A cold gust of wind tugged at me and I had to grab the trunk of a nearby tree to hold myself steady. I stamped my feet to get feeling back in them and then I ventured back through the clearing in the trees. I walked toward that red manor house that Erin had told me about, the one that had been restored by Barnabas and his second wife Ida.

As I walked past the front steps, the door opened and there, just inside the door stood a rugged looking old man with a weathered face. A long clay pipe was clenched in his teeth. His cheeks and chin were bedecked with long curly white whiskers. He wore a long blue coat and blue cap with a wrinkled leather bill that shaded a pair of dark eyes that regarded me with suspicion. I offered a little wave of the hand toward him. He pulled the pipe from his mouth, turned his head away and closed the door.

As I walked down the hill, I looked off toward the horizon. The cove and the whole world lay below my feet stretching beyond the forest of snowcapped trees. It was such a stunning sight to behold. The pier and the boat that brought me in were so tiny like child's toys that I could reach down, pick them up and hold them in my hand.

I began to stagger in the deep snow once I reached the bottom of the hill. The effort needed to make the climb and the cold wind stole away my remaining strength. I stopped and leaned against the trunk of a tree. I took a deep breath of the bracing winter air and looked up the hill from where I had come.

If hope is the belief that you have a future, then I supposed that I was beginning to have hope again. I found myself taking a liking to this place called August island. But most of all, it was Erin O'Neill who had me wanting to stay. I think I had found the woman of my dreams.

Chapter 12

"Where have you been?" Constance O'Neil demanded to know as she met me at the back door to the Inn. I followed her into a large room that was dominated by a giant fireplace whose mantle rose well above our heads. A fire was raging in the hearth and filled the room with a blast of heat. Cassie placed an iron pan covered with thick dough into one of the ovens built into the wall. She was dusted all about her face and dress with flour. As she closed the door with a long iron hook, she gazed over at me and offered a giggle and then a smile. "You look half frozen," she said.

"Erin has been looking all over the house for you," said Constance.

"I wanted to go out and see the island from top of the hill," I told them.

"It's very dangerous up there this time of the year, with all that snow and ice," said Constance. "You could have slipped off the edge. I wish you had said something to one of us first. I'm sure Roddy would have been willing to take you up there."

"I feel much stronger," I said. It was a lie. The walk up the hill had drained me of my strength and I struggled to stand erect so she would not know just how weak I felt. But I was not going to falter. I had learned how to summon my strength. Days and weeks of having no food taught me how to keep walking even when I was so weak. I was afraid if I dared falter I would not get up again and die by the roadside as so many others had done back in Eire.

"I am glad you are making a good recovery of your strength," Constance replied. "Because the captain wants you to go up to his house to see him as soon as you feel you are up to it. I'm not sure what they have decided. The captain left a message with me through his son Roddy that he wants to see you as soon as possible."

"Do you think that they are going to take me back to Boston?" I asked.

"Yes. I suppose that is what they have decided," Constance replied.

"When will I have to leave?"

"Why don't you come down to the parlor so we can have a little talk? You haven't told me much about yourself," said Constance. She wiped the flour from her hands onto her apron and led the way through the door down a hall toward the front of the house. She turned and led me through another doorway into a room off the right of the hall. I followed her into a large room furnished with simple wood armchairs arranged in a semicircle before the fireplace. Another large roaring fire was built in the hearth and the wind of heat reached out to warm my face. The outer edges of the room were still bitter cold from a draft of wind blowing through the windows.

"I use the parlor as a schoolroom for the girls," said Constance. She pointed to the shelves of books and colorful maps that were tacked to a wall over by the right corner of the room. Constance invited me to take a seat before the fire.

I found myself wanting to close my eyes again to the flames. I wondered if I could ever look into a fire again and not be reminded of what had happened on that Christmas Eve night.

Constance invited me to take a seat in one of the chairs near the hearth. She seated herself in the chair beside me. She saw me staring into the fire in the hearth and turn my head away and I must have shown my fear.

"You are still afraid of fire aren't you?" she asked. "I saw you look away. Don't worry, Billy, there's nothing wrong with being afraid of the fire after what you have been through."

I nodded.

"How is your arm? Does it still hurt terribly?"

"It aches," I replied. "But the pain is not so sharp as before."

"That's good," said Constance. "It's going to begin to itch. You must resist the need to scratch it. You'll be getting new skin to cover what burned."

"No I won't scratch it," I said.

"Billy, I know it's going to be difficult to return to Boston after losing your family," said Constance. "Have you given any thought about what you want to do with your life?"

"I don't think I will be allowed to stay here in America," I replied. "I haven't told you the truth about the fire." I looked away from her then. I wasn't sure how much I could tell her of the truth. By the look on her face, I was wishing that I had kept my mouth shut.

"Oh?" said Constance as she leaned toward me.

"I don't know where to begin," I said.

Constance reached over and placed her hand over mine as it rested on the arm of the chair. "Don't worry Billy. Anything you say to me will not be repeated outside this room."

I told her the whole story right then. From the eviction of my family in Kilkenny, to the Christmas Eve fire in Boston. It all came out so quickly. I could not stop myself. I had to tell someone the truth. I couldn't hold it in any longer. By the time I had reached the part of the story where I had pushed my father into the stove, Constance's face had turned pale.

After a long silence, she asked. "You blame yourself for the fire, don't you?"

I nodded. "I should have done more to protect Terrance from my father. I knew my father was bent on killing my brother. I should have taken him away with me when I had the chance. None of this would have happened if I had done more to protect my brother. If it weren't for me, my sisters and brother would still be alive."

"What about your mother? You didn't mention her," said Constance.

"I lied to you. She's not dead," I replied.

"Oh now, Billy, don't you think she needs you and would want to know where you are?"

"No," I replied. "I did some bad things. I gambled with cards and beat up the son of the man she worked for. My mother found out and threw me out of her house."

"I'm sure she will forgive you, Billy. She is your mother."

"She let my father beat me and my brother," I said.

"Your father must have been a very sick man," said Constance.

"That is what my mother told me," I replied.

"Your mother must have been afraid of him. Now, I know that's no excuse. But Billy, you must find a way to forgive your mother. You must go find her."

"We will both be sent back to Eire," I said. "The port officials told me that if any member of our family were to end up in jail, that the rest of us would be sent away from America. If they find me, that is what they will do."

"Then they mustn't find you," said Constance. "I know how they treat the Irish in Boston. My brother James came to visit me in America. He traveled through Boston and was spat upon. That was during a very bad time in Boston. There was a riot and a Catholic convent was burned. Oh, but I should burden you with these stories. You have seen enough hardship of your own."

"I'll will do what ever I must do to survive," I said. "I'm not afraid of hard work."

"I know many Irish who are willing to work but no one will hire them," said Constance. "They accuse the Irish of being lazy drunkards. It is hard to make these people understand that a man needs to maintain his dignity. How can a man hold up his head when he is refused work and not allowed to earn the right to put a roof over his head and take proper care of his family? What can they expect a man to do with idle hands and a wandering soul?"

"Then you're telling me that I am doomed to fail here in America?"

"Oh no," said Constance. "You must never think such a thing, Billy. That is the beginning of failure, to let your hope falter."

"If you say that I will not be hired because I am Irish, then what can I do?" I asked.

Constance tapped my hand and smiled. "I have an idea," she said. "I just remembered. Jack Wolcott is looking for a boy about your age to become a cut tail. You see he is going to promote Roddy. He's going to allow him to have his own line and give him a share in the catch."

"What is a cut tail?" I asked.

"Well, it's something like the job of a cabin boy in the larger ships at sea," said Constance. "You would cook and serve meals to the crew and prepare bait for fishing. The term cut tail comes from the idea that you would cut the tails of fish that you are allowed to catch on your own. They would be counted and you would receive wages according to how many fish were counted with such marked tails."

"I've never fished before," I said.

"You can learn how, can't you?" Constance replied.

"Do you think captain Wolcott would hire me?" I askcd.

"It can't hurt to ask, can it?"

"No. I suppose not," I replied.

And then it came to me all of the sudden. That was the way I could stay on August Island. "If the captain hires me…that means I could stay here on August Island, couldn't it?" I asked.

"Yes," Constance replied. "Would you really like to stay? It can be a very hard life as a fisherman's cut tail."

"Yes, I want to stay," I replied.

"What about your mother?"

"I don't know," I said.

"I'll tell you what I can do," said Constance. "I have friends in Boston who can try to find out where your mother is. At the least, we can get a message to her to inform her that you are safe. If she wants to come north to Maine, I'll make the arrangements. I have a house in Portland where she could stay."

"There's something else," I said. "Does a cut tail need to know how to read and write?"

"Why yes, I'm sure Jack would want you to know at least how to count your sums."

I looked down at the floor.

"Don't worry Billy. If Jack will hire you, I'll tell him that I'll teach you how to read and write and know your sums."

"When should I ask him?" I said.

"You'll have to do it soon before he makes plans to take you back to Boston."

"Can I go now?"

"Do you feel strong enough? Would you like me to accompany you?"

"No" I replied. "This is something I have to do by myself."

"There you are," said Erin. She stood at the parlor door with her hands on her hips. "I've searched this house from the cellar to the attic rafters looking for you."

"I'm sorry," I said. "I went outside to climb the hill."

"So you've gone out and seen this little world on your own, have you? Now you know I was telling you the truth," said Erin. "I can imagine that you are more than anxious now to return to Boston."

I got up from the chair and walked toward the door. "Pardon me," I said, as I was about to leave the room.

"Where are you going now?" she asked. "You should be back in bed, you still look very pale."

"I'm going up to the Wolcott house to ask captain Wolcott if he will take me on as his cut tail."

"You're going to do what?" Erin asked. She looked stunned.

"I'm going to work for the Wolcott's as a fisherman, if they will have me," I said.

"You really should go back to bed," said Erin "You must be delirious. Aunty please tell him."

"It was my suggestion," said Constance.

Erin shook her head. "Am I the only sane person left on this island?"

"Erin, mind your tongue," said Constance. "Billy has a right to make his own decisions. He doesn't want to go back to Boston."

"After all the things I told you about the Wolcott family?" said Erin. "You want to go work for those people?"

"What did you tell him about the Wolcott family?" asked Constance. "Have you been spreading gossip again? I warned you about that. It'll get you nothing but trouble, young lady."

I felt caught in the middle. I wanted to leave. I thought that maybe I should take Erin aside and tell her the same story that I had told her aunt. But I was afraid to tell her so much of the truth about myself. I was afraid she would think less of me.

"You go on Billy and I wish you the best of luck," said Constance.

"Oh yes, go on Billy. But remember what I told you. I warned you about them," said Erin.

"That will be quite enough, young lady," said Constance.

Tired and weak as I was feeling, I was determined not to show it and I knew I had to summon all the strength I could muster to climb back up that steep hill to the Wolcott house and convince captain Jack Wolcott that I was worthy and strong enough to work for him as a fisherman. I went back out to the kitchen to put on the coat I had borrowed. I told Cassie that I was going back up to the Wolcott house. I was almost out the door when Cassie came to me and gave me a small piece of paper that was folded in her hand. "When you go up to the house would you please give this to Roddy? Please don't read it or let anyone else see it," she said with a smile and a giggle and then she added quickly: "Oh and I think you are a very nice boy, despite what my sister says."

I returned the smile but said nothing in return. She had me wondering. What did Erin think of me? I went back out into the cold windy street and climbed my way back up the hill. As I reached the top of the hill and approached the house, I was worried that the old man would come to the door and turn me away. But I could not allow myself to lose my courage. I knocked on the door and held my breath.

The door opened and a kind faced woman appeared. She had a look of surprise in her eyes as if she wasn't expecting company. "Oh dear me, come in young man before the wind takes us both away," she said. I noticed she spoke with a strong brogue of the old country. I followed her into a narrow little room that was surrounded with doors and a cramped set of steps.

"This way into the parlor," she said. "You look chilled to the bone. Get by the fire and warm yourself up. You're the boy the captain brought in from Boston aren't ye?"

"Yes Ma'm," I said. "I've come to see the captain."

"He'll be down shortly," said the lady. "Oh and allow me to introduce myself. I'm Lotty McKennon."

I nodded a greeting. "My name is Billy O'Shea."

"Well it's good to meet you, young man. I've already heard much about you. I hope you are on the mend. Your voice has returned. I hope that poultice on your arm has helped your wounds heal. It was my recipe."

"Yes, thank you ma'm," I said.

"Oh you may call me Lotty. Everyone calls me Lotty. There is no need for formality with me. Of course you must always address the captain as the captain. And, master Barnabas is always called the commodore," she said.

I gazed about the parlor. It was furnished with the same kind of simple ladder back chairs as I had seen at the parlor back at the Inn. They were arranged before the large fireplace that dominated one entire wall that was surrounded by dark wood panels. Above the hearth was a long thick mantle made of stone and above that, was hung a small portrait of a woman with bright red hair. It flowed down to her shoulders and about the sleeves of a dark blue dress that was open at the collar to reveal her bone white skin. I stared up at her dark eyes and they appeared to follow me as I moved from one end of the hearth to the other. I thought the picture might come alive and the lady might speak to me from above.

I was startled by the sudden arrival of captain Wolcott as he ambled into the room while I was gazing up at the portrait. The captain looked up at the painting and smiled. "That is Ida, my dear departed mother. Aught, that was painted when she was a young lass. But even in her later years, she had not lost any of her beauty."

"Yes sir, uh captain," I replied.

"Billy, It is good to see you up and about but you still look very pale," said the captain. "You'll need some more good nourishment to build up your strength beyond sipping broth."

Lotty stood by in silence. The captain turned toward her. "Set another place at the table will you? Billy, will you stay to dinner with us?"

"Yes sir, captain," I said.

"Good, you and I have much to discuss. Constance told you I wanted to see you?"

"Yes sir, captain, sir," I replied.

"Your voice has come back strongly. I'm happy to hear that. And I trust that your arm is healing well?" he asked.

"Yes, captain," I replied.

"Well I'll go see to dinner," said Lotty "I'll leave you two to talk. Nice to make your acquaintance young man."

After Lotty left the room, the captain invited me to sit in one of the chairs set before the hearth. He took a seat beside me. I left my coat on because it was still cold in the house despite the fire.

"Well, now that you are on the mend. We need to discuss your future. I suppose you are quite anxious to return home to Boston."

"Sir...uh...captain," I said. "Constance O'Neill told me that you were looking for a young man to take on as your cut tail."

"So she told you about that, did she now? Did she explain to you what a cut tail is?"

"Yes sir, captain, sir," I replied.

"I am somewhat baffled," said the captain. "I thought you would want to return home to your family. They must be quite worried about you."

"Captain, sir."

Captain Wolcott smiled. "You may call me sir if you like or captain, which ever is easier for you."

I thought I should call him captain if I was going to work for him. I had to keep that in mind. "Captain," I said. "My family is gone. Only my mother survives and well, it is hard to say this, but she doesn't care about seeing me again. I've done a lot of things I am sorry for. The truth is, if I return to Boston, the port authorities will place me on a ship and send me back to the old country."

The captain reached up and ran his right hand through his beard and the scratched his left cheek. "I see. "You broke the law did you?"

"I gambled with friends on the waterfront."

"Gambled, you mean card games?"

"Yes captain."

"You didn't steal?"

"No, never, " I replied and hoped he believed the lie.

"Gambling is a sin in the eyes of the Lord. I can understand why such a thing would upset your mother, but it's hardly a reason to deport you. Are you sure that is all you did?" asked the captain.

"The fire...I started it," I said.

"Oh, did you now?" said the captain. "Now, that is quite another matter."

"It began as an accident," I said. "I was trying to save myself from my father. He wanted to kill me. I pushed him into the stove and it exploded."

"Your father wanted to kill you?" said the captain. He rose from the chair and walked over to the hearth and turned to face me. "I think you had better start from the beginning and tell me all about this."

"Yes, captain," I said. And then, I told him the same story I had told Constance just an hour before. I spoke with a rush of words and was exhausted by the time I had finished. The captain stood before me and nodded once in a while as I retold the story.

"That is the honest truth," I said. "I suppose I'll have to understand if you don't want to take me on as your cut tail."

"Oh, wait a minute son. It's not that simple," The captain replied. "It's not that I wouldn't like to take you on. The trouble is, you have no experience at sea. I need a boy who has grown up knowing this life from the beginning. It would be a very difficult adjustment for you."

"I'll do what ever you ask, captain," I said.

"I do like your gumption, young man," he replied.

"Then you will take me on?"

"Slow down son. There are many things to consider," said the captain as he returned to sit down in the chair beside me. "You would have to learn all there is to know about being a sailor. I don't suppose you have ever done any sailing?"

"No captain, but I did spend six weeks aboard a ship," I replied. But I dare not tell him of my encounter with the first mate and my failure to be trained as a fetch boy.

"Seamanship is very hard work, son," said the captain. "A sailor's job is to navigate the sea. We are always at the mercy of the wind and the current. A big blow can arise at any time. It calls for a quick mind and a pair of fast hands and feet. You would need to be good at following orders. There is no time to ponder or lollygag on a ship. One wrong move and it could mean the death of one of your fellow sailors. Do you understand me so far?"

I nodded. "Yes captain," I said as firmly as I could.

"That's just the beginning, Billy," the captain went on to say. "There is also the fog. In these parts, the fog is more dangerous that the wind and the current combined."

I was sure he was trying to frighten me. But, at this point, I was so desperate to be hired. It didn't matter how dangerous the job was. I was ready. I felt I needed to tell him something about my own experience. I had gone through the story about my bad time after the eviction but I don't think I said enough to make him understand just how hard it was to survive.

"I've already faced death many times before, captain," I said. "I'll do what is necessary to survive."

The captain nodded. "I just wanted you to understand what you would be facing, son. I can see now that you are a young man of fair courage. I still need to think on it some before I make my decision. I want you to meet the rest of my family. You've met Roddy already. I heard from him that you both have already struck up a friendship. I'm happy to hear about that. You will be working very closely with Roddy, should I decide to take you on. It is his position that you will be replacing. Roddy has been our cut tail since he was nine years old. He's a man now. And deserves to work along side his father and brother and drop his own line."

The captain rose from his chair. "Come down to the basement with me," he said. "We have a carpenter's shop set up there. My eldest son, Jarrod makes fine furniture. He fashioned these chairs for us. He is also a good ship's carpenter. You'll find that Jarrod is much more mature and taciturn that his younger brother. He can be a bit moody, but don't take his attitude the wrong way. He doesn't take to strangers right away like Roddy does. After you have worked at his side for a time and gain his confidence, you would not find a more loyal friend."

I accompanied the captain to a back stairwell that led down into a dark room that was lit with a single lantern hanging from the ceiling. In the shadows, I saw two figures moving about. The air smelled of freshly cut wood and the floor was covered with its shavings. There was no fireplace to warm the room and the air was bitter cold.

"Boys, stop your work for a moment. I've brought Billy down to see what you're doing," said the captain.

Roddy emerged from the dark shadows and came to my side.

"How can you both see what you're doing? Get a few more lanterns down here or you'll bother render yourself blind," said the captain.

Through the dim light of the lantern, I looked about as my eyes grew accustomed to the darkness and the shapes of woodworking tools emerged on shelves and some hung from the ceiling rafters as well as parts of furniture.

"Come forward, Jarrod. I want you to meet Billy O'Shea. I am considering the possibility of hiring him on as our new cut tail," said the captain.

Upon hearing the news, Roddy's smile broadened. He turned and slapped my shoulder with his hand. "That would be great. You and I could work side by side."

"Now don't be getting too excited," said the captain. "Whether I take Billy on or not will be left up to the commodore."

Upon hearing that, I felt my heart sink, but I tried not to show it.

"Grandpa will agree with what you ask of him," said Roddy.

"We'll see," The captain replied. "We'll discuss it further after dinner."

"You're staying for dinner?" Roddy said to me. "That's great. Then I can take you up to the captain's walk and show you the island from there."

So far, Jarrod had said nothing. By now, I could see him in the dim light. He bore a strong resemblance to his father with his dark features. He was shaving part of a chair leg with a blade. He didn't even bother to come forward to greet me. Jarrod then dropped the piece of wood and stared up at me. "I didn't think you would take on a stranger," he said with an angry voice. "I thought it was decided that you were going to hire my friend Paul Frommer from Portland."

"Paul is too old and he's been in trouble before. I told you that," said the captain.

"And what do you know about him?" Jarrod asked as he pointed the blade of his tool in my direction.

"I say we give Billy a chance," said Roddy.

Jarrod reached down and picked up the chair leg he was working on, turned away from us, and did not say another word.

"Come upstairs," said Roddy. "Pa, can I show Billy the rest of the house and take him up to the captain's walk before dinner?"

The captain smiled. "You both do as you like. But heed Lotty's call for dinner."

"I wish I had thought of it," said Roddy as he led me up the stairs to the second floor and then up again to a winding staircase that led up to the attic. It was so very dark even during the daytime that I had to feel my way along. Roddy knew the way without seeing. I don't know how they lived like this. Every part of the house was freezing cold and yet Roddy went about with no coat to offer him warmth.

"This is my sleeping room," Roddy announced. "I won't bother to light a candle to show you. There's only a bed and a sea chest. Oh and watch your step climbing the ladder," said Roddy as he stood under the roof rafters and pointed to a ladder that led up to a hatch that was barely visible in the ceiling of the attic. "You go first," he said. "I want you to see the view first."

I climbed the ladder and pushed my shoulder up against the hatch and it moved upward and a blast of cold air rushed downward into my face. I climbed up the rest of the way and found myself up on a square platform atop the roof of the house. There was a sturdy guard rail built along each side to keep someone from falling over. The cold wind sucked away my breath as I got up on my feet and stood at the rail to take in the view. From this platform, every part of the island, north, south, east and west was visible. What I had not been able to see before from the top of the hill, was the snowcapped roof of the forest that grew along the north and south sides of the island and surrounded the house on three sides. From this point, I could see the long peninsula that formed the cove far below. There was the pier and the ship and I could even see the roof of the Inn and the smoke rising from the chimneys. I think the most astonishing part of the view was that, for the first time, I could see that this was a tiny world unto itself lying in the middle of an endless sea.

Roddy came up by my side and pointed to the west. "You can't see it through the haze today, but on a very clear day you can see the mainland. That would be Portland, Maine, and the islands of Casco Bay."

"Erin told me about the island," I said.

"She hates August island," said Roddy. "I wouldn't take what she says to heart, it's a fine place to live. I was born here and I expect to grow old and die here."

"I like Erin," I said.

"Oh I didn't mean to say anything against her," said Roddy. "But she does like to tell tales. I suppose she told you about my uncle Daniel. If you hear it from her, she would make you believe that my uncle is the Devil himself."

"She was lying to me then?" I asked him.

"Oh then she has been telling you tales?" asked Roddy.

I didn't want to get Roddy angry with me. After all, it was his family. But, I didn't see why Erin would choose to lie to me. She sounded very convincing.

"Erin always gets the story about my grandfather wrong, especially the dates," said Roddy. "If she is going to tell tales about my family, at least she should get it right. She would have you believe that the commodore began his navy career with the war of eighteen twelve. The truth is he joined the navy as a young boy. He went back into the navy after becoming a fisherman to help fight the British. That is when he achieved the rank of commodore. He won many medals fighting at sea. We still call him the commodore."

Now I had to wonder which stories Erin had told me were true and which were not. I didn't think it was wise to ask Roddy about Mildred Schuster. I honestly didn't care about family gossip.

"The note," I said aloud. I reached into my coat and pulled out a small piece of paper that Cassie had handed to me to deliver to Roddy. I handed it to him. "It's from Cassie," I said.

Roddy smiled and pocketed the note. "I'll read it later," he said.

"I like Cassie," I said. "She's very happy most of the time."

"Not like her sister Erin, that's for sure," said Roddy. "My brother tried to woo Erin. He didn't have much luck. I don't think she likes boys very much. She's so self involved. She spends most of her time alone up in that studio of hers in the attic."

"She has a studio?" I said. "I've never seen it."

"She keeps herself locked in there, many times through a whole night," said Roddy. "Since you came, we have seen more of her than ever before. You're lucky you know. You are the first person who has ever occupied so much of her attentions."

"I like Erin," I said. "I don't mind that she isn't always smiling. She is very smart and has a mind of her own."

Roddy reached over and playfully punched my right shoulder. "I do believe you are smitten with her, aren't you?"

"Smitten? What does that mean?"

"Oh, it means that you've taken to her, you know..."

I suppose I did know.

Roddy pointed to the sky. "When it gets dark, I'll take you back up here and show you the stars," he said. "My grandfather taught me how to read the constellations and how to navigate by them. They take on all different shapes; A bull, a lion, a horse, A man with a bow. I could spend hours showing you the stars. I like to come up here on summer nights to sleep. I can stare up at them as long as I like and dream about making long journeys. Did you know that even if you travel great distances, the sky does not change so much? If I am out at sea and separated from those I love, I can look up at the sky and know we share the same view of the stars."

I could only think of Erin. She was going to be leaving the island some day soon and I might never see her again. I couldn't bear the thought of it. I had to find a way to win her heart before she left August island. I thought Roddy might be the key. He seemed to have a way with romantic thinking. He knew how I felt about Erin without my saying a word about it. I wondered how he could know such things.

"Your brother doesn't seem to like me," I said.

"My brother Jarrod is the quiet type," said Roddy. "Don't be put off by his manner."

"Does he still like Erin?" I asked.

"Yes, he does," Roddy replied.

"What would he say if he knew that I wanted to court Erin?"

"Oh, I wouldn't try, Billy," said Roddy. "She'll only bring you heartache."

"I can't help the way I feel about her," I said.

Roddy nudged me again with his elbow. "Oh you've got it don't you, you really are smitten?"

I nodded.

"I hear the dinner bell," said Roddy. "Lotty is calling. We best get down to the dining room. We wouldn't want to keep the commodore waiting."

Chapter 13

The Wolcott family was evenly divided as to whether I should be allowed to join their crew as a cut tail. Before we gathered at the table for dinner, I was introduced to the commodore, Barnabas Wolcott. He had been the old man that I had seen standing in the doorway earlier in the day when I made my first journey up the hill. Upon meeting him, he did not offer to shake my hand. He just nodded in my direction before we took our seats at the dinner table.

It was difficult enough trying to consume the strange tasting stew. They were all stunned when I admitted that I had never eaten fish before. It aided the commodore in his argument that I was not suited to be a cut tail. He began to pummel me with questions there at the dinner table. "What do you know about sailing? Had I ever worked aboard a ship before? What had I done to support myself back in Boston? Where was my family?"

The captain tried to break in just as the commodore posed the question about my family. By now, I had grown angry. I was ready to leave the dinner table and this house and forget about my intentions of staying on August island. I got up from my seat at the table. "I lost my family in the fire," I said. "I have no one but myself. I'm smart and strong enough to make my own way. I can and will do what ever it takes to survive."

"Sit down son," said the captain. "Finish your stew."

"I'm sorry captain. I've lost my appetite," I said. "If you will excuse me, I'm going back to the Inn." I left the room quickly and ran out to the hall. Roddy came out just as I was about to open the front door.

"Please don't go," said Roddy. "My grandfather's bark is worse than his bite. He didn't mean anything by what he said. Come back and have dessert with us."

"It's no use," I said. "Your grandfather doesn't like me and neither does your brother Jarrod. I guess I'll be going back to Boston. You can tell your father that I am ready to go."

"No, we want you to stay, Billy," said Roddy.

"I wish that was true," I said and then left the house. I regretted having to leave Roddy looking so sad.

"It's a blessing," said Erin. "I'm glad they refused you. A fisherman leads a terrible life," she said as she met me in the hall after I had returned to the Inn. This was one time I had wished that Erin was not the first person I would greet when I returned. At that moment, I didn't want to speak with anyone about what had happened. I followed Erin into the parlor. She took a seat before the hearth. I still had my coat on and was standing by the window looking out at the ship that would soon take me back to Boston and a most uncertain future.

"Why don't you come and sit by the fire," said Erin. "You look chilled to the bone. You're hands are shaking. Maybe you should go up to bed and rest."

"Will you stop treating me like a baby," I said, speaking in a voice louder and harsher than I meant to use.

"Well now, that's something I haven't heard out of you before, a voice of anger," said Erin.

"I'm sorry. I didn't mean to shout at you," I replied.

"Look at that map on the wall behind you, Billy," said Erin. "It's a map of America. Think about all the open land that it represents, and all the opportunity. Why would you want to settle down in a tiny, desolate place such as August island, when you could choose any spot on that map to call your home? You were once a farmer weren't you? Wouldn't you prefer to have your own piece of land? Can't you imagine owning a farm where you could raise a family without worrying about being evicted by some English landlord?"

"When I go back to Boston, I will be deported," I said. "I'll never have the chance you speak of."

"No, you won't be deported. Not if I have anything to say about it."

I turned to see who else had spoken. There in the doorway to the parlor stood the commodore. He was bundled up in a thick wool winter coat and he wore that same cap I had seen before. He supported himself with the aid of a finely carved wooden cane with a silver knob. He lifted it up and swung it back and forth and then let it rest by his foot.

Erin rose from her chair and scowled at the old man. "Excuse me. I'm needed in the kitchen," she said and then rushed out of the room without further word.

The commodore strode into the room and stood before the hearth. "Sit down son," he told me as he pointed to the chair with his cane.

I took the chair Erin had occupied.

"So you want to be a cut tail do you?" he asked me.

I wasn't so sure anymore. But I nodded anyway.

"A nod is not sufficient, young man. Speak up! Do you want to be a cut tail or not?" The commodore growled.

"Yes sir, I do, sir," I replied.

"Do you know what it really means to be a cut tail? Has anyone explained to you what the life of a fisherman is like?"

"The captain told me a few things," I replied.

"Have you ever slit open the belly of a fish and allowed the blood and entrails to slip out over your fingers? Have you ever cut up stinking fish parts to use as bait?" asked the commodore.

"No sir, I haven't," I said.

"The smell of fish, you would have it on you always," he went on to say. "You would eat fish; breathe fish, live with their blood on your hands. If you cut your hand on a fish hook or slice it through a line, no one will stop to mollycoddle you. You'll have to just bear up and go on working. Are you ready for that?"

"I would do anything not to be sent back to that place of death I used to call home," I replied.

"I see," said the commodore.

"I just want to be given a chance," I said. "That's all. If I don't measure up, you can take me back to Boston."

"How old are you?" asked the commodore.

"Fourteen," I replied.

The commodore sighed, "Ah...fourteen, I started my living as a sailor in the navy when I turned just eleven. I lied and said I was fourteen. It didn't matter. They would have taken any boy who had a beating heart and a swift set of feet and hands. At first I was called a green hand, for that was the color of my skin during the first voyage to sea. I spent my first hours aboard a ship with my head hung over the side of the rail. I begged for mercy. But instead, I was made to climb the mainmast and crawl out to the end of a yardarm. God help the poor soul who was standing down there underneath me to catch what had dropped from my stomach," said the commodore with a brief chuckle.

"I have been aboard a ship," I replied. "During the voyage to America, I found my sea legs pretty quickly," I added.

The commodore raised his eyebrows. "Oh so you do know a little about seafaring after all, don't you?"

I wasn't about to tell the commodore about my run in with the first mate that led me to be ordered below with the women and children.

The commodore stroked his beard with his fingers. "It'll be a rough time for you son. Those first days are always the hardest. You have a lot to learn, son. Today is the Sabbath. Tomorrow, the crew will begin work on the deck of the Dorothy, refitting her for the spring. If you are really determined, I'll notify the captain and he'll be coming down here to rouse you out of your bed long before the sun rises. You'll start your first day as a green hand aboard the Dorothy."

"Thank you sir," I said. "I promise I won't disappoint you or the captain."

The commodore had no more to say to me. He left the Inn just as abruptly as he had arrived.

Constance came into the parlor. She was smiling. "I couldn't help but overhear the commodore's words," she said. "I'm very happy that they are going to give you a chance. We are going to have to start your lessons very soon. If you are going to begin your life as a fisherman, you will have to know your sums very quickly so you can count your first wages."

I lay awake for hours that night, thinking about Erin. She was angry with me that I would choose to stay. I wish I could make her understand that I was staying because of her. But I was so awkward in my way of speaking; I couldn't yet find the words to explain how I felt about her.

The commodore was true to his word. Captain Wolcott appeared at the bottom of the stairs at the Inn before the sun rose early the next morning and barked an order that I should come down to the pier to begin my training. I found my way down to the pier in the darkness, slipping and sliding about on the ice and snow while trying to balance a tin of hot coffee in one hand and breakfast biscuit in the other.

The captain told me that there was no time to eat meals at my leisure that I should gulp down my coffee and eat my biscuit and be quick about it, because there was plenty of work to be done. To my disappointment, we were not going to be taking the Dorothy out to sea any time soon. The orders of the day were to strip the boat of her rigging and replace it with new fittings.

I was frustrated by my awkwardness. I found a way to stumble over every coil of rope or tool in my path and my hands became chafed in the bitter cold working the scraper to remove paint from the hull. My left arm was still very tender and sore. The burn was healing and Constance was right. My arm had begun to itch something terrible and it took a lot of willpower to keep my hand away from scratching myself raw.

By the end of the first day, every muscle in my body had an ache and my hands were worked till they were raw and bleeding. Still, there was something about being part of a team that made me forget about the pain. For the first time since I had left the potato plot back in Eire, I felt useful.

As another day passed and then another, I began to feel as part of the team. I could begin to recall the names of the different working parts of the boat. I knew the difference between a sheet and halyard line and what was their purpose. I began to recognize the schooner as a working machine and I marveled at the way she was built.

Roddy became my closest companion aboard the Dorothy. Because he had been the cut tail and I was replacing him, it was his responsibility to show me about the galley below deck. He taught me how to fix a fire in the stove and how to cook meals for the crew. Roddy explained to me that getting the meals ready was the most critical part of being a cut tail. He told me a story about the first time he had ever made a stew on board the ship when he had first started. He had put too much salt in the stew and it had to be thrown overboard.

I learned that the commodore was retiring from the sea this year. Roddy told me that he gave over command of the Dorothy to his son long ago but that the commodore continued to go out with them to the banks each season. I was a bit relieved that the commodore would not be present during my first sea voyage. I felt I had so much to prove to him. I knew it would be easier to please the captain and yet, I found the captain to be a hard taskmaster as well.

The captain took me aside after the first week of training and told me that I was faring well but that I needed to pay more attention to what I was doing. He explained that once we were out at sea. There was no margin for error during a squall. Every man would have to pull his weight.

I was soon to discover that the world aboard the Dorothy was like a little kingdom. The captain was the king, Jarrod was his second in command, Roddy was the junior and I was the peon, that is the word Erin used to describe my position aboard the schooner Dorothy.

Constance O'Neill insisted that I begin my studies in her parlor during the evening hours after I had come back from a hard day's work aboard the Dorothy. She would have to ply me with lots of her strong coffee to keep me awake during her lessons, for Jack had worked me well through by sunset, so that I was dragging myself to Constance's school to study by candlelight.

I began to wonder who was the harder taskmaster, the captain, or Constance O'Neill. After my struggles began with the alphabet and counting sums, I could see that learning to read and write was going to be a harder task than learning to be a sailor and a cut tail aboard the Dorothy.

Erin did not make it easy for me in school. She was such a brilliant young woman. She chided me for my slowness. I was glad that Constance was so patient. She gave me a book called the McGuffy reader and told me that, when the time came for me to go to sea, that I should carry this book with me and study it when I had the chance.

Being kept so busy with training aboard the Dorothy by day and studying my lessons at night, I had not taken measure of the time as it was passing so quickly. Before I knew it, the captain was offering some praise for the way I had adjusted to my new duties aboard the Dorothy. I was growing anxious for the Dorothy to get underway for our first journey to the fishing banks so I could test what I had learned. The captain could give me an order and I knew what to do. We had completely replaced the rigging on the Dorothy and laid down a fresh coat of paint on her hull and bulwark. I had developed a quick light step and could move about the deck without stumbling. I had also learned how to tie many kinds of knots.

I wished I could report the same progress in my studies with Constance. Becoming a cut tail was the simplest task in the world compared to learning how to read and write. I didn't think I would ever manage to write a single sentence that made any sense or read a page of a book that didn't take more than an hour's time. It didn't help that Erin was becoming a constant source of irritation. Were I not so smitten with her, I would have told her to shut her mouth long ago.

Erin loved to bring up the subject of her imminent departure from the island. She had told me shortly after I had arrived that, come springtime, her aunt Constance would be taking her to the mainland. I dreaded that day. I knew it would be coming soon because the winter cold was giving way to balmier days. The snow was beginning to melt away and green shoots of grass were showing themselves on the slope of the hill.

By the first week in March, I knew I had a birthday, but I didn't tell anyone about it. The captain told me that we would be leaving for the fishing banks on the second Monday of the month, and that we would not return until some time in mid May.

Constance told me that she was taking her nieces back to the mainland shortly after our return and that in fact we would be escorting them to Portland aboard the Dorothy. I knew I had so little time to explain to Erin how I felt about her. I still loved her, even though she had treated me so harshly at school.

Erin would disappear for hours at a time. I knew she was hiding herself up in her studio behind that locked door in the attic, located just across from my room. I would stand and put my ear to the door and listen. I could hear the creak of a chair rocking back and forth. I dared not disturb her in her work. A certain aroma came through the door. It was the oil and turps of paint, not unlike the smell of the Dorothy's freshly painted hull.

Cassie took me aside one day and tried to explain what her sister's troubles were. "Erin hates the dark and cold of winter," she said. "Aunty calls it winter melancholy." After hearing Cassie describe her sister's condition, I began to understand that might be the reason for her angry attitude towards me. Somehow, I had to make her understand how I felt about her before she would leave the island.

Time was running short. Before I knew it, the last Sunday had come before I would depart for the banks. I had only a day to make a difference. If I lost my chance this day, then there might be no other.

It was midmorning and I was invited up to the Wolcott house for dinner at three sharp. I knew I could not be late for that, so I had just a few hours to persuade Erin to come out of her studio and take a walk with me. The snow was giving way at last to the green of spring, but it was slow in making progress. Much of the hill was still barren, brown and slippery with mud from spring rains. The sun was peeking through high lofty clouds that rolled over the island. It was a fine day for a walk. I hoped I could persuade Erin to leave her studio and accompany me.

I went to the door and knocked. There was no answer. I put my ear to the door and listened. The rocking chair was creaking back and forth.

"Erin," I said. "It's a fine day. Would you like to come out and walk with me? It is my last day, you know. I'm leaving for the banks tomorrow. I'll be gone until May."

There was no answer.

"Erin?"

"Leave me alone," she replied.

"Please come out and take a walk with me. You'll be leaving after I return from the banks. We won't have much of a chance to speak after that and then you'll be gone forever."

I put my ear close to the door again. The rocking stopped and I heard footsteps approach the door. I listened as she turned the latch on the lock and slowly the door opened. The odor of turpentine and paint was strong coming out through the door. The door opened wider and I saw Erin's pale and drawn face. She had a shawl wrapped about her hunched shoulders making her appear like an old woman. Through the door I saw the rocker and beside that, a table in which had been placed a tray of uneaten dinner and another plate dotted with mounds of color. There was a stand of a kind, built with thin legs that held up a square of wood. On the square of wood was painted a portrait of Erin.

"Come in," she said as she opened the door wider.

I pointed to the picture. "It's you," I said.

"Yes of course it is me," she replied.

"I like it very much," I said.

Erin walked toward the easel, grabbed the picture and it appeared as if she might throw it to the floor.

"Stop," I said. "Why would you do that?"

"It's terrible," she replied. "The angles of my chin are all wrong. The shape of my eyes, the color in my cheeks, there is too much red there."

"Might I have it?" I asked. "If you are going to throw it away?"

"Nonsense," she replied. "It should not be seen by anyone."

"I will keep it for myself," I said. "I'll not show it to anyone, I promise."

"Why do you want a picture of me?" she asked.

My face became hot. Was it time to declare myself?

"Oh of course," said Erin. "How could I be so blind?"

"Blind?" I asked.

"The look in your eyes and the blush in your cheeks speak for you," said Erin.

"And what do they tell you?" I asked.

I wasn't sure I wanted to hear her answer. I could not bear the feelings that were coursing through me. I was on the verge. Say it now, I was thinking.

"You are smitten with me, aren't you?" she asked.

"Yes," I replied.

"Oh Billy," she said.

I hated the way she spoke my name, with a sound of pity in her voice. She made it more hurtful by shaking her head at me. I didn't know how to respond.

"How old are you Billy?" she asked.

"I just turned fifteen," I said.

"Do you know how old I am Billy?"

"No I don't," I said.

"I'm going to be nineteen in July," said Erin.

"I love you Erin. I don't care how old you are or how much younger I am." There, I said it. I declared myself at last, but I could see from the expression on her face that it did little good.

"You're just a little boy," said Erin. "I'm too old for you. One day you'll meet a girl your age and later on you'll find a wife. I'm not the person you want. Trust me, Billy. You'll find someone who will make you happy."

"I'm not a little boy," I said.

"No, that was a mistake. I'm sorry I said that. You are not a little boy but you still have a lot to learn about women," said Erin.

"How am I going to learn?" I asked.

"I'm not the one to teach you," she replied.

"You don't like me then?"

"I like you, even though you are stubborn and immature. You are like most of the boys I have known. There is no reason why I should expect you to be any different," Erin replied.

"Can't we at least be friends?" I asked.

"Well I suppose that is possible," Erin replied.

I breathed a sigh of relief. I thought she was on the verge of rejecting me completely. I couldn't bear that. "Then will you take a walk with me as a friend?" I asked.

"Yes," she replied. "But I want to make it clear to you. Nothing you can say will change my feelings. We will never be anything more than just friends. I know how boys think. They believe they can coax a girl to do just about anything if they put on enough charm."

"I'm going to miss you," I said.

"Are we going for that walk, or are you going to stand there and gush at me?" asked Erin.

Chapter 14

I am not sure which made my heart beat faster, the rigors of the climb up the hill or the presence of the young woman in my company. Out of politeness and a manly sense of responsibility, I offered to hold Erin's hand as we charged up the hill. Instead, she chose to walk at my side without my assistance and then she began to run up ahead of me just as we reached the summit.

"I could climb this hill blindfolded," she shouted back to me. "I know the position of every rock and tree."

As we reached the top of the hill, Erin surprised me by wrapping her arms around the trunk of a tree. She swung herself playfully back and forth and then she let go of the tree and ran along the path through the forest toward the edge of the cliff. I had to run fast to keep up with her.

I could already feel and hear the pounding of the waves against the cliffs. I followed Erin down the path toward the opening of the forest that led to the end of the world place. That is what I called it. I found myself drawn there many times after my first visit to watch the sunrise.

Erin was standing so close to the edge of the cliff that I had a fear she might topple over.

"Don't go so close!" I shouted.

"Do you remember what I told you about the commodore's first wife?" asked Erin. "Mildred Schuster went mad and jumped to her death from this very spot."

Erin moved a little closer to the edge and looked down. "My but she must have hated this island," said Erin.

I ran forward, grabbed Erin's hand and pulled her back from the edge.

"What are you doing?" she asked. "Why you silly little boy."

"I've never seen the other side of the cove," I said. "There is that little hill there that I wanted to climb over by the beach. Let's go away from here shall we?"

"Did you think that I was going to jump?"

I looked away from her. "Cassie told me that you suffer from winter melancholy," I said.

"Winter melancholy? Well, that is a quaint way of inferring that I am going mad, is it not?" said Erin.

"I don't think you are going mad," I said. "You are just unhappy."

"Well, Billy, You have surprised me. I think you might understand me after all."

"I want to try and make you happy," I said.

"Do you now? And how will you accomplish that?" Erin replied. "Oh, so I was right about you too. Even after the things I have told you. You just can't give up can you?" said Erin. "Well I'm going to tell you this now and I want you to hear me very clearly. I do not have the desire to marry any man, not now, or in the future. I am going to be a painter. Do you understand me? I don't want to be a mother. I have no interest in the domestic life, not the wifely duties or the waiting for a man to come back from the sea, spending so many of my days alone on this godforsaken island. By God then, I would certainly go mad. You would return one day and find me at the bottom of this cliff."

"No," I said. "It would not be that way. I would allow you the freedom to do as you wished."

"You would allow me?" Erin replied. "And who would grant you the right to decide what I should do with my life?"

"I love you," I said. "I want to make you happy."

"Love me?" said Erin as she grimaced at me. "You're just a little boy. You don't know anything about loving a woman except perhaps your mother."

"I know more than you think," I replied.

"Have you ever been intimate with a woman?"

My face turned hot. "I can't speak about that," I replied. "It's not decent."

"Your flush cheeks speak for you," said Erin. "Was it at some brothel?"

"Please, I can't speak about that," I said.

"You think that is love?" she asked.

"No," I replied. "I feel different about you."

"I should hope so," Erin replied.

"I didn't mean..."

"Look Billy," said Erin. "Some day, you'll meet a young woman who will strike your fancy. She'll no doubt be the marrying kind, like my sister Cassie. She'll provide you with a happy life and a house full of children. And you'll live happily ever after by the sea."

"I don't want just any other girl," I said. "I want you."

"You are just like my father and all the other men and boys I have known. You're stubborn and hardheaded. Well, none of you shall ever have control over me, never, do you understand me Billy? Do I have to pick up a rock and hit you over the head with it to knock some sense into that thick Irish skull of yours?"

"I'm sorry," I said.

"You should be," Erin replied.

"Can we still be friends?"

"No," said Erin. "You will always want something more and that is not possible." She then turned and walked away, back through the gap in the trees and disappeared down the other side of the hill.

August Island became a tiny dot on the horizon as the Dorothy made her way swiftly out toward the open sea. I stood near the stern and shielded my eyes with both hands cupped above my eyebrows so that I could still see the island as it disappeared behind the rays of the early morning sun that radiated out from the eastern sky. Roddy came up by my side and grabbed my shoulder. "I know that look," he said. "I'm going to miss Cassie too."

Roddy and I had become close enough to be brothers. It had happened so quickly and naturally so that it seemed as if I had known him all my life. We worked together and had begun to share the secrets of our own desires. I repeated to him what I had told Erin on that Sunday walk that I had shared with her. I was jealous of the kind of closeness Roddy shared with Cassie. But I didn't admit that to him. Cassie was indeed the marrying kind of girl and I was sure that she would offer Roddy the life he dreamed about.

I told Roddy that it didn't matter that Erin rejected me. I was not finished with her. Roddy told me that I had pushed too hard and had spoken too openly. Of course, I knew he was right. I had been so stupid. I lost control of my urgings.

I had to struggle to get Erin out of my mind. It was an impossible thing to do. I saw her out there floating on the waves, taunting me. She was present in every dream. I finally gave in to it and accepted the fact that she would be present during my entire journey to the George's Banks. I had a fear that my first journey to sea would be a disaster. I was sure that I would forget everything I had learned and would find myself stumbling about the deck, wondering what I should do next. It did not help that I had Erin on my mind.

After two days at sea, I had come to cherish the brisk wind at my back and the feeling of freedom that one received from the sensations of moving so swiftly through the waves. I was given my chance to take hold of the tiller. I could actually feel the power of the sea currents as they traveled from the rudder through the tiller arm, into my hand and up to my shoulder.

I still favored my burned left arm and kept it stiffly at my side most of the time because it still ached and itched. I would take a look at it and see the red mark that was the tender new skin that grew over the burn. It would be a permanent reminder of the past. Every time I would look at that pink scar, I would see the flames and my father's blackened skull. I would be reminded of the bad things I had done. I did my best to push the guilt aside. That was one benefit of falling in love. I could place thoughts of Erin in the way of the guilt and it worked for a time. But even so far out at sea, I could not bury the past entirely. I did have moments when I wondered where my mother was and what had happened to my good friend Jason Brody.

We arrived at George's Banks after a third day at sea. In the predawn light, I could see the many sails of other schooners dotting the horizon before us. We made our way forward between the other vessels until Jack gave the order to drop our anchor and lower the sails.

I knew not a thing about cod fishing except what Jack had taught me. There had been no practice runs. He had shown me the gear and explained what each item was and how it was used. I had taken part in the effort to load the barrels of salt that had been stored in a shed at the head of the pier. Jack told me that when the salt was all wetted with fish, the Dorothy would be homebound.

Back on August Island, Jack had brought out a strange triangular shaped thing about three feet long, gray brown in color and hard as wood. He told me that it was a cod fish that had been salted and dried under the sun. He told me that the stew I had eaten was cut from that thing.

After we had dropped anchor and lowered the sails, the gear was brought out and we donned this strange looking suit of oilcloth that covered us from the head, over the shoulder, to the knees. We each pulled on boots of heavy red leather that came up to our hips. Atop the oilcloth garb, we put on these leather aprons. I was handed a large oilcloth hat with a floppy brim that Roddy called a sou'wester.

I watched the captain and his sons grab wool cushions to pull over their hands. The captain explained that it was used to protect the hands from being cut by the line when they were dragging them in. The captain handed me this long pole widened at the end like an oar to a boat. He told me that I should strike the head of the fish once it was thrown to the deck.

The captain and his sons positioned themselves along the starboard side of the schooner and dropped their lines. I had no real expectation of what was to happen next. So that when the captain heaved the first giant fish upon the deck, I stared at it and watched it wiggle, as it tried to jump back toward its home in the sea. The captain shouted out at me. "Do your job boy. Finish him with the stick!"

I raised the stick high above the head of the fish. Its black eye was staring up at me. I brought the stick down hard. I felt so awkward. My aim was so straight and yet, each time I attempted to strike the fish, the end of the stick hit the deck and the fish continued to wiggle and struggle about. Jarrod handed his line to Roddy and came up beside me. He grabbed the stick from my hand and slashed it down in a direct hit upon the head of the fish. It finally stopped wiggling and lay flat on its side. The black eye was still open and stared up at me.

Jarrod told me to get my knife and split the fish open from the tail to the gills. I had a long rough edged knife stored in my apron. I brought it out and leaned down to the fish. I kept looking at the open eye. I positioned the knife but for some reason, I could not bring myself to plunge it into the fish.

Jarrod grabbed the knife from my hand, squatted down toward the fish, rammed the blade into the fishes belly and slashed it wide open. A flood of blood, pink ooze and fish entrails ran out upon the deck. I turned my head away and ran to the other side of the boat. I lost my breakfast over the side. I understood then, the true meaning of the term, green hand.

"Come back and do your work," the captain shouted to me. "The daylight is wasting."

This was a terrible mistake. I was not suited to be a fisherman. There was no place to run. I was a captive on this little ship and right then, the captain was angry enough to throw me overboard and order me to swim back to Boston. I swallowed hard and stood ready while the captain and his sons added to the mountain of cod that soon covered the entire deck. I was supposed to slit all their bellies, scrape their innards out and haul the fish into the hold to be laid upon the salt in the barrels in layers. I was falling behind and the captain ordered Roddy to give up his line to help me finish gutting the fish and to haul their carcasses into the hold.

It was one thing to slit and scrape out the fish. It was another test of strength to have to lift these giant fish, one after the other and heave them over the lid of the hatch and into the hold for storage. Their bodies were slippery and the deck was running slick with blood and ooze so that more than once, I found myself on my knees or flipped on my back. If Erin could see me now, she certainly would have a laugh at my expense.

After a few hours of back breaking labor, I was told to go below and prepare dinner. I considered it an easy task compared to the rigors of getting the fish below. However, I was not a trained cook. Roddy had tried to show me how to prepare the stew and how much salt and flour to add to thicken the gravy. Just the smell of the cooking fish made my stomach churn. I was not about to taste it to make sure it was right.

Roddy came down and grabbed the tin of stew and was about to bring it up to serve his father and Jarrod. "Have you tasted it to make sure it's right?" he asked. I rubbed my stomach. "I can't," I said. Roddy nodded and then smiled. "Don't worry, Billy. I got sick on my first time out, you'll get used to it soon enough." He then dipped the ladle into the stew, brought it up to his lips and tasted it. He winced, dropped the ladle into the pot, and spit out the stew he got into his mouth. He looked about and then saw the bait bucket. He rushed over to the bucket and emptied the stew into it.

"Thank God I caught it in time," said Roddy.

"That bad?" I said.

Roddy nodded. He then went to a cabinet above the stove and pulled a handful of hard crackers out of a small canvas bag. "I'll break the news to the captain that we'll be having pilot bread for dinner." He then grabbed the small bag of salt and threw it up in the cabinet. "Stay away from the salt, Billy." He frowned upon speaking and then his smile returned shortly afterward.

The captain knew that I had ruined the stew but said nothing. They did not stop work to eat their hard crackers. They chewed on them while they dragged in more fish. I did not have a chance to eat at all and, the way I was feeling, it was just as well.

I suppose the commodore would have looked upon it as mollycoddling because the captain had decided that Roddy should give up his line for the duration of this trip to stay by my side and teach me how to clean fish and store them in the barrels. Most important of all, the captain insisted that Roddy should teach me how to cook before starvation could set in among the crew.

Despite the fact that there was a shortage of crew to bring in the fish, the captain was happy with the amount of fish that he and Jarrod managed to catch over a period of six weeks. There was no way to measure the time other than by the passing of the sun and by the notations Roddy kept in his little fisherman's almanac that he had stuffed in his back pocket. After the first days on the banks, I had become adjusted to the schedule. I spent my days gutting and cleaning the fish, cooking the meals, scrubbing and cleaning the blood and fish entrails from the deck, and then, I shared responsibility to keep watch at night.

On the Sabbath, we lay down our gear and spent the day to rest. Everyone but myself, for I still had the duty to cook and scrub the deck. On occasion, on one or two given Sabbath days, a skipper from one of the other schooners would come aboard and share a story with us. The captain and his guest skipper would share tales of the big blow of forty six that had sunk many boats in it's wake and had drowned many of their old friends.

Roddy showed me the proper way to make duff. It was a special treat made from fried dough and molasses. Roddy told me that his father would look highly upon a cut tail who could prepare the duff the way he liked it. At last, I thought, I could do something right that pleased the captain. I'm sure it was just plain luck that the messy concoction came out tasting good.

I have to mention another part of the fisherman's life that I had begun to enjoy and that was the sharing of song. There was a song for every duty of a fisherman or a sailor: from the chant to hoist the sails to bringing in and preparing the fish to be salted. The men had strong voices that carried over the waters so that you could hear the other crews singing from nearby schooners and, combining their voices to our own, we sounded like a manly church choir.

The next part of the life that I favored was the night watch. It was the only time I was allowed to be alone with my thoughts. It was so peaceful. The only sounds you might hear were the lapping of the waves against the hull, the snores of the crew below deck or the singular song of another sailor doing his watch on a nearby schooner, lamenting about the wife or girl he left at home. Hearing the faraway lament led me to consider the foolish way I had treated Erin. I was bound and determined to win her heart no matter what I had to do.

The day had finally come when the homebound flag was raised and all the fish were wetted with salt. The captain was proud of what we had accomplished. He counted almost nine hundred quintals of fish in the barrels. He stated that it was an amazing feat for such a tiny crew. The captain singled me out for praise. "Look at the young man will you? His body has grown thick and hard and his sun burnished face displays the pride of a born fisherman. You started out badly son, but you really showed you are an able seaman. The commodore will be happy to hear about that."

August Island had been transformed. The desolate scene of winter with its bleakness of snow and ice were replaced with the bright colors of the blooming spring. I stood on the deck of the Dorothy and gazed at the beauty of the sight before my eyes, as the schooner sliced her way through the waves and sailed inward toward the cove. Roddy stood at my side with his fisherman's almanac and read off the date. "It was Saturday, May fourteenth, the year of our Lord, eighteen forty eight."

The island appeared just as Erin had painted it. But the colors were made so much brighter by the light of the afternoon sun as it shone down upon the slope of the hill. The vivid red and yellow wildflowers stood out so sharply that I thought I could reach out and pick them from the deck of the Dorothy.

As we entered the cove, the captain ordered Roddy to sound the bell to announce our arrival. Roddy let loose and the sounds of the bell echoed out toward the shore of the cove. The front door to Inn opened and Cassie came running down toward the end of the pier. Constance came out next with Lotty McKennon at her side. They met Cassie down at the end of the pier. They were waving at us with handkerchiefs that blew gaily in the afternoon breeze. I scanned the waterfront and there was no sign of Erin.

Roddy was so excited to see Cassie again that he almost stumbled and fell overboard when it came time to bring the Dorothy up fast to the pier. He had a rope coiled about his shoulders and threw it out to snare the pier with a loop and it fell short. He leaned so far out from the deck when the Dorothy angled closer to the floating barge that he lost his balance. He caught himself just in time before he tumbled into the cove waters.

I ran down to the bow to help him secure the Dorothy with the lines. Roddy was first to jump across the gap onto the floating barge. He then scrambled up the ladder to the top of the pier. He ran to Cassie, wrapped his arms around her and planted a kiss on her mouth in front of everyone. I was second up the ladder and continued to scan the waterfront for some sight of Erin. And then I spotted her. She was sitting in the grass about halfway up the hill. Her figure was partially hidden in the tall grasses. A small easel was set before her and her paints and brushes were laid out in the grass beside her. It was sad for me to remember that in just a few days, we would be taking our catch to the Portland Market and would be escorting Cassie, Erin and Constance O'Neill to the mainland. I could not imagine August Island without them.

Once we had all come up to the pier, we exchanged kisses and hugs from the women. The captain looked a bit lost. I think he was hoping that his dear wife would have been present to greet him even it had been so many years since she had been gone. I felt a bit lost as well. I would have loved it if Erin had joined the welcoming ladies. Roddy made a joke about my first efforts at making stew. He told them about hiding the salt bag from me. The captain was ready with his own quip. He reminded Roddy that he had made the same mistake on his first journey out as a cut tail.

Lotty came to my side "Don't you be worrying Billy," said Lotty. I'll teach you a few secrets about making stew. You'll have the crew eating out of your hand, you will."

Jarrod was the first one to ask about Erin.

Cassie pointed up to the hill. "She's painting."

Jarrod had never spoken to any of us with regard to his feelings for Erin. Roddy had told me that Jarrod had hoped to persuade Erin to marry him but she had spurned his advances. I was happy to hear that. Jarrod left us at the pier and strode toward the hill. I watched him follow the path up toward where Erin sat. I felt the blood rush to my face when Jarrod reached down to take Erin's hand to assist her to her feet, and my heart began to pound loudly when I saw her kiss him on the cheek. They folded hands together and walked arm in arm up to the remaining distance of the hill and disappeared beyond the trees. I wanted to run up that hill and tear her away from him. I would use my fists to teach Jarrod a lesson.

"Billy?" I felt a hand grasp my shoulder. I turned and saw that it was the captain. "What's wrong Billy? You look fit to be tied about something."

I couldn't understand it. Erin had told me that she didn't want any men in her life and yet she was acting so friendly with Jarrod, letting him take her hand and kiss her cheek. I wanted to confront her and ask her why she had lied to me.

The Wolcott's and the O'Neill's gathered at the big red house atop the hill to share a home coming dinner. I could hardly eat a bite of food. Nor could I muster a smile while Roddy told more stories about my awkward first days as a cut tail. I could not help but look at Erin as she sat across from me at the table. Jarrod was at her side and they were making eyes at each other. I wanted to rise from the table and leave their presence.

After we finished our dinner, the commodore invited the ladies to join the men in the parlor. I was up from my chair first and led the way. The commodore came up beside me and put a hand on my shoulder as I was making my way toward the parlor door. "The captain gave me a good report about you," he said. "You had a rough beginning, but he tells me that you came about very quickly. I'm glad to hear it." I wanted to smile but then Erin and Jarrod came up from behind and I turned. Erin glared at me and then turned toward Jarrod and smiled.

Before long, the women had formed their own little discussion group in the far corner of the parlor while the captain and the commodore stood at the hearth. Each lit their pipe and exchanged words about the weather and the size of the catch.

I stood over by the window alone. Roddy was sitting with Cassie near the women. I was jealous because Roddy was so lucky to have Cassie. It was sad to think that Cassie would be going away and leaving him. I wondered what Roddy would do without her.

Erin had left Jarrod's side and joined her Aunt Constance in a spirited discussion about the upcoming conference of women in Seneca, New York. At the same time, I over heard the commodore tell his son that he was happy that the Mexican war was at an end. He expressed hopes that President Polk would spend more of his time paying attention to the affairs of the New England states rather than the needs of the adventuring westerners.

The captain spoke of an upcoming election. He expressed hopes that Daniel Webster or some other New Englander would take office. "We need a man who will pay heed to the business of New England. We don't need any more western rubes like hizzoner, Mister Polk. If we take on all that new land in the west, it will be to the peril of we New Englanders. I say let Texas have their independence and let Mexico keep California."

Erin was sounding off loudly about women's rights and their need to be given the vote. So loudly in fact, that the commodore and the captain turned and order her to hold her tongue and commented that she was being impertinent. That brought a stern reaction from Constance but she did not say word to counter them.

The party broke up just before sunset. I hoped that finally, I might have a chance to speak with Erin. I was about to follow Erin down the hill. Roddy stopped me before I left the house. He told me that I didn't need to go back to the Inn. He was happy to tell me that I was invited to come and live up at the house and share his room in the attic. Now that the O'Neill's were going to leave August Island, the Inn was going to be closed.

We would be departing for Portland on Monday and tomorrow was another Sabbath day. It was the one day I would be free. It would also be the day that Erin liked to hide herself up in her studio. There was so little time left to convince her that I should be the one to provide her with a happy future.

Roddy was trying to put on a strong front about the upcoming separation with Cassie. She was not holding up so well. I watched her break down and cry more than once during our homecoming celebration. Roddy escorted her down the hill to the Inn after dinner. I saw them from the window of the parlor. Roddy was holding Cassie's hand and they walked as closely as if they were a single person. As they moved along, they were kissing and touching. It was too private a thing to watch but I could not take my eyes off of them. I felt such a longing. If only Erin and I could share that kind of closeness. Roddy took Cassie's hand again in his and he led her off the beaten path. They both disappeared into the darkness of the forest.

Jarrod offered to accompany Erin down to the Inn. I watched them walk together down the hill. I wanted so much to be the one to walk beside her.

"Billy, will you accompany me to the Inn?" I turned and Constance was by my side at the window. "There are things that need to be sorted," she said. "I have blankets and quilts for you to take back up to the house. And there is a box of books I am going to leave with you so that you can continue your studies after I am gone." I nodded but continued to gaze out the window at Erin and watched as she and Jarrod walked arm in arm down the path until they disappeared below the hill.

"She's too old for you, Billy," said Constance.

"You know?" I replied without turning to face her.

"I have known for some time," she replied.

"Erin told you?" I turned finally to face Constance and she nodded.

"I love her. I can make her happy. I know it," I said.

"In time, after she has been away, you'll come to realize that she was not right for you," said Constance. "I know she told you and you must accept the truth. Erin is not the marrying kind."

"What about Jarrod?"

"They have been friends since Erin came to August Island. Jarrod has matured. He knows where Erin's heart lies. He has accepted it, you must do the same."

"But she kissed him on the cheek," I replied. "...and they hold hands."

"Only in friendship, Billy," said Constance.

"Why is she always so angry? Why does she shut herself away in that room?" I asked.

"She's a very private person," Constance replied. "Erin needs her time away from everyone. She's an artist. People like that have special needs. She'll be much happier now that we are returning to the mainland."

"May I write her a letter?"

"You can ask her," Constance replied. "I'm sure that would be fine. I hope you will keep a correspondence with me. I want to see progress in your penmanship and writing skills. I want to hear from you about your new life here."

The captain entered the room. I told him that I thought I should spend one more night at the Inn so that I could assist Constance with the final packing. Of course my real reason for wanting to go back was to make one more attempt to convince Erin that I was worthy to be her suitor.

After helping Constance pack some trunks, I went upstairs to spend my last night in that room in the attic. Constance told me that I could choose a room on the second floor but I insisted on keeping my old room. I lay in that bed and thought about the first moments when I opened my eyes and saw Erin for the first time. It was such a time of fear, pain and suffering for me. And yet all I could keep in my memory of that time was the sight of Erin's pretty face and those green eyes. I would miss her terribly. I thought this kind of heart ache was far worse than the pain I had felt after the fire.

I could not give her up so easily. I got up from the bed and got dressed again. I walked across the hall to Erin's studio. The door was partly opened. That familiar odor of paint and turpentine filled my senses. I had begun to associate that aroma with Erin. The easel stood as a black silhouette in the light of a full moon that shone inward through the window. I walked toward the easel and noticed that her portrait was still there leaning against the easel. I knew it was stealing, but I had to have that picture. I reached out to grab it just as I heard footsteps approach from the hall. I turned quickly and there stood Erin holding a candle in her hand. She was still dressed and wearing a shawl about her shoulders. The candlelight made her face appear angelic.

"What are you doing up so late?" she asked.

"You didn't destroy the portrait," I said.

"No, in fact, I made some improvements. I'm going to keep it after all."

"What will you do with it?" I asked.

"Jarrod likes it very much," said Erin. "I shall give it to him."

"Jarrod!" I shouted.

"Shh," she whispered. "You'll wake up aunty and sis."

"Erin...you have to give me another chance, please."

"Oh Billy, we've been through all this already. I thought you understood by now. It's nothing against you. Please understand that."

"Might I write you then as a friend?"

"I don't think so, Billy."

"Why not?"

"I don't want to encourage you any further," Erin replied.

"I'll write you anyway. You can burn the letters if you like. I won't give up."

"You're a very sweet, considerate boy, Billy. I know you'll find someone who will offer you the love you desire."

"Might I give you a farewell kiss? Just on the cheek of course. It's all I ask. I'll give up my quest." I had one last hope that a kiss might change her mind.

"Very well, on the cheek," Erin replied.

I leaned toward her and instead of bringing my lips to her cheek, I moved my mouth to hers and kissed her soft lips. She pulled back quickly and almost dropped the candle dish. She raised her free hand and slapped my cheek as hard as she could. "Why you stubborn little boy," she said. Her green eyes were blazing with anger in the candlelight. "You're always reaching out for what you know you cannot have."

"I'm sorry. Please forgive me," I said.

Erin ran back down the stairs. I turned and stared at the portrait of her face that shone in the dim moonlight. I wanted to tear it to pieces.

Chapter 15

I rushed back to my room, lay down on the bed and stared up at the ceiling. My heard was thumping fast as if I had made a run up the hill. I was so angry with myself for having lost control over my urgings. I had ruined everything. There was no chance left in the world that Erin and I would ever be together.

The captain came to the Inn before dawn to rouse me out of bed. I had not even closed my eyes since I had left Erin. I spent the night hours thinking about her and the foolish thing I had done. The captain was calling to me from the hall downstairs. He ordered me to go aboard the Dorothy and prepare space in the hold for the O'Neill's baggage. I was more than happy to be kept occupied so that I did not have to face Erin. I wondered if she would tell her Aunt Constance that I had made unwanted advances toward her. I hoped not. I didn't want to lose Constance O'Neill's respect or friendship.

Constance greeted me in the kitchen. She showed no signs of knowing what I had done to her niece the night before. She handed me a tin cup of hot coffee and a breakfast biscuit to carry with me aboard the Dorothy as she had done during my weeks of training. This woman had given me so much. She had tended to my arm and it healed well. She had also taught me how to read and write. I was so grateful to her. I wish I could think of some way to repay her for all her kindness toward me. I hoped she couldn't read the look of guilt on my face.

I found Roddy and Cassie walking along the side of the street. Cassie was crying and Roddy was doing his best to console her. That was the thing that I thought was most unfair. Roddy and Cassie were obviously meant for each other. Roddy had told me that his father and Lotty McKennon had gone to Constance and tried to persuade her to allow Cassie to remain on the island. Constance refused their request. That was the one thing that angered me about Constance. She and her niece Erin had a cruel streak about them that was most unappealing

Roddy vowed to me more than once that he planned to marry Cassie and no one was going to get in their way. He was already planning ways to stay in Portland. He told me that he was willing to defy his father and even go so far as to move to the mainland and take a job on the waterfront so that he could be with Cassie. I understood how he felt.

Once the Dorothy was ready to get under way, Erin came strolling down the pier with Jarrod at her side. She was making a great effort to show everyone how happy she was to be leaving August Island. She glanced at me and looked right through me, as if I was an object of furniture on the deck.

Once aboard, Erin pranced about the deck "It's a beautiful day for a cruise!" she exclaimed.

"Sit down young lady," the captain groused at her. "Or you'll find yourself swimming to Portland."

This comment drew angry stares from Constance.

Erin responded to the captain's orders by making a face at him. She then slipped below deck through the cuddy hatch.

I noticed that relations had soured between Constance and the captain as of late. Roddy told me that his father had made an effort to persuade Constance to extend their stay for another month or two before returning to the mainland. Constance was adamant about leaving. Erin had already explained to me that their main reason for leaving in May was to avoid the visit by the captain's brother, Daniel Wolcott, come the first week of July. I'm sure Erin had a lot to do with coaxing her aunt not to give in on the captain's request.

Once the sails were raised and we were under way, Constance found a seat on a bench that was anchored to the port side of the cuddy. Roddy and Cassie sat on a bench attached to the other side of the cuddy, facing starboard. Cassie was constantly dabbing her eyes with a handkerchief and, at any given time, she would burst out into sobs. The captain was at the tiller and Jarrod was standing ready to trim sail or make the moves necessary to change tack. There was little for me to do but stand about, so Constance invited me to sit beside her.

At the beginning of the voyage, we were surrounded by fog, so that there was little to see beyond the deck other than a few yards of choppy seas. After an hour, the bright morning sun began to burn a hole through the mist. Out from the fog, there emerged the shapes of small islands that dotted the western horizon as we drew closer to the mainland. The sight of other ship's sails emerged as well.

The fog horn blared from Portland harbor. It was a sound that brought back memories of my arrival in Boston just a year ago. As the sun burned a hole through the rapidly fading mists, there appeared a rocky prominence on the distant coast. There above the rocky cliff, stood a tall white tower that overlooked the nearby harbor.

"That's the Portland Head Light," Constance told me.

As we made our way into Portland harbor, I was again reminded of my first sight of Boston with its mist shrouded hills rising up on the distant shore. I remembered how my mother looked as she stood on the deck of the Saint Gerard with the view of the new world within her sights. Mother held her rosary in her fingers and offered a prayer for deliverance. Looking back at the year that had passed, I had to conclude that her prayers did us little good.

Poor Terrance, I missed him. I was imagining what a joy he would have had standing upon the deck of this schooner and what a frolic he would have had out on the fishing banks. He would have made a finer cut tail than I, I'm sure. He didn't deserve his fate. But then the world was a cruel place and maybe it was better for him to be in the company of angels in heaven than down here to suffer the pain of being an unwanted child.

Constance was telling me something about the history of Portland, but, I was only half listening. She mentioned a poet called Longfellow and then she began to describe a fire that had ravaged the city during the American Revolution. My thoughts had turned once again to Erin. It made the occasion more melancholy to think about those whom I had lost and then to consider what I was losing this time.

At that moment, Erin reappeared on the deck from below. She looked about and noticed that we had entered Portland Harbor. Uttering a squeal of joy, Erin pranced about the deck until the captain ordered her to sit down, lest she fall overboard. Erin made another face at him and turned toward me. She raised her chin and then looked away toward the emerging pier.

After the captain had maneuvered the Dorothy to our berth and we made fast to the pier, Constance took me aside while the captain and Jarrod were below deck in the hold, gathering their baggage. "Do not spend the remainder of your life out on that island, Billy," said Constance. "You learned reading, writing and sums very well. You proved to me that you have a good mind and a strong will. Go someplace where you can improve your education. You needn't think that you are only fit to be a fisherman or a farmer. There are so many other opportunities for a young man like you in America. Above all, you must never allow the way others treat you to lead you to believe that you are something less because of where you were born."

I knew she was speaking about Daniel Wolcott.

Constance looked about her to make sure that the captain was not able to overhear her words to me. She then leaned close and spoke softly "I want you to avoid the captain's brother in any way you can. He's a dangerous man," said Constance.

I nodded back to her.

As we escorted the O'Neill's to the end of the pier with their baggage, I suddenly felt lost. Only a few months ago, I was a stranger among these people and, as we parted company on the pier, I felt like a stranger again. And yet, in other ways, these people seemed like family to me, as if I had known them all my life. How could it be that now they were like strangers again? It made no sense to me. We all stood by and watched in silence as Roddy assisted Cassie up into a waiting carriage. They held each other closely and exchanged hugs and kisses. Roddy let go of Cassie's hand as the carriage began to move forward. Erin hadn't said a single word to me. She shook hands with Jarrod and allowed him to kiss her on the cheek. She did not even glance in my direction.

Constance took charge of the loading of the carriage and I had no chance to say goodbye to her again. Before I knew it, they were riding up the street in that carriage. Roddy turned away from us and wiped the tears from his face. He watched the carriage turn a bend in the road. He ran up the street after it, calling out for Cassie. I was about to follow him when the captain came to my side and grabbed my shoulder. "Let him go," he said. "Roddy knows his way about the city. He'll be back soon."

The captain tried to make the best out of a sad time for all of us by offering to take us to a café for some refreshments before we took on the task of unloading the fish from the hold. First, he insisted on taking me on a tour of the waterfront and the fish drying operations. He escorted Jarrod and myself to the wharves where fish were laid out atop wooden platforms to be dried under the sun. The captain called them flakes. The salted cod were stretched out upon the wharf as far as the eye could see.

After a drink of cider and a hearty dinner of boiled lobster and potatoes, we set about the task of heaving the fish laden barrels from the hold of the Dorothy and loading them onto a wagon to take them to market to be laid out and dried. Roddy had not yet returned so that the labor was shared among Jarrod, the captain and myself. The captain was visibly angered that his son had not returned to help unload the fish.

The captain proposed that we would stay in port that night and take on new barrels of salt in the morning. We were going straight out to sea after that and not returning to August Island. I thought it was better that way, now that the ladies were gone. The island would seem so lonely. Only Lotty and the commodore remained there. I knew that the captain was doing this to help Roddy get over the loss of Cassie. But no expedition to the banks would accomplish that.

I was on night watch when Roddy returned to the Dorothy sometime before midnight. He held his head down and shuffled his feet as he made his way along the pier. As he climbed aboard, he would not look me in the eye. I knew he was ashamed to let me see his tears.

"Did you get to see Cassie again?" I asked him.

Roddy nodded but did not look up. He kicked a coil of rope lying by his feet. "I'm still going to marry her and no one is going to stop me," he said in a hurt but defiant voice.

"Then you saw Erin too?"

"I have this for you," said Roddy and he reached into his pocket and pulled out a small folded piece of paper. "Erin asked me to tell you that she was sorry she was so hard on you."

I was about to open the note to read it. Roddy told me to wait until we left port. "It's not what you think," he said. "She has not changed her mind about you. She wants you to be a friend, nothing more. She would like you to write her and tell her how you are doing."

"She told you that?"

Roddy nodded.

"You didn't read the note then?"

"No of course not. That's a private thing between you and Erin."

"I'm going to read it anyway," I said as I unfolded the paper and brought it over to the lantern to read.

Dear Billy,

I know you are sorry for what you have done. You took me by surprise last night. I am willing to forgive you, but you must accept the fact that I only offer my friendship. If you accept, you may write me as often as you wish.

I hoped you would have more ambition than to spend your life out on that island as a fisherman. You have more courage than most boys I have known. I would hope that you would spend that courage to do better things with your life.

Your loyal friend,
Erin O'Neill

I wasn't going to admit this to Roddy, but the note had renewed my hopes. At least she still wanted to correspond with me and that was better than nothing.

"So, what about you and Cassie?" I asked him as I folded the note and put it in my pocket. "Will you find a way to marry her soon?"

"Yes," he replied. "I asked her tonight. She is willing. We'll run away if we have to. I'll have to wait until the end of the season at least. Mark my words Billy. Cassie and I will be married."

We left Portland harbor early the next morning and made our way out to sea. That next fishing expedition to George's banks was not as trouble free as the first journey. Because it was later in the season, we were plagued by thick o fog and daily squalls that soaked us to the bone despite the fact that we wore oilcloth coverings to protect us. The rain came at us in a horizontal fashion and the wind stirred up the waves to giant proportions that threatened to drown us.

I had dreams during those nights aboard the Dorothy of riding that other ship bound across the angry sea from my old home. The cold and the wet and the sound of the wind reminded me of that deathly time. I dared not admit even to Roddy, how frightened I was by the angry sea that surrounded us.

The mood was not good among us during that fishing expedition. The Captain was angry that the catch was meager. Jarrod had spoken hardly a word to any of us and Roddy was feeling melancholy about leaving Cassie behind. There was little song shared and the Sabbath days were spent sleeping.

We returned to August Island at the end of June after making our return trip to Portland Market with our meager catch. Roddy used the opportunity to go see Cassie. He returned to the Dorothy and announced to me that Constance and Erin had left Portland to travel to Seneca New York to attend a woman's conference.

Upon our return home, our view of August island was obscured by thick o' fog. It was a treacherous time navigating our way into the cove without crashing into the rocks that formed the outer breakwater. It was Monday morning, the last week of June, eighteen forty eight, according to Roddy, who pulled out his fisherman's almanac and announced the date for anyone who wanted to listen. He also brought up the fact that the Fourth of July holiday was approaching, and that uncle Daniel and his family would soon arrive. To this bit of news, the captain grumbled, "Just another two weeks left of God's peace on August island."

The captain told us he was not going to bring the Dorothy right up to the pier. We would have to lower the dinghy and row ourselves back to shore. We dropped anchor in the middle of the cove. From the deck, I could not see the distant pier or any part of the island.

This was not a happy homecoming as the last return from the banks had been. No one met us at the pier. We slogged up the hill through the thick fog. We could not see the top of the hill as we climbed and could not see the bottom once we reached the top. We did not see the big house until we were just a few feet away. Lotty greeted us at the door with a frown. She announced to us that the commodore had taken to his bed with a bad cold in the chest. It seemed as if nothing could go right, and to make things worse, there was the threat of the arrival of Daniel Wolcott and his family. Roddy dared not say another word on that subject after seeing his father react the last time he mentioned them.

The captain told me that there was little that we could do until the fog lifted. That made the situation worse. With all this idle time on my hands, my thoughts turned back to Erin. I found myself taking out that note and reading it whenever I thought of her. Jarrod had disappeared from the house that afternoon after we arrived. Roddy told me that his brother had a secret project he was working on down in the boathouse

I felt lost and alone again. The Wolcott family had become a group of strangers once more. Even Roddy had seemed distant after our last journey to the banks. I wondered if it might not have been better that I stayed in Portland and tried to make a new living there. At least I would have had a chance to see Erin. Even though it would only be as a friend.

I wandered about the island that first day after our return even though there wasn't much to be seen in the fog. I wished that there was someone else to talk to.

I found my way back up the hill and almost bumped into Lotty as she was kneeling at the edge of a garden behind the big house. She was pulling up weeds that surrounded the green shoots of potato plants that dotted the ground. I recognized the plants so well. Beside the potato shoots there were other plants lined up in rows that faded away into the fog. I kneeled down beside her.

"Oh you needn't get yourself all muddied up," said Lotty.

"I don't mind, really," I told her. I had forgotten what it was like to feel the moist soil in my hands as I used to pick out the smaller plants to thin out the rows. I could have told Lotty that it was something I was doing since before I was old enough to walk.

"Yes, that's the way you do it," she said as I grabbed a few tiny shoots and pulled them out. "You look like you would have the makings of a good farmer," she said.

"I like fishing better," I replied.

"The men are all in sour moods," said Lotty. "The catch was poor and the world looks bleak to them now. But, don't you fret, it won't last long. It's the fog I think. It can make a man feel lost within himself, like a cold winter's day when the wind blows and there's nothing to do but to sit and try to keep warm before a fire. It's sad that all the women have left. I'm going to miss their company as much as you men."

I wondered how Lotty could stand the loneliness. But I was afraid to pry into her feelings. It helped me to be able to do something to occupy my time. I asked Lotty if I could help her tend the garden each day and she agreed. She told me that there was always plenty of work to be done on August island. She told me that there were two goats that roamed the north face of the island. She said that she had a secret method of luring the goats into the pen so she could milk them. She also talked about storing up food in the cellar for the winter. "You men think your work is done after you return from the banks. But my work never ends," she complained.

I saw stacks of firewood piled up against the house. I knew that the commodore was in no condition to chop wood. Lotty must have done it. And along with that, she cooked all the meals, cleaned and scrubbed the clothes, fetched water from the rain barrels, kept the privy house tidy and I wondered how she found the time to do it all by herself.

I pointed to the woodpile. "You chopped all that wood?" I asked.

"That I did," she replied.

"Doesn't anyone help you?"

"Oh Billy," Lotty sighed. "If you're going to get things done, sometimes you just have to do it yourself or it never gets done. If I had to rely on the captain or his sons to do this work, we'd all freeze and starve to death."

After a week long plague of fog, the sun finally broke through on Saturday afternoon, the first of July. The captain gave orders that we should bring the Dorothy back in to shore to get her deck and hull stripped and painted and to repair the sails and rigging for the next voyage to the banks.

The mood was still dour among the Wolcott men. The commodore was still taken to his bed and I had offered to help Lotty with the chores around the house so that she could tend to the commodore's needs. The captain did not offer praise for my willingness to take on the new duties.

Those were just a few reasons why I began to have doubts about how long I would remain on August island with the Wolcott family. It came to the point that I was ready to tell the captain that he should take me back to Boston. Roddy had ignored me and was sulking in his room in the attic. Jarrod had disappeared altogether down in the boathouse. Only Lotty paid me any attention, so that by the time the fog did lift and the sun brightened the island, I was ready to face the captain and tell him I wanted to leave and return to Boston.

Roddy surprised me on that first sunny afternoon by emerging from his room to invite me to take a skiff out onto the cove so that he could teach me how to sail it on my own. I had some hope by the return of his smile. Maybe Lotty was right, it must have been the fog. I walked beside Roddy as we descended the hill. He stopped midway and cupped his hand over his forehead to block the rays of the bright sun from his eyes. He gazed out at the open sea along the horizon.

"They will be coming soon," said Roddy. "My cousin Brent will be here and we'll have a good time of it."

I remembered Constance's warning. I felt a strange foreboding about the coming arrival of the captain's brother, but I said nothing to Roddy about it. We walked down to the boathouse and found the door locked. Roddy banged on the door. "Jarrod!" Roddy shouted. "Pa gave me permission to take out a skiff. I'm going to teach Billy how to sail it."

We heard someone approach the door and turn the lock. The door opened and Jarrod appeared. His plaid shirt and work pants were dusted from shoulder to foot with wood shavings. He opened the door wider and we got our first look at his secret project. It was the long sleek hull of a boat that rested on some long planks supported a few feet off the ground on some old salt barrels.

"She's almost ready to launch," said Jarrod. "Some pitch and paint on her hull and then I'll fit her out with her rigging."

"Will she be seaworthy?" asked Roddy. "Her draught is so shallow."

"She's built for speed," Jarrod replied. "I'll race her."

Roddy scratched his chin. "Racing, not fishing?"

I went over to the hull and ran my hand along the smoothed surface of the planking.

"Uncle Daniel will be arriving soon," said Jarrod. "You remember last year? He boasted that his Victoria was the fastest schooner afloat?" Jarrod rubbed his hands together. "This year, we'll have a race around the island to prove which is faster, his Victoria or my Marauder."

"Does pa know about this?" asked Roddy.

"I suppose he does," Jarrod replied. "I borrowed the supplies from his stock. I'm going to replace everything I used."

Roddy pointed up to a long shelf toward the rear of the boathouse. Other smaller hulls rested there. I helped Roddy lift out the hull of a skiff as well as a mast, a folded sail and a pair of oars.

"You'll come back and help me fit her out won't you?" asked Jarrod.

Roddy winked at me. "And you'll let us take her out on a cruise, eh?"

"We'll see," Jarrod replied.

"No bargain then," said Roddy as we carried the skiff hull to the door.

"Is it not bargain enough to watch me make a fool of uncle Daniel?" asked Jarrod.

"Aye, that it would be," Roddy replied.

We carried the little skiff hull along the waterfront street to the other side of the cove and then to the beach. We followed a path along the ridge of a grassy hill that ran precariously close to the water's edge. I wondered why we had gone through all this trouble to carry this heavy skiff hull so far around the cove when we could have launched her from the boat ramp located right in front of the boathouse. We had to descend the hill over a rocky slope to the beach. The tide was rising so that the beach was narrow, giving us little room to get a running start to push the hull of the skiff into the water. We dragged the skiff out into the waves. Roddy jumped in first and asked me to hand him the tall pole that would serve as the mast. I gave it to him and he planted it upright at the most forward point of the hull.

The waters of the cove were very cold. As I waded in and the icy waters washed around my feet and ankles, a flash of memory struck me. I had visions before me of those cold black waters of Boston harbor the night I tried to end my life.

"What's wrong? You can swim can't you?" Roddy shouted to me.

My throat tightened and my stomach churned. I couldn't understand why this was happening to me. I stared down into the water and could not see the bottom, even though I knew the waters here were shallow.

"Come on," Roddy shouted. "Come and climb in."

I gathered my courage and tried to block out the memories. I waded forward to the skiff and Roddy reached out with his hand to help me climb in. I had the sleeves of my plaid shirt rolled up so that the scar from the burn was in full view. I had become used to the sight of that long pink gash and so had Roddy and we never spoke of it.

"What happened?" Roddy asked after I found a seat in the skiff at the stern. "You looked like you were afraid to go into the water."

"It's just colder than I expected," I lied.

"Your arm does it still hurt?" asked Roddy.

"No," I replied. "But at times it can feel stiff."

"Do you ever think about the night we saved you?" asked Roddy.

I looked away from him and out to sea. "I'd rather not talk about that," I said.

"My pa might have never told you," said Roddy.

"Told me what?"

"How much he's happy that you've come to stay with us," said Roddy.

"He doesn't seem so happy to have me about. He never talks to me," I said. "I was thinking that I should start making new plans for my future."

"New plans?"

"Maybe I should go back to Boston," I said.

Roddy looked confused. "I don't understand, I thought you and I were like brothers. I thought you wanted to stay with us."

"I don't know if I am ready to spend my whole life out here on August island," I said.

"Oh I know what you mean, Billy. But you are just fifteen. You don't have to decide now what you are going to do for the rest of your life. I'm almost eighteen and I'm not even sure what I am going to do later on."

"Of course you do. You're going to marry Cassie and have a house full of sons. You'll be a fisherman just like your father," I told him.

"Now you see. That's what I mean. You know me better than I know myself. Now why would you want to leave?"

"It's your uncle Daniel," I said. "Constance O'Neill warned me to stay away from him. I'm afraid of what will happen when he arrives."

"Nothing will happen," said Roddy "We'll have a picnic on the waterfront. We'll watch fireworks. Uncle Daniel brings some every year. We set them off out by the breakwater. It is an amazing sight. Wait till you see. Oh and you'll meet my cousin Brent. He can be a snob but he's a good friend when his father isn't about. He's going to be staying for the rest of the summer. He comes every year and stays with us until he has to go back to school. Before you came, he was my only friend."

"Your uncle hates the Irish," I said.

"He doesn't have to know that you are Irish."

"I won't hide what I am from anyone," I replied.

"No I suppose not. But you needn't worry really. My father will protect you. He really has grown fond of you," said Roddy. "I know he doesn't show it much lately. He's had a very hard time. Grandpa is sick and the meager catch has hurt our business."

"The coming of uncle Daniel makes it hard on all of us every summer at this time," Roddy went on to say. "After he leaves, Pa will be in a better mood. In fact he has a surprise for you. I probably shouldn't say anything but, after you've told me about wanting to leave, maybe I should tell you."

"Tell me?"

"My pa wants to adopt you as his son."

"Adopt me?"

Roddy nodded. "He would be angry if he knew I told you this. But he saw that night in Boston as a miracle. He thinks of you as a divine gift from God. He sees you as the son he lost when my mother died. He was sure he was right after you came up and asked to work for him and then you went out and proved yourself worthy as a cut tail. He was so proud of you. But he's not the kind of man who shows his feelings well."

"He told you he wanted to adopt me?"

Roddy nodded. "We took a vote. Even the commodore agreed that it was the right thing."

"Even Jarrod?" I asked.

Roddy nodded.

I didn't know what to say to Roddy. It was completely unexpected.

"The day is wasting," said Roddy. "Let's get you out in the cove for your first lesson at sailing."

"When was your father going to tell me about this?" I asked.

"After uncle Danicl leaves," Roddy replied. "Please don't tell him I told you."

"No, I won't," I replied.

"Here take an oar and let's get her out into the cove," said Roddy.

We both rowed the skiff out into the deeper waters of the cove. I found myself gazing up toward the hill at the house. I tried to imagine what it would be like to be the captain's son, to be part of that family. I thought about my father and how cruel he had been. I wondered if I was betraying my family heritage. Dare I take another name and surrender my Irish name? What would my mother think of me if I were to deny my very identity as an Irish born child of the O'Shea family?

The thing that bothered me most was that, if I became a Wolcott, I would be related to that Irish hating man. I hadn't even met Daniel Wolcott and I already hated him. Were Erin to hear of this news that I would become a Wolcott, she would shake her head at me and scold me. "What kind of fool are you?" she would ask.

I was glad that Roddy had told me about this before the captain could pose the question to me himself. I was not yet ready to become his son or a member of the Wolcott family. I didn't want to hurt Roddy's feelings or the captain's. I didn't yet know what my final answer would be. I turned my gaze away from the house and the hill outward to the open sea. The mainland of America lay not twenty miles from the cove. It was such a large place and, as Constance had told me, it was filled with new opportunities. I felt it beckon to me. I wanted to start my own family and perhaps, own a bit of land to plant my own crops and build a house where no could come and evict me or my wife and children. It would be a place were we could live out our lives in freedom.

I was in a daze, thinking about the future when, out on the horizon, I caught sight of a speck that quickly grew into a sail. Roddy pointed toward it. He stood up a little too quickly and his weight tilted the hull of the skiff toward the lee. He lost his balance and fell sideways into the cove. He swam about in the waves and bobbed his head up above the water to shout. "Sail ho, it's the Victoria!"

Chapter 16

Roddy swam to the beach instead of climbing back into the skiff, so I rowed the boat back to the beach myself. By now, the Victoria loomed large on the horizon as she neared the entrance to the cove. Jarrod must have heard Roddy's call, for he had come to stand at the end of the pier. He rang the bell to alert the rest of the family up at the house. After a short time, I was surprised to see the commodore leave the house beside his son. There was no sign of Lotty.

"Where is Lotty?" I asked Roddy as he shook the water out of his hair.

Roddy frowned. "Lotty would rue the day she would come out to greet my uncle," he said. "She'll be moving to the Inn until uncle Daniel's visit is over."

"It is because she is Irish too?"

Roddy would not reply.

"I suppose you'll be wanting me to move back to the Inn, won't you?"

"It might not be a bad idea, Billy," said Roddy.

"Then Erin was right," I said.

"Erin tells lies," said Roddy.

"I'm not going to hide," I said. "I'm not ashamed of being Irish."

"Oh no, Billy, you misunderstood me," said Roddy. "It's not because of that. The house is going to be crowded. You might feel better if you had your own room back at the Inn until Daniel leaves. My aunt Abigail takes over the house. You wouldn't want to be any part of that, I'm sure."

"No, you're right. I wouldn't. Erin told me about her too," I said.

"Forget about what Erin told you," said Roddy. "It's all lies."

"Even about the suicide of Daniel's mother?"

Roddy's face turned red. "You must never repeat a word about that to anyone, please," said Roddy. "You have no idea what kind of trouble it would cause you."

"Don't worry. I won't say a thing about it," I assured him.

"Let's get the skiff back to the boathouse before my father sees me like this," said Roddy. "I don't want him to know I fell into the cove. It's not very sailor like, if you know what I mean?" And then he grinned at me. "Don't look so serious, Billy," Roddy added. "The visit will only last about a week and then life will go back to normal."

We said nothing more as we carried the skiff hull back down the street toward the boathouse. The captain and the commodore met us out in front of the Inn. The captain studied Roddy's wet hair and clothes. "You decided to go swimming did you?" the captain asked Roddy.

"Uh...not intentionally," Roddy replied.

"Get the skiff put back and then go up to the house and put on dry clothes before you come out to meet your uncle," said the captain.

"Yes pa," Roddy replied.

"Billy," The captain turned to me. "I have some chores I need you to perform at the Inn. Lotty will be moving there for the duration of my brother's visit. You go find Lotty and ask her what she needs of you."

"Are you going to make me hide too?" I said.

"Hide?" asked the captain. The commodore grumbled something under his breath and the walked away from his son toward the pier.

"I'm not ashamed of being Irish," I said. "I'll not hide myself."

The captain turned to his son. "Roddy what have you been telling Billy?"

"It's not me, Pa. It was Erin who told him," Roddy replied.

"Oh. I see," The captain replied. "Son, you can handle that skiff the rest of the way can't you? I need to speak with Billy alone."

"Yes pa," Roddy shifted the hull forward on his shoulder as I let go of one end of it. He had a strong pair of arms and I could see that he could have carried it by himself all along.

After Roddy had left us, the Captain put a hand on my shoulder. "Now I want you to forget what Erin told you," he said. "My brother can be a difficult man to get along with, that's true, but he is not a bad man." The captain scratched his beard and pointed toward the Inn with his other hand. "I think it would be better for you if you moved back to the Inn while my brother and his family stay with us. There is not much room up there at the big house. That's the only reason why I would ask you to move. It will only be for a week."

"Yes sir," I replied.

"Don't look so down, Billy. You can still join us at the picnic and watch the fireworks," the captain replied.

"Does your brother really hate the Irish?" I felt I had to ask the question even though it might cause trouble. The captain would not look me in the eye at that moment and I had my answer before he could speak. "Let's not dwell on trouble," the captain said.

"I'm not going to hide the fact that I am Irish," I said. "I am not ashamed of being Irish."

"Don't make any unnecessary trouble, Billy," said the captain. "Remember, you are a guest on this island. This is a family gathering. You're trying my patience. Just go and do as you are told."

I ran up to the front steps of the inn without offering a reply. I opened the door, went in and slammed it closed behind me. Lotty came rushing down the hall from the kitchen. "Billy, was that you slamming the door? What's has gotten into you?"

"The captain told me I have to move back to the Inn," I said.

"Oh Billy," said Lotty, after uttering a long sigh. "It's the best thing, you know. Daniel Wolcott is a most disagreeable man, and his wife, well she..." Lotty frowned. "She loves to lord it over everyone, that woman." Lotty then reached out and touched my shoulder. "You and I shall have a fine time of it down here amongst ourselves. We don't need them now do we? You come along into the kitchen. I'm making up a batch of my soda bread. You can help me build a new fire in the hearth. There is some firewood left there in the parlor. Would you go in and fetch it for me and carry it back to the kitchen?"

"Yes ma'm," I said.

"Call me Lotty if you would."

"It's not right you know," I said. "You are a member of their family, not a servant."

"Now...now," said Lotty. "I've been living with this family a lot longer than you have. It's only a week or two out of the year. I'd much rather spend that time down here at the Inn in the company of a handsome young Irish cut tail than with that arrogant so and so." Lotty was about to say more but stopped herself. "Enough of this, go fetch the wood will you Billy? Build us a nice fire. The nights are still cold. You might think about going out to get more wood for the upstairs."

"Yes," I was about to say ma'm and remembered. "Yes Lotty."

I was about to gather up an armful of wood when I caught a view of the Wolcott family reunion on the pier from the parlor window. I was interested in seeing the face of the man who hated the Irish. Erin was right. He looked so different from his brother, the captain. Daniel's hair was yellow and cropped close to his head. Although I was not close enough to see his eyes, I guessed that they were blue. Despite those differences, both brothers were of almost equal stature and height. Behind the captain's brother stood a short woman attired all in black. Tucked under her arm was the bible Erin had described to me. I guessed that she was Abigail Wolcott.

Clinging to the folds of the woman's black dress was this little girl who had long flowing blonde hair that was blowing wildly in the summer breeze. I was still a good distance from the pier and yet, I could hear the screams from that girl as she pulled on her mother's dress to get her attention and yet no one was paying her any mind. I watched as she let go of her mother's dress and ran up the pier to the street. This must have been Victoria, the young brat that Erin had threatened to drown in the cove.

 Just as I turned back to watch the captain shake hands with his brother, a teenage boy with a head of short cropped yellow hair, appeared beside Daniel. He was round in the face and the stomach and stood a head shorter than his father. He was dressed in a fancy blue sailor's pea coat. He held a sailor's cap in his hand. I guessed the boy was Daniel's son, the boy Erin called Brent. He was the spoiled snobbish whiner, according to Erin and Roddy.

Behind the guests there stood a pair of servants. One was a sailor and the other was a young lady, wearing a tan dress and bonnet. The young servant girl watched as little Victoria ran away. The servant girl ran after her.

Roddy appeared on the street coming down from the house. He had changed into dry clothes. He met Victoria on the street and tried to stop her. She grabbed his hand and it looked as if she bit him. I heard Roddy shout at her and she screamed again and ran from him. Roddy raised his hand to his mouth and sucked on the edge of his palm. I couldn't hear what he was saying but the angry look on his face spoke more about what he was thinking.

Roddy walked down to pier and met Brent. They shook hands and then locked arms as they walked back up the pier to the street. Roddy pointed to the Inn. I wondered if he would have the nerve to bring Brent in to introduce him to me. I moved back from the window before they could see me. I remembered that I was supposed to get wood for Lotty's kitchen fire. I went to the hearth and gathered up an arm full of wood when the door to the Inn opened.

"Billy, are you in here?" asked Roddy.

I carried the wood out to the hall.

"Billy this is my cousin Brent," said Roddy.

I shifted the weight of the wood in one hand and reached out to shake Brent's hand with the other. I grabbed a palm full of hot mushy flesh. It was as if the boy had no bones in his fingers at all. Roddy told Brent that I was the new cut tail aboard the Dorothy, but nothing else. He already knew that I was told to move down here to the Inn. He looked at me and then grinned from ear to ear. "I have a good idea, boys," said Roddy. "What'd you say, let's camp down here at the Inn and let the elders have the house to themselves?"

"I will if mother will allow it," Brent replied sheepishly.

"We'll have a grand time of it," said Roddy. "We can stay up as long as we like and tell stories. Did you bring some chewing tobacco?" Roddy asked Brent.

"I hid it in my other pair of shoes," Brent replied.

"And the fireworks, did your father bring the fireworks this year?" asked Roddy.

"He did," Brent replied.

Roddy clapped his hands together. "We're going to have a grand Fourth of July holiday!"

Lotty appeared from the kitchen. "Billy where is that wood? Oh, you have guests. Roddy and Brent, good day to you," Lotty said as she nodded to them.

"We're going to sleep here tonight," Roddy told Lotty. "Would that be alright with you?"

"As long as the captain agrees, yes, that would be fine," said Lotty. "Here give me that wood now. I'll get the fire started myself."

"No," I said. "I'll do it."

Just then the front door to the Inn opened. Little Victoria ran past me so quickly that I nearly lost my balance trying to stay out of her way. Some logs fell from my arms and rolled out onto the floor. The young servant girl came in after her and ran down the hall. Victoria had run up the stairs and was screaming all along. The sounds echoed throughout the Inn.

"My Lord," said Lotty "What has gotten into her?"

Seconds later, the young servant woman came back down the stairs with Victoria tucked under her arm. She dragged her out of the house, still kicking and screaming.

Brent did not appear to be very bothered by his little sister's behavior. He looked away from us toward the door. "I should go and help mother and father unpack," he said.

I went in to get the fire set up in the kitchen after Roddy and Brent left the Inn. They promised to return in a few hours with their blankets and pillows to set up a night camp. I was beginning to have some hope that the visit of Daniel Wolcott might not be so bad an event after all, as long as I could live at the Inn and stay out of his way.

Roddy and Brent returned after the dinner hour. I spent my first dinner alone with Lotty. She fixed up a feast for the both of us. I asked her who was doing the cooking up at the house and Lotty admitted that she was cooking for both places. She had already prepared the dinner for the Wolcott's. She cooked it from the Inn and carried it up herself when it was ready. I didn't think it was fair to treat a family member like a servant, but Lotty didn't appear to mind it, so I said nothing about it to her.

Brent, Roddy and I set up a little camp up in my attic room. I chose to return to the attic rather than sleep in the rooms once occupied by the O'Neill's. It was bad enough that the studio stood empty. I would look inward and remember the easel with the portrait of Erin sitting by the window. The smell of paint and turpentine still lingered about the room. I still had that little note she wrote to me. I kept it in a safe place and would read it again and again when I was feeling lonely for her. I hadn't given up hope yet that one day I could convince her that we could be more than just friends.

We decided not to start a fire. It was still very hot and stuffy up in the attic. Roddy and I gathered candles from other rooms and lined them up on the mantle. It brought back memories of the times Jason and I had back in that cellar when we would set up the candles for our card games.

"If only Jason could see me now," I said aloud without thinking.

"Who is Jason?" asked Roddy.

"A friend from Boston," I replied.

"You are from Boston?" asked Brent.

I didn't see any harm in admitting to that.

"So am I," said Brent. "What part of Boston are you from?"

"I wasn't sure what to tell him. My family lived in the north end but I lived at Fort Hill. I knew that once I had revealed that to Brent, he would know of my heritage and yet, I was determined not to hide my Irish identity. "Fort Hill," I replied finally.

Brent came closer. He began to study me more closely. "I thought there was something about you, the way you speak."

"What do you mean, the way I speak?"

"You speak like the servant lady downstairs."

"You mean Lotty?"

"Yes, she's Irish and so are you, are you not?"

"Yes I am Irish and I'm proud of it," I said with a firm raised chin.

"My father taught me that the Irish are the scum of the earth," said Brent while offering a smug grin.

"Brent," said Roddy. "That's no way to speak of a friend of mine."

I reached over and grabbed Brent by his collar with both hands and pulled him toward me. "Scum you say. I'll show you."

"Billy, don't," said Roddy.

"Let go of me or I'll…" Brent whined.

"You'll what?"

"I'll tell my father on you," said Brent. He had begun to cry.

My god the boy must have been at least sixteen or seventeen years old and he was acting like a blubbering infant. I let go of his shirt and stepped away.

"Let's go back to the house," said Roddy to Brent.

I turned toward Roddy. I hated to see our fun end, but what could be said to repair the damage? And why would I want to spend any more time in the company of a boy who thought I was scum. I'd be damned if I would apologize for being called scum by that blubbering little baby.

On Wednesday, the morning of the Fourth of July, the captain came to see me at the Inn. I was sitting at the kitchen worktable, eating a bit of breakfast. Lotty was down in the cellar pantry getting the ingredients for her pies.

The captain took the seat across from me. "I meant to come earlier," he said. "Roddy told me what happened last Saturday night. I thought I told you not to make any trouble."

"I didn't make any trouble," I said. "That fat boy called me scum. What was I supposed to do, kneel down and lick his boots and tell him I was sorry that I am scum?"

The captain regarded me through squinted eyes. "No of course not, but I would expect you to hold your temper."

"I did hold my temper," I replied. "I didn't hit him, much as I wanted to."

"Roddy thought you were about to," said the Captain.

"I was," I replied. "If that fat boy had said another word."

The captain sighed. "Oh I suppose you would have had the right,"

"Sir, I am beginning to think that the time has come for me to leave August island," I said.

This brought a look of surprise from the captain. "Oh now let's not be so hasty. A little bad blood between a pair of boys is no reason for you to decide such a thing," he said in reply.

"Why do you ask me to hide myself down here at the Inn? Why do you still treat me like an outsider?" I asked him.

"Aught, you're not an outsider, Billy. I'm just trying to keep you out of harms way," he replied.

"Then I was right. Erin was telling the truth," I said.

"Partly, yes, But my brother is still a member of my family. Nothing can change that. It is only one week out of the year that we have to suffer his presence," said the captain.

"Do you really want to adopt me as your son?" I felt I had to ask the question even though Roddy begged me not to speak about it.

"Oh, so Roddy told you about that, did he?"

"He begged me not to speak about it until you told me. But I need to know the answer now," I said.

"It is true," said the captain. "I was going to tell you after my brother left next week."

"You don't act like a father to me," I dared to say.

"Oh and how is a father supposed to act toward a son?"

"Not like a stranger," I said.

"We have our own ways here, Billy," The captain replied. "I don't know what your father was like. I am not the kind of man who shows a lot of emotion. My sons received all the affection they needed from their mother when they were just babies. My boys are grown up men now. Jarrod and Roddy know I love them dearly. I would give my life for them. They know that. And, you must understand Billy. I have come to be very fond of you. You have shown your courage and worthiness more than once as a member of my crew and aye, it goes beyond that. After I rescued you from that harbor, I felt responsible for a life I had saved. I don't know if Roddy told you, my wife died carrying my son in her womb. He was born dead. I've always wanted more children but I didn't want to sully the memory of my dear wife Dorothy by marrying again. I just couldn't do that. You came here to the island and measured up. In so many ways you filled that void. If I were to have another son, you would be the boy I would choose. I can tell you no more than that. The decision is yours to make. I can only offer you the love and respect I give my other sons. Understand this, Billy. I am not a perfect father by any means. I have a bad temper than can get the better of me at times."

"My father hated me," I said. "He tried to kill me and I had to kill him first."

The captain leaned over and stared at me with eyes wide and eyebrows raised. "My god, you never said anything about that to me before."

I remembered telling the captain my story the day I asked him to hire me as a cut tail. Had he forgotten everything I told him?

"You had told me about the fire and about your father's cruelty to your brother. You thought your father had killed him didn't you?"

"He did kill him. I found my brother's bloody coat," I replied.

"Son, there's no need to dwell upon the past anymore. You're safe here. You have a home with us if you want it. It's your decision to make. Once my brother and his family have left the island, we'll sit down and have another talk," said the captain. "Now, I want you to come out and join the family for the picnic. I want you to have a good time. You earned the right. You worked very hard these past months."

After the captain left me, I felt more confused than ever about making the right choice. Lotty urged me to go outside and join the Wolcott's. I was reluctant to meet Daniel Wolcott and his wife. They would know right away by my manner of speaking that I was Irish. I wasn't about to try to change my manner of speech to hide who I was, even though I had practiced by listening to Roddy.

It was a perfect day for a picnic. The fog was nowhere to be seen. The sky was clear and by the early afternoon, it had become hot and the air was heavy but there was a slight sea breeze coming in across the cove that made it comfortable. The day promised to be an exciting one. I knew that Jarrod had finished the work on his new sloop, the Marauder and it was ready to be launched. Roddy and Jarrod had hopes that they could challenge their uncle Daniel to a race around the island. There was the anticipation that after sundown the fireworks show would be set off at the breakwater on the other side of the cove.

I helped Lotty carry heavy clay jugs of cider that she made herself from apples brought from the mainland and stored in the food pantry. I set them about on the long food table that was placed on the street in front of the Inn. Rocking chairs were set about the street near the table for the guests to rest themselves. Daniel Wolcott and his wife Abigail were already settled in their chairs that faced the waterfront so that they could catch the light breezes coming across the cove to cool them from the hot sun. Abigail still wore her black dress and a bonnet with a veil that shielded her face from the hot sun. She held that little bible in her lap.

I thought it best that I avoid them. But, as I passed her chair on my way back to the Inn, Abigail leaned forward a little and pulled back her veil to reveal a pale face. She was not an ugly woman by any means. Her eyes were wide and dark brown, so unlike her children who took after their father with their blond hair and blue eyes. "Young man," she said with a quiet whispery voice. "Go fetch me a glass of cider would you?" It was not the kind of voice I would expect out of a woman who supposedly preached from the holy bible, not a voice that commanded a presence. I didn't want to act as her servant boy. I remembered what Erin had told me about how she was treated by them, like a lady in waiting.

I went and fetched the cider and brought it back to her. Abigail studied me some more. I was ready to leave when she asked. "Where are you from, young man? You do not look like New England stock."

New England stock, I thought, was that some kind of animal?

The captain appeared at my side. He overheard the question. I wondered what lie he would concoct to satisfy her curiosity. "Billy is from Ireland," said the captain.

Oh God, He had done it now. I thought.

"He is working as one of our crew. His family suffered a terrible tragedy. I took him in. He has proved to be a very hard worker and able seaman," the captain went on to say.

I looked over at Daniel Wolcott and watched for a reaction from him. He had been rocking back and forth and appeared to be dosing off to sleep. But, after he heard his brother mention Ireland, he sat up straight and began to study me with those steel blue eyes of his. He offered me a look that was colder that ice. "You didn't say anything to me about this, brother," Daniel said to the captain. "Have you been hiding the boy away?"

"Oh no, brother, there wasn't enough room at the house for Billy to stay, so I had him move back to the Inn," the captain replied.

"So you let members of your crew live at the house with the family, do you?" asked Daniel.

"Aught, Billy is more than just a crewman," the captain replied.

"Oh I see," said Daniel with raised eyebrows.

I wish the captain had lied.

"Young man," Daniel turned his cold gaze back toward me. "What port did your family come through?"

"Brother, what does it matter where his family came from?" the captain asked Daniel.

"Boston," I replied.

"Now brother, don't intrude further. The boy's family was killed in a terrible fire last Christmas Eve. There's no need in bringing that up now," said the captain.

Daniel's face began to turn red and there was this large vein in his left temple that bulged out purple. He rose from the chair to advance toward me.

"You lived in the north end didn't you?" he asked in a voice that was growing louder. "Tell me boy. Was that fire in the north end?"

"Yes sir," I replied.

"You goddamned Irish!" Daniel shouted as he advanced closer to me. "You dirty hooligans burned up an entire block of my houses."

"Husband, do not blaspheme," Abigail scolded him.

Daniel turned back toward her and then back towards me. The captain had moved in between his brother and me, blocking his brother's path. "Brother, you can't blame this boy. It wasn't his fault. It was an accident," he said.

Oh Christ, I thought. Let the captain say no more.

"What, are you telling me that this is the boy who started the fire?" Daniel asked.

"No, of course not," the captain replied.

"Then how do you know it was an accident?"

"How does any fire start?'" asked the captain.

"I don't know," Daniel replied. "Maybe we should ask this young man."

"You leave Billy alone," said the captain. "What's done is done. You can't bring back those houses or those who died in them," the captain replied.

"No, but I can prosecute the man or boy who is responsible. You can't shelter this boy from the law. He is a wanted fugitive," said Daniel.

"You're not the law," said the captain.

"No, but I have the means to see that this boy is punished for his crimes!" Daniel shouted.

"Your houses were not fit for pigs," I dared to say.

The captain turned toward me. "This is not the time, Billy. Please go up to the house."

"I won't hide from him anymore," I said.

"Not fit for pigs you say? Well then, I know for sure they were fit for the Irish," Daniel replied.

"Let us stop this now," said the captain.

By now, Lotty was standing over by the food tables overhearing every word. Roddy, Brent and Jarrod had come over to see what the shouting was about. The commodore appeared from around the corner from the Inn and advanced toward his sons. I began to move away after the commodore reached us.

"So is it to be this way again?" asked the commodore. "Every year, it's the same old battle of wills. I've had quite enough of it."

"That boy!" Daniel shouted and pointed toward me.

"What about the boy?" asked the commodore.

Daniel sputtered. I thought that purple vein at his temple was going to burst open. Jarrod dared to come forward. "Pa, I need Billy to help me set up the rigging on my sloop." I breathed a sigh of relief. I had Jarrod to thank. I moved toward Jarrod's side and we began to walk away.

Daniel called after me. "I suggest that you find some other place to hide, boy, The law will get you one day soon if I have anything to say about it. Half this island belongs to me. I don't want any Irish here to foul up this family sanctuary."

"The boy stays," said the captain. "I'm going to adopt Billy as my son and you'll have nothing to say about it."

"Adopt him? A fugitive from the law, have you taken leave of your senses brother? The boy belongs back where he came from and I plan to send him there," said Daniel.

"Over my dead body," The captain replied.

"Sons, make an end to this," The commodore warned.

"I'll make an end," said Daniel. "I'll find a legal way to take possession of this entire Island. I'll make you wish you never took that wretched Irish boy into this family," said Daniel. "By God I will do whatever is necessary to make sure that the Irish urchin never becomes a Wolcott!"

"Brother, you left this island when you were a boy. You have not contributed anything to this family or our business," said the captain. "You come here every summer to make life miserable for us for one week out of the year. My wife was Irish. My mother was Irish. My sons are all half Irish, and, I am proud to take this young man into my family as well. Tell me something brother, if you hate the Irish so much? Why do you still come back here?"

Jarrod and I had stopped to listen. Brent and Roddy had joined us. We all watched the spectacle of these two grown men arguing back and forth like children. They traded more barbs until it appeared that they would raise fists against each other. I was no longer the focus of the argument. They were speaking about their childhood. Jack's dark leathery face had turned blood red and he had flecks of white spittle that flew from his mouth as he shouted epithets at his brother. His beard flew up and down while he shook his head and waved his fist in his brother's face. The commodore imposed himself between them and tried to push them apart.

"This is much worse than last year," said Roddy. "I think pa is going to hit uncle Daniel this time."

"He'd better not," said Brent.

"What started it this time?" asked Roddy.

Jarrod looked over at me and offered one of his infrequent smiles. "Don't blame yourself, Billy," he said. "They would have found some reason to have a row. Let's go to the boat house. We have work to do there."

I followed Jarrod to the boat house along with Roddy and Brent. We began the work of rigging out the sloop. It was a relief to have something to keep me busy. I was worried about what I had heard today. Daniel Wolcott said I was a fugitive. What did that mean? Did they blame me for the fire? I knew that I would either be sent to jail or sent back to my home country if I returned to Boston. If the captain was going to adopt me, I had to accept his offer. Even though I was still feeling uncertain about a future here on August island, I no longer had a choice.

Brent and Roddy had left Jarrod and me alone after a time so that they could go back to the picnic table and stuff themselves with cakes and cider. I wanted to know if it was safe to return. Jarrod told me I had nothing to fear from Daniel. I wished that were true.

Jarrod and I returned to the front of the Inn just before sunset. Roddy and Brent were still sitting at the picnic table munching on pie. There were no adults about. I breathed a sigh of relief.

"Mother has gone up to pack," Brent mumbled the words through a mouthful of apple pie. "They are leaving first thing in the morning if the wind is agreeable."

"Thank God," Jarrod replied.

I wondered about the outcome of the argument. Who had won? But I wasn't going to ask. The captain came down the hill. I was ready for him to announce that he would be taking me back to Boston to face the law. But instead he smiled at me. "Don't you worry about a thing Billy," he said. "I meant what I said. My brother is leaving tomorrow. I don't think we'll be threatened with his presence next year or any future year."

The captain then realized that Brent was sitting just a few yards away at the picnic table. "Brent you are still welcome to spend the summer with us, I don't want the bad feelings between my brother and me to hurt you. This has nothing to do with you, son." Brent nodded toward the captain and continued to stuff his mouth with apple pie.

The fireworks display was cancelled. The captain told us that there were quite enough fireworks set off for one day. Roddy was the saddest among us to hear that news. Jarrod tried to make him feel better by allowing Roddy to take the helm of his newly christened sloop Marauder for a cruise around the island. I had to admit, I was still worried about Daniel Wolcott. Would he come back and take me to Boston himself to face justice and deportation? The captain assured me that he would not allow that to happen.

Chapter 17

I stood before the parlor window at the Inn and watched Daniel Wolcott help his wife Abigail climb aboard the Victoria. Lotty came up beside me and rubbed my shoulder with her hand. "We'll have peace now," she said. "I hope this is the last summer to see them come."

I was thankful that the fog had not returned and that it was the beginning of a fair, windy day and good for sailing, so that there would be no delay in the departure of the Victoria.

"I have this for you," said Lotty. She handed me a rolled up newspaper. "Daniel Wolcott came down to the Inn very early this morning before you were awake and left it here. He told me to give it to you. I was going to throw it into the kitchen fire but then I realized, it's not for me to decide to keep it from you."

I took the newspaper from her and noticed that a slip of paper that stuck out from the center.

"I'll leave you," said Lotty. "Come into the kitchen and I'll give you a slice of soda bread and a cup of coffee when you are ready to have breakfast."

I waited until Lotty left the room before opening the newspaper. I unrolled the paper and pulled the note from the middle. I wanted to throw them both into the fireplace. I turned the notepaper over and there was a message written on it.

It began:
 To whom it may concern:

I will make good my threat. If my brother proceeds with the adoption, I shall do everything in my power to have you deported back to Ireland. I have many friends and much influence in the government. You would have no means of recourse. You must leave August island by the end of this summer and never return.

I plan to make an inquiry about your past activities in Boston and about your family. If I find out that you had anything to do with starting that fire, I shall have you hunted down and brought back to Boston to face justice.

Heed my warning. Leave my brother's home or you shall face more trouble than you could ever imagine. I suggest that you read the third column on the

second page of this newspaper. It will give you some understanding about how we Americans feel about you and your invading hordes.
                    D. Wolcott

I crumbled the note in my fist and then raised my arm up into the air. I was about to throw the newspaper across the room but I was curious about what the newspaper had to say. I opened the newspaper to the second page. There, in the third column was a small title that read: Sending the Irish Home. I then read the lines underneath. It was a listing of family names. They were being deported on the second week of June. It listed certain crimes beside their names. Under the lists of names was a message:

To all those Irish born who read this, take heed: We are coming after you and we will not rest until the remainder of your horde are packed up and shipped back to Ireland. Be kind and wise enough to do the city of Boston a favor and leave of your own accord. It will go better for you.

I folded the paper, twisted it in my fingers and then ripped it in half and then again into smaller pieces. I let the pieces fall to the floor. I looked around the room and then out through the window. Daniel Wolcott was still there at the pier with that sailor. They were making ready to get under way. I wanted to run out there and tell that man that he could not frighten me.

I felt enclosed in the parlor. I needed air to breathe. I ran out through the front door and around the back of the Inn to the base of the hill. I looked up at the big house. I wanted to see the captain and tell him about the note. I ran up the hill and reached the door of the house just as Roddy and Brent were coming out. I stopped for a moment and then ran past them toward the clearing in the forest that led to the cliff's edge. I ran to the very edge and looked down at the crashing waves. The captain could not save me if I decided to jump. No one could. But as I peered down at the splash of foam and the dark rolling waves, I realized what a stupid thing it was to even consider ending my life. I can't let him win. If I jumped, he wins. He is rid of me. I turned around and saw Brent and Roddy standing under the canopy of trees. They were watching me from just a few yards away.

"What's wrong Billy?" asked Roddy.

I formed my hands into fists and walked toward Brent. And then I raised my fists to within just a few inches from his face. "You can tell your father that I have no intention of leaving August island. He can do as he wishes to me. The captain wants to adopt me as his son and I am going to become a Wolcott whether your father likes it or not. So you can just go down there and tell your father that his threats don't frighten me."

Brent reared back. "You better not hit me," he whined.

Roddy came forward and grabbed my shoulder but I shook it off.

"Billy, I'm on your side," said Roddy.

"His side?" Brent complained.

"Shut up Brent. You'll just make things worse," said Roddy.

Brent turned and ran through the path between the trees.

"He's such a baby," I said.

"His father and mother treat him that way. Once they have left, Brent will act differently. You'll see. He's not such a bad fellow," said Roddy.

"I don't really want to hit anyone," I said. "I just can't stand to be treated like this. Your uncle has vowed revenge against me. What am I going to do if he tries to carry out his threat?"

"Don't worry. Pa will take care of it," Roddy replied and then he left me and went to find Brent. I walked back through the trees to the summit of the hill. I sat down in the tall grass and watched with a great feeling of relief as the Victoria maneuvered her way out of the cove.

The captain had not gone down to see his brother depart. He came out of the house and found me sitting in the grass not far from the front door. I stood up beside him. He looked angry about something.

"Billy, I thought we had already talked about fighting," said the captain. "Brent came and told me that you were about to hit him again. We can have any more of that."

I then told the captain about the note and the article in the newspaper that Daniel Wolcott had left at the Inn. I watched as the captain's face grew redder with anger. "Aught...he had no right to do such a thing," the captain replied. "I can understand you being so angry. But there is no use in taking it out on Brent."

"I know," I said. "But that boy is such a sissy. Just looking at him and to hear him whimper like he does..." Suddenly, I was struck by a memory. I was thinking about Terrance and how he used to whine and complain. It would cause my father to strike out at him. I realized that I was acting like my father. Was Brent any different that my brother? Were they both just so scared? What was I doing?

"Billy, what's wrong?" asked the captain.

"My little brother…I was thinking about him and how my father treated him because he was so weak and I realized I was falling into the same habit," I said.

"It's good that you can see that," said the captain. "You really are on the verge of becoming a man."

I had my doubts. My father was a man and he never saw the reason why he did things.

"We're going to Portland in a few days," said the captain. "We'll lay in our stock of salt and make our last journey out to the banks for the season. While we're in Portland, I'll go see the magistrate to find out whether the adoption papers are ready. I hope you don't mind, but I took the liberty while we were last in Portland. I asked the court to draw them up. You have to understand. It is a special thing. I asked a favor from an old friend of the court who has influence in the Maine legislature. There are no laws governing the adoption of a foreign child. So they had to make up a special law for this case. I have been assured that it will be legal and binding, at least in the state of Maine. You needn't worry about my brother. I will take care of him in due time."

I looked across the top of the hill out toward the sea.

"Do you still want to be my son?" asked the captain.

I turned to him. "Yes captain," I replied.

The captain put out his hand to shake and I took it. He moved closer to me and used his other hand to grip my shoulder. He looked me straight in the eye. It was such a new thing for me to feel wanted. And by the look in the captain's eyes, He wanted me to be his son. And to me, that was more important than a name.

We headed for Portland on Monday morning. During the time before we left, I tried to make it up to Brent for the way I had threatened him. Roddy was right. He wasn't just such a bad sort once his parents had left him alone. We had a short talk alone one day, before we left for Portland. He told me that he knew Tim Gardner. In fact they went to the same school in Boston. Brent didn't like Tim because he was a bully and a snob. Brent told me that he had even considered going to one of Jason Brody's card games. He told me that he didn't go to Fort Hill because he was afraid that his mother would find out. She would have whipped him had she known he was gambling.

Still, even after our talk, I could not trust him and there was some part of him that I didn't like; it was his arrogance, inherited from his father, no doubt. There were times when I thought Brent was still like his father, especially during the voyage to Portland. Brent did not want to go to the courthouse to witness my adoption. Maybe he was afraid that his father would ask him about it and if he saw it himself, he would have to tell him what he saw. I would have been glad to have Brent witness the event so that he could report back to his father that the deed had been done.

As we headed to the courthouse, I did still have second thoughts about giving up my name. Was I betraying my Irish heritage by becoming a Wolcott? But then, what did that mean? I hadn't given any thought to my family heritage until all this trouble arose. It really didn't matter before. I was who I was. No one ever stopped to demand that I be something else to suit their needs. I couldn't understand why my identity was so important. How different was I from anyone else?

The courthouse was a forbidding looking place. We stood before a magistrate who sat behind a desk that was piled high with papers of one kind or another. The man shuffled through one pile and then another searching for our documents. The man stared across his desk at me. I felt as if he was trying to look straight through me. Even the title of Magistrate had me feeling some bit of fear, for it was the very title of the man who came to my house and ordered us to leave on the day of our eviction.

He finally found the papers he wanted and he laid them out before him.

"Young man, can you read and write?" he asked.

"Yes sir," I replied.

"Do you understand what this proceeding means? Do you know what happens when you agree to become this man's son?"

"Yes sir," I replied.

"I must make it clear to you, young man, the seriousness of this step you are about to take. Do you have any other living family?"

"I'm not sure," I replied. I didn't want to lie and say no, and yet, I didn't want to hurt my chances by saying yes.

"What do you mean, you are not sure?"

"Some of my family were killed in a fire back in Boston and other members died during the journey from Eire. I had three brothers that were left back in Eire. I don't know if they live or not," I said.

"I see. Your parents are both dead?"

"Yes sir," I replied. I knew it was a lie and the captain knew it was a lie, but what else could I say? How was I going to explain to this man about my mother? I would have to tell him the whole truth about what happened back in Boston and I was sure that would mean trouble. It was easier to lie. I hoped my mother would forgive me for that. Too much was at stake this time.

"You must understand, young man. There is no provision in the regular law for an American citizen to adopt an alien minor child. It took a special act of the legislature to allow mister Wolcott to make you his legal ward," said the magistrate. "I cannot guarantee that you will become naturalized upon the moment which you become mister Wolcott's adopted son. It may take another act of the legislature. I do believe though, that as long as you have cleaved yourself to the Wolcott family and that you spend a number of years working with them and in addition, you prove yourself to be a model citizen, I don't think that your naturalization will be disputed."

I was frustrated by the man's words. I wished that the captain had explained to me more about what these words meant before I had to decide. The word disputed bothered me the most. I knew what that meant and I thought about what Daniel Wolcott had told me. He was ready to dispute my claim to be the captain's son. The magistrate pushed a paper toward me across the desk. I looked down at the official looking paper with the big round seal stamped up in the corner. "Read the entire proclamation," said the magistrate. "And then, sign at the bottom when you are ready."

I looked back at the captain.

"It's all up to you now Billy," said the captain.

The magistrate stood up from his chair. "I want to make it positively clear to you. Once you sign that paper, mister Wolcott will have all the legal responsibilities over you. You must obey him afterward as your legal father. In addition, you must leave behind the allegiances to your former country of origin. Are you ready to do that?"

I nodded, took the quill and signed the paper, using my old name. I realized it might be the last time I use the name O'Shea. I hoped that those O'Shea's who were born before me would forgive this act. I hoped they would not begrudge me the chance at a better future.

"Does this mean that I will become an American?" I asked after signing.

"You will have a chance to declare your intentions," the magistrate replied. "There are favorable provisions for minor alien children in the laws of naturalization. Once you reach the age of twenty one, you may petition the court and, after a waiting period of five years, you would be able to obtain your right to become a citizen of the United States of America provided that you do not commit a felony."

"A felony?" I asked.

"A serious crime," the magistrate replied.

The captain came up behind me and placed his hands on my shoulders. "I can assure you sir. This young man will not be committing any crimes. He's an honest boy and a hard worker. He'll make a model citizen one day."

To become an American, I wondered what that really meant. Constance O'Neill had taught me something about the laws of America and some history, but there was never enough time to have it fully explained to me. I still could not fully grasp the meaning of the words, freedom and liberty. I thought of Daniel Wolcott's threats and wondered how much freedom and liberty there really was in America. Were they just words spoken or did they have and real meaning in truth? Erin O'Neill loved to remind me more often that I wanted to hear, that the men who held the wealth in America had the power to rob the liberty and freedom from those who had the least.

I asked Constance about this. She was quick to explain that, at least, in America, I had the chance to aspire to wealth. She told me that my station in life as a poor dirt farmer's son from Eire, would not prevent me from earning what ambition and hard work might build for me during my future life in America. I wanted to believe Constance before I accepted Erin's view of the truth. But after meeting Daniel Wolcott and having become a victim of his threats, I wondered who was telling me truth.

The captain was first to shake my hand after I signed the paper and then Jarrod and Roddy came forward and we all huddled together for a moment before the magistrate's desk. The realization came to me as I looked into the faces of these men. They were my family from now on. We left the courthouse together as a family. The captain wanted to celebrate so he took us a local restaurant for a feast.

Brent Wolcott had decided to remain aboard the Dorothy and had not attended the courthouse signing nor did he accompany us to the feast. I thought it was just as well. His presence would only have served to remind me that his father's threats still loomed over me.

After dinner, Roddy wanted to go pay a visit to see Cassie. I wanted to see the house where Erin resided. I knew that she had not yet returned from New York so I would not get a chance to see her. Roddy told me that the house was decorated with Erin's paintings. That they hung from every wall and above every mantle. That was worth seeing even if Erin was many miles away.

Roddy and I left the captain and Jarrod at the pier. I was still used to calling the captain, the captain. I did not know whether it was proper for me to call him father and then, what would I say? Roddy called him pa. I wondered if I would have to ask permission first.

The O'Neill house was a narrow two story tan house with dark brown shutters, positioned on a quiet tree lined street at the far edge of a town square. The narrow front yard was filled with bushes and surrounded by a waist high black iron fence. The house reminded me of the Inn. But we were in the center of town and there was a lot of wagon traffic rolling through the center square. I had not been in a town since I left Boston. This town was much more peaceful than Boston. There were so many more trees and green grass and the smell of the ocean filled the air. I did not feel any threat from these people. They did not stare at me. But of course I was dressed like Roddy in sailorman's garb of a flannel shirt and dark work pants of duck cotton. I wondered if it wouldn't be foolish of me to blacken my hair so that I looked more like Roddy, so that I could appear more like a Wolcott.

Cassie met us at the door. She asked us to be very quiet. A baby was sleeping upstairs. She invited us into the parlor. It was much fancier than any place I had seen before. The furniture was built of rich woods and the chairs were padded and covered in soft silk like cloth. There above the mantle was another painting of August Island. This one was painted from a view farther out in the sea. I thought it must have been imagined. Erin could not have painted such a scene from the deck of a ship. Strange that Erin would tell everyone that she hated August Island and yet she had done so many paintings of that place. I felt her presence in the room just by the sight of that painting.

I thought I should give Roddy time to be alone with Cassie in the parlor. I made some excuse to go out for a walk. I had had a full meal. I needed the walk, I told them both. Truth was, it was hard to stand in this room and look at Erin's painting. It reminded me of my greatest failing.

Before I left, Cassie told us about the women who lived in the house. They all sought refuge from terrible circumstances; harsh husbands or poor living conditions. One of them had just come off the boat from Ireland and had brought her baby. Her husband had not survived the voyage. They had come through the port of Boston. Were it not for Constance's charity, these women would have died in the street or worse, become slaves in waterfront brothels.

I only walked around the square and then returned to the house. I asked Cassie for some paper so I could write a note to Erin for Cassie to pass on to her when she would return from New York. I asked Erin to forgive me for my brutish behavior. I was willing to be her friend, even though I still had hopes that we would become much more than that one day in the future.

Roddy had a heavy heart as we left the house. I waited out in the hall and allowed them their privacy to say goodbye. On our way back to the Dorothy,

Roddy expressed a new resolve that he would marry Cassie before the end of the year.

We left Portland early the next morning for the fishing banks. It was mid summer. And, as we made our way out to the banks, the captain warned us all about the dangers of the thick fog during this part of the season and he told us to be ready for fast moving rain squalls and gale winds.

Brent Wolcott and I made our peace. He knew that I had a new position of importance. I was no longer some orphaned Irish boy from Boston; I was one of the captain's sons. Just a day after we had arrived at the banks, Brent got a fish hook stuck through his thumb. I was the one who had to pick him up off the deck after he fainted from the sight of his own blood. The captain was ready to throw him overboard for all his wining and complaining. The captain told Brent that he would have to shape up or he would be forced to swim his way back to Boston. Brent was frightened into silence. He did not utter another complaint in the presence of the captain after that, because he knew that the captain meant what he said.

I felt sorry for Brent. I had felt the captain's wrath of anger during my first days out. I felt like a veteran sailor this time, even though I had not even worked through a full season. I continued to call my father the captain because I felt it was a better way of showing my respect. I still could not yet get used to the idea that he was my father.

By the end of our expedition to George's Bank, Brent and I had begun to work together. Roddy was right about Brent. It was just a matter of time before Brent developed a backbone. Roddy told me it was this same way last season. It took about a week's time out on the banks before Brent came into himself. After six weeks of hard labor, Brent had lost some of the puffiness in his body and his light pink face had become bronzed by the sun. I only wished that the change would be complete. Brent could still whine and complain when he didn't get his way, but never in front of the captain.

We raised the homebound flag by the end of August. The captain was beaming from ear to ear as we set sail for Portland to deliver our catch to market. We had more than made up for the bad catch in the late spring. The weather had favored us this time out and the captain boasted that we had reached the high line. We caught almost one thousand quintals of cod. It was an amazing feat for such a small crew. The Dorothy's hold was groaning with the weight of our bounty.

"Twenty eighth of August," Roddy declared as he read from his fisherman's almanac. He told me he was counting the days toward the time he would see Cassie again and he marked them in his little book. The pages of the almanac were curled up and stained with fish blood. The almanac was made more ragged each time Roddy stuffed the journal back into his pocket or pulled it out to read it so that by now, the book was in tatters. By Roddy's reckoning, we would make Portland in three days time, with a good wind at our backs. The captain agreed.

Despite all the hard work and the long days at sea, I felt a bit melancholy that the season was coming to an end. I hated to think that I would have to wait until next spring before we went out again. Roddy told me that his father and the commodore had decided that it was wise not to venture out in the fall season because of the treacherous seas that they would face. It was not worth the danger for a price of a few barrels of salt cod.

We gathered upon the deck during a bright sunny afternoon of the twenty ninth of August. Roddy's prediction of a good sail had come true for at least the first day. But then, by the second day, the wind had disappeared. The captain was standing at the stern by the tiller. He could only steer by the current because there was no wind to carry us forward. He was wiping his brow with a handkerchief as he gazed out at the still seas that surrounded us and then he looked up at the hot August sun that burned down upon the deck.

"How much fresh water is left, Billy?" the captain shouted.

I had not looked, but I knew it was more than enough to serve our thirst until we reached Portland. "We have more than enough to see us to Portland, captain," I replied.

"That is if we make Portland in good time. Without a brisk breeze, we might be staying out here a few days longer than planned. Go see to the water Billy," said the captain. "Tell me how much is left in the barrel. If need be, we might have to portion it out more carefully."

The captain had ordered us to make use of the idle time by scrubbing the deck. I rose from my kneeling position to go below to check the water barrel. It was one third full. "One third," I told the captain as I returned to the deck. I looked about as I wiped the sweat from my brow with the back of my hand. The sun was hotter than ever and its light reflected brightly off the shining waters. The only sounds came from the sloshing of the gentle waves against the hull and the groaning of the timbers below the deck.

"Best you boys stop work and conserve your strength," said the captain. "Let's rig a stay sail over the deck to give us a bit of shade from the sun."

By late afternoon, we lay about the deck hoping for a merciful ending to the hot day. The captain ordered a ration of water for each of us, half a cup instead of a whole. He was worried about the lack of a wind. As the large orange dome of the sun hovered above the horizon in the western sky, the wind began to pick up a little. Its southwest direction put a frown of worry on the captain's face.

The still seas began to roll once more and the waves took on an ominous look to them. They wore foamy tops and their froth washed over the deck and wet us all to the bone. We scrambled to take down the stay sail and replace her with the mainsail. The captain ordered us to trim her up to half as the wind was blowing hard on us and twisting the Dorothy about. A dark mass of clouds moved ever so swiftly toward us from the southeast. Flashes of light flickered on and off from their dark underbellies. The heavens shook with the rumble of thunder. "Tie yourselves to something on the deck!" The captain shouted. "She looks like a bad blow. We'll have to ride her out."

Chapter 18

Day had turned to night. The wind howled about our ears and the rain fell in torrents. Only intermittent flashes of lightning allowed us to see the waves that rose high above the deck of the Dorothy. They appeared like tall giants who brought their arms down to encircle us and then closed in to crush us. Each flash of the light brought an ear splitting explosion that made us think the world beneath us would be torn asunder at any moment. We keeled so far to starboard that the mainmast was touching the tops of the waves. The captain was at the helm struggling with the tiller to bring her up. He shouted above the tempest that we should all hold to the port side.

I had tied a line about my chest that secured me to the base of the foremast. The line had become loose and I had to wrap my arms around the base of the mast. The waves washed over me again and again. Each time, the great hand of the giant threatened to wrench me from the deck to swallow me. I felt as if I was back in the hold of the Saint Gerard. I was trying to keep my head above the water so that I would not drown. But, the weight of the water bore down on me with such force, that it took every ounce of strength in my arms to hold my position on the deck.

The captain was still shouting but I could not distinguish the words above the howl of the wind. More lightning flashes brought back the day for an instant and revealed the scene of turmoil. The captain was still at the helm and Jarrod was at his side. Roddy was holding to the roof of the cuddy just a few feet away from me.

Another flash of light lit up the deck. I turned and heard a scream. It was Brent. He was down at the bow and holding on to the windlass. He saw me and let go of the windlass to make his way toward me. His hands flew upward and he was carried backward by a wave of water and the wind. He screamed out again as the giant's hand had a hold of him and was pulling him backward. He screamed out again. "Help!"

I loosened my grip on the foremast. I had been hugging it with both arms. I saw a loose line flying about and grabbed hold of it. It burned my hand as the giant tried to pull it from my grasp. I saw another line that was tied to the mast and reached for it as another flash of light allowed me to see for an instant more. I had to let go of the foremast and tugged hard on the line to make sure it would hold me. Once I knew it was secure, I made my way toward Brent. He was at the side of the port bulwark and the giant hand was at the ready to pull him over the side. I reached out to Brent with one hand while trying to keep a hold of my line with the other. "Grab hold!" I shouted.

"I can't!" Brent screamed out.

Another wave swept over us. And then a flash of light revealed Brent's position. He was huddled in against the bulwark with his head tucked down between his legs. Soon, the giant would have him in his grasp and pull him overboard. I strained to stretch out my arm as far as I could so that I could reach Brent. I got close enough to pull at his ear. I gave his ear a hard enough pull to cause him to reach up with his hand. I grabbed his hand and pulled him over toward me. I wrapped my free my arm around his shoulder and pulled him toward the foremast where we both managed to get a hold around the base with our arms.

I had no sense of how much time had passed since the storm had begun. Brent was screaming in my ear at the top of his lungs. I shouted back at him to shut up so that I could hear the captain's orders. The light flashed again and I looked to the stern. The captain was still at the helm. Roddy had not been able to move away from the cuddy. Jarrod was nowhere to be seen.

Lightning turned night to day once more. The ear splitting thunder came at the same instant. I gazed up and watched in horror as a giant wave that was taller than any that had come before, towered above our little boat. It then came crashing down upon the deck. There was a loud snap and a cracking sound that followed. Another light flashed just as the wave swept down upon us. I looked up to watch as the mainmast was twisted by the force of the deluge and broke at its center like a twig. With each flash of light that followed, I watched with fright as the rigging came falling down to the deck upon our heads. I ducked my head down as the lines fell and created a tangle about me.

I looked aft and through another flash of day I saw that the captain was still at the helm. High above my head, ripping canvas sail flew apart as the top gaff spar from the mainmast was ripped away and carried out to sea by the wind. Another giant wave rose up above our heads. I ducked my head down once more to fend off the force of the water as it crashed over me.

Another flash of lightning followed. I looked up to see a long spear come flying through the air toward the deck. It was tangled with line and shreds of sail. As the spear came closer, I recognized it as part of the broken mainmast and gaff spar. The broken mast was being thrown back at us by the force of the storm. The long spike hit the deck with a loud crash and then I heard a human cry.

"Pa!" Roddy shouted.

Another flash of light revealed the tangle of line upon the deck. I looked aft and there lay a figure trapped under the fallen rigging. A broken stretch of mainmast rested across the legs of the man I recognized as the captain. I wasn't sure if I was imagining it or not, but I thought the wind had lessened its pull and its roar. The lightning and thunder was coming at longer intervals and fell off toward the distance. I looked aft and saw Roddy kneeling over the figure of the captain, his father; our father. "I need help!" Roddy shouted. "We have to get pa out from under the rigging." Just then, The Dorothy began to keel again toward the lee. She was spinning out of control.

"Man the tiller!" I shouted. The lightning flashes were not coming as often and I was frustrated not to be able to see. I could only hear Brent whimpering at my side.

I shouted out to Roddy. "Where are you? I can't see you."

"I'm at the helm!" he shouted back. "I need you here. I can't handle her myself."

The wind appeared to be easing up and the seas were becoming calmer. I thought I could take the chance at letting go of the foremast and make my way to the stern. "You stay here and hold on to the mast," I told Brent and then I let go and grabbed hold of the tangled rigging that lay about the deck. I used it to guide my way back toward the stern. Another wave crashed over me just as I let go and almost pulled me off the deck. I jumped forward and landed on my knees. My arms descended into a tangle of line. I looked down and another flash of light brightened my view. Below me, lay the figure of the captain. A long bloody gash crossed his forehead. His face was deathly pale and his lips were tinged blue. I looked down at his chest and saw it heave.

"Can you see pa?" Roddy shouted.

"I see him," I said.

"Is he alive?"

"He breathes," I replied.

"Come help me take control of the helm!" Roddy shouted. "I can't hold her much longer."

I stumbled across the wreckage on the deck and made my way toward the stern. I reached out in the darkness and touched wet skin. It was Roddy's face. He reached up, grabbed my hand and placed it on the oaken arm of the tiller.

"Try and keep her straight, while I go see to pa," said Roddy.

"Which way?"

"Just keep her steady as you can."

The storm's fury had begun to wane. The waves were still tossing their froth across the deck but the wind had quieted to a low moan from a wild howl. I could feel that the deck was still slanted down toward the lee and I had to hold onto the tiller with one arm and use the other to keep from sliding right off the deck into the sea below my feet.

The warmth of the day had been sucked away by the cold winds of the storm and I found myself shivering. My hands were growing numb so that I was losing my grip on the tiller. I could feel the power of the ocean reach up through my arm to my shoulder. It wanted to rip my arm from my shoulder and I had not the strength to keep a hold. "Roddy!" I shouted. "I can't keep a hold of her." The lightning was gone and the world was in total blackness around me. I called out again for Roddy.

"I'm here," he said and I felt his fingers wrap themselves over mine. We both used up our remaining strength to keep a hold of the tiller to steady the Dorothy's course.

After what seemed like so many hours, struggling in the blackness to keep the Dorothy from floundering, a feeble streak of gray light began to show itself in the eastern sky. The dim light revealed the outlines of the wreckage that covered the deck of the Dorothy. The mainmast was twisted and broken at midpoint. Tangled lines were strewn about the deck and parts of ripped sail lay across the forward hatch and the cuddy. Farther forward, the figure of Brent could be seen huddling about the base of the foremast. He was still whimpering. I think he was praying.

The new light of day revealed the terrible sight of the broken part of the mainmast that had been driven back toward us during the storm. It crossed the deck and lay over the legs of the captain; my father.

"I can hold her steady," Roddy told me. "You have to try and get pa free."

I looked at the thick pole with its jagged points. Part of the spear had driven itself into the deck and tore a hole in the bulwark as well. Water was gushing in across that part of the deck. If we dared move the mast, it would bring on more water and we could not stay afloat after that. "I can't move the mast!" I shouted. "We'll sink. Water is coming in around where she's driven into the deck." I knew I couldn't have budged such a large chunk of wood anyway. It was nearly a foot thick and three times that around.

"Get to pa. See if he's still breathing," said Roddy.

I went and stood over the captain. I couldn't help it. I knew he was my father. But it was too soon to think of him as such. It had only been a few weeks time since I had signed the paper making him my father. I think I would always think of him as the captain first. I looked down at his face. It was so pale and his beard was matted down with salt water. His chest heaved ever so slightly so I knew he still breathed; but for how long? The bloody gash in his forehead had been washed out by the sea water so that it was ugly black and purple. I couldn't understand how he managed to get here beside the aft hatch from the helm. I looked about and remembered Jarrod. Where was he? I hadn't seen him since the beginning of the storm.

I looked up at Roddy. He knew his brother was swept away by the storm and lost at sea. He was my brother too. But I had not lived with him all my life as Roddy had. I could not imagine the pain he must be feeling. His brother was gone and we knew not whether his, our father, would survive his wounds.

"We're not far from the sea lanes," said Roddy. "At our last position before the storm hit, pa said we were just a day's sail west from the banks. I don't know how far we were taken out by the storm."

Brent released his tight hold of the foremast and came stumbling across the deck toward us. "How are we going to get home?" he cried.

"Shut up!" Roddy shouted to him. "I don't want to hear any more of your whining."

The deck of the Dorothy suddenly slipped to the lee. I fell sideways and grabbed a line to keep from sliding downward into the sea. Brent slid downward and got a hold just in time to keep himself from falling overboard. I knew that we must be taking on water below deck.

"The fish," said Roddy. "The weight of the barrels will sink us. We have to go below and bring then up and throw them over the side or we'll sink for sure."

"We're going to sink?" Brent cried out.

"I told you to stop you're whining," said Roddy. "You have to help Billy get the barrels over the side."

I climbed down into the forward hatch. Water came up halfway to my knees. It took every ounce of strength I had to get a hold of the massive barrel. I found a grappling hook nearby and used it to wedge into the iron rim and tugged at it to pull the barrel along. I couldn't do it myself. "Brent you have to come below!" I shouted. I need your help. You don't want to sink and die out here do you?" I hoped to frighten him enough into realizing that he couldn't just stand and watch.

Brent appeared from above.

"Grab hold of this end of the hook and I'll get underneath the barrel and hoist it up," I said. "Once we have it over the lid of the hatch, let it slide down the deck into the sea."

Once we had managed the first barrel, it became a bit easier to bring the rest to the deck. One after the other, I pushed and Brent pulled. Soon, we had half the barrels lifted and let them roll down into the sea. It seemed like such a shame to discard the fruits of our hard labors. But it was a matter of survival now. We had thrown twenty barrels of salt cod over the side, but the Dorothy was still taking on water.

"Go below to the galley," said Roddy. "You'll find some extra sail, a distress flag, and a wooden box that contains a signal pistol in the upper cabinets."

I came up with the wooden box. Brent had the flag.

"Don't just stand there. Help Billy raise the flag on the foremast," Roddy told Brent.

Brent was looking out toward the horizon. "There's smoke. I see it, don't you?" He pointed toward northeast not far from the dome of the rising sun.

I thought it must be an illusion. Anyway, it must be so many miles away; they would never catch sight of us from such a long distance. Brent reached out to grab the wooden box that contained the signal pistol and almost caused me to drop it into the water in the hold. I grabbed it back from him.

"We must fire the pistol," said Brent. "How will they know we are here?"

"It's too far away," said Roddy. "We have to wait and see if it draws closer."

"We can't wait. We're going to sink. I know it. We're all going to die out here," Brent cried.

"If don't stop your whining, I'll throw you overboard myself," said Roddy.

With every hour that passed and as the sun rose high above us, I was becoming overwhelmed with a sense of doom. The Dorothy would surely sink by nightfall and we would all drown. We had slowed the taking on of water by throwing most of the cargo of fish overboard. I didn't have any more strength to lift another barrel. I could not remember the last time I had any food to eat and I could not locate our barrel of fresh water. I might have thrown it over by mistake. All we had to drink was what was left in that clay jug of sour cider.

The smoke on the horizon gave us false hope. It disappeared by early afternoon. It did not even make an advance in our direction. Roddy told me he was certain that we were not far from the shipping lanes. "Something will come south," he said. "There is a steam packet that runs south from Nova Scotia to Boston."

I wondered how long the Dorothy would stay afloat. I searched and found a small hand pump and I took it below and tried in vain to flush out some of the water that was still rushing in through that hole made by the broken mainmast through the side of the hull. Roddy ordered Brent to stay by the captain's side and to give us a report about his breathing. It was the easiest task Roddy could think of to keep Brent occupied.

I needed food to keep my strength up. I remembered that we kept pilot bread in a nook above the stove. I found that the bread had been soaked by the sea. At the least it was easier to chew and it was better than nothing.

We were blessed with calm seas after the sunset. A brilliant display of vivid color formed a magnificent panorama around our scene of destruction. I feared the return of night. There would be no lightning this time to show us the way. I feared the end would come as soon as the light faded into blackness. Roddy was not so afraid of the night. He pointed toward the east and the emergence of the bright stars that appeared as soon as the bands of purple and pink gave way to inky blue night. We were also blessed by a bright half moon that showed its crescent halfway up into the heavens. Its glow bathed us and the ruined deck of the Dorothy in a soft blue light.

It must have been divine providence that we did not sink into the ocean that night. Somehow the Dorothy held her own. I continued to work the pump and Roddy kept us from drifting by keeping hold of the tiller. Thank god the rudder was still intact. Brent had assisted me in rigging a staysail across the foremast to the broken stalk of the mainmast. I knew we could not survive another day and a night. The deck of the Dorothy had dropped lower and it would only be a matter of time before she would go under and take us with her.

Chapter 19

Brent and I worked on and off all night long working the pump, hoping to keep the Dorothy afloat until we could be rescued. Roddy remained at the helm and tried to keep the Dorothy from drifting further out to sea and beyond the reach of help. When I had a chance, I went to see how the captain was doing. His chest barely moved and his face had turned from a pale white to an ashen gray. I had to lean down and place my ear against his chest to feel the slight movement and against his lips to hear the slight breaths. I knew that he could not survive much longer.

I was the one to spot the plume of smoke that rose against the northeast sky about an hour after the sun rose. This time, it was coming in our direction. It was not long before I could see a tall black smokestack protruding from the deck of the ship. It was a strange sight to see a sailing ship with that pipe sticking out of her like a cook stove and the smoke poured out to form a grayish white plume that left a trail across the morning sky.

The ship quickly bore down on us. Roddy loaded the signal pistol and pulled back the hammer to fire. But there was no report. Roddy reloaded the powder and inserted another percussion cap. He pulled back the hammer and this time a loud report echoed out over the waves and the flare shot well up into the sky and arched down to hit a distant wave.

"Look, they are passing us," said Brent. "Shoot again."

Roddy reloaded and fired another shot. The ship moved south of our position and appeared as if it was going to leave us behind.

"Shoot again," said Brent.

"We have no more firing caps," said Roddy.

Brent ran to the edge of the deck, waved his arms and began to shout at the top of his lungs. "We're here. Please come. Don't leave us behind!"

I had to go below and work the pump some more. The deck of the Dorothy was leaning downward toward the bow and the water line was just inches away from the top edge of the bulwark. It was only a matter of time before the deck would drop below the water.

"She's stopped," said Brent. "Look!"

I came back up from below and the ship had grown larger once again. Roddy tapped my shoulder and pointed in the opposite direction. An ominous bank of fog was moving in toward us. In a matter of minutes we might become invisible. I hoped that we were discovered before the fog could encircle our boat.

I told Brent to go below and work the pump some more, but he wanted to stay on deck. Roddy grabbed him by the arm. "You do as you are told," Roddy told him. "We can still sink and drown out here. Do you want to die before we have a chance to be rescued?"

Brent went below as he was told. I watched from the deck as the ship grew larger and I was able to see more of the detail on her decks. A large rounded structure covered the middle section of her deck and the name Nelson was painted on her side.

We watched as some men scrambled along the deck toward a dory that was suspended from davits. The dory was manned and then lowered over her side to the surface of the water. The dory made her way toward us. In a short time, the dory came up along side the Dorothy. Roddy and I both reached out to help the first man board our deck. He was a tall muscular fellow with a thick head of blonde hair and a face marked with a sea of dark freckles.

"I am Charles Proctor, Boatswain's mate of the Nelson," he said.

Roddy explained to the ship's officer what had happened during the storm and pointed to our fallen father. "He's trapped under that section of the mast. He's still alive. We need to get him some help right away."

Brent came up from below. "I can't stop the water from coming in," he whined, and then he saw that the rescue crew had boarded and he began to cry.

"Get aboard the dory," Proctor told us.

"What about my father?" asked Roddy.

"We're going to free him as soon as you leave. Once that section of mast is pulled, this boat is going to sink very quickly. Now we don't have any more time. Get aboard the dory and wait."

Brent was more that willing to be the first to leave the Dorothy. Roddy and I reluctantly followed him. Right after we left the deck of the Dorothy, the four men together lifted the section of the mainmast that trapped the legs of the captain. Two of the men rushed to the captain's side to lift him away while the other men dropped the section of the mast. Water gushed out of the hole in the deck and the Dorothy slid downward into the waves. Roddy and I reached out to help the sailors climb back aboard the dory with the limp body of the captain before the deck of the Dorothy had dropped below the waves.

Once the crew of the Nelson and the captain was helped aboard the dory, Proctor ordered his men to row the dory away from the sinking hulk of the Dorothy. Roddy and I watched as a plume of water shot upward from the damaged section of the deck and then the deck dropped under the waves. At first the top of the cuddy and the broken mainmast still rose above the waves and then they disappeared so that only the very top section of the foremast could be seen. The distress flag still flew about in the morning breeze. Slowly the remaining section of the foremast sank under the waves. There was a swirling of the waters as the Dorothy completely disappeared and the distress flag floated about where the Dorothy had been.

The captain was laid upon the floor of the dory. His legs were bent at an odd angle. I knew in my heart that he could not possibly survive this; but I could not give up hope. I wondered if prayer would do any good. I was not worthy of rescue. But this man was. Please God let him live. He has done nothing to deserve this fate.

After we were helped aboard the Nelson, passengers gathered around us. Blankets and cups of hot coffee were offered to help us get warm. We were led to a main cabin out fitted with a stove at its center and furnished with a few long tables and benches. The captain was carried in by crewmen and laid out on one of the tables located nearest to the stove. A call was made among the passengers for a doctor.

An elderly gentleman with long white side whiskers came forward. He wore a shabby frock coat, a wide brimmed leather hat and these tiny round spectacles that were perched at the end of his nose. He professed to be a doctor and introduced himself as Amos Rutherford. He approached the table where the captain lay and gazed down at the captain's face. He leaned forward to listen for the sound of a heartbeat or to detect a breath. I saw him shake his head twice. I hoped Roddy wasn't looking. Roddy had moved toward the doctor's side. "He's my father," said Roddy. "Can you do anything?"

"Has he waken or said anything?"

"No sir," Roddy replied.

"I need some cloth to bandage the wound on his head," said the doctor.

"Is he going to live?" asked Roddy.

The doctor avoided looking directly at him. "I'll do the best I can to save him but I do believe he's in God's hands now. It will be up to his maker to decide if he lives or dies." The doctor then looked back and noticed all the curious passengers crowding their way in to see what was happening. "Stand back please. If you would like to help, give me some blankets to keep him warm." One finely dressed lady came forward and offered her shawl. Two other men came forward with blankets that they had draped about their own shoulders.

Mister Proctor came forward with the captain of the Nelson. Doctor Rutherford explained to them that the man could not be moved until they reached port. Captain Meyer told the doctor that it would be at least another two hours before they reached Boston.

Roddy stood there holding his father's hand and rubbed each of his fingers to warm them. I didn't know what words I could use to make him feel better. He was my father too. But the captain had not brought me up. I had only known him for a few months. I stayed to the side and let the doctor move in closer beside Roddy. Brent had stayed in the background. He was in a merry mood because he was on his way home. He boasted that his father would come to get him.

I knew what returning to Boston could mean for me. Daniel Wolcott would have what he wanted. I would be at his mercy if that is what he wished, but it didn't matter, I would not run away and abandon my brother and my father in order to save myself from trouble.

We entered Boston Harbor by five o'clock in the evening. It was two days after the storm and I guessed that it was the last day in August. Roddy was not thinking about that almanac or counting the days. It was more like minutes. How long would it be before the captain drew his last breath? Could the captain's life be saved at all?

I went to Roddy and put my arm around his shoulder. We huddled close to the outstretched figure of the captain. The doctor stood at the other side and neatly wrapped the captain's head with a cloth that had been handed to him by another member of the crew.

Once we had reached the berth at the wharf, Brent left the Nelson to go find his father. He came to Roddy's side and promised that his father would see to it that the captain was taken to a good hospital. It was a terrible dilemma for me. I had to hope that Daniel would come and offer the best care for his brother. I knew what that would mean for me. But it didn't matter. All that did matter was taking care of the captain, my adopted father.

Daniel Wolcott arrived with his son Brent about an hour later accompanied by two men who carried a folding hammock. Daniel immediately took charge of the situation. He did not look my way or acknowledge my presence. I moved away from Roddy's side and soon found myself in the background. I know I should have remained at Roddy's side. But I was worried that Daniel might cause trouble for Roddy and his father and it might delay the help that the captain needed most. The captain was lifted from the table, placed upon the hammock and carried out of the cabin. Daniel Wolcott went to Roddy's side and placed a hand on his shoulder. "Jack will get the best care in the city. I'll make sure of that, son," he said.

I was a bit surprised to hear Daniel speak in such a kind voice to his nephew. "You will come up to the house with Brent," Daniel told him. "You can get into some dry clothes and get something to eat."

"I want to go along with pa," said Roddy. He then looked about. "Billy, where are you?"

I came forward and Daniel scowled at me.

"Billy and I will go to the hospital to be with our father," said Roddy.

"No, you will go to the house," said Daniel. "You can see your father later on after the doctor has seen to his needs."

"But what if pa wakes up? I want to be with him when he does," Roddy replied.

"I am in charge now," said Daniel with a firm voice. "I am your uncle. I am going to do what is best for all concerned. You'll get to see your father as soon as the doctor allows it."

"We should be allowed to be with our father," I said.

"Your father?" Daniel spat out the words.

"Pa adopted Billy," said Roddy.

I watched Daniel's face grow red in the cheeks and that large vein on his temple began to bulge and turn purple. "I see," he replied in a very stiff voice.

"I want to be with pa," said Roddy. "You can't keep us from him."

"You will do as you are told," Daniel replied.

"I'll go find him myself," said Roddy. He then ran out of the cabin.

I was about to follow him when Daniel grabbed me by the arm.

"Let me go," I said and wrenched my arm free from his grasp.

"Don't get any foolish notions that you are going to be treated like a member of this family," said Daniel.

I glared back at him before I turned and left the cabin. I saw Roddy on the wharf standing beside the wagon. He was being held back by one of the men who carried out the captain. Roddy was shouting at him. "I want to see my pa!"

"Hospital rules," The man told him. "You cannot ride in this wagon."

Daniel appeared from the ship's cabin, passed me and went down to get between the man and Roddy. He grabbed Roddy's shoulder and spun him around. Roddy was too weak to fight him. I ran down the gangway to stand beside Roddy. I was ready to use my own fists if necessary. I wasn't going to let anyone stand between Roddy and his father.

"You and Brent will go to the house and wait for me," said Daniel. "I promise I will come and take you to see your father myself."

Roddy turned toward me with tears forming in his eyes. "What should I do, Billy?"

"Let's go to the house and wait," I said.

Daniel turned quickly toward me. "I didn't invite you," he said. "I'll not have a thieving Irish urchin of the streets as a guest in my house."

"But uncle," Roddy pleaded. "Where will he go?"

"That's his problem," Daniel replied.

"I'm not going to the house without Billy," said Roddy.

"You'll do as you are told," said Daniel. "...if you want to see your father."

Roddys eyes opened wide. "You would deny me the right to see my father?"

"I would and I will if you do not obey my wishes," Daniel replied.

I felt so sorry for Roddy. He looked so sad and helpless. "What should I do?" Roddy asked me.

"Don't ask him," said Daniel.

I knew that Daniel would be good to his word. Even though I did love the captain and wanted to be at his side, I felt I had no right to hurt Roddy's chances of seeing him before he died. "Go to the house with Brent like your uncle told you," I said.

"But what about you?" asked Roddy.

"I'll follow the wagon to the hospital and wait outside the building until you come, and then, we'll go see him together," I said.

"The hospital is on private property," said Daniel. "You will not be allowed near the building."

"But uncle," said Roddy. "Billy has the right to see our father."

"No he doesn't," Daniel replied. "He's not blood kin. I don't give a damn what some adoption paper says."

At that very moment I wanted to kill Daniel Wolcott and if I had the means, I would have done so with God and everyone standing about as a witness.

Roddy had a tortured look on his face. It wasn't fair and it was so cruel. He had lost so much in such a short time. And to add to that pain, this man was ready to deny him the company of his only surviving brother. Even if I wasn't blood kin, Roddy and I were much closer than brothers; I loved him as I had never loved my own blood brothers. "Go to the house with Brent," I said finally. "I'll find a way to get to see our father."

"You'll find yourself arrested and sent to jail if you try," Daniel replied.

"I'll just take that chance," I said.

"But Billy, where are you going to go? You need some dry clothes and food. I know you don't have any money," said Roddy.

"Oh he's a boy of cunning and courage," said Daniel. "I'm sure he will be welcomed back into the den of thieves from whence he came."

I followed Roddy and Brent to an awaiting horse carriage. "Don't worry about me," I told Roddy. "I will find my own way. I'll follow that wagon to see where it goes, so I'll know where the hospital is. When I see you come, we can find a way to get in to see him together. At least you'll get to see him. I hope he survives, Roddy, I really do."

"This just isn't fair," said Roddy.

"I know. But what can we do?" I said.

"I'm sorry Billy," Roddy said as he lowered his gaze and then turned and boarded the carriage.

"Don't worry about me, Roddy," I said. "I'll say a prayer for our father, and for our dear departed brother Jarrod."

Roddy gazed out at me from the carriage window and nodded. Brent dared not say a word. I turned and looked at Daniel Wolcott who was ready to board the carriage. He was smiling back at me and nodding his head and then he smirked at me and offered a little wave of the hand as if to say: "Be off with you beggar boy."

Chapter 20

I gazed about the waterfront and remembered where I was. The scene had become familiar to me again. I had run along this very wharf so many times with Jason Brody at my side, back during those days last summer when he was training me to be a fighter. It was just a short walk down through the alleyway between the warehouses to the gutter located by the rear door of the Brody tavern where I had first met Jason Brody. I thought better of going into the tavern. I didn't know what had happened after the fire. What if the port officers were still searching for me? No, I knew where I had to go next. I walked up the street away from the wharf and remembered the way toward Jason's cellar hideout. The sun had already set and the streets were growing dark. I had no idea of the time that had passed since we had arrived in Boston.

I was on my own again. I looked down at myself and realized that I looked no better now with my filthy hair, torn clothes and blackened bare feet, than I did when I came off the deck of the Saint Gerard with my family. It was a little more than a year ago. To any stranger I did resemble an urchin of the streets and I smelled of the sea and the fish.

I saw the stairway that descended down toward the cellar. I hesitated at first. What if Jason was there? Would he welcome me back as a friend? I had left him on that night of the fire. I knew he would be angry at me for abandoning him. But I was bound to end my life. What he thought of me made little difference at that time. I had no idea that I was going to survive to find myself right back where I started from.

I walked down the stairs and tried to be as quiet as I could. I first peered through the window. I couldn't see through the thick layer of dust and grime. I moved down toward the door. It was ajar. I pushed it open slowly and that familiar odor of whiskey filled my senses. It brought back so many memories. I hoped I would find Jason inside and then I feared that if he was there, he would send me away, and then I would be completely alone.

As I moved in through the door, I looked down at the floor. There lay Jason Brody, almost in the same position as I had left him. He was in a terrible state. His face was covered with filth and a growth of dark beard. His black hair had grown long and was tangled about his face and neck and matted by dirt. Bugs were crawling about his face and mouth. His clothes were more ragged than mine and his feet were just as bare, filthy black and marked by bloody cuts. His face moved with tremors and there was spittle dripping from his mouth and across his chin down onto the straw that was scattered about him. There, tucked in the crook of his arm was an empty bottle of whiskey. He clutched the bottle tightly with fingers that were scarred pink and red and the two smallest fingers of his left hand were missing altogether.

The smell coming from him was worse than a bucket of fish bait. But what was to complain about? I smelled no better than he. I leaned over and tugged at his arm to wake him. He shook violently. His eyes quivered open and then closed again. "Jason," I said.

Jason mumbled something.

I shook him again.

"Leave me be," he mumbled.

"Jason, it's Billy," I said.

Jason slowly opened his eyes. They were rimmed red and covered with a shiny film. He was staring straight up at me but it was as if I was invisible. He blinked his eyes a couple of times and then a flicker of recognition appeared. "Billy?" he mumbled. He rubbed his eyes with his scarred hands. He then gazed up at me and squinted. "Is that really you, boyo?"

I nodded.

He rolled himself over and sat up against one of the whisky barrels. He reached down and grabbed the empty whisky bottle and shook it. There was a pained expression on his face and then I saw a spark of anger flare up in his bloodshot eyes. He pitched the whiskey bottle against the opposite wall and it shattered, spraying shards of glass across the floor. "Damn it Billy, why did you leave me? Where were you? I searched the waterfront for days. I thought they had arrested you and taken you away. Of course they arrested me instead. I got blamed for that fire, boyo. They saw my hands. Look at these hands, boyo," Jason raised them before his face and spread out the fingers. "That's what fire does to flesh, boyo. I saved your life with these hands. The pain was so bad I was ready to get a butcher to chop them off."

"I got burned too," I said. "My left arm, I know about the pain too."

"Where did you go?"

"I don't think you will understand," I said.

"Understand what?"

"I tried to kill myself that night. I jumped into the harbor. A fisherman and his two sons saved me from drowning. They took me to their home up in Maine and nursed me back to health."

"And you expect me to believe that?" said Jason. "You are a true Irishman. You can tell as good a tale as the best of them."

"It is true. Otherwise, how could I be standing here before you, still alive?"

"If you have this family who saved you, then why are you here and why are you looking as bad as I do. You're lying aren't you?"

I then told Jason more of the story about how I went to work as a cut tail and then I told him about the adoption and the terrible storm at sea and then about the run in with Daniel Wolcott."

Jason was shaking his head at me by the time I finished. "I don't know about you, boyo," he said after I finished. "That's quite a tale. I suppose I have to believe it. But why in hell did you come back here?"

"I had no choice. We were rescued by a Boston bound steamship. My adopted father, captain Jack Wolcott, was badly hurt. Right now, I don't know if he is dead or alive."

"So boyo, how does it feel? You are right back where you started from," he asked me.

By the look he gave me, I thought it was best that I leave him and try to make my own way. I turned toward the door.

"Going to run away again, boyo? Where are you going to go now? Your new family has rejected you and your old family, well, I happen to know that your mother and your brother Terrance were deported back to Eire."

"My brother Terrance is dead," I said. "My father killed him. That's how the fire started. He was going to kill me too."

Jason struggled to get to his feet. He used the whisky barrel to support himself. He leaned over and looked as if he was about to fall over. I moved toward him to help him. He reached out with his hand and pushed me away. "I can get up by myself," he said. "As for your brother, his face was cut and bruised and his nose was broke, but he was very much alive when I last saw him. He was with your mother. They were among those survivors who fingered me for starting the fire."

"Why did they blame you for the fire? Why didn't you tell them the truth?" I said.

"I tried to. I made you sound like a hero, boyo," Jason replied. "I told them that you went back in to the burning house to save your sisters and you never came out again. Your mother thinks you are dead, boyo."

"Why did you tell them that?"

"Because it sounded good, and you did try to go back. I'm the one that stopped you. The fire had already spread too far to save anyone," Jason replied.

"Terrance is alive," I said aloud. "I killed my father for no reason."

"He might have killed you, boyo," said Jason. "It's too late now. You can't change what was."

"You say my mother and Terrance were deported? How do you know that for sure?" I asked him.

"I know boyo. Because I saw them board the ship. They were ready to deport me too, but my father stepped in and brought me off the ship. I know he bribed the port authorities to let me stay," said Jason. "My father was going to send me away to live with a cousin in New York City," he added. "But I got into more trouble. I got sent to jail for trying to rob a store with a gun. It was a lie. The judge saw my hands and knew I couldn't hold a pistol. He took pity on me and sentenced me to a few weeks in jail. My father was so angry and momma was disappointed. My father told me after I got out of jail that I had had to find my own way in life and that I couldn't come home."

"There wasn't much else I could do to survive other than to steal," Jason went on to say. "I stole from home mostly. And I've been living in this cellar room. My father knows I live here and so does momma. They know I steal from them, but they don't report me."

Jason raised his hands before his face. "It took a lot of practice to get these fingers to deal cards again. I had to chop the two little ones off the left hand because they turned black and hurt something awful."

"What are you going to do with yourself?" I asked him. "You can't spend your life stealing and living in a cellar like this. What happened to Maddy? Why won't she help you?"

"Forget about Maddy, boyo, I have. She ran away with a sailor a few months ago. She is with child."

"That sailor?"

Jason shook his head. "It's mine, but I'll never see it, just as well don't you think? What kind of a father would I make?"

"So then what are you going to do?" I asked him.

Jason flashed one of his broad smiles. There was just enough light left in the cellar to see his mouthful of yellowed and blackened teeth. He reached into his torn shirt pocket and withdrew a curled up piece of paper and waved it in the air. "I've decided to leave Boston," he said. "I'm going out to California to get some of that gold I've heard they found out there."

"Gold?"

"That's right boyo, gold; riches beyond imagining," said Jason "I got that flyer from a sailor who came in to port. He had just come off a ship that sailed around the horn. He's been in a place called San Francisco. He said that the gold is still a secret in most parts of the country.

"How come he gave it to you?"

Jason went silent for a moment. I couldn't see his face in the deepening darkness of the cellar, but I heard him gulp. "I can't talk about that boyo. I had to do things to survive. I had to give certain...uh...favors...uh, never mind about that. At least I know where I'm going and I know where my future is."

"San Francisco?"

"Yep," Jason replied with a grin.

"Where is that?" I asked.

"Out west, on the other side of the country, as far from Boston as you can imagine," he replied.

"How are you going to get there?" I asked him.

Jason let out a chuckle. "Before I leave this town, boyo, I'm going to take a bit of Boston's bounty with me. Just enough to pay for a fine stateroom in a steamship bound for the isthmus to a place called Chagres. And then, I'll make my way to Panama City and then board another steamship to travel up the coast to San Francisco, California. It's easier than trying to travel over land."

"More thieving?"

"Look boyo, I don't expect you to get involved. You go back and find that new brother of yours, what's his name? Roddy?"

"I don't know what to do," I said. "Daniel Wolcott told me that he would have me arrested if I tried to get to see the captain. What if he's already dead? I don't want to be deported."

"Then come with me, boyo." said Jason. "We'll have a good time of it. Just think, you and me out in that place called San Francisco. I hear they have all night gambling and drinking parlors out there. It says it on that paper. But I can't read it."

"If you can't read it then how do you know what it says?" I asked him.

"The sailor read it to me," Jason replied.

"I can read," I said.

"Open it up, boyo. Read it to me again."

I unfolded the piece of paper. There was just a bit of light left of the day. I turned toward the window and squinted to see what was printed on the paper. It was decorated with a picture of a log house out in the woods with the words Sutter's Mill printed underneath. Below those words, there was a map of the country with lines drawn to show the different routes to California. I traced my finger along the overland route. It didn't appear so long a distance on that small piece of paper. It had printed across the bottom in large letters: Eldorado!

There was not much else to read. I guessed that it was the sailor who told Jason about San Francisco from his own experience.

"What does it say about the gambling, boyo?" asked Jason.

"Nothing," I replied.

"Nothing?"

"That sailor was telling you tales," I said.

"Naw, boyo. I know he was telling the truth."

"It's late," I said as I turned and looked out the window. "I've got to try and find that hospital where they took the captain. I have to try to find Roddy. He'll be wondering what happened to me."

"Forget them, boyo," said Jason. "You don't want to be a fisherman for the rest of your life do you? Do you want to live out on some deserted island? Do you want to die out in some shipwreck during a storm? I heard about those storms at sea, boyo. That sailor told me he was almost killed in a storm like the one you said you were in. It can happen any time. That's no life for you, boyo, to risk get killed again. You cheated death more than once already. You won't get too many more chances at life, boyo."

"I loved the captain and his son's like they were family. They gave me more than my own family ever did," I said.

"Look at you," said Jason. "Your hair and clothes are ragged and filthy and you smell as bad as I do, what is that smell, fish? Christ, boyo, you want to stay poor and have the rich lord it over you for the rest of your life like the Brits did back in Eire?" Jason asked me. "Do you want to turn into a mean, broken down, drunken thief like your father was?"

I gazed across through the darkness of the cellar room. I could no longer see Jason but I knew how he looked. He could be a young version of my father, Gerald O'Shea, with his bloodshot eyes and stinking of whisky. He was every bit as much as a thief as my father ever was. But, in spite of those faults, I would follow Jason to the ends of the earth. He risked his life to save me. I owed him so much. Were it not for him, I would never have lived to meet Erin O'Neill. Were she to be here in my presence, she would tell me straight off that I should go west and not give it a second thought.

"When were you going to leave?" I asked him.

"Soon as I can plan a few little chores, get me a bit of money, a few weeks, maybe sooner. I been told that it's best to leave before winter comes," said Jason.

"I'll think on it some," I said. "I'll tell Roddy and see what he thinks. If the captain should survive, well, I don't know."

"I'm bound for California with or without you, boyo," said Jason. "I can't wait to put a thousand miles of distance between me and Fort Hill. I hate Boston. Let my folks wonder where I've gone. They don't give a damn anyway."

I thought about the gold. I remembered what it was like to have a lot of money, even though it was ill gotten. I was able to buy Terrance anything he wanted. I never worried about going hungry and I had warm clothes and a fine roof over my head. I had a good thing back on August island as well, but, with Daniel Wolcott standing in the way, if the captain died, I would have no chance to become a Wolcott. There would be nothing Roddy could do to help me. They would surely find me and deport me. And then I thought about Erin. If I had real money, I could afford to give her the life of freedom that she wanted. I could build her a great painting studio and give her other riches. If I was a rich man, I might just be able to persuade her to marry me one day.

"I have to go and find Roddy," I said.

"Are you coming back?" asked Jason.

"I have a lot to think about," I said. "I am vexed about what to do. I feel divided inside. One part of me wants to go west with you and another part wants to stay and try to make a life with my adopted brother Roddy. He and I have become closer than brothers; I can't just abandon him to go out west. Maybe he will agree to come with us. Oh...but no, he'd never leave Cassie behind, not for a fortune in gold or anything else."

"You don't have to stay away forever, boyo. You can make your fortune and come back," said Jason.

"I didn't tell you about Erin. She's a young woman I met on August island," I said.

"Ohoo, boyo, now I understand," said Jason, as he raised his eyebrows at me.

"It's not what you think. We're just friends you see," I replied.

I heard Jason move across the room and suddenly, he was at my side. "It's too damned dark to see your face, boyo, but I can hear it in your voice. You have found love, haven't you?"

"She a painter," I said. "She doesn't like boys very much. She told me that she will never marry."

"But you love her anyway, don't you?"

"I suppose I do."

"Aye boyo, I know how it feels. I still love Maddy. I only wish I had told her so before she ran away with that sailor," said Jason.

"Erin might change her mind about me if I became a rich man," I said.

Jason grabbed my shoulder. "Now that's the way to think, boyo. Hell, maybe after I get rich, I might go out and find Maddy and take care of that kid we had together, maybe I will."

"I got to go now," I said. "I have to find out what happened to the captain."

"You know where to find me boyo," said Jason. "But, don't take too long. That gold is out there waiting for us. I can't stay in this fucking city much longer, boyo. I'm going to do something crazy if I don't leave here soon."

Chapter 21

I left Jason in the cellar and ventured back out toward the waterfront. I found myself drawn there for some reason. I walked out along the edge of the wharves and recognized the very spot where I had jumped into the harbor on that Christmas eve night. I wondered why God had saved me. There must have been some good reason. Was there some task he would have me finish? Maybe I was supposed to live to be returned to Eire to take care of my little brother or perhaps it was destined that I should die at sea. But if that was the reason, then why hadn't I drowned during the storm?

It was dark and the night air was cold and I had no good coverings. My flannel shirt was torn and my feet were bare. I didn't have much hope for a good future. Would anyone care if I decided to jump again? Would anyone save me this time?

"Billy?"

I heard a familiar voice calling out to me from the other side of the street that faced the wharves. There were just a few street lanterns along the waterfront. None of them offered enough light for me to see who was calling me. I walked back toward the street and saw a figure standing at the corner. At first, I wondered if it might be one of the port officials but then, they wouldn't be calling me by my first name. It didn't sound like Jason's voice.

"Billy is that you?"

I squinted my eyes to see where the voice was coming from. I walked closer to the dark figure standing across the street and Roddy's face appeared as he moved under the light of the lantern. His cheeks were streaked with tears. He didn't have to tell me why he had been crying. I got a hard lump in my throat and there was a sinking feeling in my stomach. I knew that the captain must have died.

Roddy rushed toward me. He reached out to me with his arms and fell on me. "Pa's dead," he sobbed in my ear.

I was not used to giving comfort. Reluctantly, I raised my arms up to wrap them around his shoulders and held him close.

"I never got the chance to see him before he died," Roddy cried. "Uncle Daniel told me pa died on the way to the hospital."

I saw a bench on the other side of the street facing away from the wharf. "Let's go over there and sit," I said.

Roddy still held on to me as we moved toward the bench to sit. I was not going to tell Roddy to act more like a man. I knew how much he loved his father. I could never imagine the amount of pain he must be feeling. I loved the captain too, but, he was not my real father and I had known him for less than a year, and yet, I owed him my life. The only emotion I could muster at this time was anger. Daniel Wolcott had denied a son the only chance to be with his father in the last moments of his life. A man like that deserved to be punished. A man like that deserved to be sent to hell.

As we sat together, Roddy began to speak about his father. He brought up old memories of what life was like when he was a young boy and his mother was still alive. And then he broke down and cried some more. "I can't believe that they are all gone. Mother, father, Jarrod, why? I just don't understand why?" Roddy sobbed. "It's not fair."

"You still have Cassie," I said.

Roddy groaned. "Oh I wish she was here now."

I knew it was the wrong time to bring up the possibility that I might go west. But then again, maybe it was best that I tell him about it, maybe he would feel better if he knew I had found my own way. I decided not to bring it up while Roddy continued to speak about his childhood. The memories gushed out of him in a long stream of words. "Pa had such dreams," said Roddy. "He told me that one day he was going to build another schooner and he would make me the captain with my own crew."

"You can still do it," I said.

"What?" said Roddy.

"Build that schooner. You can still do what you father dreamed about."

"Yes, yes...I will, and I want you to be my partner," said Roddy

"I don't know," I replied. I saw the opening. I knew it was the time. "You'll need money," I said. "Where are you going to get it? The Dorothy and this year's profits are at the bottom of the sea."

"Oh, we'll find a way," Roddy replied.

"What if I were to tell you that I knew where such a fortune can be had? What if I were to tell you that I know where we can get a fortune in gold?" I said.

Roddy looked at me strangely. "You wouldn't think of stealing it would you?"

"No, I 'm talking about gold that has been discovered out in a place called California. It's a long way from here."

"California, that's out west," said Roddy.

"I met an old friend tonight," I said. "He's going to California to get some of that gold."

"I wouldn't want to leave Cassie," said Roddy. "I'll find another way."

"My old friend invited me to come with him," I said.

Roddy turned toward me with a hurt look on his face. "You wouldn't leave me at a time like this, after all that has happened?"

"No Roddy, I won't leave without you. I think you should come with me. It won't be forever, just a few months maybe. You can get your gold and come back to Cassie. You'll have the money to build her a fine house and that schooner you want."

"But it is so far away," said Roddy.

"I didn't want to bring this up now, but I guess I have to. I'm in a lot of trouble, Roddy," I said. "Your uncle wants to have me arrested and then deported. I can't stay in Boston much longer."

"No, of course not," he said. "We'll go back to Portland and to August Island. My grandfather will keep you safe. No one is going to arrest you."

"There will have to be a funeral," I said.

"Oh Billy, let's not speak of that now," said Roddy.

"I'm sorry," I said, knowing it was not enough.

Roddy leaned over toward me and rested his head on my shoulder. The next thing I knew, he was fast asleep. We spent the rest of the night on that bench. I got just a few winks of sleep before the sun arose and the clatter of activity sprang up on the docks behind us.

Roddy awoke and yawned. He looked about and remembered why he was there, but he did not cry. He took a deep breath and then let out a long sigh. "I already miss pa and Jarrod. I want to go home and see Cassie. She'll make things better," he said in a melancholy voice.

"You have to go back to your uncle's house," I said. "You need food. I don't have any money. You should rest in a real bed. You don't want to get sick."

"I hate that man," said Roddy. "How could you even suggest that I go back to that house?"

"He's still your uncle. And there will be the funeral. You'll want to be a part of that won't you?"

"Yes, of course. But you must be a part of that too. He was your father as well as mine," Roddy replied.

"Your uncle will never allow it," I said.

"But he must," said Roddy.

"I wish things were different," I said.

"You've already decided that you are going with that friend to California, haven't you?" asked Roddy.

"I don't know for sure yet, but honestly, I don't see any other way to the future. Your uncle will not let me remain free," I said.

"Damn him," said Roddy.

"You have to go back to your uncle's house, Roddy, it's the only way."

"But what about you, where are you going to stay? You wouldn't leave without saying goodbye would you?"

"No, I'd never do that," I replied.

"I'll go back to my uncle's house," he said. "How can I find you? You will stay long enough to see pa buried won't you?" said Roddy.

"I'll come find you," I said. "Where is your uncle's house located?"

"Up on Beacon Hill. It the biggest house on the corner of Pinckney Street. It has a brick wall around it with an iron gate at the entrance," Roddy replied. "But then maybe you shouldn't take chances. uncle Daniel might see you. I had better come and find you."

I didn't want to tell Roddy about that cellar room. I didn't want him to see the place where I had made so much trouble for myself. Above all, I decided that I did not want him to meet Jason Brody. "Don't worry," I said. "We'll find a way to get back together."

"I don't want to leave you," said Roddy.

"I can take care of myself," I said. "You go on now. Well see each other again soon, I promise."

It was hard to watch Roddy walk away. I wanted to follow him all the way back up to Beacon Hill and confront the man who had denied us our last moments with our father. But I held myself back. It would do no good to face that man again. I would find myself in jail. It was better that I let Roddy go alone. I knew that he was better off with his uncle's family than to stay with me.

I returned to the cellar. Jason had laid himself back down and was sleeping on the floor. The filth on the window allowed only a small amount of daylight to enter but it was enough to see that Jason was living like an animal. He had been relieving himself in the corners of the floor and it stank up the whole room. Bugs crawled along the dirt floor and through the dirty straw that was scattered about. I couldn't bring myself to get down and lay on that floor. I saw a long board that Jason once used as a table top. I grabbed it and lay in across a few barrels to make a platform. It was barely large enough for me to stretch out on.

I was so hungry and exhausted that I couldn't think. I knew I had to have sleep so that I could reason again. I lay on the platform and stared up at the webs that hung down from the rafters. I could not stop thinking about what had happened. It was as if I was living through a nightmare. But I knew I was not sleeping and it was not something I could just wake up from. The captain was dead and so was Jarrod. Roddy could not protect me from Daniel Wolcott. I knew that. It seemed as if the only choice I had, was to go west with Jason. But, before I went away, I wanted to do something to Daniel Wolcott to make him pay for what he had done to Roddy and myself. Such a cruel man deserved to be punished.

Someone was shaking my arm. I opened my eyes and in the dim light, I saw Jason standing over me. He was holding a bottle of whiskey in his right hand. He raised it toward my face and shook it back and forth.

"I brought some dinner," he said. And then he brought the mouth of the bottle up to his lips and took a swallow. "Hmm good," said Jason after he wiped the whiskey that dribbled down his chin with his filthy hand. "Here have some." And he handed the bottle to me.

I pushed it away. "I need real food," I said.

"This is all the food I got," he replied. "It's all I need, that and a good cigar."

"What is the hour?" I asked as I stretched myself out and forgot that I was lying up on a platform. I rolled right off the edge and onto the floor.

Jason stood back and laughed at me. I knew he was already drunk. I picked myself up off the floor and tried to stand up. My head felt woozy and I heard my stomach growl. How well I knew that sound and that feeling.

"I have to go find Roddy," I said. "I need to find out when the funeral will be held."

"Funeral?" asked Jason.

"My father died yesterday," I said. "Roddy came and told me."

"Sorry boyo," said Jason. "Come on now. Have a drink. It will make you feel better."

Right then, I was so thirsty. I couldn't resist any liquid. I took it from him and swallowed a mouthful. It was too much to take at once. I thought my mouth was on fire. I had to spit most of it out onto the floor.

"Boyo, that's good sipping whisky, you don't gulp it down like water," said Jason.

I coughed and bent over to puke but there was nothing to come out. My stomach was so empty.

"I forgot. You can't hold your drink," said Jason.

Even though the stuff tasted foul, it wet my lips and tongue. I still held the bottle in my hand I brought it up to my mouth and took a smaller sip. It didn't taste so bad once you got used to it.

"That's the way, boyo," said Jason.

I took a few more sips and I began to get a tingling warm feeling that reached down to my toes and fingertips. I began to feel lightheaded. The best part of getting drunk was that, the pain I was feeling was slowly beginning to slip away from me. Slowly the world began to turn about before my eyes. I had to sit down. I handed the bottle back to Jason. I didn't bother to ask where he got such fine whiskey. I'm sure he stole it from his father's best stock.

"So boyo, what you say about my plan to go west to get the gold? Are you in with me or not?"

"I guess I'm in," I said.

"Well, well, I've got to take a drink to that one, boyo. What changed your mind?" asked Jason.

"Daniel Wolcott," I replied. "He's got it out for me. He vowed he would have me arrested and deported. It's only a matter of time before they come out to search for me. I have to leave Boston as soon as possible."

"We still need traveling money, boyo."

"Daniel Wolcott is a rich man. He lives in a big mansion up on Beacon Hill," I said.

Jason raised his eyebrows. "Now boyo, do you mean to tell me that you think we ought to rob his house?"

"He deserves to be punished," I said. "He kept Roddy from seeing his father before he died."

"You want to kill him, don't you?"

"No, I'm not a killer," I said. I didn't want to admit to Jason that I had indeed thought about killing him with my bare hands.

"Those rich folk have got a lot of booty in their houses. Lots of jewelry and cash," said Jason. "We could get all we need to have a fine journey aboard one of those steamships, if you are really up for it. Were you joking or did you mean it?"

"I don't know," I said. "We can't just go up there and ask for what we want, can we?"

"I've got a pair of persuaders hidden in the wall," said Jason. "They are dueling pistols. I got powder and charges too. I stole them from under the bar at the tavern. Tory will never miss them. He's never had to shoot one of his customers. I don't think he even knows that they are gone."

"I don't know about guns. I never shot one," I said.

"I know how to load it," said Jason. "It's not that hard."

"I thought you couldn't hold a gun in your hand," I replied.

"I been practicing," said Jason.

"No, I can't do it," I said. "Roddy is there. What would he think of me, robbing his uncle?"

"Hell, I bet Roddy is as mad at his uncle as you are," said Jason.

"He is," I said. "I had a hard time persuading him to go back to his uncle's house."

"Boyo, just think about it now? We get to kill two birds with one stone. We get the money we need to go to California and you get your revenge. We're not really going to hurt anyone. We're just going to take his money. No harm done really is there?"

"No, I suppose not," I replied.

"Well then, what are we waiting for?"

"No, this is daft. What am I thinking of…thieving and then running away?" I said.

"You just told me that you don't have any choice," said Jason. "If you stay, that man will have you deported."

"Damn it," I said. "Why does it have to be this way?"

"Oh boyo, it won't be so bad. Once we put some distance between ourselves and this fucking city," said Jason.

"Why do so many here hate the Irish?" I said. "I've never done anyone wrong. Why do they treat us like this?"

"It don't matter, boyo. Once we get some of that gold, those sons of bitches who hate the Irish will get their comeuppance. We'll come back and take over this little city and make them grovel in their own gutters," said Jason.

The whiskey was working on my mind. I listened to Jason and felt the blood rise to my head. He was right. We had to show those rich bastards that we wouldn't be lorded over by them. "Give me some more of that whisky," I said.

Jason cracked a broad smile and handed the bottle to me.

I took another long slow swallow. I was getting used to the bitter flavor.

"So what you say, are we going to do it?" asked Jason.

I wiped my mouth with my hand and looked out the window through the filthy glass. I was so tired of living in filth and being hungry. I knew it was the whisky in me that made me nod my head and say yes.

We waited until it was well past midnight. We made our way from the waterfront up through the center of Boston. We walked across the common. No one was about at that hour. It was a good thing too, because we would have stood out among the crowd. Not just with the sight of our ragged clothes, but with the overwhelming stench of our bodies. It was so bad that it made my empty stomach churn inside. Maybe it was the whiskey too. But I was a long way off from getting sick this time. Maybe it was a blessing that there was nothing in my stomach that could come out.

There was also something else that would have made us stand out. It was the thick bulge in our pants where we had stashed the heavy iron pistols. I worried that mine would cause my pants to fall about my ankles so that I had to keep a hold of it as I moved along. I pointed up the hill. "I think that is the house there on the corner," I said. "See that wall? How are we going to climb over it?"

We walked up the narrow street alongside the ivy covered brick wall. I didn't see any possibility that we could get up over that wall without using the gate.

"There is only one way boyo. You'll have to climb up on my back and I'll boost you over the top," said Jason.

I looked up. The wall was higher than my head. "I don't know about this," I said. "Maybe we should forget about it."

Jason bent over and leaned against the wall. "It won't be so hard. Come on put your foot up on my back. You can grab a hold of some of those vines to get you over the top."

"What about you?"

"Once you're over, you can hang down and pull me up," Jason replied.

"This is daft," I said. "We don't know what we are doing. We're going to get caught and put in jail."

"Just shut up and put your foot on my back," said Jason.

I raised my foot and placed it in the center of Jason's back and hoisted myself up. Jason groaned underneath my weight.

"Hurry up, damn it!" said Jason.

I grabbed a few vines that were draped over the top of the wall and used the little strength I had left in my arms to pull myself up and over the top of the wall. It was too dark to see anything on the other side. I knew it was a long jump to the ground.

"Stay up there, boyo. Reach down now and grab my hands," said Jason.

I looked down. I didn't see how it was possible that I could lift Jason up over the wall myself. "I can't get you over myself," I said.

"I'm stronger that you are," said Jason. He grabbed one of the thicker vines and tested its strength. "Once I get high enough. I want you to grab my arm and pull," said Jason.

And suddenly he boosted himself up and was halfway up the wall. I reached down and grabbed his arm and he used brute strength to lift himself up to the top.

"Now you see," Jason whispered. "It wasn't that hard was it?"

"How do we get into the house?" I asked.

"Through a window," Jason replied. "That one there, it's the library window. That's where mister Wolcott will keep his valuables; in a safe in some bookshelves."

I turned toward Jason. "How did you know that?"

"It's better if you don't know," said Jason.

"You've been to this house before?"

It was dark so I could not see Jason's face to read his expression.

"I'll take care of the window," said Jason. "Let's jump down. Careful, there are bramble bushes down there."

"You didn't rob him before did you?"

"Forget about it boyo. Let's get this thing done with," said Jason.

Jason jumped first and I followed. I heard the tinkling of breaking glass. I hoped it didn't alert anyone.

"I'll give you another boost," said Jason. "You go in first. Watch out for the broken glass on the ledge."

I climbed over the window ledge and through the parted curtains. The room was filled with the aroma of sweet perfume and mixed with that, was the scent of burned wood in the hearth. I looked down and there was a feeble shaft of light coming from under the door across the room.

"Billy, help me get up," said Jason.

I turned around lifted the window sash and some of the broken glass fell out and onto the floor.

"What was that?" asked Jason.

"Broken glass fell on the floor," I whispered.

"Help me up," said Jason.

I reached over and grabbed Jason's hands and he lifted himself up and over the window ledge and climbed in through the curtains.

"Let's get the money and leave," said Jason. "The safe is behind the desk on the third shelf behind some volumes about business law."

"How are we going to get into the safe?" I said. "I suppose now you are going to tell me you have the key."

"It's something called a combination safe. If you have a good ear, you can listen to the device and tell when it is the right number and the right distance to turn," said Jason.

"How did you learn about this?" I asked him.

"In jail," Jason replied. "My cell mate called himself a safe cracker."

"A what?" I said.

"Shh…you wait by the door and listen to see if anyone is coming. I'll go take care of the goods," said Jason.

I heard some footsteps in the hall. "Jason," I whispered. "Hurry up. Someone is coming down the hall."

By the time Jason had moved toward the window, the door began to open. I saw the shadow of a figure appear in the light of the hall.

"Get the pistol ready," Jason whispered to me.

I pulled the pistol out of my pants. I had loaded it to fire earlier. I hoped that the charge and the power were still there. The pistol was so heavy; I had to raise it with both hands. The door opened wider and there stood Daniel Wolcott dressed in a long dark blue robe and black slippers. He walked into the room, lifted the lantern he held in his right hand and turned to stare directly at me. I had the gun aimed at his face.

"Close that door behind you," said Jason from across the room. "I have a gun aimed at your head."

"I thought I detected a malodorous presence in this house," said Daniel while wrinkling his nose. "It is a pair of Irish thieves."

"Just follow instructions and you won't get hurt," said Jason. "Just open that safe behind those books and empty it out. We'll take what we need and be on our way."

"Oh. You think it is just that simple?" said Daniel.

"Yes," Jason replied. "Just that simple if you want to stay alive to see the morning sunrise."

"Roddy is asleep upstairs," said Daniel. "I think I should go up and wake him and let him come down and see this. Let him see who he has accepted as a brother. Then he'll know that I was telling the truth about you."

I waved the pistol at Daniel's face. "I should shoot you for not allowing Roddy to see his father before he died."

"I will admit, I was wrong to keep Roddy from seeing his father, for that I am sorry," Daniel replied. "But, as for you, I am not the least bit sorry about refusing you the same privilege."

I pulled back the hammer to release the charge. I wasn't sure it would fire.

"Put that thing down," said Daniel. "You're not going to shoot me. You wouldn't dare. What would Roddy think of you then?"

"He won't shoot you," said Jason. "But I will, unless you go and get that money. Do it now."

Daniel went over to the bookshelves and pulled out three fat volumes and placed them on the desk. He opened the safe and pulled out a small bag of coins. "I have already been to the bank. There is just a few hundred dollars here," he said. And then, he threw the bag at me. It dropped to the floor and some coins rolled out onto the floor. There was a commotion in the outside hall.

Jason kept his gun aimed at Daniel.

"Pick up the bag, boyo," said Jason.

"Father, are you there?" It was Brent's voice.

"Go back to bed, son," said Daniel.

The door opened and Brent saw me with the pistol in my hand. I reached down to pick up the money and then he saw Jason in the corner with the gun aimed at his father's head.

Someone else was in the hall.

"Brent?" It was Roddy's voice. He came to the door and looked inward. He saw my face and then his eyes traced the length of my arm to the pistol in my hand. "Billy, What are you doing? I can't believe my eyes," said Roddy.

"These boys have what they want. They are just leaving," said Daniel. "So go back to bed. Oh, and Roddy, before you go, take a good look at the boy you would call your brother. I want you to remember this night."

Roddy stared at me with a mixed look of hurt and shock and then he ran down the hall.

"Roddy!" I called out.

Daniel laughed at me. "You know," he said. "It was worth losing a few hundred dollars in gold to see this happen."

I still had the gun ready to shoot. I had eased back the hammer. I raised it once more to Daniel's face. "Jason, come take the money from my hand," I said. Jason came and took it from me. "Let's go boyo. Our work is done."

"I'll see you are both put in jail for the rest of your lives, you Irish scum. Now Roddy knows what you are," said Daniel.

I aimed the pistol at Daniel's face. "You son of a bitch!" I shouted. I let the hammer fall and there was an explosion. The powder burned my hand as the pistol was jerked backward. A bright light flashed before my eyes. My arm felt as if it had been wrenched free from my shoulder. The smoke had strong scent to it. The cloud cleared and Daniel Wolcott was still standing. A trickle of blood dripped from his right temple. The shot had only grazed his forehead. The sound of the shot had awakened everyone in the house. I heard a little girl scream from upstairs.

Daniel pulled a handkerchief from his robe pocket and brought it up to dab the blood from his temple. He didn't appear to be badly hurt. There was the look of intense rage in his eyes.

"Let's get out of here, now, boyo," said Jason.

"I'll have you two hunted down like animals," said Daniel. "Go where you will with your bounty. I will have you found and brought back to face justice!" he shouted. "Now get out of my house!"

We ran out into the hall and down to the front door. Jason went out first and I followed. We ran through the front yard to the iron gate. We were going to have to climb over it to get out to the street. I couldn't help but to look back at the house and I wondered where Roddy was. Oh God, what had I done? I had ruined everything. It was such a stupid thing to do. But it was too late to change what was. I felt so sick to the stomach. I climbed over the gate and cut my fingers on the sharp points. I had blood all over my hands by the time I jumped to the other side and fell upon the hard surface of the cobblestone street.

Jason was already on the other side and holding the money bag. I ran to the curb and I bent over to puke. I thought my stomach was going to come up through my throat and spill out onto the street.

Jason came over and patted me on the back. "It's all over boyo. Forget about them," he said. "It was no kind of life for you to become a fisherman anyway. You belong with me. Good times are coming ahead of us, boyo. We'll leave this fucking city and make our way to California and get our fortunes. We'll have our gold and our freedom to do anything we want. No one is going to go out that far to catch us."

So it was on to California. I had already lost my excitement for it. I wanted to go back and try to make Roddy understand why I did what I did. I wanted to put everything back the way it was before the storm. I knew that it was not possible.

Jason led me down the hill to the common. We dared not return to the waterfront. That is the first place they would search for us. Jason had other ideas. He told me that there was a horseless trolley that traveled upon a set of tracks that would take us out of the city quicker than a horse carriage. I had never seen such a thing. He took me to this house that stood beside an open road that was lined with wooden planks and iron strips running above it. There before the house, stood a caravan of carriages and a big iron boiler on wheels with a smokestack like a steamship. People climbed up into the carriages and took their seats.

It was nearly dawn by the time we climbed aboard one of those carriages. We took a seat by the back because the other passengers were staring at us and wrinkling their nose at our stench. "We'll get a bath and new clothes after we put some distance between ourselves and this city, boyo," said Jason.

I felt an overwhelming sense of doom. I could not share Jason's feelings of joy. I gazed out the window as the carriage began to move away from the house. I could only think about what I was leaving behind. Roddy looked so hurt. I 'm sure I would never forget the look on his face at the Wolcott house. He would probably forget about me. Erin would find out about the robbery and she would be ashamed of me. I had no chance with her either. I had ruined everything.

"Cheer up boyo," Jason told me. "You're better off leaving. You told me yourself that Daniel Wolcott was going to make your life miserable whether you had robbed him or not. Either way, if you had stayed behind, you would have been arrested. They would be putting you on a boat bound for your old homeland. You didn't want to go back there now did you?"

"No," I replied. "It was a place of death and want."

"Buck up then boyo. Stop looking back," said Jason. "The gold is waiting for us out there in California. Can't you just imagine it now?"

Chapter 22

We were so filthy and roguish looking that Jason Brody had to offer the conductor a bribe to keep us from being thrown off the train. Our fellow passengers took a special effort to avoid sitting near us and that was a difficult thing to do in the dark cramped car. Jason was very creative with his explanation. "We have been working as laborers," Jason told the conductor. "We have only a short time to return to our families in New York City. We were not given the opportunity to change clothes or have a bath."

The conductor responded to this explanation by folding his arms against his chest, giving us a sideways glance and nodding his head up and down. He then jerked him thumb toward the exit. "You both get off my train at the next stop or I'll call in a constable," he said.

Jason pulled out a five dollar gold piece from the bag that contained our booty and flashed it in the conductor's face. He offered us a broad smile and pocketed the coin. "That'll get you through till Springfield, boys. I suggest you get off there and find yourselves a place to get a proper bath and change of clothes. I'll not let you back on the train until then," he said.

We arrived in Springfield by the early afternoon after many delays. The train made a stop every few miles to take on water and wood to fuel the boilers. I thought we would have made better time if we had hired a carriage and a team of horses. I didn't like the train. Soot and sparks flew out from the engine and came in upon us through the open windows, making us filthier than we were when we started the journey.

We left the train at Springfield and entered a small Inn that was located along the tracks. The hotel clerk greeted us with a suspicious stare. "We do not serve malingerers," he told us.

Jason was quick to pull out another gold coin that brought a smile to the clerk's face. "We are in need of lodgings," said Jason. "And, we need a bath drawn up. We are railroad workers on our way home to our families. I must ask your forgiveness for our filthy persons. We didn't have the opportunity to bathe at our place of work. We don't have much time before we must return to work.

You understand don't you? And if you might sir, could you suggest the name of a tailor or a clothing emporium? My friend and I are in need of a change of attire."

We soon found ourselves in a tiny but comfortable room outfitted with two narrow beds, a chair and a small chest of drawers. I lay upon one of the beds and wanted to remain there for an eternity to sleep. I recalled that I had not slept in a real bed in many weeks.

"You take the first bath, boyo," said Jason. "That fish stink is making me sick. We've got plenty of money. I think you should take two baths and use lots of soap."

"You're a great one to talk," I quipped back. "I bet you haven't had a bath since you left home. You might need a pick and shovel to chip all that shit off of your body."

"No kidding boyo, we both need to look respectable if we are going to be allowed back aboard that train," said Jason. "We have to get out of this state real soon. I didn't tell you about the telegraph."

"Telegraph?" I asked.

"Did you see those poles that stand along the tracks that are strung with wire?" asked Jason.

"No, not really."

"Go look outside the window. You can see them from here," said Jason.

"I don't want to get up from this bed until the bath is ready and then I want lots of food, not whiskey, real food," I said.

"Alright, boyo, you'll get your food, but you need to understand, those wires can carry messages real quick from one town to another. A sheriff in Boston can send a message to a sheriff in Springfield in just a few minutes.

"How can a little wire carry words?" I asked.

"Don't ask me," Jason replied. "I just know it does. We might not have much time to get out. So we'll have to make this a fast rest stop; just a couple of hours. So you lie there and get a few winks. You can sleep more on the train on our way to New York City."

The clerk called from the hall announcing that our bath was drawn. I got up from the bed and began to strip off my filthy clothes. "What am I going to wear after the bath?" I don't want to put these clothes back on," I said.

"I'm going out while you bathe. I'll go and try to find us some clothes," Jason replied. "We don't have time for a tailor to make us something. We'll have to settle for work pants and shirts. If I can find some boots or shoes, I'll bring then along too. You can't get back on that train barefooted like you are."

"Where is New York City?" I asked.

"It is south of here," said Jason.

"Why are we going south? Shouldn't we be headed west?"

"Boyo, listen to me. We're not going overland to California. That would be crazy. Do you want to climb over all those mountains?" Jason shook his head. "We're going by sea. The steamship we want to board is in New York City."

"Do we have enough money?" I asked.

Jason sighed. "Don't worry about those things," he said. "Just take your bath and get your nap. I'll be back with some clothes."

I sank down in that tub of water and felt my whole body go limp. The water was not so hot but it felt so good. My hands still had traces of blood from the cuts on my fingers caused by the iron points on that gate. It led me to recall the images of what had happened last night. The worst part of it all was Roddy's expression of hurt and surprise. I stared at the pink scar on my left arm that was my constant reminder of what I had done to my father. I was beginning to think that I deserved to join my father in hell after all. My thoughts turned to Erin. What would she think of me after she heard about what I had done? I couldn't let her believe that I was a bad person because of the mistake I had made. I had to find a way to get a letter to her explaining why I had done what I did.

There was a knock on the door. The man outside shouted that I had to be out of that bath in five minutes. I thought I had been there for only a few seconds. There were large towels to be had to dry myself, but I had to pay for them and Jason didn't leave me any money, so I was forced to put on my filthy pants over my wet skin to get back to the room. I pulled them off and lay naked on the bed. I pulled the coverlet over me to keep warm. I wanted so much to sleep. But the tensions in my mind would not allow me to rest.

Jason returned with boxes full of clothes that included some fine looking frock coats and frilly shirts. I complained that it all must have cost a fortune. "We won't have any money left to get to California," I said.

Jason cracked a smile. "Easy boyo, it didn't cost as much as you think," he said. "I bought these outfits from the town undertaker. They are not so well made but they will serve us until we can get something better."

"What is an undertaker?" I asked.

"Let me put it this way, boyo," said Jason. "These clothes were tailored for men who are going to be lying still for a long time, so watch how you treat them."

I didn't want to know any more than that. It was good enough to have something to cover myself that was clean and offered protection from the cold.

We got dressed and then went out to a small restaurant near the tracks and I had my first meal in so many days. My stomach ached and I had to watch myself not to eat too quickly or I would lose it all again.

Jason insisted on spending some of our hard earned booty to purchase a bottle of whiskey and a few cigars. After finishing our meal of boiled ham and potatoes, he and I stopped at a barber so we could both have a shave and our hair trimmed. Jason looked like quite a gentleman after his hair was neatly combed and his beard was shorn off. He had his hair slicked with oil and parted carefully. He donned a tall dark brown beaver hat and walked about like he was someone important. That same conductor greeted us with a smile and a nod as we climbed aboard the carriage, and so did a lot of the women. Jason would tip his hat and smile back. I was envious of him. I wish I was that handsome and had a way with the women.

I did not get much more sleep during our journey south. I couldn't stop thinking about what I was leaving behind. Jason was having the time of his life. He had his cigar stuck between his teeth and his trusted whisky bottle by his side. He had all the women gazing at him. "What more could a man want out of life?" he turned and asked me with one of his broad toothy smiles.

I wanted Erin. She would have seen through Jason at the first. She was someone who would never succumb to his charm. I asked Jason for a few coins. I wanted to buy some paper and postage to write and send a letter to Erin, but Jason refused. "We have to keep this money for the fare to California," he said.

We had a rude awakening once we arrived in that noisy, boisterous city that was called New York. We left the train depot and rushed headlong into a wild throng of people amid fast moving horses, wagons and carts. The street surface was a moving mass of mud. After walking just a few feet, we were both doused from head to foot with the foul smelling muck. I couldn't wait to get another bath.

We traversed many streets on foot searching for the waterfront and the pier where the California bound steamship was berthed. We had to dodge fast moving wagons to cross the broad avenue to reach the piers. All along the opposite street there stood large barn like structures that were even larger than the pier entrances in Boston and so many more people crowded the streets. The noise about us was so deafening, I put my fingers up to my ears to block the sounds.

Jason grabbed my shoulder and pointed to a large colorful painting of a ship floating on an imaginary sea that was surrounded by distant green mountains and tall trees that had long tapered trunks with bunches of leaves on top and appeared to wave in an imaginary breeze.

"That's a picture of the Gulf Liberty," he shouted over the din of noise that surrounded us. "We're going to California on that ship, boyo, only..." he said something after that, but I couldn't hear it because a loud steam whistle blew loudly above our heads. I looked to my left and saw that a train was coming down the avenue in our direction. I hadn't even realized that we were standing on tracks. A man on horseback was leading the train and shouted at us to move away. I grabbed Jason's arm and pulled him forward. We got out of the way just in time to watch the engine pass slowly by. "What was that you were telling me?" I asked him. "I couldn't hear you because of the whistle."

"Bad news, Billy," he said. "I should have taken better care to keep an eye on what we were spending. I don't think we have enough money to cover passage for the both of us to reach California."

Damn it. I knew something like this would happen. I knew how to count better than Jason did. He should have let me keep a watch over the money, but I was too tired to hold to my anger towards him.

"I just want another bath and a bed to sleep in," I said. "Can we at least afford that? Oh, and as long as we don't have the money for passage, there's no reason why you can't give me a few cents to buy paper and postage. I want to write some letters."

"Letters, to who?"

"Erin and Roddy," I said.

"Billy, let it go. There's no use looking back," said Jason.

"I can't," I said. "I did Roddy wrong. I want him to know how sorry I am."

"Oh Christ…alright," Jason dug into the bag and pulled out a dollar gold piece. "This should cover it and then some. Make it last, boyo. I can't give you any more."

"So what do we do if we can't sail to California?" I asked him.

Jason pointed toward the waterfront. That's west, boyo. We certainly can't walk to California. We would have to cross a lot of rivers, tall mountains and a desert."

I remembered that I carried the flyer with me that the sailor had given to Jason. I pulled it from my pocket and opened it to the map. It didn't seem so far away as I traced the distance with my finger on the paper. Maybe it wasn't so far as I thought.

We spent more of our dwindling booty to leave New York City. We did board a steamship after all. It was not a steamer bound for California, but instead, a ferry steamer that would take us to a city some miles south called Philadelphia.

I spoke with a man at the wharf once we reached Philadelphia. He told me that we could board a train that would take us to Harrisburg. And then he told me that we would have to board a canal boat to take us to the foothills of the Allegheny Mountains and then, there would be another train we would take that would get us across the mountains into a city called Pittsburgh. I asked him if Pittsburgh was anywhere close to San Francisco. He laughed in my face. "Son, San Francisco is a long way west from Pittsburgh."

During our stop in Philadelphia, we got a room for the night. I insisted on it. I didn't care what it cost either. I wanted a good night's sleep before we started such a long journey. I had no idea how long it would be before we reached San Francisco. I thought it would take at least a week or two at the most.

I took the time to write letters to Roddy and Erin. I still wasn't good with words so, in my own crude way, I asked them both to forgive me for what I had done. I told them both that I thought it was best for me to go west to California. I told Roddy that I would get the gold that he needed to buy his schooner and that I would send it to him. I told him that I hoped he and Cassie would marry soon and have a happy life together. I wrote that I hoped that one day he would allow me to return and visit him.

As for Erin, the words did not come so easily. I had to be very careful not to speak about love or my desires for us to have a future life together. I just asked her to understand why I made such a foolish mistake and told her that I hoped she would continue to be my friend.

By the time we had reached the city called Harrisburg, I had had my fill of the rattling, bouncing, head thumping steam coach travel for a lifetime. I was so tired of breathing in the black soot that coated me from head to foot. There was no way to get a breath of fresh air. The closed cabin had few open windows and the roof vents let in more soot that air, so that after a night of travel, I was ready to get out and walk the rest of the way to California.

As we reached Harrisburg, the mountains could be seen from the window of the train carriage. I hoped that California lay somewhere on the other side of those mountains. We got off that terrible train in Harrisburg and went aboard a canal boat that took us to the very bottom of the mountains. The conditions on the canal boat were no better than that of the train. The canal boat was just as crowded and cramped and stinking of human sweat and dirt.

The mountains towered over us as we boarded another train to take us up and over. I wondered how it was possible for a machine on wheels to go straight up? How would we get back down again? The mountains covered almost the whole sky above our heads. They were blanketed with dark green forest that gave off a pleasant piney smell and the air was cold and fresh. It was still early September but it felt more like December. I had nothing to protect me from the cold, except this frock coat that had begun to split apart at the seams.

Jason had not lost his spirit of adventure. He looked up at the tall mountains and announced that he couldn't wait for us to board that special train that would take us up into the heavens. But even he had to grab hold of something as we rode up that steep incline. I wondered what was holding the train in place and why we had not slid back down.

We both gasped at the view from the window. The buildings of the little town that we had left behind appeared like child's toys. It was a mountain many times taller than the hill on August Island. It was an even greater thrill when the train reached the summit and then began to slide down the other side. Jason had his arm braced against the seat in front of us to keep from falling forward. After we came down that first mountain, we looked out the window and could see that it was the first of many mountains that we had to cross. By the time we had scaled the last mountain, I thought it was much like a journey across an angry sea riding the largest waves.

I told Jason that I hoped that these were the only mountains we would have to cross to reach San Francisco. A man sitting behind us began to laugh. He leaned forward and tapped my shoulder. "Son, if California is where you are bound; you have only just begun to see mountains. The Allegheny Mountains are but mere hillocks compared to the great Rocky Mountains and the Sierras beyond. And between the mountain ranges lie two thousand miles of desert and prairie land. It is a perilous journey. It should not be undertaken by a novice adventurer such as you."

Jason turned his head toward the stranger. "Sir, we will take care to heed your advice. It is our plan to avoid the mountains altogether and head for New Orleans and take a steamer to the Isthmus and travel to California by sea."

"That is a wise choice, son," the man replied.

"What's this about going to New Orleans? Where is that?" I asked Jason.

"Shhh..." Jason whispered to me. "I don't want you to say any more about California, and, please do not speak another word to strangers about the gold. Promise me."

Chapter 23

When we finally came sliding down the last mountain, I peered out the window to gaze upon a deep valley that stretched out far below us. Wide ribbons of silver wound their way through the valley floor from separate directions to join at a point in the center to form a much wider silver band that disappeared into the haze along the horizon. Standing along the edge of the ribbons, there arose some tall chimneys that bellowed out dark smoke; creating puffy clouds that stretched out across the valley. As we descended farther into the valley, I noticed that tiny boats moved about along the ribbon's surface and they too had chimneys that bellowed out more smoke and formed their own clouds.

Once the train had reached the bottom of the mountain, we boarded another canal boat that took us into the city of Pittsburgh. We passed forlorn looking buildings of brick with dark soot covered windows. The tiny chimneys that we had seen rise above the river's edge from our view atop the mountains now loomed as giants. They spewed out clouds of smoke that obscured our view of the sky.

The truth was weighing heavily on my mind as we entered the city of Pittsburgh. No more of Jason's jokes could relieve my deep sense of dread. What had I done? I was a world away from Boston without so much as a penny in my pocket. I thought back to the storm at sea and the death of my adopted father. And then, there was the robbery and the shooting. It seemed as if all that had happened an eternity ago. And then again, I remembered it as if it all taken place yesterday.

I would not soon forget the warning Daniel Wolcott had vowed after I shot him. "You will be hunted down like animals," he said. So why did I drink that whiskey and do such foolish things? I had a real chance at a good life with Roddy and his family and I had ruined everything. But there was no turning back. If I returned now, I would be deported for sure or worse, I would be sent to prison for many years and then be deported afterward if I was to go back there and be captured.

Jason came to my side as we stood along the bank of a wide river. I heard a fellow passenger call it the Mon. Jason had the stub of his last cigar stuck between his teeth and the nearly empty bottle of whisky sticking out of his frock coat pocket. "Where can a man get an honest drink in this dark city?" he asked me as he chewed down on the stub of his cigar and flashed a smile. "There must be a saloon about here somewhere, and maybe a good card game."

I turned toward him. "You need money for those things," I said. "You told me we were out of money."

Jason spit out the stub of the cigar on the ground and pulled the whiskey bottle from his pocket. He lifted it up to study its contents. He then pulled the cork and drank the last swallow. He then threw the bottle to the ground where it shattered. He did something else then. He shook his left pocket and I heard the jingle of coins.

"You lied to me," I said.

"Easy boyo, I didn't lie. I just said that we didn't have the money to take the steamer to Chagres. I had to keep us from spending too much, so I could have enough for a good stake in a card game. I aim to win us the fare to California, boyo."

"Half of that money is mine, isn't it?" I asked.

"Sure it is, but, don't you trust me? We can't go spending it on a lot of frivolous things like hotel rooms and baths. Christ, boyo, look down there, you got a whole river of water to wash in. Besides, you're just going to get dirty again."

"We need to eat, at least I do," I said.

"What did you do with the rest of that dollar I gave you?" asked Jason.

"I ate it," I told him.

"Alright...alright, boyo," he said as reached down into his pocket, pulled out another dollar coin and handed it to me. "Make it last longer won't you?"

I was too tired to be angry or offer an argument. I followed Jason along the waterfront. It turned out that Pittsburgh had just as wild and rough a waterfront as Boston. As we passed dimly lit saloons, I heard the sounds of rowdy drunks calling from within and the strong odor of whiskey flowed out from those wide swinging doors.

Across the street from the saloons and warehouses, lay the quays and the wharves that slanted down toward the river's edge. Hundreds of boats were berthed beside the wharves, some with sail and most without. I looked up into the sky and a soot like rain fell upon my face. I then searched around us for any inviting door so that we could escape this world of gloom.

We stopped in front of a rundown looking wood frame house with a long sagging front porch. There were young ladies sitting upon the porch rail and waving for us to come forward. Jason moved ahead of me to approach a dark skinned woman wearing a tight black dress that barely covered her bosom. She sat at the bottom of the steps and made eyes at Jason.

I stood back and watched Jason put on his charm. The woman reached out and grabbed Jason's arm. She was trying to coax him to go inside the house. Jason turned to me and smiled and then he came back and spoke in my ear. "Boyo, we've come upon a paradise here. This gal told me that we can have all the fun we want for just two bits!"

I was so tired. I thought it might be worth spending the two bits just to have the chance to lie down in a bed.

"Come on Billy. It's time to have a bit of fun. We earned it didn't we?"

202   John E. Sheehan

I looked across the way at the ladies. None of them looked like Erin. I suppose that was a blessing. Most of them had brightly painted faces that looked old and tired and not very appealing to me.

"I want a good meal and a bed to sleep in," I said.

We both heard loud shouting coming from a large tent that stood beside the house. A man dressed in fancy clothes came walking out of the entrance carrying a bag that jangled in his hand. Jason called over to him. "Sir, is there a card game to be had anywhere in this part of town?"

"Sir," the man looked up and smiled at Jason. "There is no need to gamble on games of chance. Put your money on Magnus. He'll win you a fortune."

"Magnus?" asked Jason.

"Magnus McGee, the miner," the man replied. "He can beat any man on the waterfront."

"He's good at cards is he?" asked Jason.

"Go inside the tent, you'll see," the man said and then walked away.

I noticed a sign that was propped up on a barrel just outside the tent entrance. The sun had gone down and the tent entrance was illuminated by the bright flames of two torches that were stuck into the ground in front of the tent. On the slat of wood there was painted a picture of two bloodied fists crashing together to shatter a bottle of whiskey. Across the top of the picture was painted the words Blood Sport Saloon in red and outlined in black. Tacked to the tent above the sign was a paper flyer that read in big black letters: In the fight ring tonight the Waterfront Mauler, Magnus McGee, the reining champion will challenge any one to bring him down.

We heard more shouts from inside the tent. "We're in paradise, boyo," said Jason as he turned and smiled at me and then turned to wave at the lady who still sat at the bottom of the stairs in the nearby house. Jason nodded to her and then walked ahead of me and disappeared through the entrance into the tent. I followed Jason into the tent entrance and was soon surrounded in a thick cloud of cigar smoke that burned the eyes. The only light came from two lanterns that appeared to be suspended in the darkness above the moving shapes of heads that crowded the room. Once my eyes adjusted to the dim light, I could see a crowd of men gathered around a fighting ring set up in the middle of the tent.

I slipped and almost stumbled to the floor as I made my way through the crowd toward the edge of the ring. The straw under my feet was slippery. I looked up and saw the bulging cheeks of many men. They turned their heads away and spit out long streams of tobacco juice onto the floor in every direction. I had to move quickly to avoid their aimless efforts to hit the floor.

Jason came out of the darkness, grabbed my arm and pulled me backward toward a long bar that was formed by a plank that lay atop a row of barrels. Jason already had a bottle of whiskey in his hand and a cigar had appeared in his mouth. (so much for saving our money).

I turned my attention to the fighting ring. In the left corner just under the lantern, stood a giant of a man with a large head and tiny piggish eyes. He was as big around as he was tall. His shoulders and arms were as thick as whiskey barrels. He had short cropped black hair and a long drooping black moustache that dripped with blood which ran down from his nose. His nostrils flared out and the blood would spray out of them each time the man snorted to take a breath.

The man standing across from him had a head of scruffy blonde hair. He was much thinner but somewhat taller. He did not seem to me to be a fair match for the bigger man. The thinner man turned and I had to wince at the sight of his face. His bloodied nose was smashed in and both his eyes were purple and swollen shut. There was a long cut along his forehead across both eyes that dripped blood down his cheeks to his chin and onto his chest.

The thinner blonde man flashed a bloody grin to the crowd. He then turned suddenly, lurched forward toward the bigger man and bent down to butt his head into the bigger man's belly. The fat man's face turned red. He bent over and groaned and then his mouth opened and he spewed vomit from his lips out toward the crowd. The big man spat out the last of the vomit, wiped his mouth with his fingers and then he reached out with his hands and enclosed the other man's head with his long fat fingers and gave the man's neck a hard twist. The other man managed to reach up and pull away the fingers to escape the grip. Just as he was doing that, the big man brought up his right knee and slammed it between the legs of his opponent, who then let out a high pitched cry.

The men surrounding the fighters were shouting "Magnus! Magnus! Give it to him! Finish him off!"

The bigger man was about to bring a double fisted hammer blow down upon his opponent's head, when the thinner man managed to reach up between the bigger man's legs and grab him by the privates. He twisted and turned them this way and that and soon, the tent echoed with the sounds of an even louder squeal from the big man. His tiny piggish eyes were squeezed shut and sweat mixed with blood trickled down his forehead and cheeks.

 The thinner man did not let go and was squeezing and twisting the big mans balls with his fingers until the bigger man's legs began to quiver and shake and then his knees moved forward. The big man's legs finally buckled under him and then he began to fall slowly forward. The thinner man let go and quickly moved away as the big man came falling down on his face and let out another girlish sounding loud squeal. The cheers stopped suddenly and were replaced with low grumbles.

Jason tapped my shoulder and shouted in my ear. "Anybody could win a fight by doing that. It's the coward's way."

By the look and sound of the crowd, it appeared as if another fight might start outside the ring.

"Hey red!" I heard someone shout from behind me. "You old enough to be watchin this, boy, Where's your mama?"

Jason tapped my arm. "That guy is talking to you," he said.

I didn't turn my head to look.

"Hey I'm talkin to you, boy," the voice became louder.

"Watch out," Jason told me.

I could sense someone standing close behind me. I turned about and there, under the dim light of the lantern, stood a boy who was about my age and a few inches shorter than me. He had a dirty face and long stringy brown hair that drooped over his eyes. His left cheek was bulging and tobacco juice stained his thin lips. He was working his jaw and some of the juice dripped down his chin. He wore a loose gray shirt that was stained on the front with more juice. He also reeked of whiskey.

"I don't want any trouble," I said.

The kid offered me a gape toothed smile. "I asked where's your ma?" he said as he wiped his chin with the sleeve of his shirt. "I bet she's next door whorin it up."

"Hit him. Knock the ugly son of a bitch on his butt," said Jason. "You could lick him with one hand tied behind your back."

"That so?" the boy replied. "Come on then," the boy said as he took a fighting stance and raised his fists before his face.

"I'm not going to fight you," I said.

"What, you some kind of chicken shit Irish boy?"

I started to move away from the bar and the kid followed me. Jason was standing right beside me. "You're not going to let him get away with calling you chicken, are you?"

"Who the fuck are you?" the kid asked Jason.

The kid was filthy and stank of whiskey and he was standing too close. Every time I made a move in one direction or another, he moved with me.

"Get away from me," I said. "I don't know you. What do you want from me?"

The kid smiled at me through rotted broken teeth. I knew.

I didn't want to get close enough even to touch him. But I felt I had to do something so I reached out with my hand and pushed him away. He wouldn't budge.

"I said move away,"

"Make me," he replied, still smiling.

I felt the blood rise to my face. I was having enough of it now. He was standing too close. I closed my hands into fists and stared directly into his eyes. I saw him blink and that is when I raised my arm and caught him in the mouth with my fist. I pulled it back quickly. My fingers ached and I had scraped my knuckles against his broken teeth.

The boy was stunned by my sudden move. He reached up to feel his jaw and I saw his eyes begin to roll about. I didn't think I had hit him that hard and yet he wavered on his legs and then they buckled under him and he fell forward to the floor.

"Damn, you did everything right, boyo," Jason said as he slapped me on the back.

"Let's get out of here now," I told him. "…before the kid gets up."

I turned and headed out through the crowd. Some of the men began to shout at me. "Hey red, why don't you go up and take on the winner?"

I had moved well ahead of Jason.

Someone grabbed my shoulder and swung me around. At first, I thought it was the boy that I had hit, and then I thought no, he was still on the floor, out cold. I turned and came face to face with a tall lanky boy with long dirty blonde hair and half closed sleepy eyes. He wore a dirty brown shirt that hung open to reveal his scrawny chest and stomach. The ribs showed through his pale skin. He had a bulge in his left cheek and a bit of yellow juice dripped from his lip. He worked his jaw while he stared at me through those half closed eyes. I could not tell what he was thinking by his expression. He was not smiling or frowning. His glare reminded me of the eye on that dead fish back on thc Dorothy.

"That was my friend you hit," said the boy. He spoke with a slow twang.

I continued to stare at the boy, trying to figure out what he might do.

"What you got to say bout it?" asked the blonde haired boy.

"Nothing, I didn't want trouble. He started it," I said.

The boy chewed some more. His lips parted and he spit out a stream of yellow juice onto the floor just inches from my feet. He then bent down to grab something by his foot. He straightened himself and brought up a long curved knife and raised it up to touch my chin. I dared not move as the cold sharp point touched my skin.

"Cut him!" came a shout from the crowd.

The kid I had knocked down had gotten to his feet again. He came forward while rubbing his jaw and he smiled at me.

"You want I should cut his throat?" the blonde said to the boy I had hit.

Jason finally came to my side. I wondered where the hell he had gone.

"Hey boys," said Jason. He raised his whiskey bottle to show it to them. "What you say we all have a drink on me and forget about this?"

The boy I had hit came up closer. "You got one hell of a right hand. You ought to be up there in the ring," he said as he rubbed his jaw back and forth.

"You want I should cut him just a little?" asked the sleepy eyed boy.

"Naw, Lafe, it ain't worth the trouble," said the other boy and I breathed a sigh of relief. But the sleepy eyed boy still hadn't moved the point of the knife away from my chin.

A crowd of men had surrounded us. I knew they wanted this kid to cut me from ear to ear just so they could have something to watch.

"Come on boys, the whiskey is waiting," said Jason.

The sleepy eyed boy pushed the point of the knife deeper into my chin. "Don't think that I wouldn't cut your throat from ear to ear," said the boy. But there was still no anger in his expression. His face was a frozen mask and the sight of him sent a chill up my spine. "Then mebbe it might be more fun to run this blade down through your belly and spill your guts like a slaughtered pig," he said. I watched the kid work his jaw muscles and knew that he meant what he said.

"Boys, boys," came a shout from a bald headed fat man wearing a bright red frock coat who pushed his way through the crowd. "No knife fights in here. You'll get me closed down again."

The sleepy eyed boy finally withdrew the knife from my chin. He turned toward the fat man. "This stranger here got a good right arm," said the boy with the knife. "Bet he could take on that ironworker that just put Magnus away."

"And who the fuck are you, his manager?" asked the fat man.

"Never knowed him before," The kid said as he turned toward me. "What's your name?"

"Billy," I replied.

"I'm Lafe," said the boy with the knife.

Jason pushed his way forward. "If any body got a claim to be Billy's manager, it's me," he said. "I'm the one that trained him."

"Who the fuck are you?" asked Lafe.

"Jason Brody," he replied.

"Where you both from? Ain't never seen you round here b'fore," asked Lafe.

"Boston," Jason told him. "Back in those parts, Billy is known as the Boston Brawler."

"Jason," I said as I whacked him in the shoulder with my fist to get him to shut up. I then turned and tried to walk away.

"Where you goin?" Lafe asked me.

"Hell, he's not a fighter, Boston Brawler. Heh heh..." The fat man laughed behind my back.

"I'd put money on him. I saw him knock that kid down with one hard punch!" shouted one of the men from the crowd. I stopped and turned. Other men came forward and stood around the fat man trying to get him to agree to let me go up and fight the blonde ironworker who had just dropped Magnus. I had no intention of ever getting up into any fighting ring. "The fat man is right," I said. "I'm not a fighter."

Jason came over to me and put an arm around my shoulder. "My friend here is a humble fellow," Jason winked at me and smiled and I knew I was in a lot of trouble then.

The fat man was seeing profit in his eyes when he looked at me. "If you can take Patterson down, it'll be worth two hundred dollars in gold," he announced.

"Christ boyo, think about that? Two hundred dollars, that would buy us steamship fare all the way to California," said Jason.

"California?" asked the fat man. "Ain't that out in Mexico? What you want to go out there for?"

"There's gold out there," said Jason with a broad smile. Jason had told me not to say a word to anyone about the gold so I kept my mouth shut. I figured Jason was drunk and the whiskey has loosened his tongue.

"Billy, you show em the flyer, you still got it don't you?" said Jason.

"I thought it was supposed to be a secret," I whispered back to him.

"Oh no, we're among friends here," said Jason. "Show em the flyer. There must be plenty of gold to go around. Who will pay two bits to see the flyer?" Jason shouted.

Men moved forward upon hearing the word gold.

"Keep a tight hold on that flyer, boyo," Jason said to me under his breath. "We're going to make us a bit of money here tonight."

Jason pulled out his little booty bag ready to take a collection and men came forward with their coins and actually paid to get a look at the flyer.

The fat man was skeptical. "Who says this gold is real?"

"It been reported in the papers," someone else said.

"That true?" said the fat man. "Well I'll be damned. Let me see that flyer."

I kept a tight hold on the flyer and, as each man passed to get a look, he dropped a coin in Jason's bag. I was glad that the attention had moved away from the subject of fighting.

"Easy boys, don't push," said Jason. "You can all have a good look. Pay attention to the map. It'll show you which way to go. My friend and I are going by sea from New Orleans. It's easier than crossing the mountains."

I felt a tug and then someone ripped the flyer out of my hand.

"Damn it, now why did someone have to go and do that?" said Jason.

Now that the flyer was gone, the attention turned away from us. I didn't know how much money Jason had collected for a look at the flyer but I knew it wasn't enough to get us to California.

"About that fight," said Jason.

I hit Jason in the ribs with my fist. "Shut up about the fight," I told him.

Lafe came to my side. "I got money put on you. I know you can beat that ironworker. He's all beat up already. All you got to do is drop him with that right hand of yours."

"I'm not going to fight anyone," I told him.

Lafe brought his knife up and pointed it at my chin. "If I say you fight, you fight, here?"

Chapter 24

Jason took his bottle of whiskey to a rickety table set beside the fight ring. I sat down across from him on one of the half barrels that served as a chair. The boy with the knife who called himself Lafe and his partner, Ned Kramer, the one I had knocked to the floor, came around the other side of the table and leaned against the side of the ring. Lafe had his knife in his hand and he was using it to pick at something between his teeth.

Standing around the table was a crowd of mostly young men with tired, work worn faces, reeking of whiskey, and carrying that bulge in their cheeks, spitting out a stream of juice when ever they felt the need. They wore plain work clothes that were tinged with black soot and it stained their faces as well. They huddled near and begged Jason to tell them more about the gold. Jason loved being the center of attention. He smiled up at them and agreed to tell them all he knew about the gold in California as long as they paid their two bits worth. And they paid willingly.

Someone handed Jason a fresh cigar and he had it clenched between his teeth. He was smiling that Jason smile. "Anyone have a deck of cards?" he asked. And then he proceeded to tell the men about the sailor he had met in Boston who had given him the flyer. He told them about San Francisco and the place called Sutter's Mill where the gold had been discovered. When they asked him how he was going to get there. He told them that the best way to go was by sea. But, most of these men were land lubbers and I could see that many of them didn't like the idea of boarding a ship to go out to sea. They expressed their willingness to make the journey overland. I overheard a few of the men talk amongst themselves. Could they, would they leave their families behind and their job at the coal mine or at the iron mills to go out and seek their fortunes?

I was happy that the subject of the fight was forgotten, for now at least. Although Lafe continued to stare at me while he played with his knife and, at given times, he would point the knife in my direction as if to remind me of what he had told me earlier that night. I had no doubt at all that he would use that knife on me or anyone else who crossed him.

The card game had begun in the early hours of the morning. I was so exhausted that I leaned back against the fighting ring and fell asleep. It was Lafe who woke me. "It's all been fixed," said Lafe. "You're going to fight Patterson the ironworker, tonight."

I gazed over at Jason. He was still dealing cards but he was no longer smiling. As the bright light of day came streaming into the tent, only three men remained of the crowd that had gathered the night before. There was a stack of gold coins on the table.

One man suddenly stood up. He was the best dressed of the remaining souls. He grabbed his tall beaver hat from the table and placed it upon his head at an angle and tapped it with his fingers. He then reached down and gathered up the gold coins with both hands and began to count each coin as he placed them in a large black purse that he pulled from under his frock coat.

"Just stay a bit longer," Jason pleaded.

"Good day sirs," the man said with a bright twinkle in his eye and a smile broader than Jason could ever muster. The winner's teeth were perfectly white.

Jason picked up the nearly empty bottle of whiskey from the table and swallowed the last of it. He gazed over at me and winked. "You win some, you lose some, boyo. Tell me; are you ready to take on that iron worker tonight?"

"I need sleep and something to eat," I said.

"That mean you're going to fight him?" asked Jason.

I looked over at Lafe. He had finally put his knife away.

"It'll mean two hundred dollars for us, boyo. Can you just hear that steamship whistle blow?" said Jason.

"That iron worker, he's a coward," said Lafe. "You saw how he took down Magnus. He's already beat up pretty bad. You can finish him with one good punch like you did Ned here."

Ned rubbed his chin and nodded.

"No coward is going to grab me there," I said. "I'd kill him first."

Lafe smiled for the first time. It was more like a grimace. His eyes opened a little wider and his lips spread apart just enough to show a few broken and rotten teeth.

I had been in Pittsburgh for just a night and yet, I was willing to do almost anything to get out of this gloomy city. Even to risk my limbs and body by fighting that ironworker. I was so tired I could hardly stand up. If I was going to fight anyone, I had to have some food in my stomach and some sleep, real sleep, in a bed with a soft mattress, a pillow, and blankets to keep me warm.

At some time during that first night, our traveling twosome had become a foursome. I supposed it was Jason's doing. When I had awakened, I overheard Jason and Lafe making plans. I didn't like the sound of any of it, but I did not say a word. At the time, Lafe was still playing with that knife of his.

Lafe told me he knew where I could find a place to sleep and get a good meal next door at the ladies house. He admitted that he worked for the madam, a woman named Nanna. He brought in customers and she paid him a nickel for each man that went upstairs.

"I still don't know about this fight," I said as the four of us, Jason, Lafe, Ned and myself, left the Bloodsport saloon to go over to Nanna's house.

Jason placed his hand on my shoulder. "You'll do fine boyo. Just don't forget what I taught you," he said. "If you got to fight dirty to survive, you do what ever you have to do."

"I'd even lend you my knife to finish him," said Lafe. "But I s'pose that's not a sportin thing to do."

"Remember this boyo," said Jason. "If we don't get some money soon, we're going to be stuck in this city through a whole winter. Hell, we might never make it to California. And all those other men will go out and get what's ours."

"Why don't you fight him?" I asked Jason.

Jason raised his scarred hands. "With these?"

Nanna was a pretty looking woman who wore a bright red dress trimmed with black lace about her large bosoms. Her cheeks and lips were painted a matching red. She wore a sweet perfume that smelled up the whole room as she entered the parlor. Lafe told her about the fight and asked her if I could have a bed upstairs to rest and a meal served in the kitchen.

"We'll pay," said Jason.

"Pretty boy," said Nanna and she came forward and touched my cheek. "Pretty face...ah, but I see by that crook in your nose that you have fought before."

"His father did that," said Jason.

"Oh dear," said Nanna.

She then turned her attention to Jason. I saw the exchange of glances and then the smiles. It was the way Audrey used to look at Jason before they were ready to go upstairs and do business together. A moment later, Jason and Nanna locked arms and were on their way.

I was allowed to take a bed in one of the upstairs rooms under the eve of the roof. A woman's voice cried out in the next room and there was a loud thumping against the wall. The sounds faded away as the exhaustion overtook me.

I was shaken awake by Jason. He stood over me with his cat's grin. "There's a big dinner of beef and potatoes waiting for you downstairs. Go get eat your fill, boyo. The fight starts in two hours."

"Do you really think I can take this ironworker?" I asked Jason as I rose wearily from the bed. I could have slept for at least another day or two."

"You dropped Ned," Jason replied.

"Huh, that's not saying much, a good brisk wind would knock him down."

I ate three helpings of potatoes and tried the beef. It tasted and chewed like a boot sole. Jason offered me a drink of whiskey to bolster my courage. All I wanted was lots and lots of milk to satisfy my thirst.

I wondered…if we were so broke, how come Jason had come up with another bottle of whiskey and a fresh cigar stuck between his teeth? I wasn't in the mood to fight with him. I wasn't in the mood to fight anyone else either.

There was an even bigger crowd at the Bloodsport Saloon the next night. I stood just inside the entrance wondering what I was doing there and was I so daft that I was ready to get up in that ring and risk my life to earn two hundred dollars to get to California? I wondered what Erin would think of this. My guess would be that she would tell me to stand up for what I thought was right and she might have even put a bet down on my side.

I moved in through the crowd. I didn't know where Jason or Lafe had gone to. I spotted the ironworker named Patterson standing at the bar. His eyes had reopened and his face was clean of blood, but still scarred and swollen. He appeared to be much younger than I thought. Not much older than I, maybe sixteen or seventeen at the most. He did not look so fierce. He didn't even bother to look up at me. He was staring down at the floor.

The fat man in the red suit approached me. "Well if it isn't the Boston Brawler himself. Get on up there in that ring kid. The boys are hankering for a good show tonight."

"Billy, over here," Jason waved at me from the table beside the ring where he had his card game going again.

I had my eyes set on this Patterson fellow. He left the side of the bar and went to the ring and climbed up over the ropes. He had an uncertain way of walking as if he was reluctant to go ahead with this fight. He turned his head and looked at me. It was too dark really to see his expression, but for a moment as his face shone in the lantern light as he turned, I thought I caught a look of fear in his eyes. He grabbed his shirt from around the waist and pulled it up around and over his head and he lay it over the side of the rope. His arms and chest appeared stronger and brawnier without Magnus to compare him to.

I moved over to Jason's table. Lafe was sitting there beside Jason playing with his knife again. He looked up and offered the grimace of a smile that didn't make me feel very good. I didn't see Ned, that scrawny partner of his. I didn't like him much and was glad he wasn't about. He was the reason I had found myself in the middle of this. I saw that Jason was collecting bets instead of playing cards. He had another cigar in his mouth and an almost full bottle of whisky at his side.

"You do us proud now, here?" Lafe shouted to me. He raised the point of the knife in my direction as if to tell me. "You'd better win this fight, or this knife will be in your future."

I was about to sit down at the table when Jason offered a bit of news. "Lafe and Ned are coming with us to California," said Jason. "If we collect enough bets tonight, we'll have enough money to buy us all passage to California."

It wasn't fair, but I didn't offer a word of complaint. Why should I be the one to risk my life for them? I wasn't about to go all the way to California with those boys, Lafe and Ned. And I was going to tell Jason about that after the fight was over. If need be, I'd just go back to Boston and face my troubles rather than go anywhere with that blonde kid with the big knife. I knew that the time would come when he would use that knife on me.

I pulled off my shirt and left it at the table with Jason. It was freezing cold in the tent and I felt a cold sweat start to roll down my chest and under my arms. I climbed up under the ropes into the ring and stood across from Patterson. I was standing where he was and he stood where Magnus had been. Thank God, at least he wasn't Magnus.

The fat man in the red suit got up into the ring and stood between us. "Anything goes, boys," he said. "You can bite, kick, chew and gouge, just give us a good show."

I gazed down at Jason and shook my head at him. I must have lost my senses. But I was trapped. I couldn't get out of this tent alive if I tried to run away.

Jason got up from the table and came up to the side of the ring behind me. "Make believe this guy is Daniel Wolcott," Jason shouted. "He just told you that you couldn't see your pa before he died. You can't ever see him again cause of that man. He ruined your chances for a good life. If you don't kill him, he'll send you to jail for the rest of your life. Kill him, Billy. He's our ticket to California."

I had fought bigger boys on the Boston waterfront with Jason at my side. We put the terror into Tim Gardner. But that had been so long ago, or so it seemed. I didn't have the fire inside my belly. Not like I did then. Seeing my adopted father hurt knowing he had died alone, losing Jarrod at sea, watching the Dorothy sink, all hopes of that future were gone and then there was Roddy. He probably hated me now because of what Daniel Wolcott had done. And then there was Erin. The only chance I had with Erin was to become a rich man so that

I could have some of the power Daniel Wolcott had. I had to win this fight to get back some of what I had lost.

"Fight your heart out, boyo," said Jason.

I gazed across the ring at Patterson. He wiped his nose with his wrist and then took a fighting stance with his legs spread apart and his arms raised before him. He formed his hands into tight fists.

I hoped to finish him quickly like I did to Ned the night before. As I drew closer, I could see that this boy wasn't going to fall so easy. I moved toward him with my fists raised. He stepped back when I advanced and looked as if he was cowering.

The shouts from the crowd began. "Take the Irish kid down!" They shouted. "Show him that Pittsburgh Iron Mill boys don't let fancy boys from Boston take us down."

Patterson stood frozen. He lowered his arms just a bit.

"Are you ready to fight or not?" I asked him.

Patterson would not look directly at me. He offered no reply. He just stood there. I wondered how I was going to hit him. I was expecting him to come toward me.

"Come on you yellow bastard, fight!" That was Jason shouting from behind. I wish he would keep his big mouth shut. Patterson heard him alright and his eyes moved up toward me and he cracked a smile. I didn't like the looks of it either. Something was wrong with this.

"Hit him, damn it!" Jason shouted to me. "He's asking for it."

I moved closer to Patterson. How could I hit him? He was just standing there.

"Hit me," said Patterson. "Get it over with."

I leaned out with my right to hit him in the face with a direct blow to the jaw, but suddenly, he wasn't there. He had moved so quickly away and then he had his left fist ready. He brought it up swiftly to my jaw and I felt my teeth bite into my tongue. I tasted my own blood as the force of the blow brought my head back and I saw bright flashes of light before my eyes.

I tried to pull back, but then I felt another blow hit my right cheek across my nose and I saw more flashes of light. Stabs of pain shot through my jaw and cheeks as if my skull had hit a brick wall.

I heard the echo of shouted voices. I opened my eyes and the world was a blur. I caught sight of the flame in the lantern above my head. There were dark shadows moving all about me. I tried to focus my eyes. I felt my knees buckle and my legs gave way underneath me. The force of another blow slammed into my stomach and doubled me over. All the steak and potatoes came gushing out of my mouth as I went crashing down to the floor of the ring. My head hit first and there was another explosion inside my skull. For just a second, I thought I saw my father. He was pointing at me and laughing and then, there was nothing but blackness.

"Poor boy," a woman's voice murmured.

I opened my eyes and saw the painted face of that madam, Nanna. She hovered over me and had placed a wet cloth upon my forehead. I had a terrible ache in my head and I could taste blood in my mouth as I ran my tongue along my lips and teeth and felt a couple move a little. I tried to lift my head but it hurt too much to move it an inch. "Where am I?" I asked.

"Don't you worry honey," said Nanna. "You just lie there." She then made a clicking sound with her teeth. "Why would you want to ruin a handsome face like this for money?" she said as she shook her head at me.

"Where is Jason?" I asked. I moved my jaw a little to the left and I felt a sharp pain run through my mouth up to the top of my head. I grit my teeth and it made the pain worse. I had some broken teeth that rubbed together and sent a sharp chill up my spine.

"They've gone out," said Nanna

"Did I win or lose?"

Nanna shook her head again. "Honey, you had no chance to win," she replied.

"No money," I said. "I'll never get to California now."

"Honey, why do you want to go so far away? Ain't you got no family?" asked Nanna. "You seem like such a nice boy. Why you runnin round with the likes of that boy that drinks so much? Now that he's taken up with Lafe, there's no end to the trouble there's gonna be on the waterfront. It's only a matter of time b'fore the sheriff finds em and puts em both in jail." Nanna didn't have to say much more. I knew what Jason and Lafe were up to.

I spent three days at Nanna's house recovering from my beating. My nose had escaped another break, but I had lost two good teeth and I had to pull them out myself. Nanna was good to me. She fed me all I could eat from the kitchen and allowed me to lie about in that little room under the eves of the roof so I could get my strength back. All I could think about was getting out of Pittsburgh. I didn't want to go to California. I wanted to go back to Maine.

Jason came back to see how I was on the second day after the fight. He had let his beard start to grow again. I could tell by the look of his red rimmed eyes that he was doing a lot of drinking and no sleeping.

"I'm going back to Maine," I told him.

We both sat out on the far end of the front porch of Nanna's house, away from the ladies. It was mid afternoon but the sky was so dark and gray that it could have been near nightfall. We had the luck to have a bit of warmer weather but there was still no sunshine and it gave me a deep feeling of melancholy. I felt that my friendship with Jason was about to come to an end.

"They'll find you and put you in jail," Jason replied. "You can't go back."

"How are we going to get to California without money? I lost the fight," I said.

"Look boyo, Lafe and I got a plan on how to get some money," said Jason.

"That's another thing. How did that kid become such a close partner of yours?" I asked him. "Nanna told me you and him are going out and making trouble. She said that the sheriff will get you."

"Aw boyo. We got to do what we got to do to survive," Jason replied.

"That kid named Lafe would have killed me back at the Bloodsport. He would have cut me to pieces with that knife and not give it a second thought. I don't like him and I don't trust him," I said.

"Aw now boyo, Lafe is sorry about that, he really is. He's not a bad sort once you get to know him."

"I'm not going to California with him," I said.

"Now boyo, see the reason. We need him. He's got talents."

"He's a thief," I said.

Jason raised his eyebrows and smiled. "Well now, just what do you think you and I are? Did we get a written invitation to attend that little gathering in the library of Daniel Wolcott's house? Did he just give over that gold because he wanted to donate money to a pair of poor Irish boys from Fort Hill?"

"It was a mistake," I said. "I was drunk. I didn't know what I was doing. I'm not going to do any more thieving."

"You gotta eat, boyo. I know how much you like food. No one around here but maybe Nanna is gonna feed you. She won't do it forever. What are you gonna do then?"

"Get a job," I replied.

"It's gonna be hard. They don't seem to like the Irish much out here either," said Jason.

"I don't care," I replied. "No more thieving for me."

"Well it looks like we got a problem then, boyo, cause Lafe and I got it all worked out. We got a few places spotted that look like easy takings. If you don't work with us, how you expect to share in the booty?"

"I won't. I'll earn the money my own way," I replied.

"That mean you and I are going our own separate ways?" Jason asked me.

"I don't know," I said.

"There something else I should tell you," said Jason. "Lafe and I are going overland to California. He heard about some mining companies that are going out of Saint Louis in the spring. He found out about it from one of Nanna's customers. If we go that way, we can't start till March or April. That means we got to spend the winter here."

"I still might go back to Boston. It might be better than facing what's ahead," I said.

"Nothing is worst than jail, boyo, nothing," said Jason. "Take it from me. I've been there. They give special treatment to Irish boys. You might not last a day in that place. And that's the truth, boyo."

"I still can't join you and Lafe," I said. "No more thieving. I'll find a way to earn the money."

"Since when have you become so honest?"

"Since I felt that last blow to the stomach from that ironworker. I do believe it sent me a message," I replied.

Jason cracked a smile. "He did take you down hard, didn't he?"

I rubbed my jaw and nodded.

"Aw come on boyo, be a good chum. We're not going to hurt anyone, honest. We picked easy targets. It will be like taking candy from a baby."

I wished he hadn't put it that way.

I shook my head at him. "No more thieving for me."

Jason hit the porch post with his good right hand. "Damn it boyo. I thought you and I were real friends."

"We are," I said.

Jason waved his scarred left hand in front of me. "I saved your life remember?"

"I won't steal any more," I said. "Not for you, not for anyone."

Jason let out a long sigh and then shook his head. "Alright boyo, I suppose the time had to come when we had to split up. I thought we would have a good time out there in California, I really did. But, you've changed. I don't know when it happened. Maybe you were always better than I was and I just didn't take the time to notice. See ya round, boyo. Maybe we can get together again sometime before Lafe and me leave for California." Jason then turned and started to walk away. I wanted so much to follow him but I stayed on the porch and watched him leave.

Chapter 25

Nanna knew of a flophouse down the street that rented beds for sixty cents a week. She let me borrow a dollar to pay for the first week and I hoped that the remaining forty cents would buy me enough food to survive until I could get a job. I told her right off that I had no intention of joining Jason and Lafe in their troublemaking. I didn't call it thieving to her face, but she knew what I meant.

"You take care of yourself," Nanna told me as I left her on the porch. "You come right back and see me if you run into any trouble. If need be, I'll give you a job doing errands for me."

I waved to her and walked down the street. I took a look down at myself. Who would want to hire a boy dressed in these rags? My clothes were falling apart at the seams. Nanna had let me borrow a pair of man's pants. She didn't tell me where they came from. I still wore what was left of one of those frilly shirts Jason had bought from the undertaker back in Springfield. The frilly part had come undone and I pulled it off the front thread by thread so that by the time I was finished, the shirt had no collar at all. The frock coat had split in the seams under the arms and at the shoulders. Nanna helped sew part of it back so that the sleeves did not fall off altogether. My feet might as well have been bare; the tops of the shoes I wore had separated at the tip and flopped upward to reveal my toes.

I went to that flop house down the road. It was a horrible place; dark, filthy and crawling with vermin. I paid my sixty scents for a mattress that I had to carry upstairs. There were no beds. This shelter if you could call it that was hardly worth sixty cents a week. On that first night, I found myself surrounded by drunken men who snored loudly and got sick on the floor. The rooms and halls stank of human filth and vomit. It was as bad as the house my family stayed in at the north end of Boston and maybe worse because there were no women; just men like my father. I decided that I would rather sleep outside. And, after that first night, that is just what I did. I hated to waste all that money, but I couldn't stand to spend another night in that place. I found a hidden spot among some bushes and trees down by the edge of the river beyond the wharves. It was cold at night, but then, I had survived through many cold nights with little protection during those days on the road after my family was evicted from our house.

I walked for hours along the waterfront asking men along the wharves if they would hire me to carry cargo. They told me I was either too young, too weak looking or too Irish. After so much of this, I was ready to give up. I went to a café across the street from the wharves some blocks east of Nanna's house. I sat down at the table set just inside the big front window and ordered a bowl of potato soup because it was the cheapest thing on the menu. Two cents a bowl or five cents bought as many refills as I wished. That came with my choice of milk or boiled coffee. A nervous looking man came running out from the back. "Ah...guten tag mine Herr," he said.

I didn't understand his words.

He was a young man with a head of long brown curly hair that hung down about his eyes. He brushed his curly locks aside and flashed a big smile. "What can I get you, sir?" He gazed down at me with very large blue eyes that had a bright sparkle in them. "Pardon me, sir, I forget sometimes to speak English," he added quickly.

I was the only one sitting in the small dining room. The café was furnished with five little tables covered with green and white checked cloths and rounded back wooden chairs. There was a small stove standing toward the back center of the room between the two last tables. Beyond that was an opening to the back room draped with a stained white curtain. The room had a pleasant odor that came from a whole combination of cooking smells, and it made me all the hungrier for something to fill my grumbling stomach.

I pointed to the hand written card. "Potato soup," I said. "I'll pay the five cents to get refills."

The man smiled. "Very good sir, and will it be coffee or milk?"

"Might I have both?" I asked him.

"Ach, sure, sure," he nodded.

The man was staring at my collarless shirt and then he gazed down and saw my worn out, open toed shoes. I knew that look. He didn't think I could pay. I decided that I should show him my money. It was a look I had seen many times before. I hated that look. "I have the money to pay," I said as I pulled out the last nickel coin I had. I had spent most of that dollar on a bug filled mattress in a cold room up in the attic of a house down the road.

"You look very tired," the café keeper told me.

"I've been looking for work," I told him. "No one will hire me. I'm either too young, too sick looking or too Irish."

"Too Irish?" the man let out a little chuckle and then his smile faded. "Ach, I understand, I do. When I first came to this country, I was treated very badly," he said and then he reached out and offered his hand to shake. "My name is Karl Steuben. I came here from Karlsrue, Germany."

"My name is Billy," I was about to say Wolcott and then I realized that there was no use in pretending that I was a Wolcott. "Billy O'Shca," I said as I shook his hand.

"You look hungry," said Karl."I'll go get you that soup now."

When Karl came back with the soup, he had a shirt draped over his arm. He put down the tray of food and took the shirt from his arm and handed it to me. "This was left to me to pay for a meal. It's too big for me in the arms. I think it might fit you. It's wool and very warm," he said.

"I have no more money," I replied.

Karl waved his hand at me and shook his head. "Don't worry about it. Maybe you come back and pay me later or, let me see," Karl looked about the room. "When the door opens a lot of dust comes in from the street, you know? The floor gets very dirty. I have a broom out back. If you like to sweep, we will be even."

"Yes," I said. "I'll sweep your floor for the shirt."

"Tell me something, Billy. Don't you have a family somewhere? Why are you here all alone?"

I told him about Jason and a part of the story about my leaving from Boston to make the journey to California to seek my fortune in gold. But I dared not tell him the whole truth about what I had done back in Boston.

"Oh...I see, gold," Karl nodded his head.

"But I can't start out until spring," I said.

"So what happened to your friend?"

"We had a fight."

"Oh," he replied.

"So where do you sleep?" he asked me.

"Outside along the river," I replied.

"Outside?" Karl replied with a sound of surprise. "But it gets very cold at night. Winter is coming. You can't stay out there."

"When I find a job, I'll get a bed somewhere, but not with a bunch of drunks," I said.

"I tell you what I do," said Karl. "I have a tiny room upstairs. I use it for storing my trunks. I think there's enough room for a place to sleep. I can give you some blankets to place on the floor for a bed until I can find a cot or something."

"You've been so kind already. I have no way to pay you," I told him.

"I think I know a way," said Karl. "There is a man who owns a riverboat across the street beside the wharf. His name is Jonas Slattery. He transports all kinds of cargo from Saint Louis up river to Pittsburgh and makes stops all along the Ohio. He hails from Gallipoli, Ohio and his boat is named after the town he comes from. Jonas is always looking for a young man to come and shovel the ashes out of his boiler when he comes up the river. It's a very dirty job and doesn't pay very well, but it is better than nothing, no? I'm sure it would pay enough to help you survive the winter. You take my room upstairs and you can pay me by working for me, waiting tables, sweeping floors and keeping the stove fire going so that I have more time to cook. Maybe I can bring in more customers. It's hard doing all this myself."

"You're all alone?" I asked.

Karl nodded. "I came here from Germany five years ago. I left my wife and daughter with her parents. I hope to raise enough money to bring them over soon. I spent all my savings to buy this café. It barely lets me survive. In another year, if I don't raise the passage, I sell the café and go home. I miss them so much. It's not worth being away so long. My little Vera is seven years old and she will not recognize me by the time I bring her over."

"I still like America very much," Karl went on to say. "I hoped to go on to Cincinnati and get a position teaching at a University. You see I am not really a cook. I have spent many years studying at the University of Heidelberg. I hoped to start my own small university here, to teach history math and the sciences. Oh I know it's a wild dream. But what else does a man have but his family and his dreams for the future?"

I was nodding as he spoke. Karl pointed to the soup. "You eat. It will get cold. When you finish I give you refill. I have hot coffee ready. You look cold. Put that shirt on over the one you have."

I stood up and did just that. The rough wool collar rubbed against my neck but it felt so much warmer. I sat down and devoured the soup and emptied the cup of milk. He came back and refilled my bowl three more times and brought with that, three more glasses of milk and the two cups of hot coffee. And then, he brought out a small plate that held a square bit of cake for dessert. It was hard to chew with my broken and loose teeth, but I couldn't help myself. I hadn't eaten such a fine sweet treat in a long time.

I got up finally and Karl handed me the broom. "So now you sweep, yes?"

I rubbed my stomach, nodded and grabbed the broom handle.

"After that, I take you upstairs show you the room and then I take you across the street to introduce you to Herr Slattery and his two sons," said Karl.

I worked for more than an hour. I swept every corner of the café and even shook out the table covers outside and restocked the stove with wood. Karl came back out and looked about him. "Mine Gott, I can hardly recognize the place," he said as he smiled. "You do a good job. He then pulled the apron from his waist. "Now we go and see Herr Slattery about that job."

As we strolled across the street and down the sloping wood planks to the riverfront, I saw below a strange looking platform. It could hardly be called a boat. It had no curved shape and no bulwark. There was no mast, no rigging, no sails aloft, and not even a hull to speak of. It was just a flat raft resting on the surface of the river with a shack built upon its deck and a strange wheel attached to the rear. Encircling the deck was a crude open wooden fence that you might see surrounding a house on land with a large gate that faced the wharf.

Karl called out for Jonas. A man appeared at the door of the shack. He was a tall wiry man with a thin sallow cheeked face whose skin was darkened and cracked by the sun. He wore this rough outfit of blue patched up pants and a dark red wool shirt with the sleeves rolled up to reveal arms that looked like bundles of cord wood. He was a chewer and had that familiar bulge in his cheek. He came forward and spit a stream out toward the river. It fell short of the mark and hit the deck with a splat.

Karl introduced him to me after we met at the gate. Slattery asked me if I ever worked a river boat. I told him that I worked aboard a schooner. He chewed some more and turned his head to spit again. This time it reached the water with a soft plunk.

"Billy is a fine hard working young man," said Karl. "You should see my café. He just swept the place so clean. I thought he could do the same with your boiler."

Slattery chewed some more. "Roll up your sleeves boy, let me see them arms of yours. You look a might scrawny. I need a boy with a good strong back and a pair of good arms. That ash is heavy and it's mighty hard work."

I rolled up my arms. The man stared at the pink scar on my left arm.

"That looks like a burn, you been in a fire?" he asked.

I nodded. "But it's all healed," I replied.

He studied me and chewed some more. "I don't suppose you know anything about steam boilers?"

"I can learn quickly," I replied.

"Well bein that Karl thinks you can do it; I'll give you a try. You come on board and I'll show you the works," said Slattery.

"You come back after," Karl told me. "We get the room ready for you." He turned and walked back to the cafe. I wasn't sure what to say next.

Slattery kept chewing and gestured with his hand to lead me into the shack. Two very tall and muscular teenage boys sat in chairs before a table and were eating a stew. I had never seen two boys so tall and so large. They stopped eating and stared at me without saying a word. "Those are my boys," said Slattery. "If'n you get the job, I'll let you meet them."

Slattery took me into another room that was dominated on one side by a huge black iron tank with pipes coming out from the top. Beside that was a giant stove with a door in the front. The door was open and inside I could see a pile of black and grey ash about a foot thick on the bottom.

"That's the boiler and that's the engine. We feed the engine wood and it heats up the water to make steam. The steam builds up pressure and turns those wheels that turn the rods and makes the big wheel at the back of the boat turn. That's how the boat makes her way up and down the river, by churning the water," said Slattery. "It's mighty simple when you think about it some. The engine needs to be tended all the time. We got to keep the fire hot, oh, but not too hot. If the steam builds up too much, she can explode and blow us all to kingdom come."

"You don't use sail?" I asked him. I knew by the look on his face that it was a stupid question.

"My boy's job is to keep the fire goin," said Slattery. "You won't be doing that. You're job starts after we let the fire go out. You still got to be careful when you get inside. The walls are still mighty hot. I got a pair of gloves you can use to keep your hands from getting burned. The ash is still hot underneath. You got to watch for them hot embers. Fifty cents is all I can pay each time you clean it out. It might be once a week. Winter's comin and I won't be here for parts of the winter. We go back to Gallipolis during Christmas and January. We'll come back up river in the spring though. We'll load up on wood and mebbe some livestock and make our first trip to Saint Louis. But we got to wait till the river is up before we can pass the falls at Louisville."

I was nodding to him.

"You never been down river had you?" he asked.

I shook my head.

"Well, don't matter really. You'll only be needed to shovel ash."

"I'm planning to go to Saint Louis in the spring," I said.

"Oh are you now?" he asked.

"I'm going on to California," I said.

"Way out there. What you want to be goin out there for?"

"Gold."

"Hell son, there's nothin out there but mountains, deserts, injuns and Mexicans. I never heard about no gold. What is all that about?" asked Slattery

"I just heard about it myself," I told him.

"It's another one of those damned fool notions," he said. "Gold, huh...you'd do better to go home and find yourself a good wife and make a good living off the land."

"I got no family," I told him. "They were all killed."

"Look, son. I don't really care about your past," said Slattery. "You just do a good job and earn your keep. You can start now if you want. Looks like you could use something better to cover them feet. You're gonna burn your toes in that hot ash. I got a pair of boots layin over there. You put them on while you work and take em off after. Mebbe you can buy your own boots after earn your first wages."

I felt as if I had made some progress. Life did not seem so hopeless after meeting Karl Steuben and taking that job with Jonas Slattery. I knew that I was going to survive the winter at least. But I found myself worrying about Jason Brody. I still considered him a good friend even though he was a drunkard and a thief. He did save my life and he was my only connection out here to the past. I wished there was some way I could change him to make him realize that he could do better than thieving to survive.

I got so busy with all my new jobs and living above Karl's cafe that I lost track of time. The winter came very suddenly and before I knew it, the waterfront had turned white with a heap load of snow and the river was soon frozen over. It was at that point, I lost my job with Slattery for a time. He left to go down river to his home in Ohio for a good part of the rest of the winter, so that I had to survive on Karl's job only. He couldn't pay me with real money. He fed me and gave me a roof over my head. That was more than I could hope for.

I knew Christmas was coming soon. I dreaded its arrival. Christmas Eve was not a day I would look forward to. Last year it was the fire. I had lost the rest of my family. The year before that, I lived out in the cold on the road. And here I was living again on the charity of a goodhearted man from another country. At least I was allowed to work for my food and shelter so I didn't feel guilty about taking what he offered. But I knew my work was not really needed. He could have done all those chores on his own.

I wondered if there ever be a time when I could feel good about the future and not have to worry about where my next meal was coming from? I knew Karl was in trouble too. He wasn't bringing in enough customers and he worried about losing the café before he even had a chance to sell it. Karl told me that he had bought a large stock of potatoes and kept them in the storage cellar. That's all he had left so we both survived on potato soup and he made a wonderful fried pancake with potatoes that was better than the soup but when he ran out of animal lard he could not fry any food so we were left with watered down potato soup.

When Christmas Eve did arrive, Karl admitted that he was feeling most melancholy. It was his fifth Christmas away from his wife and daughter and he missed them most at this time of the year. We sat together by the stove and Karl told me about the wonderful Christmas's they had back in his old country. He vowed that one way or the other, come next Christmas, he would be spending it with his wife and daughter.

On Christmas Eve night, a terrible storm raged outside. The wind piled up large drifts of snow against the front of the café and I had to go out and dig a path to the roadside in the hopes that maybe someone might come in to order a meal. I had no winter coat to protect me from the cold. Karl let me borrow his.

The storm reminded me of last Christmas Eve. I thought back to that night of frolic in the Brody Tavern before my sister showed up and told me that my father was let out of jail and Terrance had disappeared. I looked about at the blowing snow and the waterfront of the river. I thought I saw a huddled figure running away. I was seeing things, I knew. But for a moment, I thought I saw my sister Ann standing not a few yards from the front of the café beckoning me to come to find my lost brother. Suddenly I realized what I had to do. I had to go find my friend Jason. I told Karl that I needed to borrow his coat so that I could go and find my friend. I told him that I would be back soon. He was worried about my going out alone in the storm.

I first went to Nanna's. She hadn't seen Lafe or Jason in almost two weeks. I thought back to the last time I had seen Jason. I realized that it had been two, no three months ago since we had the argument on Nanna's porch. I felt ashamed. I couldn't let this happen again. I couldn't let a friend like Jason be left alone. I had let Terrance down. I let my whole family down. I wasn't going to make the same mistake with my only good friend in the world. It didn't matter any more that he was a drunkard and a thief. He was still my friend.

Nanna told me that terrible things had happened. Lafe's friend Ned had been shot dead and Jason was in a very bad way. She said he had a terrible cough and that he was holding his stomach a lot and had blood coming from his mouth. She told me that she had given Jason a dollar to get a bed in the same flophouse where I had spent that one night in back in September. She told me she thought he would probably spend the dollar on whiskey. "That boy is going to freeze to death in some alley," she said and then she made that clicking noise with her teeth and shook her head. "He don't have any sense at all."

I went back out into the raging storm. I looked out into the world of white and could not see much beyond a few feet. Again I thought I saw that huddled figure moving ahead of me through the snow. I was ready to call out for my sister. But I knew it couldn't be Ann. She had perished in that fire. I explored every alley between every building from Nanna's house down toward the café. The Bloodsport Saloon had been abandoned. The tent had collapsed and the sign with the two fists lay half buried in a snow drift. The fighting ring was still standing and partly covered in snow and shreds of the fallen tent. I was about to pass the tent when I saw something move. I kicked away the snow and uncovered a pile of empty whiskey bottles and bits of straw. I moved in toward the ring. The platform was pushed to the side and there was an opening. I kicked one of the barrels that supported the remaining part of the fighting ring. Another section of the tent had been pulled over and I noticed that there was a hole dug in the snow, either by an animal or a person. I moved in closer.

"Is anyone one in there?" The wind was blowing so loudly that I had to shout to make myself heard. I waited and there was no reply. I shouted again, "Is anyone there?" I moved in just a little closer. Suddenly, the tent cover flew upward and the blade of a knife appeared, and then a hand and then an arm. The knife slashed out toward me and I jumped away just in time to avoid getting cut by the blade.

Chapter 26

A head popped up. I recognized Lafe's long stringy blonde hair. It was all wet and pasted to his forehead. His face was so pale, almost blue. His lips formed thin lines of purple and his teeth chattered within his sunken cheeks. His outstretched arm held the knife tightly. He couldn't see me at first. He turned his face toward me and then he blinked at me with those sleepy eyes as if I was a ghost. "It's you," said Lafe. "Leave me alone." He then turned his head away from me and pulled the part of the tent that covered him back over his head.

"Where is Jason?" I shouted to him.

Lafe pulled the cover back again and stared at me. "What do you care?"

"Where is he?"

"Dead, I spose," Lafe replied. The wind was still blowing hard. I could barely make out what Lafe was saying. But I knew I heard him say the word dead.

"He can't be dead," I said.

"Why not?" said Lafe. "He been real sick. He coughs a lot and bleeds from the mouth. Last time I saw him, he looked like a man who was ready to die."

"When did you last see him?" I asked and then I moved in closer to better hear his answer. Lafe lashed out with the knife again. "You stay away from me, here? I don't need you comin here." And then, he shut his eyes tightly and began to shudder all over.

"You can't stay out here," I told him. "You'll freeze to death."

"Go away," said Lafe. "I done well stayin alive so far without you."

"Tell me where Jason is," I said.

"Why you care? You left him alone. He don't need you either."

"Just tell me, please."

"Hell, I'm not really sure where he's gone," said Lafe. "Nanna let him have a dollar to get a bed in that flophouse down the road. You might find him there. Damned fool if he paid good money to stay in that place. Money be better spent on whisky to keep his insides warm."

"Come out of there," I said. "I know a place where you can get warm. It's Christmas Eve. Karl won't refuse you."

"Who's Karl?"

"It doesn't matter," I said. "You come out of there or you'll freeze to death."

"And who says I don't want to die?" Lafe replied. "Not been much of a life anyway. Christmas don't mean nothin to me."

"What about that gold out there in California?" I said. "I thought you me and Jason were going out there come the spring?"

"Jason told me you don't want me comin along. Ned's dead, don't have to worry bout him no more," Lafe replied.

I didn't know what else to say to him. It was true. I didn't really want him to come with us to California. I didn't trust him. But to see him now, so pale, half frozen and starved, I couldn't help it. He was just a cold, sick helpless boy. He posed no danger to me. He couldn't even keep a hold of his knife. He dropped it in the snow without realizing it.

"You just go on," he said. "Try to find Jason if'n you can. Leave me be. This ain't the first winter I spent outside in the snow."

"I'm not leaving you here," I said. I reached down and grabbed his arm to pull him out of that hole. Lafe tried to get his knife but I kicked it away before he could reach it. I managed to pull him out. He held tightly to the tent cover. I didn't realize until then, that the bit of canvas was all he had to cover him except for the tattered pair of pants.

"Why you doin this?" Lafe asked me as I got him to his feet and reached around with my arm to hold him up.

"Just come along," I said. I looked down and saw the knife. I picked it up and held it blade downward and away from Lafe's reach.

"That's my knife," said Lafe. "You give it here."

"I'll keep it for now," I said. "You'll get it back."

"You don't trust me," said Lafe.

"Not yet, no," I replied.

"Then why the hell are you tryin to save me?"

"I just am," I replied.

Karl was angry at first when he saw Lafe come in with me through the door. There was not enough food to go around. I knew that. I would give Lafe part of my share. I told Karl that. He finally uttered a sigh and told us to get by the stove to get warm.

Lafe and I settled down in chairs before the fire. I took his knife and carried it over to a table and went back to the stove to sit next to him. He turned his head to gaze at the knife. "I want it back," he said.

"You just sit there and get warm," I said. "Your knife is safe where it is."

Karl came back into the room carrying a tray with coffee and the last pieces of a cake he had made from the last bit of sugar and flour. Again, he had a shirt draped over his arm. He put the coffee tray down on a table near us and handed the shirt to Lafe. "You put this on," said Karl.

"I don't need your charity," Lafe replied.

"It's almost Christmas," said Karl. "Take it as a gift."

Lafe allowed the tent piece to drop from his shoulders to the floor and Karl let out a gasp. I looked toward Lafe and winced at the sight of his back. All up and down his spine and across his ribs up to his shoulders, there were these long pink and white ridges that crisscrossed his back at many points like wagon ruts in a muddy road.

"I spose you're wonderin what happened to my back," said Lafe. "Well, it's a long story and none of your damned business." Lafe quickly pulled the shirt over his shoulders to hide the scars. He stared back over at the knife that lay on the nearby table. "I want my knife back. I want it now," he said.

"Go get it then," I told him.

Lafe got up and reached over for it. He held it so gently as if it was a woman's hand. He ran his finger along the edge of the blade. "This knife been a good friend to me," he said. "I kill rabbits and fish for food; make a shelter, defend myself." He then ran his thumb right up against the tip. "Gettin dull. I need to sharpen it."

"Who whipped you like that?" asked Karl.

Lafe pointed the knife at Karl. "You got no right to ask," he said.

"No one is going to hurt you here," said Karl. "Accept our friendship."

Lafe looked down at his knife. "Had no friends that was worth much cept this knife," he replied.

"Where you from?" asked Karl.

"Virginia," Lafe replied.

"What's your name? Billy didn't tell me," asked Karl.

"Lafe Watson."

"Well, I'm pleased to make your acquaintance, Lafe," said Karl. He reached out to shake Lafe's hand but Lafe did not respond. He just sat there and stared at his knife.

"Do you have family down there in Virginia?" asked Karl.

"My daddy owns a ranch down by Charlottesville in a deep hollow by the Blue Ridge. It's mighty fine country. My pa raised horses, last I saw him," said Lafe.

"Did he whip you like that?" I asked.

Lafe swung his knife toward me. I had to move back quickly to avoid being slashed. "I told you it ain't none of your damned business," he said.

"My pa broke my nose," I told him. "I finally had to kill him to save my life." I don't know why I said it. Karl was staring at me with his eyes open wide and Lafe gave me a strange look.

"You kilt your own pa?" asked Lafe.

"He had a knife. He was going to kill me," I said. "I pushed him into a stove. It really was an accident. He died in the fire."

"Damn," Lafe replied. He then looked at the knife and I think he understood my fear. He offered me that grimace of a smile and lay the knife down on the floor beside his foot. "I figure you and I got a lot more in common that I thought," said Lafe. "It was my daddy that whipped me," he added.

"Why?" I asked.

"I helped my half brothers to escape, Chad and Luke. You see they was my daddy's prize bucks."

"A buck, what is that?" I asked.

"I see you don't know nothin bout slaves do ya?"

"No," I replied. And then I remembered Erin telling me about her aunt belonging to an abolitionist society that was working to end slavery. But I really didn't know what it was all about.

"A buck is a young slave man," said Lafe. "My daddy owned about five good bucks. It's not right, but he took their momma to his bed and gave me nigra brothers. My real mother died not long after I was born. I was the only son. My daddy wanted more sons but no decent lady would take up with the likes of him. He forced himself on the wenches. I don't like to talk about that much. That wench what had my brothers was more of a lady that any other woman I had met that had white skin."

"I couldn't stand to see how my daddy treated my half brothers, so I decided to help them get away," Lafe went on to say. "The first time we tried, we got all the way to the Pennsylvania border b'fore a sheriff caught sight of us and sent word to my daddy. He rounded us up, that sheriff did, put us in chains, even me, and sent us back to Virginia," said Lafe. "My daddy shot Chad and Luke in the head and tied me to a tree in the back yard and whipped me till I passed out. One of the slave ladies took me down and brought me to her cabin and nursed my back. My daddy was a mad man. He came in there and vowed he'd sell them all south if they did anything more for me."

"Didn't anyone else try to help you?" asked Karl.

"Some town folk from Charlottesville came along, but pa put the gun against them. Told em to mind their own business lest he shoot em for trespassin," Lafe replied.

"How did you get away?" I asked him.

"Jules helped me," said Lafe. "He was Chad and Luke's older brother. He didn't come with us the first time, cause he was afraid of what would happen to his momma and sister. It was Jules who went into the house and confronted my daddy after he sold his mother and sister south. He hit him over the head sose we could have a chance to escape. Jules was mighty smart. He figured everything out. I helped him knock out my daddy so we could leave. Jules and I made it across the Pennsylvania border. We split up here in Pittsburgh. He told me the only way he would be safe was if he went all the way up to Canada. I wished I had gone with him, but then somethin happened. I stole some food and the sheriff got me and put me in jail. I was just thirteen at the time. I told Jules to go on north without me. I didn't want him to take any chances at bein caught."

I was listening to Lafe's story and was thinking about Jason all the while. I couldn't accept the idea that he might be dead. I had to go out and try to find him. I got up and buttoned the coat I borrowed from Karl. "I got to go out and find Jason," I said.

I dreaded going back to that flophouse. But I knew I had to go. It was like last Christmas Eve all over again but this time, I wasn't going to fail. I stood outside that bleak looking three story wooden boarding house that faced the waterfront. The outer walls were dark gray and unpainted. Many of the windows were broken and others were boarded up or stuffed with rags and old newspapers to keep the wind from blowing through. There was a man sitting by a small stove just inside the front door. He had a little table set up to collect money. He was dressed warmly in a heavy coat with hat and gloves. He saw me come in and demanded that I pay before I went farther.

"I'm looking for my friend," I told him. "I don't need a bed." And then he eyed me strangely. "You been here before," he said. "You paid for a week and didn't stay more than a night."

I didn't want to anger the man by telling him his house was a pigs den and that no one should have to pay to stay in such a horrible place.

"Maybe you saw my friend," I said and then I described him.

The man rubbed his gloved fingers against his chin. "I see a lot of men come through here. I don't have time to get a good look at any of them," he said. "I just take their money. This ain't my house. I just collect the money, it's my job."

I looked beyond the clerk into the hall and up the stairs. Men lay everywhere; some sleeping, some drinking, many moaned in their sleep. The sounds of the coughing, wheezing and farting drowned out the howl of the wind outside.

"You can go up," said the man. "...but it will cost you a nickel."

"I'm not staying," I replied.

"It's a finder's fee," The man said as he smiled at me.

"Damn your finders fee," I said. I walked past him up the stairs. I nearly stumbled back down trying to climb over bodies. I made it up to the second floor and looked down the hall. There were no doors to any of the rooms so that I could see inside the rooms. There were more men lying about on the floor sprawled out this way and that on their straw mattresses. Some had a piece of a blanket or used a part of their clothes to cover their faces so they could sleep. All the rooms were bitter cold. There was no stove in any of the rooms or a fireplace. The sounds grew worse as I tried to make my way down the hall. The clerk did not bother to come after me. I suppose he must have been joking about the finder's fee, hoping I was enough of a fool to pay him. But he was enough of a coward not try to force me to pay.

Most of the men without mattresses sat up and were hunched over or had their faces hidden. I went to the first room and then the second and third until I reached the back of the hall. I was about to climb up the stairs to the third floor, when I stumbled past a man who was sitting on the second step groaning and doubled over with pain. His long black greasy hair was tangled about his shoulders. He had his face tucked down in his chest. His whole body was shaking with tremors and each time he coughed, his whole body jumped. I was ready to pass him when I caught sight of something sticking out of his torn frock coat pocket. I recognized the delicate white lace fringe of the handkerchief. It once belonged to Nanna.

I reached down to grab the handkerchief so that I could get a better look at it. And then the man reached out to grab my wrist. I looked down and saw the pink scars on his fingers through the grime and dirt. The man raised his head. I saw those dark brutish features that I had come to know so well. A boy who could be so handsome when he was all fixed up with a bath, a shave and proper clothes.

"Jason," I said.

Jason looked up. He had sores on his lips and a bit of blood at the corners of his mouth. Drool wet his chin and dripped down through his weeks old scruffy beard. His clothes were in tatters and his feet were bare and black with filth. He looked worse than when I had found him in the cellar back in Boston so many months ago. He raised his hands up to his face and rubbed his eyes. He began coughing. It was a terrible sound coming from within him, like his insides had grown hard and were crumbling. He was also trembling with the cold and his scarred hands were shaking uncontrollably. He finally had to tuck them under his arms to get them to stop shaking.

"Come on, I'm taking you out of here," I said. And I reached down to help him get to his feet. He shrugged me off.

"Leave me alone," he said. His voice was cracked and hoarse.

"You'll die here," I said.

"I don't care anymore," he replied.

"I care," I said. "You saved my life. I'm not going to let you die."

"You've got too soft of a heart, boyo. It's going to get you killed some day," he said.

"Are you going to sit there and feel sorry for yourself?" I said.

"Why not?" Jason replied. "Nothing better to do. Besides, I heard from a doc I met at a saloon. He told me that that I got blood seeping out of me. Says I'm going to bleed to death. I'm not sure if he was a real doc. But I know I'm bleeding. My stomach feels like somebody cut a hole in it."

"It's the whisky," I said.

"Maybe it is but who the fuck cares?"

"What about the gold?" I said. "Are you forgetting about California? We're supposed to go out there and dig up our fortune."

"Oh hell, boyo. I'm not going to live to see California or to get any of that gold," Jason replied.

"Yes you are," I said. "I'm gonna make sure you get to California. I'll carry you all the way on my back if I have to."

"I got to get this bleeding stopped first," said Jason "You aren't a doctor. You can't save me boyo. You might as well just try to save yourself. Go back home. Let that new family of yours take care of you. You don't need me. I'll just get you in more trouble."

"I'm not leaving you here," I said and then I reached down to grab his arm. He was so weak he couldn't manage to pull himself away. I helped him get to his feet. We both almost lost our balance and fell down onto each other as I helped him get down the stairs. It made me think back to the days I used to help carry him up to his room back above the tavern in Boston.

I took Karl's coat off and put it around Jason's shoulders once we reached the door. The man who collected the money just stared at me this time and didn't say a word. He got his money. I figure he was happy Jason was leaving so that there would be room for another fool who could pay. Jason began to cough again and I struggled to hold him up as we walked through the blinding snow. I saw the blood drip onto the snow from his mouth. He had that lace handkerchief clutched in his fingers. It was stained brown and dark red in its center.

Chapter 27

Karl Steuben had a kind heart. He was one of the few men I had met so far in America who would give so much of what he had to strangers. He reminded me of the captain, Jack Wolcott, my adopted father and the man who had saved my life that Christmas eve night, a year ago in Boston. The captain had given me so much more than another chance at life. He provided me with a new family, a livelihood, and a chance for a good future. I couldn't understand why bad things happened to destroy the good things men did. Why would a man such as the captain die in such a terrible way and yet men like Daniel Wolcott are allowed to live and dominate the weak?

I had a real fear that Jason wasn't going to survive this time. I got him to Karl's café and he had passed out by the time I got him through the door. Karl rushed over and helped me carry him toward the stove to get him warm. Lafe was lying by the stove on the floor. He was curled up like a baby with his knife tucked by his chin. He didn't even wake when I came crashing through the door with Jason.

Karl said nothing to me in complaint about bringing in another friend. He ran out to the kitchen to get some more coffee and some rags. We had to use a part of the coffee to wash Jason's bloodied face. There was no fresh water to be had because the well was frozen over.

Karl told me that we should get him upstairs. He insisted that we put Jason in his bed. He also told me that he knew of a doctor down the road who might come after the storm had passed. I was afraid that Jason might not live to see Christmas. I stayed at his side the rest of the night. He seemed to be sleeping better, but his cough was terrible and more blood came from his mouth. I went out and got a bucket full of snow to melt to get some more fresh water to give to Jason and to wipe his face. Although parts of his body were cold, his forehead felt as if it was on fire.

On Christmas morning, Karl came up with a hot bowl of potato soup. I had not slept much all that night. I had just nodded off once in a while but was awakened again by Jason's coughing. I talked to Jason not knowing whether he could hear me or not. I told him he had to live and that we were going to go to California together and make our fortune. We would be partners in business and meet a fine pair of ladies who we would marry and they would bear us each a house full of children.

That doctor came the day after Christmas when the storm had passed. He took a look at Jason and told me that I had to keep the whiskey away from him if he was going to survive. He told me to keep Jason in bed for at least two weeks and not let him move an inch. He had no medicine to leave me. He just told me to give Jason lots of cool water and maybe some broth but nothing solid. He said he would come back in a week to see how Jason was.

I asked the doctor if Jason was going to live. The doctor told me the same thing that that other doctor on board the Nelson told me about the captain. "That boy's life is in God's hands now," he said. "It's up to his maker whether he lives or dies. I can't do much more for him. I suggest you pray for him, son."

A few weeks after Christmas, we had a bit of a warm spell and the river ice broke up. Slattery came back up river and I had my job back for a while. By then, it looked as if Jason might turn the corner. He was still coughing but there was less blood and he was getting the strength back in his body so that he could sit up. I told him what the doctor told me, that if he wanted to go on living, he couldn't get out of that bed for at least another week or two and that he had to swear off whisky forever.

Jason knew just how closely he had come to dying and he promised me that he wasn't going to drink anymore. I told him I was going to make sure of that. I told Lafe that he had to help me keep Jason away from the whiskey.

Lafe was feeling better as well. He went back to stay with Nanna because there really wasn't enough room at Karl's for all of us to stay. Karl told me he didn't mind giving up his bed to Jason. He had a bed set up in the kitchen where it was warmer. I knew there was nothing I could do to make up for all his kindnesses. He didn't seem to care about being paid back. But once I had made a dollar from my job on the Gallipolis, I gave it to Karl so he could buy more food to keep the café going.

I knew spring would be coming soon. It was time to start thinking about finding a way out of Pittsburgh. I knew that the best way to get to Saint Louis was to persuade Jonas Slattery to take me, Jason and Lafe on his riverboat. I would offer to work my way. I told Jonas that I had two friends who wanted to go to Saint Louis. I told him we would all do something for him to earn our fare.

Slattery wanted to meet Jason and Lafe. I was a bit worried that Lafe might flash his knife and scare off Jonas. But I had to take that chance. Anything was worth getting out of this city.

We all met in Karl's café in the first week of February, in the new year of eighteen and forty nine. Jason was up on his feet again and came downstairs for the first time since I had brought him back from that flophouse. He was still pale in the face and walked slowly. But the shakes were gone and he was eating some solid food without a lot of stomach pain.

Karl had lent Jason his razor and he shaved off his scruffy beard. Nanna brought over some spare clothes that were left by men who couldn't pay her any other way. She handed us a pair of boots, a worn out but clean frock coat and some shirts and pants. At last, Jason looked presentable and so did Lafe. I made them both promise to be on their best behavior when they met Jonas Slattery.

Jonas took one look at Jason's face and told him he looked mighty sickly. I told Jonas that Jason had a bit of the fever but that he was well on the mend. Karl told Jonas that it was true. Jonas looked at Lafe's thin body and shook his head. "How you goin to heft that lumber with those stringy arms of yours?"

I waited for Lafe to pull his knife and make a scene. But he held his arms to his side. "Just try me," he said. "I can lift anything."

"Any of you boys know about horses?" asked Jonas. "I got two teams I'm transportin from Wheeling to Saint Louis."

For the first time since I had met him, I saw Lafe Watson's eyes open wide. His face broke out into that grimace of a smile. "I know horses," he said in a voice brimming with pride. "My pa owned a horse ranch in Virginia. I rodem and brokem since I could stand."

"These are fine grays," said Slattery. "No breaking needed, just someone who knows them and can tend to them till we reach Saint Louis."

"I'm your man," said Lafe.

Jonas had a mouthful of chew. He was looking about for a place to spit. He finally grabbed a nearby empty coffee cup and brought it to his lips. He spit into the cup and then rubbed his chin a little. "I'm goin to have to think on this some," he replied. "I'll discuss it with my boys. I'll let you know in good time before we leave for Saint Louis."

Karl told me he thought for sure that Jonas would take us to Saint Louis. I didn't want to get my hopes up too soon. I would not feel easy until Jonas had told me himself. There were other things I was worried about. I overheard Lafe and Jason talk about the thieving they had done last November. Lafe said he hoped that they would leave Pittsburgh before the sheriff caught up with them.

That was not the only thing I had to worry about. I had not forgotten about Daniel Wolcott's warning that he would have us hunted down like animals. No one had yet come after us, not that I knew about anyway. I knew I took a chance when I sent those letters to the O'Neill house in Portland, Maine.

In my letters to them, I asked both Roddy and Erin to write me and send their letters to Pittsburgh, not knowing then that I would still be in Pittsburgh so long. I hoped that the post office would send them forward to San Francisco. I was foolish enough to think that I would have arrived there by now.

I wondered if I would ever get an answer to those letters or had they just forgotten about me. I knew Roddy would be angry that I left before our father's funeral. I had done a terrible thing, robbing his family house and shooting at his uncle. Even if he did hate his uncle as much as I did, I knew it was something Roddy wouldn't have expected from me.

Erin might be more forgiving of my actions but it would make me look like the foolish little boy she once accused me of being. I began to think that maybe I should just forget about them and look forward to California. Maybe I should just start thinking about a new life.

Karl Steuben's cafe had an upswing in business during the winter thaw and I was made busier than ever helping Karl serve the crowd of men that came in hungry after a long days work loading cargo on the wharves. Between the work on the Gallipolis and working the Café, I didn't have much more of a chance to think about the coming journey to Saint Louis or what had happened in the past.

Jason must have been frightened by his brush with death, because he stayed away from the whiskey and Lafe was good to his word not to let him have any either. Jason was still weak and spent his days upstairs in Karl's bed playing cards with himself and sometimes with a customer. Karl discouraged that. He told Jason that he wanted no gambling in his establishment.

On the nights after all my work was done, I went upstairs to spend time with Jason. We talked about the future in California. Jason's good humor had returned and I did let him have a cigar or two. Usually it was a customer who left a cigar with him in exchange for a card playing tip.

Jason had his cards laid out in his lap before him. He had managed to train his battered and scarred fingers to manipulate the cards almost as well as the day I had first seen him do his tricks. He bragged that he would open the biggest gambling parlor west of the Mississippi. He would serve the best whisky in the world and hire the most beautiful women to entertain his customers. His mention of whiskey disturbed me. I told him to stick to the cards and forget about the drink. He offered me one of his cat's grins. "Christ, Boyo, you can't have gambling without whiskey to satisfy a man's thirst. That don't mean I have to drink it."

By the first week in March, Jonas came to the café and gave us his answer. He agreed to take us on. The occasion coincided with my birthday, my second in America. I was sixteen years old. Jason knew I had a birthday coming but I told him not to say anything. He must have told Karl because when Jonas came up to see us about telling us he was taking us on, Karl came out of the back with a big chocolate cake on a plate. Nanna showed up too, and we had a little party. Karl went out back again and brought out a big package wrapped in brown paper tied up with twine. "It isn't much," he said. "But you earned it, my boy."

Lafe let me borrow his knife to slit the twine that bound the paper. I tore it open and found a pair of work pants and two wool shirts.

"You're going to need those for the long journey," said Karl.

"I haven't paid you for the things you already gave me," I said.

Karl shook his head. "I always get these in exchange for food. They don't fit me either," he said. "I have no use for them. You should take them."

I knew it was a lie this time. These clothes were brand new, not used.

"We got to be headin along," said Jonas. His two sons had come with him this time, but even at their large size, they were both too shy to speak and sat together at a table near the door.

"We'll be leaving for Saint Louis in a few days time," said Jonas. "You boys need some time to get to know what you'll be doin. You all come down to the wharf before first light in the mornin, sose you can start your learnin."

We all had a strike of fear that very night when the sheriff appeared at the café looking for Jason and Lafe. Lafe was good at hiding but Jason was still a bit too weak to be running about to hide. I ran upstairs to tell Jason that he should keep real quiet. I came back down and Karl was feeding the sheriff a piece of my birthday cake and telling him that he'd never heard of Jason Brody or Lafe Watson.

The sheriff eyed me suspiciously and I decided that I should stay out of his way. Karl told me to go out back and wash dishes. I felt the sheriff's eyes on my back as I left the room. I wondered if was he looking at me because he thought he had seen me before?

That night, Karl told me we had better go down to the Gallipolis and stay there until it was time to leave. He had convinced the sheriff that neither Jason nor Lafe had been anywhere near the café but there was always the chance he would return.

I hated to have to leave Karl so soon. I wanted to spend more time with him before we had to go down river to Saint Louis. I told Karl about the letters I wrote to Roddy and Erin. He had been such a good friend, I was ashamed to tell him what I had done in Boston; robbing that man and blinding him. Much as I wanted to tell Karl the truth, I couldn't afford to have him reject me.

On our day of departure to Saint Louis, Karl was supposed to meet us down at the wharf. He promised to go to the post office to see if I had gotten any letters from the east. Jonas was anxious to fire up the boiler and get under way. "Daylight was a wastin," he complained. In a lot of ways, he reminded me of the captain. He had a rough outside but I knew he was a kind man in his heart.

I begged Jonas to wait just a little longer but he was bent on leaving before the sun rose. It turned out to be a fine sunny day and, for some odd reason, on that very day, the sky was actually blue and clear of haze. It would figure that the prettiest day in Pittsburgh would be the day I was leaving.

I couldn't get Jonas to wait any longer. He ordered his sons to fire up the boiler and let loose the whistle. He played a little song with it; two long low toots, two short high toots and then three very short low toots. I had gotten to know that tune real well since I began to work for Jonas. I always knew when he was coming up the Mon by that funny tune.

I stood at the very edge of the deck. Jason and Lafe stood at either side of me, facing the wharf. I didn't think it was such a good idea that they show themselves, being that the sheriff was looking for them. Even still, I was glad to have them at my side. Nanna was at the wharf waving at us with one of her white kerchiefs and sniffing back tears.

Lafe told me late one night a while back that he thought of Nanna as his momma but, he didn't allow himself to get all sentimental about leaving her behind. Hearing that from him made him sound a little bit more human and it gave me a reason to trust him a little more than before.

The Gallipolis began to move away from the wharf and I searched the waterfront for any sighting of Karl. I didn't want to leave him without saying a final goodbye. Watching the land move away, reminded me of the day I left Eire. But there was such a difference between that day and this one. Back then, I had no idea what I was going to face in America. I was angry and I was scared. I didn't trust the captain of that ship or my father. But here at my side were two friends I thought I could trust. Well, at least I thought I could trust Jason. Anyway, no matter what I faced during the coming journey to California, I had a better feeling about leaving Pittsburgh that I did about leaving my old homeland.

"There's Karl!" Jason shouted and pointed to the wharf.

The Gallipolis was out and almost in the mid stream of the river. I watched as Karl ran to the very edge of the wharf. He was waving something in his hand. I couldn't see what it was.

Jonas came up to me. "I can't stop her now," he said.

Karl was at the very edge of the wharf, calling out something to me and still waving.

"He got some letters," said Lafe.

"Letters?" I said.

"He can send then on to Saint Louis," said Jonas. "I can't go back to fetch them."

I gazed down at the swirling waters of the river. It was all murky brown and mixed with floating bits of ice and branches of trees. I then looked up at Karl. I climbed up on that fence that surrounded the deck.

"What the hell are you doing?" Lafe asked.

I didn't offer a reply. I took one big leap from the top rail of the fence and jumped into the river.

Chapter 28

I was shocked by the coldness of the water and I began to fear that I might not be able to swim all the way to the wharf without drowning. I recalled the night I had jumped into Boston harbor to kill myself. Dying was the last thing I wanted to happen this time. I wanted to see those letters. I pulled my head above water. All I could hear was Jonas calling. "You come back out of that river or I'll leave you behind, you damned fool!"

I treaded water with my arms and legs. I had to fight the current with all my strength. The cold was sapping my energy so quickly. I could barely feel my feet as I drew closer to the wharf. Bits of branches swept by my face and scratched my skin raw. As I approached Karl, he stared down at me as if I was a madman. He crouched down at the edge of the wharf and grabbed for my out stretched hands. I nearly pulled him into the river with me. I managed to get hold of the edge of the planks and pulled myself up and onto the wharf. I looked up at him and tried to say something but I was out of breath. He had a coat about his shoulders. He pulled it off and draped it over mine as I stood up.

"You could have drowned out there," said Karl. "I would have sent these on to Saint Louis."

"The letters…do you have them? Can I see them?" I said right after I caught enough air to speak.

Karl pulled a fat envelope from his shirt pocket and handed it to me. "All the way from Portland Maine," he said.

I grasped the envelope with my wet hands. My fingers were so numb I could barely feel the envelope in my hand.

"You're teeth are chattering," said Karl. "Come back to the café and get warm. You'll have to get out of those wet clothes or you'll catch a sickness."

I looked out toward the river. The Gallipolis was on its way back to the wharf. I could spot Jonas's red face all the way from where I stood. I waited until the Gallipolis had made fast to the wharf. Jonas stepped off the deck and came toward me. "I ought to leave you here, you crazy fool. You don't have the sense of a mule!" he shouted at me.

I waved the envelope in his face. "I'd do it again for this," I replied.

"Let's be going on," said Jonas with a sigh. "We've missed half a day's travel already."

By the time we got off again, it was almost noon. Jonas told me to change into dry clothes lest I catch a chill and die from a fever on the way to Saint Louis. We all gathered again on the wharf to say our goodbyes. I was glad to have been able to see Karl before we left. I promised him that I would send him a letter once I arrived in Saint Louis and I told him that I would write again once we reached California.

I wasn't sad to see the waterfront of Pittsburgh be left behind. Nor would I miss all the stacks and chimneys from the iron factories and steamboats that spewed smoky air into the sky. We made our way west along this river called the Ohio. It was wide as a sea and colored brown with the spring mud. The countryside along her banks was pretty wild in places. There were patches of woods with bent and fallen trees that arched over into the rushing currents. Through breaks in the woods, I could see stretches of farmland that reached out far beyond the horizon. Out there in the deeper woods there stood some log cabins built in the center of a sea of tree stumps.

Farmer folk stood at the banks of the river upon these stubby, rickety piers and waved to us as we passed. I saw a young boy run down the bank of the river after his dog. He got a hold of his dog and lifted him up to scratch behind his ear. I stood there and waved to him. He had light yellow, almost white hair. For a moment, I thought he could have been my little brother. I wondered if Terrance had survived the return voyage to our homeland with my mother. I knew I would never see either of them again.

I remembered I had the envelope with the letters clutched in my hand. I wanted to read them as soon as possible. I was just about to tear open the envelope, when Jonas called me over to the boiler shed. He told me it was my turn to tend the boiler. We all would have to take our turn. We had drawn lots earlier that morning and I got the first shift.

I'll admit that facing that roaring boiler fire was a frightening thing the first time. I confronted that red wall of flame and felt the blast of heat and suddenly, the memories and fearful images of the past had come back to haunt me. As I stared deep into the flames, I was sure that my father was in there staring back at me, laughing and pointing at me, taunting me. "You'll never add up to anything more than I was," I heard him shout.

I slammed the boiler door shut and then I put my hands over my ears and closed my eyes. But then, I pulled my hands away from my face and formed them into fists. I wasn't going to let him taunt me anymore. I reopened the door and stared defiantly into the inferno. I picked up the shovel and thrust it into the burning embers of wood as if to stab at the creature that lived within the fire. Be it my father or the devil, he would not have me. I decided that if he tried to taunt me again, I would thrust the shovel in after him to silence him. It was not long before I lost my fear of the flames.

I had finished my shift just as the sun dipped below the trees on the banks of the Ohio River on that first day's journey. I went out to stand at the bow of the Gallipolis. I turned to face the stern and could see the stars emerge from the darkening eastern sky. They were so much sharper than I had ever seen them before, so bright you could almost reach out and touch them with your fingertips. Roddy had taught me to recognize the constellations. He reminded me that even if we were separated by a great distance, that I could take some comfort in knowing that we shared the same sights in the night sky and that I could use these stars to find my way home if I became lost.

Before the last bit of daylight faded, I pulled the envelope out of my pocket and carefully tore it open. I unfolded the pages and was happy to see that there were two letters, not just one. The outer letter was written on fine white stationary. Tucked inside those white sheets, were two dog eared pages ripped from the back of Roddy's fisherman's almanac. The paper was stained brown with fish oil and smelled of salt from the sea. It was amazing to think that Roddy's little ragged book had survived the storm at sea.

I decided to read Erin's letter first. I suppose it was because I was worried more about Roddy's reply. Might it be a rejection? Or might he be writing just to tell me how angry he was at what I had done. I was afraid that he was going to tell me that he wanted nothing more to do with me. I hoped that Erin would be a bit more sympathetic. I didn't know why I should think so, considering the fact that she had rejected my efforts to woo her attentions. I suppose it was wishful thinking on my part.

The letter from Erin was dated up at the corner, 16 February, 1849, it began:

Dear Billy,

I hope this letter finds you healthy and safe. I must ask you to forgive me for not responding sooner. I did not see your letter for some time after it arrived in Portland so many months ago. One of the boarders had mistaken your letters for something else and had had tucked them into a drawer in the hall secretary where I found them just a week ago. We have ladies coming and going so often. I know she didn't mean any harm.

I wish to extend my deepest sympathies to you after hearing about what happened to the captain and Jarrod. Aunty and I were both in shock to hear of their deaths and about the tragedy of the storm at sea and the sinking of the Dorothy.

Roddy had sent an urgent message by telegraph to Cassie and then Cassie telegraphed Aunty Constance. We were still in Seneca, New York. We left for Portland the very day that we received the message.

After Constance and I returned to Portland, we received another message from Roddy begging us to come to Boston to accompany him to the funeral. We arrived a day after the captain was buried. Daniel Wolcott was most rude and would not even invite us into the house. Roddy met us at our hotel. He told us what you had done. I must admit, I was taken quite by surprise that you would do such a terrible thing. But I can understand your feelings of anger and betrayal. Roddy was feeling so low, both about his father and brother's death and the fact that you had left him. He was so hurt by your sudden departure. He couldn't understand why you committed the robbery or shot at Daniel. He told us that Daniel was wounded and could not see through his left eye.

I still can't muster any sympathy for that man. But you must be made to understand, Billy. Daniel Wolcott is in a rage. He will use all the powers at his disposal to have you hunted down and captured. Daniel Wolcott has power and influence that reaches far beyond the borders of Massachusetts, so remain vigilant. Daniel does not know anything about your letters. And that secret will remain with us.

I tried to explain to Roddy why I thought you had done what you did. But he would not listen. His uncle had filled his mind with bitterness towards you. It was Cassie who brought Roddy back toward reason. I persuaded him to write you his own letter, which is enclosed.

In a way, it was just as well that your letters remained hidden from us. It allowed Roddy some time to get over the tragedy of losing his father, his brother Jarrod and to ponder the reasons why you had to leave.

My sister Cassie has been at Roddy's side through all this. They are going to be married soon. But Cassie must first get the permission from our father. To that end, Constance is taking us to the continent this spring to visit my parents in Holland.

Cassie's heart is in turmoil. She wants to see our father to beg him to allow her to marry and yet, she doesn't want to leave Roddy's side. We don't have the funds to bring Roddy along. I know what the result will be. Cassie will stay behind and it will be up to Aunty Constance and me to persuade my father to allow the marriage to take place.

I am most anxious to go abroad. In fact, once I arrive in Holland at my father's studio, I am hoping to persuade him to allow me to stay with him and my mother. I have heard that mother is ill and my father is also in poor health. I fear that the time I might have with him will be short and there is so much I still have yet to learn from him about painting.

I have not given up my dream of becoming a great painter, greater and more famous than my father. The fact that I am a woman should make no difference. But alas, I am confronted with reality. It is still a man's world.

I must admit, it was a heady experience to attend that woman's conference in Seneca, New York, to meet so many intelligent women at one gathering. Well, it did give me hope for a brighter future. But, after returning to Portland, Aunty Constance reminded me that we had so much more work to do. I was blinded by all the great oratory and forgot about the political machinations and the inner rivalries between the different factions of the women's movement.

Oh I am sorry to go on about this with you. But it is very important to me. I hoped more would come out of that meeting than just a written manifesto. I do agree with every word it contains, but I fear that the divisions between the abolitionists and those who champion the rights of womanhood might lead to a failure of both causes. We need more activity, not just words on a piece of paper.

Aunty Constance tells me that I am too impatient. "We must work within the system," she reminds me. But I look at that system; dominated by men like Daniel Wolcott and I do not see much hope of change in the near future. But I will not go on further about politics. There are more important things I must tell you before I close this letter.

I'll boldly admit to you Billy, I think what happened to you is a blessing in disguise. That may make you angry to hear, but, in the long term, you will see that going out west was the best thing you could have done for yourself.

I want you to keep up the correspondence with me. I have written in the margin of this letter, the correspondence address for my father's studio in Holland. I should like you to write and describe to me what you see and what your experiences are like and I shall do the same for you. In that way, we shall live out each other's adventures. Tell me about those grand prairies and mountains and about that distant outpost on the Pacific Ocean called San Francisco, and I shall describe to you the great cities of old; London, Paris, Rome and Athens. In that way, we will become fellow adventurers.

I have no doubt that you still hold special feelings for me in your heart. Although my feelings about marriage and childbearing have not changed, I hope that you will be satisfied to become my good friend and that our friendship will mature over time.

In closing, I beseech you to explain to Roddy that the course you have taken is best for all concerned. I have enclosed his letter to you. Read through the angry lines with an understanding of how he has been feeling. Were it not for Cassie and her love and support, I do not know of what desperate lengths Roddy might have gone to exact some kind of revenge against his uncle Daniel. Write him and tell him it is not worth sacrificing his future.

At the last, all I can say is make the best of your new life, Billy. I look forward to hearing about your adventures in the western wilderness. Keep safe and healthy. Godspeed on your journey.

You're friend and fellow adventurer as always, Erin O'Neill

I folded the letter carefully and then gazed up at the night sky toward the east. I still loved Erin so much. I loved her even more after reading this letter. I still had hope in my heart that one day I could convince her that we could be happy together. We had at least found a common bond as fellow adventurers.

I was reluctant to read Roddy's letter. I unrolled the curled up corners of the pages. The daylight had gone but the moon was bright and I squinted to read the roughly printed words of my brother.

Dear Billy,

I hope this letter finds you safe, where ever you are. But, I have to begin by telling you that I cannot understand why you saw fit to rob uncle Daniel. To see you with that gun...you had become a stranger. I realized that I didn't know you even after all we had been through together.

For a time, I listened to uncle Daniel and I believed the worst about you. But Erin and Constance came to see me after pa's funeral. Erin tried to convince me that uncle Daniel was wrong about you. I didn't want to hear it then. I just couldn't understand how you could come and invade my uncle's house in the night, take his money at gunpoint and then shoot at him, right after our father and brother had been killed? And then, you just left without saying goodbye.

Many months have passed without a word from you. I began to wonder if you had met some terrible end. Uncle Daniel lost sight in his right eye after the shooting and now he is almost totally blind. His anger knows no limits. He and I are always at odds. I escaped his house not long after the funeral. Brent gave me money secretly to get me back to Portland.

At first, Brent and I were at odds too. In fact, we had a bloody fight. I gave him a black eye and knocked out two of his front teeth. Strange what happens between cousins, we became even closer friends after that fight. Something has happened to Brent since the storm. He's not as emotional and he has taken to speaking up against his father.

Sometimes, I wish that your shot had killed my uncle. I know that is a terrible thing to say. But it is true nonetheless. I hate him for all the cruel things he did to me. My pa died alone without seeing any of his sons. I can never forgive my uncle for that. But, I am angry at you too. You're taking leave ruined all my hopes for a future as a family. I hoped we could begin a partnership as fishermen.

Cassie has spoken of you many times when I didn't want to hear your name. She has persuaded me that you did not really want to hurt anyone. You were as angry as I was. Who knows? Maybe I might have done the same thing if I were in your place. Both Cassie and Erin have tried to make me understand that you would have a better life away from here. I think I understand, but it still hurts to remember what was and what will never be.

I still have a hope that one day in the future; you will have had your fill of adventure and will come back at least to visit me. I don't want to get too sentimental about this, but after losing my father and brother and long ago my mother, I realize that there is so little time to enjoy the company of those we love.

I don't hate you anymore, Billy. I just want you to know that. You will always be welcome in my home. Write me and tell me how you are getting along. I look forward to the day when we can meet again.

You're loyal friend and brother, Roddy.

I folded the letter and then gazed out upon the moonlit landscape of the river. I then turned back toward the deck. There lay Jason Brody, his snores broke the silence of the night. I owed Jason my life. I felt obligated that I should see him safely to California. And yet, here in my hand was the letter of forgiveness that I had hoped for. I had a real choice. I could go back to Maine and I would still be welcome. I didn't really want to go all the way out to California. But what else could I do? I couldn't leave my best friend, the boy who saved my life. I knew he would never survive the journey to California without my help.

I looked down into the moonlit waters of the river and watched as large boughs of trees were being carried downstream by the swift current. I remembered my struggle to swim up river against the current to reach those letters. I realized that I was free to choose my own path. I had the will and the power to fight against the current. I didn't have to let myself be pulled along. Still, it was very hard to make the right choices as to which direction I should go.

Everything I wanted; the security, the company and love of a real family, was back there in Maine. But if it was there now, wouldn't it always be there? Or would it? Was there time yet to explore and seek adventure and still be able to go back to the security and love of my adopted family?

I had such a fear of losing the good things. They moved so quickly and easily from my grasp. The world I had known back in Kilkenny was stolen from me so suddenly. My family had been thrust out into the cold world from the only home we had known since my birth by strangers who did not care about us. And then, we had to face such terrible hardship during the voyage and after our arrival in America.

Why had I been the one to survive? I should have died of the fever aboard the Saint Gerard with my sister. But how could I think of dying? I had been given so many chances at life and I wasted so many of them foolishly. I wish that I had the faith of my mother that all things would come together in the end for the good. But it was so hard to have faith in a God who would allow such suffering.

I took another look at Jason. He had been turned away from his home and rejected by his family. He had nothing to go back to. If it wasn't for Jason, I would have died in that fire. I might have been thought of as a hero, trying to save my sisters. No one would have known that I had started the fire that killed them, but I had to live with that truth always. I turned and was startled by the appearance of Lafe walking across the deck towards me.

"You read them letters?" he asked as he leaned against the fence rail and spit a mouthful of tobacco juice onto the water below.

I didn't really want to talk about the kinds of things I had been thinking about with him. I didn't think he would understand.

Lafe pointed to Jason. "I don't think he's gonna survive this journey," he said.

"I'll make sure he does," I replied.

"You'll have to carry him all the way to California on your back," said Lafe.

"I'll do it, if that's what it takes," I replied.

"I never had a friend that good cept my half brothers Jules, Luke and Chad," said Lafe "But then, I had to be careful not to act like a brother to them, cause they was nigra slaves and folk down that ways don't think they's human beins. Well, I'll tell you somethin. Those boys were a hell of a lot more human than my daddy was. I would've carried any of them on my back up to the north to save em from what my daddy did. I wish he'd a shot me instead."

"I'm glad he didn't," I said.

Lafe pulled his knife from his boot and brought it up to his mouth to pick between his teeth. "I know you're afraid of me," said Lafe. "No need to be," he added quickly.

I wasn't so sure. I could never figure out what he was thinking. I still didn't trust him even though he had tried to be more of a friend since we had left Pittsburgh. I had the feeling that some day soon I was going to have to fight him and that knife of his.

Chapter 29

We arrived at Wheeling, Virginia early the next morning and took on that team of horses. A team of four of the largest horses I had ever seen and they took up much of the open deck. When I was growing up back in Kilkenny, there were farmers who owned teams of horses to pull their wagons. They were the rich protestant landowners. In our little village outside of Kilkenny, no one could afford to own such animals. But I remembered seeing them trot down the road past our own little plot, pulling along the fancy carriage owned by our landlord's family.

Lafe Watson had been looking forward to the arrival of these big gray horses. I saw a great change in Lafe's attitude around them. He rubbed their flanks and reached up to pat their noses and spoke with such a gentle voice as if they were his own children.

I never had any experience with such large animals myself. The only beast that roamed our land back in Kilkenny, was an old milk cow with a sagging set of udders that was owned by our neighbor. She lived in their house and was usually tethered to the door by a long rope. I could recall that one time when I was about eight or nine years old, my older brothers had tried to goad me into trying to ride on the back of that milk cow. I remembered trying to climb upon her back and being thrown into a pile of manure. Mother heard all the commotion and found me out there. My brothers had a good laugh over it. My mother came and grabbed me by the ear and dragged me down to the river. She threw me into the cold water and told me not to come out until the muck was washed off.

I had forgotten all about that time until now. After our eviction, my whole childhood past felt as if it had been swept out of my memory as if it had never happened. And as I traveled farther west, some memories of that childhood were coming back to me.

During the days that followed our departure from Wheeling, we were plagued by fast moving rain squalls. One minute the sky would be clear blue and the next minute, there would be layers of thick black clouds rolling above us and then the whole world turned a strange shade of greenish gray. The rains poured down upon us with giant heavy drops and, mixed in with them were these hard little rocks of ice that bruised our arms and faces. Loud crashes of thunder rumbled overhead and bright flashes of lightning spooked the horses. It took all of Lafe's charm with the grays to keep them from galloping off the deck and jumping into the river.

I thought I was back out at sea again. I was sure this little riverboat was no more able to withstand the terrible crush of the raging waters about us than the schooner Dorothy could withstand those giant waves that wanted to devour us. I had a fear that we would all be killed.

Jonas gave us each these long poles that we were supposed to use to steer the Gallipolis away from the river banks and around the large chunks of broken trees and other obstacles that moved in our path. In many ways, this river was more frightening than the sea. At least in the sea, there was nothing to collide with but the waves. But here, on the river, we had steep, rocky banks that rose up on either side of us and large rocks rose ahead of us that would turn this boat into splinters.

The squalls passed quickly and the river became calmer. But I was left completely exhausted and terrified by the experience. Lafe tried to put on a brave face. But I knew that even he was scared by the river. Jason tried to make a joke about it. That was his way. Whenever things got rough he would smile and try to make everyone think that he was not afraid. But I saw that look in his eyes when the Gallipolis was headed toward the river bank. His face was a shade of green that I wore during my first days aboard the Dorothy. And, after the storm had passed, I found him leaning against the deck fence with his head bent over the side.

"It gets better," I said.

"I just want to jump off and die," said Jason. "I'm no kind of a sailor, boyo. It's a damn good thing we're not going to California by sea. I'd never make it."

We reached Cincinnati on the fifth day of our journey down river. At least we had calmer weather for that part of the journey. I thought about Karl Steuben as we made fast to the wharf along the Ohio River. I wondered if he would ever make it here and start that university he talked so much about.

Cincinnati was a fine looking city sitting up on the riverbank that stretched back into some hills beyond. Like in Pittsburgh and many of the other towns that we had passed, the river was crowded with barges; some ran with steam and others without. I wanted to go on land and spend some time exploring this new city. I was told that I was not going to have the chance to walk her streets. Jonas had a tight schedule to keep and he did not allow any of us to stray far from the wharves. We took on some wood to fuel the boilers and we left after only a few hours.

As we made our way farther down river, we had more visits from those fast moving storms. I was ready for it the second time, but it did not lessen the fear. The tensions from those storms and the nearness of so many of us having to share such a crowded space, had caused grumblings now and then from Jason, Lafe and myself.

The Slattery boys were getting more to eat than we were. We got to drink river water and hard bread and they got sliced bacon and apples. I knew we worked harder than those boys did. Lafe threatened one day after we left Cincinnati that if we didn't get our share of bacon he would rile the horses. This happened just as we were about to pass through the river falls before arriving at Louisville, Kentucky. It caused Jonas to change his harsh ways with us. He wouldn't admit it, but I think he was afraid of Lafe Watson.

I spent so much time in the boiler room, I had little time to sit and take in the sights of the river when the days were calm. And, after so many hours of feeding the wood to the furnace and stoking the embers, I was too tired to take any pleasure in the journey after my shift was over when the day was done at sunset. I knew I was working harder than Lafe and Jason. Lafe didn't do his turn at the boiler because he had to watch over the horses. And Jason used the excuse that his arms were not strong enough to heave wood into the boiler furnace. And added to that, he told Jonas that he might hurt his already scarred fingers, so that left me and Slattery boys to do all that work of tending to the fire. Big and strong as they were, those boys were quite willing to let me do a lot of their work too. But I didn't complain, because working kept my mind off of my troubles.

I couldn't stop thinking about those letters. I read them again and again. I would look back at the river standing at the stern and wonder why I was going forward instead of back to the east and to the home where I was still welcome. But then Jason would come over and try to joke with me to make me smile and I remembered what I was doing. I had a mission to get him to California. I was beginning to think that it might take a miracle to get him there on my own.

I tried to find a safe and quiet place away from the horses upon the deck and fell asleep after I worked my shifts, only to be shouted awake again by Jonas, to have my breakfast and to go about another shift in that hot little shed. At that time, I didn't think we would ever reach Saint Louis before I would be completely worn out.

There was an excitement aboard the Gallipolis once we arrived in Saint Louis on the morning of April ninth, eighteen and forty nine. The city of Saint Louis was sprawled out high atop this bluff on the western side of the Mississippi River. Berthed along the bottom of the bluff on the edge of the river were steamboats and barges of every size; many more than what I had seen in Pittsburgh. The Mississippi River was many times wider than the Mon or the mighty Ohio. A long stretch of wharves and waterfront buildings lined the bank of the river almost as far as the eye could see. And, clogging the river itself were dozens more moving steamboats that spewed out their silvery clouds of vapor, obscuring much of the morning sun and blue sky.

I was happy that we had made it this far, but then, I looked out at that bustling city and wondered what I was going to do next. We were not getting any money for our labors on the Gallipolis. We had agreed to work for just our passage. I figured we had earned our fare and then some, at least I know I had. It meant that we would be left in Saint Louis without any money. I had been so happy to leave Pittsburgh that I had not thought about what I was going to do once we reached Saint Louis.

Jason came to my side at the deck fence and offered me one of his cat's grins. "We're almost there, Billy," he said. "I can hear that gold jangling in our pockets now."

"What are we going to do from here?" I asked him. "We don't have the money to go any farther."

Jason raised his left eyebrow and winked at me with his right eye. That worried me. Every time he offered that cat's grin and the wink of the eye, I knew there was going to be trouble.

Lafe Watson and Jonas Slattery had been at odds about the horses since we left Wheeling. Lafe was angry that Jonas had taken on the grays because the Gallipolis was such a crude little boat and it was no way to transport such fine horseflesh. Lafe had his hands full trying to keep the horses calm during the storms and now he was treating them as if he owned them. He had taken to them so well and now he had to part with them. I think he was actually going to miss them a lot. I was glad of the fact that those horses had a calming effect on Lafe. He did not use his knife to threaten anyone during the entire journey from Pittsburgh. But, on our last day aboard, Lafe went to Jonas and demanded that he be paid extra for taking care of the team of grays.

"If I hadn't been here to keep em calm, you would have lost em," Lafe told Jonas. "They would have run right off the deck into the river."

"A deal is a deal," said Jonas. "You agreed to work your way for the fare to Saint Louis. Well, we're here. I've done my part."

Lafe reached down toward his boot and pulled up his knife. He walked toward Jonas and pointed it at his face. Jonas's boys, even as big as they were, looked frightened by Lafe with that knife. They stood well back from their father who confronted Lafe.

"I could spook those horses and they'd trample into the river," said Lafe. "You either pay up or I'll rile them up. I mean it."

"I got no money to pay you," Jonas replied. "Not till the owner comes for the horses."

"I'll stay and tell the owner that you refused to treat these grays proper like," said Lafe.

"Get off my boat," said Jonas. "All of you. We're in Saint Louis. I done my part. Get on to California and out of my sight."

Lafe had his jaw muscles set tight and he squinted at Jonas through those sleepy eyes. I knew he was ready to make a move toward Jonas to cut him.

I stepped forward and tapped Lafe on the shoulder. "Let's go," I said. "A bargain is a bargain. He gave us passage. We're here. It's time to go."

Lafe swung around and brought the knife point up to my chin. "I want what's mine," he said. "I took real good care of them grays. I deserve more," he said. "You and Jason can go on. I'm not leavin till I get some money."

"Put that knife away," I told him.

Lafe pressed the point of the blade into my chin and then flashed his grimacing smile. "Now you know better than to go against me, Billy. I'm not leavin this boat until I get what's mine, here, and not you or anyone else is going to get in my way."

Jason went over to Lafe's side. "Aw Lafe leave it be. We can get money other ways. Will you look out at that fine city?" Jason stretched his arm out toward the wharves. "Just think of all the money that's in this town? Look at all those dumb farmers walking around. I bet they got fat purses on them. It'll be just like taking candy from a baby."

Lafe turned and offered another grimace like smile to Jason. "I spose you're right. Much better pickins than this," Lafe said as he turned toward Jonas Slattery and sneered at him. He then walked up to him and pointed the knife at his chin. Jonas did not flinch. He just stared back at Lafe.

"I know the sheriff in this city, boys," said Jonas. "You had best behave yourselves. If I was you Billy, I'd shed myself of this young boy before you go on to California. He'll bring you nothing but trouble. He'll have you all endin up in jail and you'll never see the likes of California or get any of that gold you're seekin."

"Come on Lafe," said Jason. "He's not worth the trouble."

"No, I spose not," Lafe said as he withdrew the knife and put it back in his boot. I breathed a sigh of relief.

Jason was first off the deck and then Lafe and I followed. We found ourselves surrounded by the bustle of activity as we climbed the sloping wharf up toward the street. Long lines of black skinned men stood on either side of us on the wharf. They carried barrels and other cargo above their heads and onto their bare shoulders. Sweat poured down their faces and ran down their bare muscular chests and arms, down to their ragged pants and bare feet. There arose a chant among them that reminded me of our songs out at sea when the Dorothy went to the banks.

Along with the sounds of the chanting laborers was the clatter and rattle of hundreds of wagons and carts and the din of voices from hundreds of people who crowded the wharves. I had not seen so many people gathered in one place since I had arrived in Boston on the Saint Gerard almost two years before. They were dressed in simple farmer's clothes; men wearing flannel shirts, sturdy workpants and broad brimmed hats that shielded their faces from the sun. The women wore colorful calico and gingham dresses with broad flowing skirts and varieties of bonnets that framed the faces of many a pretty girl.

I looked down at myself and saw how dirty I was and how ragged my clothes had become. I held a bundle under my arm that contained the new clothes that Karl had given to me on my birthday. I was trying to save them for the long journey ahead. But right then, I wished I could strip these filthy clothes off and jump into a hot bath. But I had no money to pay for it. I looked down at the river. I suppose I could get in that water and get washed but the river water was murky brown and looked dirtier than I was. I was ashamed to have those farmers look at me as I was; and especially those pretty farm girls.

I had lost sight of Jason and Lafe among the farmers. I looked down toward the wharf and could no longer see the Gallipolis among the many other steamboats. I felt so alone and isolated even though I was among so many people. I didn't know anyone. I searched the crowd for signs of Jason or Lafe.

Suddenly, Jason and Lafe appeared from nowhere with smiles upon their faces; Jason with that cat's grin and Lafe with his grimace and I knew that they were up to no good. Jason was bold enough to raise a little black bag to show me that they had robbed some poor farmer of his purse already. Jason came to my side and patted me on the shoulder. "Come on boyo, it's time to find us a saloon where they sell some good sippin whiskey."

"I thought you quit drinking," I said.

"Aw come on Billy, you didn't really think I was going to quit drinking for good, did you? It was that bad rot gut that damned near killed me. I'm gonna buy only the best from now on," said Jason.

I shook my head at him. There was no sense in arguing with him. I knew it was a lost cause.

"Why you askin him to come along?" asked Lafe. "He didn't help. He don't deserve a share in the booty lest he goes along and helps us get more."

"Billy is my friend," said Jason "We share everything."

"But he don't share the trouble," Lafe replied.

"I'm not doing any more thieving," I said.

"What makes you think you're so high and mighty?" asked Lafe.

"I'm not," I replied. "I just don't want to go to jail, that's all."

"We won't go to jail if'n we don't get caught," Lafe replied.

"Jonas Slattery knows the sheriff. He might tell him about us," I said.

"That old man was lying," said Lafe. "He said that just to put a scare into us." Lafe reached down to grab his knife but I was quicker this time. I reached down and grabbed his arm before he could reach it and I held him still.

"Let go of my arm," he said.

"I will if you keep your hand away from that knife," I replied. "I'm not going to let you scare me any more," I said. "I'm going my own way if I have to. I'll find a better way to get money than stealing it."

Lafe wrenched his arm free from my grasp and I stepped back.

He reached down and grabbed for his knife but he didn't threaten me with it. He brought it up to his mouth and began to pick at something between his teeth.

"Aw now boyo," said Jason. "How do you think we're gonna get all the way out there to California on this little bit of booty? We got to get lots more."

"You can do all the stealing you want," I said. "I'm not going to be a part of it."

Jason let out a sigh. "Oh damn it all, alright, if that's the way you want it, fine. But I ain't paying for you to get a bath this time. And you can find your own money for food."

"That mean we're splittin up?" asked Lafe.

Jason looked at me. "That so boyo, we parting again?"

"I 'm going to see that you make it alive to California," I told him. "I'm not giving up on you yet."

Jason cracked one of his broader smiles. "I told you before boyo. That soft heart of yours is going to get you into trouble. Oh hell, boyo, I'll give you part of my share anyway, after all you done. You saved my life didn't you? I might have died in that flop house if you hadn't come to fetch me out of there. You don't have to be part of the thieving if you don't want to."

"Not fair," said Lafe. "He don't share in the trouble, why should you pay him."

Jason reached around my shoulder with his arm and let it rest against my neck. "Cause he's my best friend, in case you didn't know," said Jason.

I wasn't sure I wanted to be Jason's friend anymore. I knew there was going to be more trouble and Jason and Lafe would be at the start of it.

Chapter 30

We found out quickly that a little ill gotten money didn't go very far in Saint Louis. Whiskey cost twice as much as it did in Pittsburgh and the finest whiskey was well beyond our means. There was not a bed to be found on which to rest ourselves. All the hotels were filled to the point that clerks rented out the chairs and floor space in the lobbies. Men could be found bundled up on the curbs of the streets and in open carriages and wagons standing along the waterfront. Whole families were encamped in their wagons along the wharves. I was ready to take my place among those men on the street just to get a few hours sleep, even if I had to use a stone curb as a pillow.

We walked about the city of Saint Louis with no particular place to go. Night was coming. Jason had bought a pint of the cheapest whisky he could find and he had an even cheaper cigar clenched between his teeth. He was smiling away as if he didn't have a care in the world. He called Saint Louis a paradise too.

Lafe was brooding. He said nothing to me since our confrontation earlier that day when we arrived. I watched him closely though. He had that roaming gaze of an animal seeking its prey. He stopped and stared any finely dressed man who passed him on the street and looked as if he might be carrying a large purse. I knew what Lafe was looking for. It was only a matter of time before he found his victim.

We came upon a boarding house along the waterfront that offered beds for five dollars a night, five dollars? I could have rented a room for a month in Pittsburgh for that amount. A poster nailed to a wall beside the entrance caught my eye. It was advertising for the O'Toole Mining Company. They were recruiting men to join their ranks to go to California. I was the only one among us who could read well enough to know what the poster said. Jason pointed his cigar at the poster and asked me what it was about.

I thought it strange that Jason couldn't read. His parents had given him so much. He was eighteen years old and he had never mentioned whether he had ever gone to school. I imagined that he must have had some kind of schooling. How could he reach this age and not know how to read? Why would his parents let him grow up without schooling? I had been with him all this time and knew he wasn't ignorant. I wondered if he was faking it. I never had the courage to ask him why he couldn't read.

"They are looking for men to join their company to go to California. The poster says we should inquire inside to a man named Michael Dougherty," I said.

"A fellow Irishman, that's encouraging," said Jason.

"It costs a hundred dollars to join them," I said as I read the poster. "That doesn't include provisions."

"What's a provision?" asked Lafe.

"Food, guns, wagons and horses," I replied. I read that from the poster too. Because I didn't want to admit that I didn't know what the word meant either.

"Don't need no gun," said Lafe. He reached down to his boot and pulled up his knife. He waved it in my face just to frighten me again. I leaned back from the blade as it swept past my chest by less than an inch.

I opened the door and went in first, just to avoid Lafe's knife. Daylight was fading quickly and the room was dark except for the feeble glow of a lantern placed upon a round table set in the middle of the room. I turned quickly, once I heard a man cough. I saw his shadow first and then turned farther to see that he was sitting in a chair behind the door. I noticed that the room was crowded with different kinds of tools. Wide tin plates were stacked on another table against the opposite wall. Coils of rope, picks and shovels lay about on the floor. What caught my real attention was the stack of rifles that lay on the floor beside the man's feet.

Jason and Lafe came in after me and then the man got up from his chair and walked over to the table. The feeble light of the lantern revealed a face that was covered with about a weeks worth of dark beard and long shaggy black hair that hung down his back. "Sorry boys, no more beds left," said the man.

"You Dougherty?" I asked.

"I am. Who are you?" he replied.

"Billy," I didn't know how much I could trust this stranger, so I decided not to tell him my last name. Who knew, there might have been some message sent from the east already that Jason and I were wanted for robbery.

"You the one lookin for men to go to California?" asked Lafe

"That we are," Dougherty replied.

"So are we," said Jason.

Dougherty offered a half grin. He eyed the three of us with a shake of the head. "We don't take boys," he said.

I was waiting for Lafe to pull his knife, but he kept his hands at his side. I did see a muscle twitch in his jaw. I knew trouble was coming.

"Would it make a difference if I told you we each had the hundred dollars to pay?" said Lafe.

"You boys don't look like you have a penny farthing between you," said Dougherty.

"We can get it," Lafe replied.

"Too young," Dougherty said as he shook his head at us. "We're lookin for grown men. It's a long dangerous journey. You boys would be cryin for your mothers after the first hundred miles."

"That so?" said Lafe. I saw his jaw twitch again and he made his move to grab the knife from his boot. But, in the same instant, the door opened wider and the long barrel of a rifle appeared. I could see the gleam of the metal barrel in the lantern light.

"You just put your hands higher where I can see them," another man said as he showed himself in the doorway. He held the rifle butt against his chest and aimed the barrel at our chests. He appeared to be younger than Dougherty. He had a rounded pink face with yellow fuzz that covered his cheeks and jaw. His lips were formed into a crazed half smile, half sneer. There was a cruel kind of look in those eyes of his that were a color that matched the steel of the rifle barrel. It was a look like he would enjoy shooting any of the three of us just for the sport of it; a look more unsettling than Lafe could muster during one of his angry fits of temper.

"Who are these boys?" The man with the rifle asked Dougherty. "They give'n you trouble?"

"No, they're just asking about joining us. I told em they're all too young," said Dougherty

"You boys got any money?" asked the man with the rifle. He still had it aimed at our chests. He waved the barrel back and forth between us. And then he stopped when it was aimed at Lafe's chest. "That's a fine knife. Got one myself," said the man with the rifle. "You from the south?"

I noticed they spoke with a similar twang.

"Virginia," Lafe replied.

"What part of Virginia?"

"Down near the Blue Ridge, roun bout Charlottesville," said Lafe.

"I'm from Columbia, Tennessee," said the stranger. "Name is Rory O'Toole. I'm half owner of the O'Toole Mine Company with my brother Henry. If you got money, I want to see it."

"Don't have it yet," said Lafe. "We'll bring it tomorrow."

Rory stared at Lafe through squinted eyes. "How you goin to get that kind of money so soon?"

"Does it matter to you?" Lafe asked him.

Rory's smile grew wider. "Hell no, it don't matter as long as you can pay. You know you got to come up with your own food, guns and ammunition. Course, you can buy all that from me. I'll make you boys a good deal."

"This man Dougherty says we're too young," said Lafe.

"I'm the boss of this company," said Rory. "You come with the money; you get your share of the mine. You got to hurry though, the Belle Missouri will be leavin the wharf down the street in a few days time. It'll be headin for Westport Landin and we'll be making camp at Independence where we'll form up."

"You can count us in," said Lafe.

"You'll be in when you give me the money," Rory replied.

"Dougherty says you got no more beds?" I asked.

"You got five dollars in gold with ya?"

I shook my head.

Rory shook his head. "We got no bed for ya then."

I didn't like the looks of this man and I didn't think he was someone I could trust. He still had the barrel of the rife aimed at us and he looked like he was itching to shoot someone.

I was the first to head outside the door. Jason followed close behind me.

"I got to get some sleep," I said. "I'm ready to lay down anywhere."

Lafe came out grimacing from ear to ear. "Well boys. Looks like we got ourselves set. All we got to do is come up with three hundred dollars. I'd say it ought to be five hundred or mebbe a thousand sose we have enough left to buy our guns and food."

"Where we gonna get that kind of money?" asked Jason. "A thousand dollars? Only a bank would hold that much."

Lafe wiped his mouth with his hand and pointed toward a saloon down the block. "I saw that there's a big card game goin on in there. A lot of men with fancy clothes are playin poker. I saw one man who's winnin real good. I say we wait till he's done and follow him home. We'll take his winnings right out of his hand."

"I'm not going with you," I said.

Lafe glared at me. "You don't have to be the one that robs him. You can be the one that keeps an eye out while Jason and I take care of him."

I shook my head.

"Aw now Billy. This is our big chance," said Jason. "Hell boyo, we're not goin to hurt him. We'll just take his purse. It's not like we're taking on an innocent man. This guy won his money at cards. Just think of those days back in Boston when we took all that money from those rich boys. You didn't feel so bad about it then."

"I've changed since then," I said.

"Boy, don't I know that," said Jason. "It must have been that new family of yours. Honest to a fault are they?"

"I just don't want to go to jail," I said.

"Oh hell, let's leave him and go get it ourselves," said Lafe. "Let him starve out here. He'll find out soon enough what it's like to have nuthin."

"I already know what it's like to have nothing," I replied.

"Just come along with us," said Jason. "I'll give you part of my share like I said. When we go after the card player, you can go and hide somewhere. You don't have to be part of it."

I should have known better, but I agreed to follow them. We went into that saloon and watched the group of men play cards. At least I had a chair to sit on and then I fell asleep. Jason jarred me awake. I opened my eyes and saw the card game breaking up. There was this man wearing a white suit and hat who had the biggest part of the pot gathered in front of him. He pulled the stack of coins across the table toward him with both arms and then he dropped each coin into a green velvet bag. Once he had filled the bag, he got up, grabbed his hat and left the saloon.

Lafe told us to wait till he went down the block before we went out after him. Lafe turned down the street and we walked through some dark alleys between saloons and hotels until we reached the other side of the block. Lafe knew exactly what he was doing. Somehow he had figured out all his moves earlier without telling Jason or myself what his plan was.

He stopped in the dark alley just before we reached the street. It was late at night and no one else was about. Lafe, Jason and I stayed in the alley. I told Jason that it was my time to leave, but Lafe told me to stay. And in the dark, I felt the point of his knife push up against my stomach. "You stay or I'll slit your belly, here?" Lafe whispered.

I froze. Jason was too scared to say anything or, more to the fact, he was too drunk and leaning against the wall. I heard a snore out of him and realized that he had fallen asleep standing up. We were within sight of a lamppost, one of the very few that offered some light to the otherwise dark street. I watched as a man in a white suit approached the alley. He was happily swinging his arms back and forth and whistling a tune to himself.

Lafe stood ready like an animal ready to pounce on his prey. Just as the man passed the alley, Lafe jumped out in a flash, grabbed the man around the throat and dragged him into the darkness of the alley. "Get his purse," Lafe told me.

"No," I said.

The man was struggling to get free. I could not see his face but could hear him trying to call out for help. Lafe had his arm wrapped around the man's face to muffle his cries. Seconds later, I heard a groan and a cry of pain. Lafe let go of the man and gave him a hard push. The man staggered out of the alley and toward the street while clutching his stomach.

I heard the jingle of coins. Lafe had his booty.

I watched the man stagger a few more steps and then he crumbled to the ground and lay on his face by the curb just under the lamplight. A puddle of blood formed underneath his still body.

"You killed him," I said.

"I ought to kill you too," said Lafe and I felt the knife point press against my belly again. "I told you to get his purse. Your fault I had to get it myself. Your fault I had to kill him."

"Just let me go on my way. I won't tell anyone about this," I said.

"No, course you won't, you're just as guilty as I am. They catch you, you'll go to jail anyway," said Lafe.

Jason coughed and started to move about. "What's going on here?" he asked. And then he saw the man lying in the pool of blood under the lamppost. "Damn it, Lafe. You didn't have to kill him, did you?"

"Had to," said Lafe. "Billy here wouldn't do what I told him to do."

"Let's get away from here," said Jason. "Before somebody comes."

I felt sick to my stomach and it was empty of food. I couldn't stop looking at the poor man with that white suit that was becoming drenched in dark red by his side. The man's eyes were wide open with a look of terror in them.

"You can cut me up too," I told Lafe. "You can't stop me from leaving."

"We got the money to go to California right here," said Lafe. "There's at least seven hundred dollars in gold here. Bein that I'm in a generous mood, I'll lend you both a hundred and some more for food and guns. I'm keepin four hundred for myself cause I did all the work. Hell, I ought to leave you both with nuthin. Serve you both right."

"Aw come on Lafe," said Jason. "Billy is no good at thieving."

"And you're just a lazy drunk," Lafe told Jason.

"Are we partners or not?" asked Jason.

"I'm out of this," I said. "I'm going to try and find way to go back to Maine. I was a fool to think I could get you out to California alive," I told Jason. "You're just going to have to find your own way. No more killing, no more thieving for me," I said.

"You go back east, you'll get put in prison," said Jason.

"And if I stay with you, I'll get killed for sure. I'll take prison any day over losing my life," I replied.

"Those boys in prison will have their way with you," said Jason. "I know all about that. You won't survive through the first day."

"I guess I'll just have to take my chances," I replied.

"So this is finally the end of the road between us, heh?" asked Jason.

"You can come back east with me if you want," I replied.

Jason waved his hand and shook his head. "Hell no. I'm not going back there."

I started to walk away. Jason pounded the wall with his fist like he had the last time we parted. This time I knew it was probably for good.

"I'll be down by Slattery's boat by morning," I shouted back to Jason. "I'm going home. I got too much to lose now. I hope you make it to the mines. Thanks for saving my life." I turned my head away and walked down the block. I turned back once to take another look at that poor man lying in a pool of blood under the lamppost.

I walked back down to the waterfront. I was already regretting that I had left Jason behind. I knew Lafe wouldn't take care of him, but then, I didn't think there was much more I could do for Jason. He was never going to change his ways. I walked down the wharf to where I thought the Gallipolis had been berthed. It had been situated between two larger steamboats. It was too dark to make out the individual boats.

I was so tired that I couldn't walk another step. I decided that I would try to find Slattery's boat in the morning. I went over to a stack of crates located halfway down the wharf. I lowered myself down, leaned my head against the splintered wood and closed my eyes. The sight of that dead man lying in that pool of blood appeared to me, even though my eyes were closed. It was only my own total exhaustion that allowed me to sink into a deep sleep. I knew that when I woke again, the nightmare would not end and that poor man would still be lying in a pool of blood and I had done nothing save him. The guilt would follow me whether I returned to face justice in Boston or whether I went on to California.

End note from the author:

The city of St. Louis was the gathering point for one of the largest movements of people in American history. The most important year of that movement was 1849. Combined with the thousands of farmers who sought to find their version of the promised land out west, another group of predominately single men were bound for the newly discovered gold in California. The route both groups would follow would be called the Oregon Trail. The trail was not a single road but consisted of many roads and many routes to cross the western frontier from St. Louis. The actually kicking off point was St. Joseph or Independence Missouri. These emigrants, both gold seekers and farmers boarded steam ferry boats in St. Louis and made their way up the Missouri river to these jumping off points.
An important figure in this great migration was the trail guide. Many of these guides were mountain men or native Americans who had previously traveled these western lands either trading or trapping furs or were members of tribes of native Americans who spent their lives wandering about these lands they considered their homeland.
In the opening of Book II of the continuing Billy'O epic. Billy O'Shea finds himself facing a Hobson's choice; return to Boston and face prosecution for his crimes and then be put on a ship bound to return him to Ireland, or to continue his journey to California even though he faced overwhelming odds.
Billy O'Shea was stranded and penniless and he wandered the busy wharves of the Mississippi waterfront in St. Louis hoping to find a boat to take him back to the east. Providence brings a much hoped for rescue in the form of a crusty old veteran trail guide by the name of Noah Caleb and thus begins the next important chapter in Billy O'Shea's journey across America in Book II.

Made in the USA
Columbia, SC
22 December 2019